Farewell

Farewell

Fleeing Repatriation

Barbara Sorensen Fallick

Gold Street Publishers

CONTENTS

CONTENTS

To Donald Fallick
For his unfailing love, encouragement and editing
insights.

Prologue

Our dear grandchildren,

You are very familiar with the Church's encouragement to write our personal histories. I have long hesitated, not only because English is a language I stumble around in, but more because there are some things in my personal history that I fear will trouble you. I cannot leave all of the troubling things out and adequately tell my story. I have enlisted Kenretta, our skilled family writer, to spruce what I say into proper English. Mamochka will also tell her part of the story from her point of view; also, with Kenretta's probing for details we may leave out, filling out the story.

Some of you still have the innocence of youth. I admonish you to guard it as something very precious. Don't rush into the adult world even by reading of the sins, cruelty, and wickedness done by men in this world, thinking of it as mere entertainment. I once heard a story of a girl who wanted to see an inappropriate movie. Her mother invited her to make a cake with her. As the electric beater was mixing the ingredients, the mother threw in the eggs—shells and all. The girl protested, "Mother! You just ruined the cake. You'll never get the eggshells out." The mother said, "The inappropriate things in that movie are eggshells. Once you get them in your mind, you will never get them out."

Our story has eggshells in it. War is ugly and heart-wrenching. Anyone who has been through a war has eggshells in their mind. Wait to read our story until you have experienced some of life's cruelty after you have committed some sins you regret and after you have been bitterly disappointed. It is easier to handle eggshells in our minds after we have become a bit calloused.

I also want to remind and caution you of something. When Mamochka and I met, we were not members of the Church. We had not been taught the law of chastity. We did not know of the Word of

Wisdom. We violated the law of chastity, and smoked, and drank, and did not know it was wrong. This did not save us from the consequences of those actions. I believe the commandments of God are more like laws of nature than suggestions. Saying, "Live the Law of Chastity," is more like saying, "Don't jump off a cliff because you will fall and be hurt," than saying, "Don't date until you are sixteen." You don't have to believe in the law, or even know of it, to be hurt by violating it.

Now, you may be saying, "Well, it turned out all right for you. I'll just repent later." You are in a different field than we were. You know God's commandments. If you violate them, you are adding "rebelling against God" to the list. It's a whole 'nother ball game to deliberately make yourself an enemy of God.

Well, enough said. You young, innocent ones, put this down and come back in a few years. You seasoned warriors, read on, and maybe learn something from life's hard lessons as Mamochka and I have done.

All my love,

Papochka

Part I

Kamchatka, *Proshchai*

Farewell, beloved Kamchatka
Farewell, roaring volcanoes
Farewell, my native land
God knows if ever I'll see you again
-Adaptation of Theodore Bikel's
translation of *"Proshchai"*

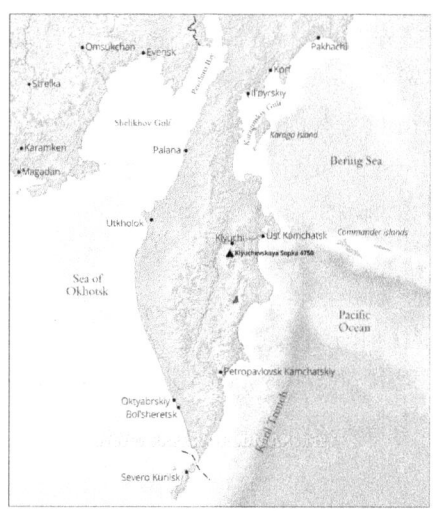

Unwanted Refugee

Salt Lake City, Utah 1948

Just inside the church, Valentina hesitated, wondering why she ever thought it would be a good idea to talk to the bishop. When Douglas made his pronouncement, it had seemed that she stood in immediate danger. But no one really knew who she was. Despite what Douglas had said, she didn't believe he even suspected. Why did she think the bishop could solve her problem? Just knowing her situation would endanger him. Could she just ask him something innocuous and leave? That would not justify her request for an hour of his time.

Hand on the door handle, vacillating between staying and going, Valentina jumped when an inner door opened, and Bishop Bullock followed Sister Peters into the foyer.

"Thank you, Bishop, for your advice and your time," Sister Peters purred, adjusting her hat on her tight gray curls before heading for the outside door.

"My pleasure. Please let me know how it goes," Bishop Bullock responded. A smile crinkled his face as he turned to Valentina. "Sister Waters, please come into my office."

Bishop Bullock stepped aside to allow her to precede him into his office, and Valentina schooled herself to put on her *I really know nothing about this. Nothing you say will ruffle me. I'm innocent* demeanor while reminding herself that she hadn't come to be interrogated. She came seeking his help, which undoubtedly would require a confession.

"And how may I help you, Sister Waters?" The bishop moved behind his massive mahogany desk. The wooden chair squeaked as he lowered his tall frame into it.

Even though it had been a week since Douglas had unknowingly caused her crisis, Valentina still had no idea how to begin. Trying to keep her composure, she stated what she hoped the end result would be. "I want to become clean before the Lord, and I don't know how." Valentina suddenly realized that that sounded naive, and she might receive a pat answer, but that would give her a chance to leave without revealing anything.

Bishop Bullock stretched his legs and interlaced his fingers over his midsection as if to indicate that she had all of the time in the world to unwind her tale. "Yes?"

"Well, it's now been three years since I joined the Church. When I got baptized, I vowed I would never sin again, but I have. I don't know what the Lord would have me do, nor how to become clean again. I'm not sure the Lord would have me do the only thing that would seem to make it right."

Now it would be awkward to back out. She must continue, for better or worse, for life or death. She glanced briefly at her hands resting primly in her lap and returned the bishop's gaze, sensing the caution he must be feeling.

"And what is it you have done?" Bishop Bullock adjusted the knot of his blue tie as he probed for more information.

"I stole medicine from the Ft. Douglas Veterans' Hospital where I work." Well, she had done that, and she probably needed to repent of it, but that was barely the tip of the iceberg. Still, Valentina's unflinching gaze met his, her hands calm in her lap.

"That's easy enough. You confess to the hospital and pay for what you took." He gave her a one-size-fits-all answer.

How tempting it would be just to thank him and leave! But it had taken gut-wrenching courage to come in to talk to the bishop. If she didn't do it now, she knew she would never do it again. If this visit sealed her doom, she would accept it as God's will to end this way. That seemed far better than continually waiting for someone like Douglas to stumble upon the truth and report her and Alex to the authorities.

"Yes, on the surface, that would seem easy enough, but they most likely would want to know why I took it, and I'm afraid that would come out if I confessed." Valentina didn't dare blurt out the whole thing at once. Little by little, she would lead him into the web.

Bishop Bullock's brow furrowed. "Oh, and why did you take it?"

"Because a very sick man at my house required medication, and I saw no way to get it." She knew that each answer just complicated rather than clarified his understanding.

"You couldn't just buy it?" His voice and his wrinkled brow now showed his confusion.

"I didn't have enough money, nor did I know where to buy it. I had just arrived here. He seemed in danger of dying. If I just replaced the medicine, would that take care of it?"

"Perhaps. Why couldn't the man at your house go to the hospital to receive what he needed?"

Well, this would get them to the heart of the matter quickly. "I was-- I am hiding him. He's still here. He lives here."

"This man, is he a relative?"

"No, he was a soldier in the war."

"So, you live together. I thought you were single."

"We don't live together that way," Valentina hastened to explain. "We just live in the same house, as roommates.

"Where does he work?"

Valentina felt they were playing "find-the-object," like she used to play with her brothers. *Cold. Warm. Warmer. Hot.*

"He can't work." She smoothed the skirt of her lavender print dress and crossed her feet. She clasped her hands but did not grasp them in any sign of the distress she felt. Her training served her well, but instead of pretending that she knew nothing, the time had come to be more open.

"And why is that?"

"He doesn't speak English." *Warmer.*

"A refugee? Jewish?" Bishop Bullock asked his own searching questions since she revealed so little with each answer. "How did he come to live at your house?"

She gave a tremendous sigh, no longer able to keep all emotion from showing when they approached so close to the full truth. "Well, you might say I am responsible for him."

"Even with all of the returned soldiers, there are jobs non-English speakers can get. Maybe I could help make some contacts, get him the papers he needs."

She momentarily bit her lip before dropping the bomb. "You can't. You see, he is Russian."

Bishop Bullock leaped to his feet. "A Russian! Surely, you know of the repatriation act signed at Yalta. You could be arrested for un-American activities and be sent to prison for harboring a Russian. You are in deep water."

"To the Russian government, Russian prisoners of war did not exist. They were all traitors, to be executed or sent to Siberia for risking their lives in defense of their country." All composure dropped away. Her eyes snapped and flashed as she rushed on. "That also goes for anyone who served Russia in the west in any capacity during the war. Displaced persons who were captured by the Germans and forced into slave labor are included as well. The truth of the matter is, all of these people saw how the Russian government had lied about conditions in the west. How could any Russian deny the prosperity and freedom that he saw? If that were known in Russia, the government would be toppled."

Bishop Bullock sat down and spoke in controlled tones: "You are in very dangerous territory. How did you get mixed up in this?" His voice intensified to match hers.

If only that were all there was to tell! she thought. *But there is still so much more. He still only knew the first few meters of the iceberg, the kind of iceberg that sinks ships.*

Her manner became contrite. "I suppose you read about Nina Pavlovna?"

He shook his head at her apparent non-sequitur. "The Russian spy who was caught in New Jersey last week?"

"She is not a spy!" Valentina's voice broke, and she momentarily bit on a knuckle. *Keep your composure!* she reminded herself, and her practiced mask fell back into place.

"The newspaper said she spied for Russia in England during the war."

Valentina practically whispered. "Well, that is true. She worked for the Allies in training spies. But she didn't come to America to spy. She came as a refugee and hid here only because the U.S. does not permit Russian refugees. There is no way a Russian can legally remain here or in any other western country. They must all be repatriated, by force if necessary."

"How do you know all of this? How did you get involved? Are you part of a spy ring?"

Hot. Valentina bowed her head momentarily, then looked him straight in the eye. Very softly, she said, "I am Nina Pavlovna's daughter."

This bomb left him so astounded he could not speak for a moment. "You, you're Russian? But you speak English perfectly."

"My maternal grandmother lived in England as a child. I've spoken English since my infancy." She said it calmly as if her words didn't mandate her own repatriation, but this was what she needed to know. What did Heavenly Father expect of her in these circumstances?

"Well, are you a spy?"

"No. Well, not now. I spied for the Allies during the war in France, but I went underground when I decided to defect. The Russians don't know where I am. The Americans don't know who I am. If I am repatriated, I am certain I will be executed. Maybe one could say I deserve it, but Alex, the man living in my house, doesn't. Is that what Heavenly

Father would have me do? Confess that I defected and came to the US under a false identity? Actually, that happened before I joined the church, but I don't know if the sin was washed away in my baptism as I haven't forsaken it." She gave another huge sigh, hoping he looked upon her with compassion.

"I understand they imprisoned your mother. They did not repatriate her." The bishop did not directly address her concern as if he were still so bewildered by all of this he had not yet gotten his bearings.

"For the time being, she is imprisoned. So I might also be imprisoned either for the rest of my life or eventually be repatriated and probably executed. So, is that what Heavenly Father wants of me? To confess?"

Bishop Bullock gave his own huge sigh as he tried to grasp this situation. "Do you have other family still in Russia?"

"My father was taken before I left for England. I do not know if he is still alive. I also have a married sister, but, of course, we have not had any contact since before I left Russia. I don't know what has happened to her and her family since I left Moscow. I have no idea what kind of danger my sister and her family face because of my mother's discovery or if it will be better or worse for them if I confess. I suspect it could mean their deaths or being sent to labor camps. I don't know what to do, but I live a lie every day of my life. What would Heavenly Father want of me? I don't know if I am worthy to partake of the sacrament." Now she wrung her hands, with no more pretense that this didn't affect her deeply.

Bishop Bullock still looked as if his head spun. "I think I better hear this story from the beginning. Let's back way up and tell me how all of this came to be."

"Well, my real name is Valentina Markovna. In Moscow in the early spring of 1943...." and it felt like she time-traveled, living it all over again.

Moscow, Early Spring 1943

Just as Valentina opened the oven and slid the *kulich* in, she heard the knock at the door. She glanced at the clock. Too early to be punctual Comrade Chirikov. She hoped it wasn't him. She planned to run and change out of her flour-smudged frock before he arrived. The door-knocker pounded again. Perhaps *Papochka* would get it.

"Valushka, could you please get the door?"

"Yes, Father." She smoothed her hair with her hand and then realized she'd just wiped flour across her head. She didn't have time for this. It would set her back even more if she had to tidy up her hair. Valentina ran down the hall and pulled the heavy door open. The cold blast of snow flurries contrasted with the heat of the kitchen. Comrade Fyodorovitch stood there. Tiny icicles formed on his bushy, gray mustache, but his quick smile and twinkling eyes warmed her. She gave a curtsy to show her pleasure in seeing him.

"Miss Valentina Markovna, how nice to see you again." He took her hand in his and gallantly kissed it, tickling it with his damp, bushy mustache.

"It's so good to see you, Comrade Fyodorovitch. I hope it is good news which brings you by."

"Oh, yes. I expect, anyway. All I know is that your mother has requested that I deliver this directly to you. I am never permitted to read them."

"Won't you come in for a cup of tea?" As much as she liked Comrade Fyodorovitch, Valentina hoped he would say no. Comrade Chirikov would be here directly, and she needed to finish preparing for his visit.

"I would dearly love to, but...," he smiled again, his eyes communicating genuine regret. "I was given to know that this note is for you only, and I would have to make up reasons for my coming by if your father should answer the door."

He handed her an envelope and tipped his hat. She searched her apron pocket for a kopeck, and finding one, handed it to him. "Thank you kindly," he smiled again before she shut the door.

Leaning against the carved wood of the door, she closed her eyes and savored a moment of excitement. Why would Mamochka send a letter just to her? Only her birthday had merited a personal note since mother went abroad. Valentina glanced at the postmark. February 24, 1943. Three weeks ago. Mother would have heard of Andrei's death by then and, possibly, Mikel's. Father could certainly know that Mamochka sent her a note of sympathy. If only she were to see this message, it must be important and something other than condolences!

"Who was at the door?" Papochka called.

"Oh..." Valentina searched for an explanation he would accept without further questioning. "Just.. uh... Olga, returning some..." she almost said sugar but stopped herself in time. No one had sugar anymore, not even themselves, as she used the last smidgen of their privileged supply in making the kulich. That would be a dead give-away. "Olga, returning some books. I'll be in my room dressing for Comrade Chirikov's visit."

With the envelope clutched tightly to her chest, she rushed down the hall and up the stairs, oblivious to any response from her father. In an act of sheer discipline, she lay the envelope on her stretched canvas cot and changed into her best navy-blue dress, with a stiff, white collar and cuffs. She liked the way the dress turned her eyes a deep blue. To save time, she just lightly brushed the flour off her hair and pinned it into a crown around her head instead of rebraiding it. Then, as if the ritual of dressing up made her worthy of the news, she sat on the high-backed chair the authorities hadn't wanted when they confiscated all of their fine furniture to distribute among the less privileged. She picked up the envelope, the chill of the room eclipsed by her excitement.

It had been drummed into her head since infancy that, because of Mamochka's importance in espionage for Mother Russia, they lived in such a large house and enjoyed many other privileges. In the great equalization under the Soviets, the large house had been partitioned among five other families, the kitchen and living room communal.

With Natasha married and the boys in the army, she and Papochka each had a cot in her bedroom, which at one time had been a servant's bedroom when the house had belonged to Count Voskinsky. The five other families evacuated during the battle for Moscow, leaving only her and Papochka to rattle around in the huge house, and Papochka had moved back into his upstairs bedroom. Even if they were grand and important people, the house was too much for the two of them, too much cleaning, too much expense to try to keep even the rooms she and Papochka used warm, too many aching memories of those gone. She would have gladly traded all of it just to have Mamochka back. Missing Mamochka translated into a hollow ache filling her whole insides. Maybe this letter contained some consolation.

The return address read: The Embassy of the Union of Soviet Socialist Republics, London, England. It sounded so formal, but a message from Mamochka nestled inside, much more intimate than any other letter she could receive from anyone else. She slit the envelope, and in slow, reverent movements, removed the letter. A glance at the page told her this letter had escaped the eyes of the censors. None of the heavy dark lines characteristic of most of Mamochka's letters marred the contents of this one.

> *Darling,*
>
> *I received the news of Andrei's death, and my heart is broken. I must keep busy working so that I cannot think too much. War is such a terrible thing. I hope that you are handling this dreadful news well. Two sons left and still in danger. I cannot risk thinking about them.*
>
> *After much thought and concern about your own safety, I have decided to recommend that you be sent to England to work in espionage. I imagine you will be sent into France if England invades, which I expect they will at some point. Your French and English are both excellent, enabling you to pass for a native speaker of either language. This will qualify you for the service.*

Astounded, Valentina kissed the paper and clutched it to her. England! France! A tremor of excitement shot through her. Who would have ever imagined she would find her way to those exotic lands at merely seventeen years of age? Tutored from infancy in the English her grandmother learned living abroad as a child and the French that all Russian nobility had spoken in the last century; Valentina always hoped the day would come when she would visit those far-off lands. Who would have thought that it would be war that would open a door for her in an increasingly closed Russia? She continued reading:

> *Arrangements are being made for you to be trained as a nurse before you leave Russia. A touch-typing course will also hopefully be included. These will be your cover.*
>
> *I do not think all the pieces can be in place for you to begin before fall. Your father will not take kindly to this news…*

No, he certainly would not. Short of having no choice whatsoever, no way existed where Papochka would ever allow her to follow her mother into espionage.

> *…and it is only because I feel it will be safer for you here than there that I have taken this step. Do not tell your father until an official appointment arrives. He will have no option then but to accept its dictates.*
>
> *May you be well, my precious. I am not sure if I will be able to see you when you arrive without endangering both of us, but I will look for an opportunity.*
>
> *All my love,*

She may actually get to see Mamochka again soon! Would Mamochka even know her? In the almost three incredibly long years since Mamochka left, she had changed from a silly kid to a seasoned young woman.

Mamochka wrote this, evidently not knowing of Mikel's death, not knowing that there would never be a future between her and Mikel. But his death forced her to move on and, bless Mamochka, a way just opened up for her to put the painful past behind her and have something to look forward to.

Oh, oh...the kulich. Valentina reverently replaced the letter in the envelope and slid it under her pillow. Thank goodness she would not have to be the one to persuade Papochka. His fury would erupt like a volcano. Valentina dashed down the stairs, into the kitchen, and pulled the oven door open. Barely within the range of perfection, the kulich smelled divine. Another few minutes, and it would have been overdone. Hmm... Just in time. Once again, knocking resonated throughout the house. It must be Comrade Chirikov this time.

Valentina curtsied as she opened the door, "Good-day, Comrade Chirikov." She heard the excitement in her voice. Her father would guess something was afoot if she did not settle down. How did one settle down when her insides somersaulted for joy. and that smile just would not stay off her face?

"Pretty and pert as usual. Good-day, my dear," Comrade Chirikov set down a satchel and swept her into the fatherly hug that characterized his visits since she grew too big for a toss in the air. He bent over and made a kissing sound as he brushed his lips across the top of her head. "I see two stars in the window. I heard of Andrei. Who else?"

Ah, thank you, dear Comrade Chirikov. That settled her in a hurry. Genuine tears thickened her voice as she spoke, "It wasn't one of my brothers. A special friend..."

"Oh, I am so sorry." He opened his arms to her, and she slid into his embrace a second time, burying her head against his chest. "War is a terrible waste of young men. I feared when General Winter loosened his grip, Russia's casualties would increase. Would that the Germans had retreated!"

Comrade Chirikov no longer mentioned the loss of his only son over a year ago in the battle at Stalingrad. He may still grieve in private, but he was the face of compassion to others.

Taking a moment before feeling herself back in control, Valentina whispered, "Papochka's waiting for you."

Comrade Chirikov gave her a last reassuring squeeze before releasing her. "This trip to Kamchatka will be a good antidote for his grief. If you can't solve a problem, sometimes the best thing to do is to go far away and put your mind on something else." He gently wiped a tear from her cheek before untying the ears of his *ushanka* and shaking off the snow that clung to its fur before hanging it on the hook. Slipping out of his coat and boots, he shook the snow off each one, and placed them on hooks and racks. Then he reached for the mop.

"Don't worry, Comrade Chirikov. I can do that."

He gave her a dimpled smile, "Now that my wife is gone, I do it all the time. I do not mind. I know you have to do all of the housework now. I want to save those pretty little hands for something more delicate."

Comrade Chirikov always pampered her in ways her father never did. Valentina led him to the door of the study and announced, "Father, Comrade Chirikov is here."

"Thanks, dear." Her portly father paused in pouring a glass of vodka and turned to look at them. His blue, knit sweater turned his eyes a deeper shade, but he wore the garment for warmth, not vanity.

"Hello, Anatoly. Come, sit by the fire. Valushka, please bring us some refreshment."

Valentina felt satisfaction swell in her as she went to the kitchen and sliced the perfect kulich. She snitched a piece to see if the raisins, dried apricots, and dates made up for the inadequate amount of sugar. Yum. It tasted good to her.

Her father always ate absentmindedly. He didn't know if he ate caviar or beets and cabbage. In contrast, Comrade Chirikov applauded her every effort. Just for the pleasure of watching him enjoy the results of her labor, she attempted to make something lavish each time he visited, which proved to be a significant challenge with the limited war-time rations.

Valentina paused in the doorway to see if her return would interrupt their conversation.

Comrade Chirikov lifted his satchel to his lap. "I expected I wouldn't be able to obtain copies of the books by the seventeenth and eighteenth-century foreign explorers, but I got them, both of those I have been seeking. Such chance! Early Russian explorers' detailed descriptions of Kamchatka still seem to be the most definitive Russian statement. I guess the place doesn't change much."

"A wildlife preserve limited to scientific study is not supposed to change. At least we can thank Stalin for that." Her father raised his glasses and rubbed at his left eyebrow where a scar still troubled him obtained when an errant shovel hit him in digging trenches during the defense of Moscow.

"We can thank him for that and allowing us to go on this trip. I never dared hope that we old codgers would be so rewarded after doing our part in chasing the Germans out." Comrade Chirikov turned and acknowledged her with an appreciative sniff, "Um! Um! Easter Cake. So few still commemorate our Savior's resurrection and then only in the privacy of their homes, amongst trusted friends. The knowledge of the resurrection is such a comfort when we suffer the loss of loved ones. Thank you, Valentina, for this sweet reminder."

Comrade Chirikov had never mentioned his Christianity to her before in her memory. For her family, Easter had been another excuse to eat and drink, not a religious holiday to be celebrated. The fierce, patriotic fervor that beat wildly in their breasts when they watched the soldiers march in Red Square before leaving for the front had now dissipated. In the cold reality that many of those beloved defenders would never return, the atheistic doctrine of communism provided no comfort. How she would love to believe that someday in a far off hereafter, she would again see her brother and Mikel, that there was an Easter, a day of the dead resurrecting.

Comrade Chirikov took a piece of the kulich from the proffered tray and took a bite. Closing his eyes as if to maximize his enjoyment, he savored the eating experience. "Perfect, as always. Thank you so very much. Do I detect a hint of sweetness?" He reached for another piece.

"It is, unfortunately, the last of our sugar." Valentina sat the tray on the table and handed a cup and saucer to each man, "I apologize for the bitter tea. I'm not able to get anything else on our rations."

"That's fine, that's fine. No one gets good tea anymore, although I have squirreled some away for the trip." Comrade Chirikov dismissed her apology, as she knew he would. He gave her a smile that caused his dimple to show before turning back to her father. "Now, as I said, I miraculously obtained the books by the early American and French explorers. Regretfully, they are in English and French. Wish that Nina were here to help. By the way, what do you hear of her?"

Papochka gave an audible sigh as he shook his graying head of hair. "Precious little. She is in England. Everything is so censored she can't really say much. I have heard nothing since sending notice of Andrei's death."

"Would she have any associates who know French and English well enough to be able to translate? I have a little in the way of money or goods with which I can pay."

Valentina caught her breath and looked at her father, wondering if she dared say anything. Father didn't even glance at her but answered before she could. "Anatoly, Valentina can do it. She's fully fluent in both English and French." This showed his implicit trust in Comrade Chirikov. He rarely revealed this fact to anyone.

"Indeed!" Comrade Chirikov turned suitably impressed eyes upon her, and Valentina felt warmed by his approval. "Well, that's wonderful. How is it Mother Russia hasn't required her services yet?"

"You mean, beyond digging trenches for the Battle of Moscow? Isn't three sons enough?" Papochka clasped his hands over his protruding stomach.

"War is greedy."

"Yes, it certainly is! Valentina's linguistic skills are not something we choose to broadcast. She learned from Nina's mother and Nina herself, but her language abilities are not known outside of the family, and I intend to keep it that way." Her father looked at her, his eyes warm with paternal love.

Proof that it was not a misapprehension to think he would be furious to learn Mamochka had recommended her for espionage.

"This guide we have in Kamchatka has requested we bring some books. The cost is to be deducted from our fee." Comrade Chirikov quickly shifted the subject away from this sensitive topic as well as the war, a topic everyone wearied hearing of. It always seemed to be the same dreary news, only with different names for where the fighting occurred and those killed. Valentina appreciated most about Comrade Chirikov's visits because he brought more than the war to think about. "The guide seems to be some kind of intellectual who doesn't know that the only books readily available are the works of Lenin and Stalin. The list of books he wants is as long as your arm."

"Well, that seems better than having a dullard. Give the list to Valentina. It will give her a good excuse to spend time in her favorite haunt, and maybe she can find a buried treasure or two." Papochka graced her with a smile.

Comrade Chirikov offered her the list and an envelope. "There should be enough money in the envelope to cover the purchase. I think the bookstore on Povarsky has reopened." Valentina scanned the list. Books about birds, flowers, Czar Nicholas and Alexandra—that would not be available, Tolstoy's *War and Peace*—for the Kamchatka guide? What kind of guy read these? Certainly not the stereotypical ignorant native.

Valentina startled at the unexpected banging of the door knocker.

"I'll get the door, father."

She bounced into the hallway, her mind a daze of anticipation at the luxury of being sent to a bookstore. She flung the door open and stood in stunned disbelief, then wanted to slam it in that moment, to run and hide from the truth the gray-clad government messenger brought. He handed her the buff telegram. "I'm sorry."

She dumbly took it, her body aquiver inside and out. No! No! No! No! Why? Why another one? How many would it take before the gods of war accepted the sacrifice?

"What is it?" her father called.

She walked back to her father's side, tears streaming down her face. She sunk down at his feet and buried her face against his knee. She barely felt him remove the telegram from her clenched fist. Dmitri or Mark? It hardly mattered which one. So close that either would feel his heart amputated without the other, she could not imagine how one would survive alone. Did they even know of Andrei and Mikel's deaths?

The heaviness of her father's grief weighed on the silence, but she didn't hear the telegram rip open. She glanced up at Papochka. He stared at the telegram as if it did not become fact until he read it, and he staved off the inevitable as long as possible. Finally, after a long moment, he handed it to Comrade Chirikov. "I can't do it." His voice caught on each word.

Valentina's eyes traced Comrade Chirikov's veined hands as he tore open the grief-bearing missive and held her breath in suspended horror as Chirikov silently read. He dropped the missive to the floor and passed his hand across his eyes.

Valentina glanced from Comrade Chirikov to her father and back. Her father slumped forward, his forearms on his legs, his hands clasping and releasing, "Which one?'

Comrade Chirikov gave a shuddering sigh, "Both."

"Both," her father whispered, "Both. At least they won't miss each other."

A long, wracking silence held them before her father continued. "But me, three sons, three sons and... and nothing."

He paused again, the very silence punctuating their anguish. "Are they shipping the bodies back?"

Comrade Chirikov shook his head.

"Perhaps that is better. I don't know if I could bear to see them."

The moments stood suspended as all groped with nothing to say, nothing to ease the devastating news. Finally, practically in a whisper, Comrade Chirikov said, his voice gentle, "Mark, you could postpone the trip if you need time."

That focused Papochka's thoughts into words, "Oh, no, no. What I need now more than anything is to get away. What is there for me here except the ghosts of memory to torment me?"

"Yes, something else to think about, a change of scenery, it will be good for you to go to Kamchatka. What about Miss Valentina?"

"Valentina? Oh... she is planning to begin work at a factory. There are still a few small ones that are not in the Urals. She will stay with her sister."

"Mark, take her along. With her language abilities, Mother Russia could easily require her skills abroad. In Kamchatka, she is away from danger for a season."

Valentina's eyes flew to her father. Go to Kamchatka? Her?

"She does not qualify," Her father closed the subject just as firmly as the Kronotsky Nature Reserve remained firmly shut to all but scientists.

It would be okay to stay here if she could launch right into the espionage training, but that would not happen until fall. To stay at Natasha's, do the drudgery of factory work, and to try to keep from thinking, her heart would break from the weight of her grief. She'd strangle from the oppressiveness of it. Markuska. Dead! Dimitri, Dead! Andrei, Dead! Mikel, Dead! Each one dead. Never, never, never, never coming back. For her to go to Kamchatka, speeding on a train far from memories, far from crushing thoughts, far from the reality of her loss, that seemed a much better option.

"Think about it. We are permitted to take a cook," Comrade Chirikov stood. He looked at the two foreign books he had brought in, at Valentina, and back at the books, silently communicating they were there for her to read. "The same friend who processed our travel permits could do hers."

Papochka did not respond. Valentina followed Comrade Chirikov to the door.

"I'm so sorry about your brothers. You are welcome to come along if you want."

"Thank you." She managed a tremulous smile.

"The application is inside the books if you choose to go." He practically whispered, "It needs to be submitted this week. I'll drop by tomorrow to pick it up."

"Thank you." Valentina accepted a hug from him.

Salt Lake City 1948

Bishop Bullock glanced at the clock, and Valentina realized her allotted time was up.

Bishop Bullock spoke, "And this trip to Kamchatka is pertinent to the situation you are in today?"

"Yes. That is where I met Alex."

"We are out of time tonight, but I would like to meet with you again. Next Tuesday, at the same time?"

Valentina nodded.

"I want you to bring Alex with you the next time you come."

Fear gripped her. She never permitted Alex to go and come in the daytime because she didn't want anyone to realize he lived there. If she left the house with him, what would they make of it if any neighbor should see? "What difference does it make? You can't talk to him."

"Though not fluent, I have studied Russian. I served in intelligence in the war after I was injured. I understand fairly well. I think to be fully helpful to you, I need to meet him. I need to hear his side of the story."

To be fully helpful or to turn you both in at once? Is that what the bishop contemplated? Valentina swallowed hard, and her mind raced. She had not anticipated this. Having opened up this much, she saw no way to turn back. She tried to calm herself. Bishop Bullock didn't look at her malevolently. In the bishop, there existed the possibility of someone who might help. She believed this man to be inspired by God. By coming and revealing as much as she had, she had relinquished control of the situation. As hard as it was, she now needed to go with the flow. Maybe they could find a way around it. Maybe, hopefully, the bishop was just trying to find a way to help. "Alex doesn't have any shoes. He's worn out his own shoes. I've been able to pick up a couple of shirts and pants from patients at the VA who've died; but his feet are wide, and I haven't found any that will fit him."

"What does he do when he goes outside?"

"He never goes outside except when it is dark. He must not be seen by anyone who would ask questions."

"He is a virtual prisoner of war."

"That is one way to look at it."

"What is it like to live with him?"

How to state that briefly? "It is like living with a caged bear."

"Does he mistreat you?"

"No. I wouldn't protect his life if he did that. I would abandon him to whatever fate became his if he didn't stay within the boundaries I've set."

"Whoa," Bishop Bullock gave a low whistle, "This is amazing. Bring the outline of his feet on a piece of paper on Sunday. I'll come up with some shoes for him."

Valentina decided she needed to be more explicit. The bishop didn't see the danger. "But I'm scared if others see him. How am I going to explain him to others? How am I going to explain that he can't speak English? If anyone realizes he is Russian, we are both doomed. Could you come to my house?"

Bishop Bullock pondered that for a moment. "No, it would not be appropriate for me to come to your house. It would totally be misinterpreted if I went into the home of a single sister everyone thinks lives alone and come out an hour or two later. The neighborhood never misses things like that, and then I'd have to explain why to my chain of command. We'll come up with a tale you can use."

This gave her some reassurance that the bishop did not intend to turn them in, and she saw the wisdom in that explanation. Still, her heart thudded with fear. "I'll have to trust you on this. I am terrified."

"The Lord will bless you. It seems he has so far."

She stood, and suddenly, the bishop said, "Didn't I see you with Douglas Parkins?"

So, others had noticed. "Yes, we've been dating."

"Be very careful. He is an--, um, a flaming patriot and could be very, very dangerous to you."

The panic that gripped her since Douglas' declaration to track down every Russian secretly hiding in the United States rose like bile in her chest. "Yes, I know. That is what prompted me to come in to see you."

"Has Douglas met Alex?"

"Not exactly. They've seen and glared at each other, but Douglas does not know that Alex is Russian."

"I'm sorry Douglas has any part in this." The bishop stood and ushered her out the door.

*****

As soon as the door shut, Bishop Greg Bullock sank to his knees. It wouldn't have done to admit he felt terrified himself. He needed so badly to talk to someone, but he fully realized what Sister Waters presented as her problem had now become his problem. He now knew of not one but two Russians with a direct and intimate relationship to the just-arrested Communist spy Nina Pavlovna. He'd have to go back to those newspapers and see if the articles mentioned her daughter Valentina.

If he didn't report them, he would be breaking the law. Should he do that? Could he send them, and perhaps Valentina's sister's family as well, to their deaths? Would he then feel he'd done right before the Lord? She had come to him in confidence as her bishop, seeking guidance in this perplexing situation. Would not turning them in be like what those who had turned in the Jews did for Hitler? When he had parachuted into a tree in France in the opening days of the Allied invasion and hung there helplessly, it had been a Russian who had cut him down, tenderly administered to his needs, hid him when the Germans came close and alerted the Allies. In the face of all of that, how could he feel justified in assuming all Russians in the United States were spies, as Senator McCarthy so loudly proclaimed?

He couldn't talk to his wife about this; he couldn't talk to his counselors; he couldn't talk to the stake president. Anyone he might talk to would then be in exactly the same quandary. Should he have the authorities pick them up at their home or when they showed up next week? Should he help them continue to perpetuate the illegal deception? He bowed his head to his clasped hands to consult with the only friend who could give him comfort and advice.

Alex Meets the Bishop

Salt Lake City 1948

Greg Bullock sequestered himself in his office at the university. Glad that his secretary had kept old newspapers for his fireplace, he poured over the articles about Nina Pavlovna. During the war, she had been stationed in England working for the Allies. She evaluated and instructed possible spies to be sent into France. After the war, she disappeared. Last week a soldier she had trained as a spy recognized her in New Jersey at a parent-teacher conference. She had trained him in English, but he remembered hearing that she was actually Russian and had disappeared. The soldier received a nice award for turning her in.

Nina lived under the name of Janice Holmes and taught French in a high school in Newark, New Jersey. Nothing was known of her husband. Nina had three sons, all killed in the war, one married daughter still living near Moscow, and a younger daughter named Valentina, who also disappeared after being sent into France as a spy. How did they know all of this? Had Nina Pavlovna freely disclosed it? Probably not since it could endanger her daughters. Had it been tortured out of her? Or were there records kept concerning Russians who had worked in Western Europe during the war?

The paper went on to say that Valentina evidently did not live with Nina Pavlovna in New Jersey, as no one who had any acquaintance with Nina under her US alias had any knowledge of a daughter.

Investigations continued to see if any hint could be discovered leading to Valentina's whereabouts. A tempting reward would go to anyone who could lead the authorities to her. And Douglas Parkins, despite his avowal of patriotism, would be enticed by the reward. Greg could only hope that Douglas was as clueless as he himself had been before Valentina's revelations.

Since Nina Pavlovna might be part of a communist spy ring infiltrating the United States, she had not been repatriated as the Yalta agreement mandated but had been imprisoned and was being interrogated. There seemed to be no evidence that she currently worked as a communist spy. Valentina's story could be completely true. She and her mother may well have come to the States as refugees, with nowhere else to hide.

Sunday, when he greeted Valentina with an enthusiastic handshake, Bishop Greg Bullock thought he discerned a little strain in her eyes, but she kept her voice light, her smile big. He tried to imagine what it would be like to live under the fear that at any moment someone might discover the truth about you and, all of a sudden, a life constructed like a house of cards would come tumbling down. He had not reported her yet, and would not unless he got a clear answer from the Lord. He compared it to the killing of Laban in the Book of Mormon. One could not do such a thing without a clear witness from the Holy Ghost that God demanded it of him. He had prayed fervently for the Holy Ghost to give him such a witness if that was what God wanted. He had received no witness to take that path.

Valentina handed him a folded piece of paper, and Greg tucked it in his pocket as he asked, "Can we change the appointment to nine PM on Thursday night?"

"No. I work Thursday night."

"Wednesday at nine?"

She nodded. Greg thought it best not to have his appointments with her during his regular interview time. He did not want to have her go through his executive secretary to set them up. The interviews' length and the frequency could raise a red flag that something out of the ordinary went on in these sessions. However, he would have to explain to Gayle that he would have yet another regular demand on his time. She was the perfect bishop's wife, never complaining about all the demands this calling made on their family time, bless her heart. She understood that he must keep the confidence of others. She never pressed for details. Still, it amounted to a monumental sacrifice for her.

Valentina had no sooner entered the chapel than Douglas Parkins appeared and enthusiastically shook Bishop Bullock's hand. "Bishop," he said, running his hand over his smooth, slicked-back hair, "There is something, or more accurately, someone I need to talk to you about."

"Set up an appointment through Brother Knott. I have time set aside on Sundays and Tuesdays for interviews."

"I'll do that."

Greg felt a knot begin to form in his stomach. He didn't like to be caught in the middle of an issue between two ward members, doubly so when it posed a clear and dangerous threat to one of them.

Once on the stand, Greg noticed that Douglas had seated himself next to Valentina, and it appeared they were holding hands.

Later, behind his closed bedroom door, Greg pulled out the piece of paper Valentina gave him to see if, by any chance, this Alex might be a shoe size similar to his own. Not at all. The wide though not long, shoe size would make it hard to find a match. No shoes at Deseret Industries approximated the size. At the Army Surplus store, he found soldier boots a bit long but wide enough. Tucking a couple of pairs of socks into the boots, he dropped them by Valentina's home. No one answered the door, so he left the bag on the porch. He felt caught in his own web of deception. Once again, he praised his wife's trust when it came to their finances. She never asked to know where the money went that he spent without giving any accounting to her.

Greg did not see Douglas Parkins' name on his interview list for Tuesday and hoped this was a bullet he might dodge but felt it premature to breathe a sigh of relief. It wasn't Douglas' nature to just let something like this drop.

*****

As Valentina tied a scarf on her head, her hands shook almost as much as her voice, "Now you know what you are supposed to do?"

Sasha nodded, weary that she intended to go over it again.

"Tell me."

His reassurance was not good enough. "I'm to wait about five minutes after you leave. Then I leave by the back door, go to the little alley behind the house, turn to my right, go to the first major east-west street, turn left. Walk past one major street and turn right on the next one. Walk one block. On the corner is a big stone church with no cross on it. The church looks something like a medieval castle. Enter the church. Be as inconspicuous as possible."

She gave a huge sigh as if she wasn't satisfied but didn't know what more to do about it. Sasha watched her walk down the sidewalk, turn right, and she was out of sight. It was night. How much trouble could he get in? Who would see him that would care? Was it really as dangerous as she feared? He let himself out of the back door, threaded his way through the small street and onto the major street. He didn't quite understand the whole point of this. How was this bishop, this man of her church, supposed to help them anyway? Say some kind of incantation, some prayer to a supposedly powerful god who got involved with the petty problems of mankind, and everything would magically be better? Then he would be able to speak English fluently without a discernible accent. Then he would be able to get a job with false papers, and then what? Valentina would be free of him and could pursue her fictional life in this unwelcoming land without fear that he would somehow reveal that they were Russian, and the ruse would be up. Maybe it already was. She had already told the bishop they were Russian. Surely a hard labor camp couldn't be any more boring than living in a comfortable

American house day after day with practically nothing to do. Even a quick death did not seem to be that bad of an option.

*****

Wednesday night, as he waited for Valentina and Alex to show up, Bishop Greg Bullock pondered what kind of story they could use to explain Alex's existence and inability to speak English. Did Alex physically resemble the Eskimos of Alaska? Kamchatka lay just over the Bering Strait from there. Would Russian be his only language?

On Wednesday, Valentina arrived alone. Greg saw her quickly case the surroundings as if she verified that no authorities lurked in the shadows, waiting to apprehend her. How must it be to always live in such fear, never to know if anyone could be trusted?

"Alex is coming from a different direction. I didn't want to be seen walking with him. He should be here shortly."

Just then, the door opened, and a man entered. Valentina said something to him in Russian. Bishop Bullock's first impression of their relationship was the obvious lack of it. They neither touched nor looked at each other. Alex looked neither at him nor at Valentina for clues of what to do or not to do. He shuffled stiffly in the new boots to a chair and sat down.

The Alex Greg had anticipated was totally different from the man in front of him. He had expected that Alex might have at one time been husky, but the second-hand clothes hung loosely on his almost emaciated frame. Alex did not have the black hair or physical characteristics of the American Indians or Eskimos, so they would not be able to make up a story to pass him off as one of them. His features suggested Caucasian, European. What story could they come up with to explain his existence and his lack of English so he could be released from his house prison? Greg extended his hand to Alex and greeted him in Russian.

Alex's eyes met his for the first time, and a flicker of interest flashed there. He nodded but did not take his hand and did not speak.

"Thank you for not reporting us," Valentina said in English as she seated herself.

Feeling it important to include Alex, Greg responded in his halting Russian. "I not think you spies."

While maintaining a cautious guard, Alex's eyes stayed on him as he spoke. The man seemed very uncomfortable, as if out of his element, which undoubtedly he was, having been a house prisoner for what? Maybe as long as two years, with no one to associate with except Valentina.

"So," Greg said to Valentina, but continuing in Russian. "I talk Russian. If not make sense, please translate. If I not understand Alex, please translate."

Wishing he spoke the language with more adeptness to create a more relaxed atmosphere, he just hoped Alex would be willing to open up.

"Tell me about she come to Kamchatka."

For the first time, Alex glanced at Valentina, and Greg wondered if Alex did not understand his request. She merely nodded as if giving him permission to tell his story.

Alex looked at his hands for what seemed like a long time before finally raising his eyes. When he did, Greg saw a flash there that spoke of the strength and resentment that smoldered in this imprisoned body. He could well be said to resemble a caged bear. With a voice much stronger and deeper than his physical appearance suggested, Alex began his tale.

"At that time, I went by Sasha, not Alex. Alexanders are often called Sasha in Russia. I will tell of her coming as I remember it."

Kamchatka 1943

The waves crashed rhythmically against the rocks, punctuated by screams of seagulls and quacks of ducks. Though a lone birch bowed and wildly waved its twisted branches, the wind passed right through the thick, moist, white curtain shrouding the countryside without disturbing it. Standing on a bluff above the shore, Sasha despondently knew his desire to have the fog lift carried even less power than the wind to make it happen. But, still, he wished it. Outwardly, he appeared to have the patience of a wolverine crouching high in a birch tree, waiting for a hungry reindeer to discover the moss the cunning predator dropped at the base of the tree. Inwardly, his thoughts churned in impatience. He, too, sought an arrival, but his intent was not to destroy.

Last summer, when the war canceled all scientific expeditions to the Reserve, neither the lost money nor the lost work troubled Sasha. He missed the good teas, abundant vodka, plentiful cigarettes, and the new shipment of books the scientists always brought. This summer, fortunes brightened.

Knocked to its knees by the formidable, unpredictable Red Army weapon, a Russian winter, the German Army pulled back from Moscow. Though the war still menaced around the edges, it no longer threatened to unravel the very web of normal life and allowed two expeditions to be scheduled this summer. Sasha wanted the first one to happen at all costs, but not for the tea, cigarettes or vodka, or even the books.

Though stone-faced, he struggled not to fidget in impatience. He understood the expedition of scientists not arriving last week as scheduled because of the hurricane, but the little black storm birds seen dimly darting through the fog flew high today. No storm brewed. His cousin Boris, who ran the boat service, trusted his compass. A blinding fog would not deter him. They should be coming.

Reaching into his saddlebag, Sasha withdrew his binoculars and discovered little spiders crawling all over them. Evidently, a spider's nest had hatched in the saddlebag. He shook the tiny spiders from the binoculars and felt a tickle on his hand. One of them just lunched on him. Squashing the spider, Sasha put his chilled binoculars to his eyes in a futile attempt to penetrate the shrouding fog. His lens only caught a seagull in its successful attack on a puffin. He, too, had enjoyed the leathery meat of this shoreline delicacy for his own lunch. He fingered the massive orange bill with its green base, which now hung from a cord of plaited seal hair around his neck. He didn't subscribe to the superstition that it warded off bad spirits if a shaman placed it there.

The scientists wouldn't know that he put it there himself. Some of them might even think he was a shaman. Ha! All the better.

Even as the wind ruffled Sasha's sable fur hat, the cold mist did not penetrate his reindeer skin suit. He ignored the cold biting his eyes and nose, letting the pregnant possibility of the summer warm him. His life, as cyclic as the changing seasons, would soon change forever. A comet shortly would plunge through the orbit of his predictable days, thereafter illuminating even the ordinary.

The excitement sparked a restlessness in Sasha. It reminded him of the excitement he felt as a youth. Each summer, as he prepared to return to Babushka's yurt, this kind of excitement held him captive until he could wildly abandon himself to the lush, joyous sights and sounds of summer on the Reserve. Or the inverse feeling, when summer grew old, and he climbed onto a sledge and coached his dog team to dazzling speeds as he returned to Petropavlovsk. There, he soared to far-off places and other times in words and pictures in every book he could get his hands on. Chirikov's coming spawned that kind of excitement.

Sasha heard the slap, slap of the oars before he saw the boat. He untied the horses' halters and slipped a bridle on the saddle horses, one for himself and one for each of the four scientists on his list. As the boat approached land, Sasha put away his binoculars, the most visible evidence of his modernity, and finished his preparations to greet his guests. He briefly debated skipping this little ritual, wondering if it would ruin or enhance his chances with Chirikov, but even Chirikov needed to prove his mettle. Sasha dug his fingers into the soft mud making sure to cake his fingernails with the gooey substance. Smearing a little on his face, he smelled the rich earthy odor. He wiped the rest of the mud on his reindeer-skin suit. He would not disappoint them. He would look like what they would expect from reading the explorers.

"*Tétk oun, oukhtchitch!* (Look out! A girl!)" Boris called in the Kamchadal language.

Why a girl? Restricted explicitly to scientific study, the Kronotsky Nature Reserve held no appeal for girls. The rules prohibited children of the scientists from coming because of the impossibility of guaranteeing safety.

"Enokitch? (What?)" Sasha responded in Kamchadal. But something else held Boris' attention, and he did not answer.

Standing at a distance, Sasha folded his arms across his chest and watched them disembark. Of the scientists, only Chirikov's reputation preceded him. Would he be able to identify him by appearance only? He could eliminate the woman scientist. Wait a minute. There was no woman in that boat, only a girl and three men. A short, stout man climbed out of the boat first and extended his hand to the girl. She stepped into a shaft of light that broke momentarily through the dense, white curtain. Because of the wisps of fog wafting around her feet, it seemed that she floated on a cloud rather than walked on land. He shook his head as if that could clear the cobwebs created by the mystical impression.

Sasha looked back at the boat. Only two men scientists remained in it. He did not see a woman scientist. This small, teenaged female could no way merit the honored badge of scientist. How had she ever wangled permission to come? Volunteered as a cook? Why would she want to take a trip like this? Why, when handed the opportunity of the lifetime to work with Chirikov, should a threat to his very safety sully that? Leo rotted in a prison camp because of an accident of a careless female scientist on his expedition, and Kolenkhov died by hanging after supposedly raping a cook. Women only spelled trouble, especially young ones.

Sasha shifted his attention back to the men. Two of them fit his expectations: middle-aged, with the spreading waists of office-working city-dwellers, at least as near as he could tell from their abundant wraps. The other man, though considerably older, moved with athletic spryness. Hopefully, this man would prove to be Chirikov. He already esteemed Chirikov to be a champion in spirit. He wanted him to be one in body also. The older scientist wore a coat, but the wind-tossed his white hair.

As the men began unloading their gear, the young woman floated right up to Sasha, interrupting his thoughts and forcing him to focus on her. She appraised him with the unabashed frankness of a child through eyes a darker blue than any autumn sky.

Sasha appraised her as she did him, trying to weigh her appearance against his experience with women. She must have purchased her reindeer-skin coat in Petropavlovsk. The silk embroidery shone in vivid blues, oranges, and yellows, and the glossy beaver fur ornamenting the collar and cuffs, typical of Kamchatka, testified to the newness of the coat. She pushed the foxskin hood off her head, revealing two headscarves worn in the Russian fashion. A blue, checkered one covered her forehead. A white one created a halo around her head, twisted under her chin, around her neck, and knotted at the nape. Not a wisp of hair escaped from under the scarves.

Her sensible dress did not allay Sasha's apprehensions. If, by some miracle, she were an astronomer as the registration claimed, why would she come in the summertime when sunlight lasted practically all night long? Something was amiss.

"I'm Valentina Markovna," she said, her voice like lilting music. "You're the expedition guide?"

Sasha nodded.

"Do you speak Russian?" she asked.

How would he have understood her first question if he didn't? How else could he lead them? She should know everyone spoke Russian here. Sasha nodded again.

"What's your name?" Her questions buzzed like the Herculean mosquitoes that plagued Kamchatka all summer long.

"Tatischev." He couldn't swat her except figuratively, but he could ignore her. He turned his back on her and scratched the spider bite on his hand before untying the halters on the pack horses.

"Your first name." She did not accept his dismissal.

Maybe he couldn't ignore her. He resented this push for intimacy. "You do not need to know my first name."

"You don't expect me to call you Tatischev do you?" She went with frequent emphases like the endless song of a skylark.

"Yes. That's what the scientists call me on these expeditions."

"But I'm different, you see."

Yes, Sasha could see the difference. Not a man, prettier, smaller, and brasher than the local women. With that combination, he needed to ignore her beauty and remember both her youth and brashness. If he overstepped his bounds, the consequences could be severe.

"Well...," she said, tapping a tiny foot clad in a sealskin boot, "Are you going to tell me your name?"

Without answering, Sasha raised his eyebrows and, turning away from her, led the pack horses on a diagonal path from the bluff down to the boat. He caught a glint of amusement in the scientists' smiles, and Boris openly grinned at him.

Sasha growled, "Let's load the horses."

Boris tossed Sasha a disappointingly small package. Sasha's features momentarily softened in pleasure with the knowledge he held at least some of the treasured books he had requested. He consciously dropped all expression from his face when he realized Valentina was watching him. He stored the books in his saddlebag, patted the horse's rump, and turned back to meet the scientists.

In a flurry of introductions, Sasha learned the older man was Chirikov. Though no flicker of repulsion could be read in Chirikov's expression as he shook Sasha's mud-smeared hand, no interest sparked there either. Of course, Chirikov would not have come expecting to have his research channeled through a native he surely presumed to be ignorant when he himself reigned undisputed as supreme among ornithologists in the Russian empire. He would not value Sasha's council until he saw him as an invaluable resource. Sasha knew he could have Chirikov begging at his knee. He could definitely lay the groundwork, if not spring the trap if Chirikov rode back to camp next to him.

Valentina hung back and let the men lash the seal skin boxes of supplies onto the pack horses. The wooden support saddles creaked and groaned under their weight. As Sasha tied the ropes securing the boxes, he watched the scientist identified as Mark Kaflov help Valentina onto her horse. Each man took the rope of a packhorse and mounted his own riding horse. Valentina immediately reined in next to Sasha at the head of the group. Kaflov followed them, and Chirikov and the zoologist took up the rear. Seeing no way to reshuffle the order so that Chirikov rode next to him, Sasha sent a longing glance towards the greatest ornithologist on the face of the earth, who rode two horses behind him and one to the left, and then glared at the silly little female next to him. The path wouldn't become wide enough to change positions until just shy of camp.

"If the fog lifted, could we see the volcanoes from here?"

Her incessant chatter started to buzz around him again.

"Yes," Sasha answered. Had she come to sight-see? The Reserve prohibited tourists. Who agreed to bring her?

"Tolbachik?"

So he couldn't classify her as totally ignorant. "When it's clear, Tolbachik can be seen. It is not on the Reserve. We will be closest to Mount Kronotsky. It is the most beautiful cone-shaped volcano on the peninsula."

"I so wanted to see the beautiful sights as we came in, but the fog has hidden everything." Passion filled her voice. She tied her reins together and hung them over the saddle horn. Her hands took flight as she talked.

"In his book, the American explorer Kennan is so poetic in describing Kamchatka."

She went off into what sounded like a memorized quote extolling the beauties of Kamchatka. Sasha barely listened to her prattle. He didn't need to see Kamchatka either through her eyes or this Kennan's that she parroted.

"Well?" she asked.

"Huh?" he said.

"Doesn't that just thrill you? That's the Kamchatka I came to see."

He scarcely heard any of what she said. Her description of the Kamchatka she hoped to see did not give her a right to be here.

"Hold onto your reins tighter. If you give the horse his head, he'll run away with you."

"You're not even listening," she pouted.

Ignoring that, he said, "You need to remember you're on a horse in a fog. You're not on a stage."

"Okay, okay." She took the reins more firmly. "Do you know of Kennan?"

Sasha shook his head. He knew nothing of foreign explorers to Kamchatka, and he didn't expect.t a female child to be his teacher.

"He explored here in the 1860s. He was sent here to prepare for the telegraph to go over this part of Russia." Her voice showed that his ignorance clearly astonished her. "You've got a real treat ahead. I brought his book."

Read about the beauty of this place when one could see it in person? That would be like reading about a beautiful woman even as she stood before him waiting for his caress, waiting for him to hug her, kiss her, taste her, have her. Sasha knew Kamchatka as an intimate lover. He knew her moods, the expressions of the weather upon the face of the land. He knew the joy in the brightness of her glorious days and the fear of her tempestuous anger expressed in hurricane winds and volcanic fury. He knew the meaning behind the shifts in her colors and sounds. He adored her and was devoted to her. Never would he leave her for another land. Even now, in fog-shrouded Kamchatka, he knew her as a lover in the dark.

"Of course, you would have to read English to read Kennan." Valentina jerked his thoughts back to her. "Do you read English?"

"*Nyet*." Sasha spit the word out. Read an American to learn about Kamchatka? Talk about ridiculous.

"I read English fluently. I speak it too, with an English accent so good I could be a spy." She urged her horse faster as it lagged behind Sasha's.

A little braggart, a *pokazuka*. Let her leave this paradisaical land to be a spy. Excellent idea.

"Maybe if we get rained in, I could teach you to read and speak English."

With Chirikov here, the thought that he would spend time with her if they got rained in struck him as preposterous. "I have other plans if we get rained in."

She looked at him, her voice and face shocked, "You do not know me well enough even to think such a thing."

He did not resist laughing. A man did not have to know a woman at all to think that, but his thoughts went elsewhere this time. "Excuse me. It's you that thought that not me. My other plans do not include you."

She sent him a dark look, but it silenced her a while, but only a bit.

Her face petulant, she threw out another line, "If you prefer, I could teach you French. A French explorer also wrote a book. He explored here long before Kennan. He's quite funny. You'd enjoy reading him."

"Look, I don't intend to learn about Kamchatka by reading foreign explorers." Sasha shook his head, determined to be taciturn. He didn't know of any French explorer who wrote about Kamchatka, and he didn't care to learn. He wanted to learn from Chirikov, although he expected to end up being the teacher as much as the student.

"So you're going to restrict yourself to the Russian explorers? They are so dry."

"I didn't learn about Kamchatka from reading explorers." His voice dripped with exasperation.

She turned to him in amazement as if that eliminated all possibilities. "How did you learn?"

"I was born here. I learned from living here."

"No." She shook her head. "You're not a native. Even though it's been two hundred years since the Russians explored here, Kennan described the natives the same only a hundred years ago. Native characteristics would not have changed that much in the last hundred years. Your hair is blondish-red and curly. You have blue eyes. You can't be a native."

She turned her head aside as if categorizing him as unworthy of further discussion.

Sasha knew his physical characteristics did not fit the historical Kamchadal described by Russian explorers. Generations of interbreeding had erased the flat nose, slanted eyes, and straight black hair in Sasha. He did have the squat figure typical of his Kamchadal ancestors, and his lifestyle endowed him with the leathery skin others portrayed them as having. It always amused Sasha that the scientists from the west couldn't seem to see either the curl or the blondish-red of his beard and shoulder-length hair. He deliberately designed his costume to bind them to a blind acceptance of their preconception, but this child-woman pierced beneath his facade and unmasked him.

"Didn't your Kennan mention all of the Russians who have been here since the 1600s? Did he mention the custom of Kamchadals offering their wives and daughters to visiting travelers to warm their cold nights? Maybe you're too young and innocent to understand that." He almost enjoyed sparring with her, stripping away her pretense of knowledge.

"I'm neither that young nor that innocent. I'm seventeen, and I have known a lover."

And bragging about it, but seventeen? Six years younger than himself. A bit older than he expected. Well, that reshuffled the cards, but Chirikov still trumped. If she insisted on playing, she'd be playing old maid. No way would he allow her to distract him from his opportunity to work with Chirikov.

"So you are one of those children of disputed parentage?" she asked.

"Not me. My grandparents and also some of their ancestors. French, Russian, maybe even American. Maybe Kennan is my ancestor."

"No. He didn't mention having fathered any children here. I guess that doesn't mean he didn't. That's an intriguing thought. You could be descended from any of the early explorers."

"A hundred years ago, some of my Russian ancestors were sent here to do agricultural experiments and civilize the natives by their industry."

Valentina cast a sidelong glance at him and laughed. "Evidently, the natives still resist being civilized."

Sasha clammed up. He didn't like the way she poked fun at him and doubted his word.

"Why do the horses not sink in the spongy tundra? Kennan said it would be exhausting for a horse to walk through the tundra because he would sink to his knees with every step."

She didn't know how to be silent. Words burst from her like lava from a volcano.

"Kennan didn't have me for a guide. I have charted a path to our campsite of either rocks or boardwalk. If you took off across the tundra, the horse would sink." Sasha half hoped she would take off across the tundra just to see what would happen. That would quickly flush out the party responsible for her in this group.

She glanced away from the path but seemed able to resist the temptation. She stayed at his side. "Have you ever been to Moscow?"

"*Nyet*. I've never left Kamchatka, and I don't intend to."

She laughed. "You don't have to be huffy about it, but you may get your chance. The clutches of the draft can find you here."

"They won't take me. Both of my parents spent time in prison camps. Even though my father died there and my mother served her term for some trumped-up charge, I am not to be trusted because I am the offspring of enemies of the people. It's fine with me if they kill off all those fine patriotic boys and leave us enemies to father the next generation."

"It is ironic, isn't it? But you may not be as safe as you think. A lot of fine patriotic boys have been killed. They are getting more desperate for soldiers. They'll use you before they'll lose the war." A catch in her voice finally forced her to stop speaking. Someone who mattered to her must have died in the war.

They rode in silence for some time. Sasha peeked back at Chirikov and, even at that distance, could almost see his ears perk up at the barely discernible trumpeting of swans. The fog gradually began to dissipate, and Valentina emitted little squeals of delight at each new beauty revealed. "It's just as Kennan said. I bet he saw this very site."

Or one of a hundred others just like it. Kennan, Kennan, Kennan. At least they could claim allies in this, equally appreciating the actual beauty of the snow-clad volcanoes, stark against the deep blue skies, and the meadows generously sprinkled with shattered rainbows of color from the profusion of wildflowers. The lush grass caressed their knees even on horseback. Abundant bird songs blended in a rich symphonic melody. No one ever adequately described the beauty of this place.

"Is it really light all night?" Valentina jumped into his thoughts again.

Sasha nodded. "Essentially. Since you knew you could not expect to see many stars from Kamchatka in the summertime, why did you, an astronomer, come on this trip?"

"I'm not really an astronomer. Astronomy is my passion. I know the constellations, and I can identify the commonly seen planets. The form asked what kind of scientist I am, so I put the most accurate answer since I am not really a scientist. Still, I would love to come in the wintertime with the long, long nights, to see the stars. I can just imagine the northern lights painting the frigid, winter sky. It would be so romantic."

Beautiful? He thought, yes. Romantic? Freezing temperatures didn't strike Sasha as romantic. "So why did you come on this trip?"

"Because my father agreed to bring me. Mark Kaflov is my father."

"You should not have come."

"Why not?"

"It's dangerous here. Both Bering and Krasheninnikov lost their lives exploring here, and they are not the only ones. They just have monuments to them, but there have been others."

"What would happen to you if something happened to me?"

Sasha shuddered. Was she setting him up? A precedent existed. "Prison Camp."

"Then, it behooves you to take care of me."

"I'm not hired to rescue damsels in distress. If your father brought you, he should take care of you."

"He should, but he does not face the same danger you do if something goes wrong."

Sasha sent her a dark look and urged his mare faster, moving the packhorse over to occupy the space next to him, leaving no space for Valentina. She dropped back and rode next to her father.

So, another layer of fog cleared, illuminating the reason for her coming on this trip. Someone she loved died in the war, and her father spoiled her by taking her on a trip. She somehow targeted Sasha for something: Romance? Entertainment? Childish, boastful, baffling, and intriguing all described her, but poison crowned the list. He would be best served to have as little to do with her as possible. Pampering her would be her father's job.

3

Sasha's Camp on Kamchatka

Salt Lake City 1948

Valentina didn't dare look into Bishop Bullock's eyes when Alex finally fell silent. She couldn't even speak. Had she really been so bad? He remembered other details of their meeting with amazing accuracy. Could his portrayal of her be just as accurate? Had she really been the immature, self-serving girl Alex described? If only she had stayed aloof and truly had nothing to do with him! Coming to Kamchatka would have been but a fleeting memory, not a persistent problem risking both their lives.

"Valentina?" Bishop Bullock prompted when she continued to say nothing. "Would you care to pick up your side of the story now?"

She did a quick side-line glance at Alex. He also looked at her. Did she detect a gleefulness in his expression? Probably her best defense would be humor—portraying herself as the same spoiled girl he had. She couldn't deny there had been elements of truth therein. She began with the feelings she had experienced at his reeking rejection, amazed at how well she could still call them up.

Kamchatka 1943

Well. Well! Didn't he think he reigned supreme! He would soon learn he had met his match. Though the indulged younger sister, her three brothers, and Mikel, through their own teasing and rebuffs, had carefully tutored her in the art of getting the best of an over-inflated male. This guide, this...this red beard, this Barbarossa would be begging for her attention before this trip ended. His tea without sugar would taste good to him compared to the words he would be eating.

"So, what do you think of our guide?" Her father asked as she took her position next to him.

"He's a stuffed shirt, full of himself."

Her father chuckled. "And what stick do you use to measure him by?"

He might as well have said what her brothers always taunted her with, "It takes one to know one." She didn't answer, nor did she find it amusing.

Valentina nursed her smarting ego, trying to devise her next offensive in this conflict with the potential of escalating into a war. She might be young, she might be female, but she would not tolerate being treated as non-important. Barbarossa would be taken down a notch, not her. The path widened, and Valentina regained her position next to this native who thought his experience far superior to her learning. She preferred her father's company to Mr. Know-it-All, but she would need lots of contact to wear him down. Even though next to him, she assumed the posture and attitude of a queen, disdaining him as if his only value consisted in showing her the way. She did not find him worthy of her conversation.

She broke her silence as they rode into what must be their camp, "I'm so glad the *balagans* have not changed!" Surely he'd be impressed that she knew the word for the conical shelters standing like hats with wide brims on high pole pedestals. "I feel that I have gone back into history, and it is still the same."

"It hasn't changed because it works. We are not a museum trying to recapture the world described by explorers here two hundred years ago." He seemed determined to remind her of her ignorance despite her book learning. "Even nature changes. The volcanoes blow their tops off."

She smiled to herself. He answered her, though reluctantly. She would enjoy breaking him down. "I'm still glad the balagans haven't changed." She jutted her chin out in a gesture of defiance and hoped her blue eyes darkened as they snapped. She knew ways to subdue a man that only a woman could use.

A litter of four white pups with curly tails tumbled from the shade of a balagan, yipping a greeting. The bitch watched from the shade, raising bursts of dust by thumping her tail on the ground. Valentina jumped from her horse and scooped a squirming puppy in her arms, caught in the moment of the excitement of actually being here in the world of the explorers. She buried her face in the dusty fur and turned to Barbarossa, "Oh, they are so cute! Do you run a sled?"

"I have my own team."

Now that would be interesting. "I wish I could be here in the winter. I would love to ride on a dog sled."

"Come back in the winter." His voice grated with insincerity.

"Maybe I'll surprise you. Maybe I will come back in the winter." Although it would be interesting to ride on a dog sled with an expert, his frosty manner didn't make it seem very inviting.

Barbarossa laughed harshly and shook his head.

So readily he dismissed her, the heathen! He probably had not even the slightest idea of how to charm a woman. Well, she knew how to charm a man and leave him dangling with desire and no possibility of fulfillment. He'd wish he'd never met her.

The leather creaked on Barbarossa's saddle as he climbed down from his horse. He uncinched the saddle and lifted it off his horse, hanging it by one stirrup from the stump of a branch on a silver birch. Barbarossa glared at her. "You need to take care of your horse."

Valentina turned her back on him without answering and continued to cuddle the puppy. She knew her father or Comrade Chirikov would pamper her in this matter. She watched and counted as the trees' canopies swayed under the sudden uneven weight before slowly regaining balance as each scientist hung his saddle on a branch stump. Someone had hung up her saddle.

Barbarossa knelt by his horse and buckled some straps around its front legs, dismissing her as she did him, even though she stood but a few feet from him, cooing to the puppy. He arose and slipped a bell belt over the horse's head and swatted the horse on the rump. It jumped off, the bell clanging at each leap. The other horses followed. Valentina could smell the robust, horsey odor on him even as the horses disappeared into the trees.

"Won't the other horses run away?" She asked, determined to make him acknowledge her.

"No." He looked at her father as if seeking advice on dealing with this childish peppering of questions. Her father met his eye squarely, smiled, and shrugged as if to say, 'You deal with her as you want.' Barbarossa indulged her with an explanation. "Every time there is a group of horses, one tends to be the lead horse. If that horse is hobbled so it can't go too far, too fast, the others will stay near it. The bell tells me where to find it."

Each time he gave in with a response, Valentina cheered at the tiny victory. She eyed the shelters and baited him. "So, why do we need three balagans?"

"Sometimes the expedition parties are large," Barbarossa explained, indulging her again. "You'll use this one for lodging," he pointed, "and that one for storage. Scientists on these expeditions tend to bring a lot of stuff."

Valentina didn't hide her smile as he gave in and responded again. "And the third one?"

"My quarters."

Valentina turned a twinkling eye on him and pushed the scarves off her head, revealing the braid twined around her head, which she knew shone like a golden crown in the sunlight. His eyes registered appreciation before he glanced away. Score.

"Your own quarters, huh?" Her voice teased. "None of the explorers mentioned the natives having their own quarters apart from visiting guests."

He turned away in deliberate dismissal.

Not surprising. A battle of subterfuge, not all-out attack, necessitated some apparent defeats. In the meantime, she had lots of interesting things to investigate before her next attack.

Valentina went to the base of the balagan indicated as lodging for the scientists during the expedition. A notched log ladder ran at an angle from the ground to the platform running around the balagan, which she guessed to be twelve feet high. She attempted to climb the notched log ladder, but after the first couple of feet, it turned, dumping her in the dust and knocking the breath from her. She didn't have to look at the others to know if they watched her. They made no effort to contain their laughter. She stood and brushed herself off. She would show not only Barbarossa but all of them that she could do this. She climbed higher and fell three more times before she heard Barbarossa say to her father, "You'd better go hold the ladder steady for her, so she doesn't fall near the top."

Although aware her father slowly loped in her direction, she didn't wait for him. She let her father and Comrade Chirikov pamper her in some things, but she would prove her merit in others. Confident she had figured out how to climb these crazy poles, she no longer feared falling. She climbed at least eight feet and kept on going. She would be at the top before her father reached her unless the log turned. If it did, well, she didn't want to think about that. It would show that pride ruled to the point of her making a very foolish choice with perhaps serious and long-lasting consequences. She expected everyone, including herself held their breath, hoping that she would be successful. No one made a human sound against the abundant bird songs and the distant tinkle of the horse's bell. She poked her head through the round hole in the platform and climbed onto the flat surface, her triumph only overshadowed by her gratitude for her safety. She deliberately looked at Barbarossa and thought she read relief on his face before he quickly turned away.

The men resumed their chatter and went back to unloading the gear from the pack horses. She watched Barbarossa expertly scramble up the notched log ladder of the storage balagan, and let down a rope that the scientists tied to the seal-skin boxes. With muscles bulging and sweat glistening, Barbarossa hauled the boxes up to the platform. If one liked the tough and rough macho man, he could be considered attractive. Barbarossa's build reminded her of Dmitri's, but Dmitri's city living left him less trim with fewer observable muscles. Both Andrei and Markuska had sported their mother's long limbs, while Mikel had been tall and very slender.

Valentina pulled herself back from her momentary reminiscing, which couldn't be indulged in or it would lead to tears. She went in and investigated the lodging balagan. After assessing it and measuring it against her expectations, she came back out of the low door and accused Barbarossa as if he tricked her. "There's a stove in it and windows. It has changed."

Barbarossa paused in untying a box. "Be glad," he called. "This one hasn't. It is nice and dark and will fill with smoke to burn your eyes and lungs and dirty your hair when you build a fire. I don't find anything charming about it, but you can have it for your own personal quarters if you desire."

Valentina eyed him a moment, then looked from the platform to the ground. She would check it out. Just coming to Kamchatka felt like a trip back into history, especially since she traveled on the words of explorers here a century or more ago. She would like to see it and maybe even experience it as they had.

Feeling a hesitant fear, Valentina edged backward onto the log ladder. "Please don't turn, please don't turn," she chanted to herself as she gingerly crawled down the log ladder. Allowing herself one glance at Barbarossa, Valentina found his eyes fixed on her. Despite his protestations to the contrary, she knew there would be repercussions on him if she came to injury, but the higher cost would be hers in this instance. Successfully reaching the ground, she went over and climbed the notched log ladder of the storage balagan a little more confidently while her father held the base. Peering into the dark recesses, she admitted that she too preferred the stove and windows.

Salt Lake City 1948

Valentina kept her eyes on Alex as she spoke and saw in his eyes a challenge to her, to be honest. She felt him responding to the type of sparring they had engaged in so long ago on Kamchatka. There was none of that in their ill-defined relationship now, partly because she had proved herself and mostly because he was totally dependent on her. He had been a totally different person when he was independent. She couldn't imagine that in their current circumstances. Who would he be if he could be independent here, in Utah?

She nodded at Sasha to pick up the tale, knowing his continual portrayal of her would be as unflattering as before.

Kamchatka 1943

From the time they approached camp, Sasha reluctantly admitted to himself that any courting of Chirikov's favor would have to be postponed at least until after they settled in. After storing all the boxes except those to be used immediately, Sasha looked around for Chirikov and found him standing on the lodging balagan platform with his binoculars to his eyes. Feeling his own hunger, Sasha reminded himself to be patient until after a meal. He knew that Valentina would be the cook even if she were a serious scientist and despite her youth. Being female gave her the job. Though an absolute pest, he could tolerate her constant questions and know-it-all attitude for the far superior food he would undoubtedly enjoy.

Valentina withdrew the urn-like metal container of the samovar from a box set aside with the cooking gear and turned to him, "Where is your water source?"

Sasha pointed to a cluster of larches a hundred feet away. "A fresh-water spring surfaces there." He stepped to where a yoke rested on branches between twin stone birch trees. As he lifted it down, the buckets swung on ropes attached to notches on the tips of the shoulders of the yoke. He handed it to Valentina. Without taking it, she eyed the yoke warily, "That is too big for me."

Sasha shrugged, set the yoke down, picked up his package of books, and headed for his own balagan. When he reached the platform, he glanced back to see her father shoulder the yoke and head to the spring just as it should b—them solving their own problems without relying on him.

It annoyed Sasha that the little female's taunt about him having his own quarters made him uncomfortable. He indulged himself in private quarters to store his books and artifacts from the tribes and specimens from nature he accumulated. He didn't show these to others because the natives would mock him, and the scientists would seek to profit from his treasures.

When Sasha returned to the campsite, he enjoyed the sight of Valentina kneeling on the ground, her rear in the air, trying to blow life into the banked coals from his morning fire which she had put in the cylindrical tube of the samovar. She stood, glared at him, and removed a tea from a box he recognized as imported from India. Evidently, the war hadn't made every luxury unavailable. He made his teas from locally grown herbs, but he much preferred imported teas. While the water in the samovar came to a boil, Valentina made the strong tea mixture called *zavarka* in a teapot. Into each glass seated in a metal holder, she poured a little of the zavarka and then added boiling water from the samovar. Sasha took one sip and spat it out.

"No sugar?" he asked.

Ryabtsev, the zoologist, answered, "Though much in Moscow has resumed some semblance of normality, the food is still scarce and will continue to be for some time. The men are away fighting, and the women are trying to do the men's normal jobs and extra ones created by the war. Women largely staff munitions factories. Those left to farm are fewer and fewer." He shrugged as if apologetic.

That level of deprivation had not reached Kamchatka. Sasha went to his own stash. Valentina and the three scientists accepted his offer of the coarse brownish lump of raw sugar that they held in their teeth as they sipped their tea through it with a gratification characteristic of one long denied a basic joy.

As he swallowed the warm liquid, Sasha debated whether this would be a good time to show his skills to Chirikov. The esteemed scientist intently listened to bird sounds and attempted to sight them in his binoculars. He occasionally made notes. Sasha decided to hold off a bit, observe how Chirikov worked, and let him feel overwhelmed by the sheer plethora of birds to catalog on the Reserve. After a few days, despite his considerable knowledge and experience, Chirikov would be very appreciative of Sasha's abilities.

Sasha shifted his attention to Valentina's father, wondering what she inherited from him besides his name. Nothing physical except maybe height. Kaflov sported a squat, short figure. Valentina's shortness appeared petite because she lacked the breadth of her father. His hair may have been blond like hers at one time, but now it lay gray and lifeless against his head. His light blue eyes held nothing memorable about them.

"Does fish form the mainstay of your diet here?" Ryabtsev interrupted Sasha's thoughts.

Sasha nodded and watched the portly scientist rub his tightly trimmed black beard.

"Where do you fish?" Valentina's father peered around as if he expected to see the source. Sasha slowly pushed himself to his feet, swatting at the flies and mosquitoes buzzing around him. "I'll show you." The puppies immediately began to jump and nip at his feet.

Sasha accepted the good, pre-rolled cigarette offered by Kaflov. Valentina also stood and took a cigarette. Kaflov struck a match, lit his own cigarette, and then each of the others. Taking a deep drought and exhaling in pleasure, Sasha lifted a fish net from a nail on a balagan pole. He led the way to the little freshwater pond created when the lava flow sealed off the stream's path. Valentina scooped a puppy into her arms and trotted along behind. Sasha realized that she would be ever-present, just like the puppies. He puzzled over what drove her. Curiosity? What did she really expect to accomplish on this trip?

Seeing the fish dart through the clear water, Kaflov asked, "What kinds of fish do you have here?"

"Trout, loach, and a red salmon that adjusted to spawning in the shallow lake."

Valentina lay on a rock jutting over the edge of the pond and trailed her fingers in the cold liquid.

The fish swam so lazily in the still, blue water that Sasha could catch them with his bare hands. That never worked for Muscovites. Their very presence seemed to stir up the waters with impatience. He handed the net to Kaflov, who splashed the net in the water, and the fish scattered. Kaflov made several futile dips until Valentina said, "Here, let me do it."

Still lying on the rock, she held the net still in the water until a trout swam right into it. She tossed her catch to Kaflov, who obligingly cleaned it while she caught another.

Sasha turned back to camp, unwillingly impressed. They wouldn't need him there, for that he could be grateful.

Sasha retrieved his *balalaika* from his balagan as the evening fell. He strummed it as the men gathered around the fire. Eventually, Valentina joined them as she finished the dishes. Ryabtsev broke out a bottle of vodka and passed it around, much to Sasha's satisfaction. The men drank right from the bottle. Valentina poured a half glass and drank it without a cough or sputter, giving evidence that her father no longer viewed her as a child in her drinks. What a baffling combination between an adult and a child!

Sasha again watched Chirikov as he made a crude drawing of a three-toed woodpecker. Sasha had assumed that Chirikov did the artwork in his book, but evidently not.

"Will you show me the sarana lily?" Valentina called Sasha's attention back to her. "I want to dig the root and dry it in the sunshine and make flour out of it for bread."

Doesn't she ever quit? Sasha wondered. He glanced at the Ryabtsev and Kaflov. They didn't bother to suppress the smiles that played across their lips. Even Chirikov glanced from Valentina to Sasha before going back to his drawing. Evidently, they viewed Sasha and Valentina's inter-actions as a major source of entertainment on this expedition.

The alcohol seeping through his system warmed Sasha's sarcasm. "I thought you knew everything about Kamchatka."

"No. Not everything." She turned her pretty back on him.

Sasha smirked to see her bristle, glad to have discovered a way to keep her in check, and then realized he idly played "Dark Eyes." He'd better be careful to steer away from love songs. Who knew how this young damsel might misinterpret his intent. He switched to "I'll Sow Goose Foot," and she spontaneously broke into song in a clear, soprano voice as lovely as any songbird on the reserve. "I'll sow goose-foot on the shore. I'll sow goose-foot on the shore. My large seedlings. My large greens." He stilled the balalaika.

"Well--will you?" she said after a moment when he said nothing more.

"Will I what?"

"Show me where the sarana lily grows."

"The sarana lily does not even bloom until mid-July, and then the whole countryside is covered with its bright, cherry-red flower." His hand swept the panorama. "You cannot dig the root until fall.

Valentina's face took on a petulant look like a spoiled child denied her way, "Did you dry some last fall?"

"Yes, I have some."

She brightened. "Will you teach me how to make bread with it?"

Sasha smiled in spite of himself, worn down by the childish charm in her persistence. No wonder she expected to get her way.

"Yes, but not today. Maybe tomorrow."

"Will you show me cloudberries to put in it?"

Sasha shook his head and said impatiently. "*Chort,* lady! Cloudberries are just white blossoms now. You'll have to use dry ones." He wanted to listen to the men talk.

She flashed him a smile of apology and lightly touched his arm. It disconcerted him for her to play the child and woman at the same time. He knew how to deal with the child, but not the woman. He turned his back on her.

A scarlet rosefinch, a nuthatch. Determined to shut out any interference from Valentina, Sasha mentally cataloged the birds Chirikov would be hearing. A goshawk, a black-legged kittiwake, a--

"It amazed me to see all the German tanks mired and rusting in the snow." Ryabtsev's voice snatched up Sasha's thoughts and quickly transported them to another time, another place. "Did we ever take them by surprise! No weapon of theirs could fight against General Winter."

Sasha set the balalaika aside, wanting to concentrate on the war talk.

"General Winter fought impartially," Kaflov responded with a bitter tone. "We suffered tremendous losses too. The tragedy of seeing both a Red horse and soldier frozen still standing haunts me,"

"But those Siberian boys knew how to do battle." Ryabtsev persisted in seeing Winter as fighting on Russia's side, "Germans freezing all around and the Siberian boys dug away the snow to ground level, packed it into walls, lined the floor with evergreen branches, put a tarpaulin on for a roof. With an oil drum and a piece of piping, they had a stove that made it as toasty as home."

Kaflov merely growled.

Sasha momentarily watched Valentina as she smoked a cigarette and listened to this talk, and then she said, "I hoped you'd got tired of rehashing all that on the long train ride getting here. Do we have to hear it while we are here too?"

"Just because we went away doesn't mean the war went away. It is still going on and will continue to until long after we've returned." Kaflov said dryly.

Ryabtsev chuckled, "Did you read of those Germans captured in women's fur coats, jackets, even silk underwear? Now why they would have thought that would keep them warm, I don't know."

Valentina stood up abruptly. "Will you walk with me?" She asked Sasha.

Sasha shook his head. He actually liked to hear these first-hand accounts of the war. In Petropavlovsk last winter, he heard and read some of the war, but, once the news got there, everyone tasted its staleness no matter how vividly told. No one doubted the victories were wildly exaggerated and the defeats minimized in typical Russian fashion. He wanted to know more about how it really was.

Sasha viewed the war as safely removed from his world, another man's quarrel, another man's pain. Native Kamchatkan tribes still thought of Russia as a foreign invader and saw the oppression much more clearly than any benefits. That left them indifferent to whether Russia won or lost this war. Could Hitler be any worse or any better a leader than Stalin? Sasha didn't imagine his life would change much regardless of which man ruled. Moscow's remoteness seemed untouchable, Germany's even more so. As long as they kept their quarrels far from Kamchatka, Sasha cared little for what happened. Still, he felt a curiosity to hear about it.

"It's a wonder that we can even hold our own after the great purges of 1938; so many of those with military expertise, executed." Ryabtsev unfaltering steered the conversation to more war topics.

"And it hasn't stopped there. Pavlov was executed just a few months ago for losing a battle, and he was trying to do only what Stalin ordered. Sometimes one wonders if the greatest danger is internal or external." Kaflov tossed some sticks at his feet into the fire, sending sparks flying.

Sasha quickly glanced at the others to see if anyone reacted to these traitorous words. No shock registered on anyone's face. Valentina looked at him with bored pleading. Ryabtsev drew on his cigarette and blew a cloud of smoke in the air. Of course, Ryabtsev's words had been tinged with the same criticism.

Chirikov cleared his throat and made his first contribution to the conversation. "Without the people volunteers digging the trenches around Moscow, we could not have kept the Germans out."

"Are there that many men still in Moscow?" Sasha fed the conversation.

"No. Just old men like us. Too old, too weak, or too sick to be much good in the service. Zhukov said over 250,000 women and teenagers moved almost three million cubic meters of earth with no mechanical help. They..." Chirikov cut himself off as he heard the distinctive *zick* call of the yellow-breasted bunting.

"May I?" Valentina reached for the balalaika.

Sasha shrugged, and she picked it up and began to strum with expertise that surprised him. She started to sing, "He called me maiden, He persuaded me, Come with me maiden, Come to the open field for a walk." Sasha ignored the sweet invitation of her words.

Chirikov continued to keep himself aloof from the war talk. His eyes and ears constantly researched, even in camp. Without being too obvious, Sasha observed his methods while listening to the others. Patience coupled with immobility and making a "shh, shh" sound comprised his only techniques in drawing birds to him. Sasha noticed that within the bounds limiting him, Chirikov experienced amazing success, but Sasha knew his own unique skills would be a wondrous liberation to him.

Sasha aided him by silencing Valentina on the balalaika by asking her, "Were you in the trenches?"

"I helped dig some, and then I was sent to my sister's place near Tula for safety."

"Safety?" Ryabtsev snorted. "That was in the very path of the Germans. Did they reach the village where you were?"

"Oh, yes." Valentina put the balalaika aside. Evidently, she did not object to the war talk if she were the topic of the conversation.

"How did the people receive them?" Ryabtsev rested his forearms on his legs and leaned forward, giving her his undivided attention.

Valentina preened to it. "Like a liberator. People ran door to door crying, 'The Germans are coming! Hurrah! The Germans are coming!'"

"Traitors," Kaflov muttered.

"Come on. We were defenseless, just women, children, and a few old men."

"So, what happened when they came?" Sasha did his part to keep her talking.

"We all lined the streets like a grand parade was coming. First, a large detachment of motorcycles zoomed down the street. The riders had on field gray uniforms, not like our drab green ones. The helmets looked different too, more of a flair at the bottom." Her hands talked even as her words described what had happened. "They all looked straight ahead as if we were not even there. Then came columns of tanks, massive tanks. Each had the swastika flag draped over it. The people called, "*Willkommen! Willkommen!*"

"Hey, what happened to 'Here and there Hitler beware! Bet your boots, Hitler's *kaput!*'?" Kaflov's words had a more teasing quality to them than confrontational. "Let a little personal danger arrive, and 'We'll do whatever you want.'"

Still, Valentina reacted defensively, her voice growing petulant. "The Red Army retreated, not protecting us, leaving us to our fate of these German soldiers. We could hear the explosions as the Soviets blew up everything in their retreat. We well knew that some of us would hang for assisting, feeding, or hiding the Red Army. No one wanted that to be them."

"The Germans are a people without honor or conscience. They have the morality of animals. Hadn't the young women heard the German soldiers sever the breasts of virgins and eat them?" Ryabtsev's hatred of the Germans was evident in the snarl of his voice.

"Considering the tight sweaters most of the girls greeted them with, I don't think they worried about that, though Natasha made me wear head-scarves to hide my maiden braid and a shawl to hide myself." Her voice suggested she resented this.

"So you didn't get involved with the soldiers?" Only Kaflov as her father, could ask this direct personal question.

"Hardly, with Natasha watching me like a hawk. But they were devastatingly good-looking. Tanned. Blonde. Muscular." Her eyes grew dreamy, her voice wistful.

"Women!" Ryabtsev exploded. "Disloyal creatures. Embrace the enemy without a backward thought at the first opportunity!"

Valentina's slight laugh effectively communicated she was deliberately baiting Ryabtsev. She did like to get a rise out of men, Sasha surmised, and she had quite an arsenal to accomplish it. "Next came the grenadiers smartly marching and singing, really quite beautifully—scores and scores of them. We threw chrysanthemums at them, wilted chrysanthemums. As they started to disperse, we presented them with small trays with bread and salt. Bowing from the waist, we said, 'Welcome to Mother Russia, in the Lord's name.'" She did a graceful demonstration.

At Ryabtsev's snarl, she smiled. "Well, we didn't all say that, but the old people did. Even though they could not understand the words, I think they got the message. They accepted the gifts and said in broken Russian, 'Russky our friends. Bolsheviks kaput!'"

"So, how friendly were they?" Ryabtsev finally realized she was playing with him.

"Not at all. They took over all of the finer houses in the village for their billeting," Her voice hardened, now overlaid with a tinge of tears as her hands tore the grass from the ground at her feet. "Once they realized the Soviets had destroyed everything of worth to them, they hung a few of the older men and a couple of women for helping the Red soldiers, raped a few of the girls, and burned the village. We all escaped the best we could. A bunch of us went through the forests until we got back to Moscow."

"The Germans are not human," Ryabtsev spoke. "Now the word 'German' has become the most terrible swearword. Let us not be indignant. Let us kill. If you do not kill the German the German will kill you. He will carry away your family, and torture them in his damned Germany."

Sasha recognized this as a quote from Ilya Ehrenburg.

"And we have. The French couldn't take us in 1812 and the Germans in 1942." Kaflov clasped and unclasped his hands. "It appears that Stalin is right. 'Our cause is just. Victory will be ours.'"

"And on that positive note, I am going to call it a night," Chirikov picked up the pack he had set by the log near the fire. "I want to be up with the birds."

Sasha set himself to banking the fire. Valentina arose and handed the balalaika back to Sasha. He shook his head, "You may use it while you are here." He wouldn't mind hearing her sing again.

The next day, Sasha showed Ryabtsev a copse of white poplars which formed a natural blind to enable him to see the bears, Arctic sheep, deer, wild horses, and other animals which might come to water and graze. He showed Kaflov a meadow dotted with blue marsh violets, sprinkles of red columbine, and accented by the unique black Kamchatkan lilies against the emerald green grass. He led Chirikov to a lake fed by several streams where he could see seven varieties of geese and nine varieties of duck. Valentina, he taught how to grind the sarana lily flour and make the bread, adding dried cloudberries for flavor. Sasha laughed, not surprised when all of the scientists politely tasted it and then left it alone. The flavor would grow on them if made daily.

Now with everyone settled in, Sasha decided the time had come to show Chirikov his stuff.

*****

Salt Lake City 1948

And this was the one thing Alex could brag about. Valentina still stood in awe at his ability. It was the one place she gave him due respect. Could it somehow be an answer to their current dilemma? She didn't go there because surely the trust and charge he had given her in Moscow would come up, and she would have a confession to make. Maybe if she did it here with Bishop Bullock, he would shield her from Alex's anger. Alex had never mistreated her, but there were things he didn't know which might be an earthquake to a volcano, causing him to erupt.

Valentina Entices Sasha

Kamchatka 1943

The next evening, confident Chirikov would now welcome his help, Sasha set the stage. After the evening meal, he positioned himself near Chirikov with paper and pencil in hand. Each evening they had heard the piercing scream of the black Stellar eagle, but Chirikov failed to sight it. This evening, as the eagle screamed, Chirikov sharply turned his head and put his binoculars to his eyes. The eagle called again but remained hidden. This time Chirikov stood and stealthily crept in the direction of the call as if he thought he could sneak up on the crafty bird. Just as the bird lifted off at Chirikov's approach, Sasha cupped his hands around his mouth and gave an echo to the scream. The bird changed direction so suddenly, it seemed to stand still in flight. Chirikov's eyes darted between Sasha and the bird in amazement. The bird flew within sight and perched. By repeatedly raising the cry each time it rose and circled, Sasha kept the eagle returning in search for this audacious, invisible invader of its territory until he sketched it in photographic accuracy.

"Incredible!" With a one-word whisper, Valentina broke the silence that gripped all of the scientists as Sasha worked. Her voice held an awe that approached reverence.

Sasha sent her a withering glare for daring to interrupt this moment with Chirikov.

"Can you call a bear like that?" Ryabtsev also showed his brashness in trying to refocus the moment on himself.

"Can you mimic the calls of other birds?" Chirikov asked.

Sasha could hear the breathless eagerness in his voice. He smiled inwardly at the evidence of the success of his effort on Chirikov. Ignoring Valentina and Ryabtsev, Sasha tried to sound casual as he responded to Chirikov. "Virtually all of them."

"Is there some way I could entice you to spend the early mornings with me?" Chirikov asked.

"Late mornings with me?" Ryabtsev asked.

"I speak afternoons. I could definitely use some drawings of the plant life." Kaflov also tried to stake a claim on his time.

"I get evenings," Valentina giggled as she spoke, and Sasha realized that, while Ryabtsev and Kaflov were serious, Valentina joked—at least he hoped so.

Trying to instill some dignity back into the situation, Sasha rolled a cigarette as if he pondered the ramifications before committing. He lit the cigarette and slowly exhaled.

"I'll pay you extra," Chirikov said.

"So will I," Ryabtsev and Kaflov chorused.

"So will I," Valentina laughed.

Sasha shook his head, "I don't have time for all of you." He turned to address Chirikov only, "Money's not important, but time is. I'll help you. We can start tomorrow morning."

"Can I come too?" Valentina pleaded. "Please?" All jesting dropped from her voice and manner.

Chirikov and Sasha looked at each other. Sasha didn't intend his little ploy to hook her. Chirikov seemed hesitant.

"No. You'd have to be absolutely quiet." Sasha implied that would be impossible for her.

"I can. I will. Please."

Sasha didn't believe her for a second. "No." He wanted to be able to spend this time alone with Chirikov. He didn't want her to distract them from their research.

She gave him her spoiled child pout face and then suddenly brightened. She picked up the picture. "May I keep this?"

Sasha shrugged his assent. He'd drawn the black eagle many times. In his balagan, he stored drawings of every bird and the rest of the flora and fauna on the Reserve.

Chirikov reached for the drawing. "I'd like to keep it if I may."

"It's yours," Sasha said.

"But you said..." Valentina protested.

Sasha shrugged and reached for the picture. She reluctantly surrendered it to him, and he handed it to Chirikov.

*****

Valentina rose early the next morning, determined to become part of Barbarossa and Comrade Chirikov's expedition. Comrade Chirikov habitually indulged her, but it would certainly be naive to think that she would be more important to him than his work. Barbarossa's display of his skill awed her. The complexity of this guide went beyond her original estimation of him. True, even she wanted to stereotype him as an ignorant native. Native? Yes, by his own admission. Ignorant, no. How quickly she forgot his shopping list for books. Evidently, the man read ravenously and must have all of the kinds of thoughts that went with reaching outside the known world on this remote reserve. His expertise on the balalaika went beyond rudimentary as well, but his skills of mimicking birds sounds and his incredible drawing ability could not be learned in books. Exceptional skills like these would be respected in any culture.

Valentina brewed the good Indian tea provided by Comrade Chirikov for him and Barbarossa before they arose the next morning. She poured a cup for each of them and quietly listened as they talked. She would prove that she could be quiet when important. She would need to do this to get her way. As they finished their tea, she took their cups and washed them out. Barbarossa and Comrade Chirikov slung their binoculars around their necks and picked up their packs. Valentina stood and dared them with her look to refuse to let her come along. Neither said anything as they strode out of camp.

Valentina struggled to keep up. No doubt Barbarossa deliberately walked fast to keep her trotting and breathless. He kept the conversation heavily sprinkled with huge technical words. She expected he did this on purpose to make everything unintelligible to her. She dared neither to complain or question, the advantage not in her favor. She knew Barbarossa well enough by now to realize that should she make her presence an inconvenience in any way whatsoever, he would look at her with that withering way of his and tell her to scamper back to camp like the naughty child he liked to treat her as. Not even dear Comrade Chirikov would rise to her defense. Even he hesitated at the suggestion that she be allowed to accompany them. Last evening, he reverentially referred to Barbarossa as a national treasure.

She chose to be here because she wanted to. She even admitted to herself only that Barbarossa's ability to talk to the birds captivated her. She knew people's languages but never imagined learning the language of birds, nor did she fancy she or anyone else could. This arrogant native really did have something to be proud of, and no one existed in all of Russia to value it more than Comrade Chirikov. Barbarossa obviously preened for this ardent admirer in his own masculine way, and Comrade Chirikov's lavish praises rewarded him well.

Comrade Chirikov stopped walking and listened intently. Valentina used the moment to sit on a fallen log and try to catch her breath.

"It's an Asian Rosy Finch," Barbarossa identified.

"Can you bring it in? Comrade Chirikov asked.

Barbarossa's smile revealed the self-satisfaction he felt in the recognition. He pursed his lips and made an indistinct harsh "cheep" sound. Evidently, the quarry didn't recognize it as an impostor because, within moments, a bird with a gray head and buff collar perched on a bush, looking this way and that for the invader. It flitted to a tree, rosy tints on its feathers highlighted, and repeated its song with greater vehemence. Barbarossa chirped back. The startled bird puffed out its breast, and its volume increased in this territorial dispute. Valentina could not restrain a giggle. Sasha scorched her with burning eyes. She suppressed the giggle.

Comrade Chirikov let out a sigh of extreme contentment. Barbarossa quickly sketched the bird with enviable accuracy, and Valentina regretfully noted that he only used a lead pencil, unable to capture the pink on the bird's body. The lack of superior tools with which to wield his trade only slightly handicapped him.

Valentina listened and watched without comment as Barbarossa called in, identified, and sketched a gray bunting, a white-backed woodpecker, and a red-throated pipit. Her awe in Barbarossa's ability grew as each bird made its visit.

Once Valentina, Barbarossa, and Comrade Chirikov returned to camp for breakfast, Valentina felt she could venture to speak to Barbarossa. As she served him, she somewhat timidly said, "Thanks for letting me come. I know you didn't want me to."

He merely grunted as he pushed the buckwheat kasha topped with berries into his mouth. Valentina knew acknowledging her would be tantamount to giving permission. Obviously, he would not go that far.

"May I come again?" If he didn't just give permission, she would ask for it, daring him to deny her.

He looked at her, sizing her up, not a spark of warmth in his eyes, "I told you not to come last time, and you came anyway. Will you stay behind if I say no this time?"

Initially uncomfortable with the scorn in his gaze, she suddenly felt lighter, more confident. He just deferred to her, acknowledging that she did what she wanted regardless of what he said, and he couldn't stop it. She laughed her gay little laugh. "No. I just wish you did not resent me so much."

He growled and said no more. She took it as unwilling permission and reveled in it.

Valentina continued to follow Barbarossa and Comrade Chirikov on their outings. To her credit and, she expected, Barbarossa's amazement, she kept a strict silence. She didn't succeed in hiding a smile, though, when Barbarossa began accommodating her by walking slower, helping her across streams, explaining things to her when she turned her questioning blue eyes on him. She felt confident he hated himself for giving in to her. He did not surrender by nature, yet he did just what she wanted, like a puppet dangling from a string. She did feel a certain fragility in her triumph as if it could tumble like a house of cards, and she guarded the parameters diligently.

Barbarossa worked with Comrade Chirikov in the early mornings and evenings when the birds vocalized the most. Her father brought snippets of flowers and foliage back to camp for identification and information. Barbarossa answered Comrade Ryabtsev's questions about animal habits, but he staunchly resisted being absorbed into either her father or Comrade Ryabtsev's day-time research. Valentina would have liked to flatter herself that he worked around camp to be near her, but evidence indicated otherwise. Nevertheless, he still spent most of his days in camp doing this and that, and she tagged him around, pelting him with questions.

"What kind of fur is that you are putting on the harnesses?"

His eyebrows knit. "Bear."

"What purpose does that serve?"

He growled, "Decoration. Bring me a puppy."

She obeyed and captured one of the wriggling bundles of energy in her arms and lugged it to where Barbarossa held a knife in one hand while he reached for the puppy.

"No!" Her eyes widened in horror. "What are you going to do?"

"Castrate it. I can only keep one male for breeding purposes." He took the puppy from her grasp, "Now, go get another one."

Instead, she plugged her ears with her fingers and turned her back on him. In spite of blocking the sound, she heard the yelp of pain, and

Sasha mutter as he brushed past her, "You're about as useless as the tribal gods."

"Well, you're about as rude and uncouth and undesirable as an insufferable varmint!" She heard his chuckle and realized that, once again, she had taken his deliberate bait. She stalked off to the balagan where the scientists lodged, expertly climbed the pole, and pulled Kennan's book from underneath the bed ledge. Coming back into the sunshine, she lay on the raised platform, reading while pretending to ignore Barbarossa, but she caught every surreptitious glance he sneaked in her direction.

Salt Lake City 1948

Bishop Greg Bullock felt the stakes rising in this unlikely relationship, but also his personal curiosity intensified. "Show me bird song." He wished he knew more about how to say that as a request instead of a command.

Alex shrugged as if it were no big thing, and cupping his hands around his mouth, emitted a cheery, familiar bird sound. "Valentina says you call that a Robin. We don't have them on Kamchatka."

"Yes, very common. You draw it?" Greg pushed a piece of paper and pencil across the desk to Alex.

Alex leaned forward and quickly sketched a robin so lifelike Bishop Bullock could imagine the song coming from it. "Have color pencils?"

Alex shook his head.

"I guess I should have gotten him some. Funds are kind of tight, and I just didn't think of it." Valentina inserted

"I give you color pencils." Bishop Bullock addressed Alex, feeling he needed to be validated instead of speaking through Valentina. "You find work draw?"

"But there is the problem of the language," Valentina voiced her concern.

"Yes. We find way. Have books, read?"

Alex shook his head. "I don't have access to anything in Russian."

"Library?" Greg addressed Valentina, knowing Alex could not go there.

"Yes, but I must not let anyone know I have any interest whatsoever in Russia or the Russian language."

"Yes," he said, acknowledging the issue. He turned back to Alex. "I find you book."

Switching to English, he asked Valentina, "How do I say are you bored?"

Valentina rephrased the question in Russian.

Alex raised his eyebrows. "Yes, I am very bored. I would love to be able to read something."

"Please, nothing in Russian," Valentina plead. "I don't dare have anything in Russian in the house."

"Important learn English." Greg ignored Valentina's comment and spoke directly to Alex.

Alex glanced at the floor and then met his direct gaze. "It is a crazy language."

"Crazy, yes. Important, yes." Bishop Bullock glanced between the two. "What next?"

Alex again picked up the story.

Kamchatka 1943

Feeling uneasy because he anticipated Valentina mocking him for doing women's work, Sasha prepared to make himself a new *kuklianka*, the traditional knee-length, winter outer-garment. Historically, a man would have felt gelded to be caught doing this, but today only the tribal babushkas knew how the young women having left their yurts for the city life.

He began by using a stone knife to scrape the flesh and fiber off the reindeer skin. He rubbed it with fresh fish roe, twisting and then treading it with his feet until it softened a little. Valentina did not even raise her eyebrows as she watched him work while pretending to read her book. He couldn't tell if it were the French or English one, only that it didn't use the Roman alphabet. She thought she was so smart because she knew these foreign languages, but he saw no use for them. It made him wonder what she was up to as she read while he worked. Her reading must fill some calculated purpose. She didn't just read. She read and looked at him and read some more. She constantly checked on him and his activity, even though she acted like she read. Well, he could, and he would ignore her. No way would he give this little snippet of a female any power over him.

Repeating the process of twisting and treading many times until the skin became soft and supple, Sasha continued to tan the skin by rubbing it with the alder tree bark shredded into tiny pieces. Completing his work for today, he stowed the skin away, then picked up a basket and headed to the pond. He needed a cache of dried fish for the winter. Since he spent the bulk of the winter in Petropavlovsk, he would not need a large supply for himself, but Baba counted on him replenishing her supply. Not surprised to see Valentina put her book down, he chuckled as she scampered down the log and followed him.

"Now, what are you doing?"

"Looking for ways to make you ask more questions."

One day as Valentina occupied herself with the laundry, Sasha sneaked off to indulge in one of his favorite pastimes—bathing in the hot springs. He found tolerating the strong sulfur odor a small price for the pleasure of the hot water. In his personal, nature-made banya, he stood in the shallow lake below a waterfall created by the springs running off a small cliff. Washing himself, he bellowed out any song or animal sound that came to mind. He turned to rinse the soap from his hair and saw Valentina reposing naked on the little cliff above him, watching him. Her hair cascaded to her waist, half revealing, half concealing her, making her as delicious as one's dream of a mermaid.

"I thought the natives believed demons or evil spirits are in the hot springs," she mocked him.

"They are. Which are you, a demon or an evil spirit?" he taunted back. He tried to focus his eyes on her face alone. He never before saw a woman's naked body glistening in the sunlight. Desires stirred inside him Sasha didn't know if he could resist.

She stuck her tongue out at him. "Meow. I guess you know that for Russians, the devil's symbol is a cat. Catch." She jumped off the small cliff towards him.

Salt Lake City 1948

"Enough." Valentina jumped in. Alex would certainly be delighted to tell all of the embarrassing details, totally unaware of how inappropriate it was to discuss such things in front of the bishop and uncaring that it would shame her. "Suffice it to say I tried to entice him to sleep with me. I didn't know it was wrong, then. Please believe me, Bishop."

Bishop Bullock seemed to be restraining a smile. "So what happened?"

Alex cleared his throat, looked at Valentina for a long moment. She thought she saw both teasing and desire there. He continued. "I left her there."

Kamchatka 1943

Striding away from her, Sasha began pulling his clothes on. Valentina stood under the falls, the water splashing from her baby pink body, her hands on her hips. The visual image of her enticed Sasha like a powerful magnet. His heart pounded; he felt breathless as if he just finished vigorous exercise. He felt hot, even though the brisk air cooled his body from the hot springs.

"Why do you run from me?" she demanded.

"What do you want from me?" Sasha responded, not looking at her.

"I want to lie with you."

"Why?"

"I like you."

"Take your poison elsewhere. I don't trust you. I don't believe you."

Sasha left without looking back. Fighting the memory of seeing Valentina naked took all the strength of resistance within him. He didn't dare look at her again.

He could remove himself from her, but he could not remove her from his mind. What would it be like to give in to her temptings? His imagination ran wild, refusing to obey his efforts to shut her out.

Why did she do this? What motivated her? Was she a spy? Was she really English or American and came here because she spoke Russian like a native? Maybe she wasn't Kaflov's daughter at all. They didn't resemble each other that much. Maybe she planned to trap Sasha into lying with her so she could scream rape and have him clapped in a prison camp until old, bent, and gray. But what had he ever said, ever done to merit that? He minded his own business. He did his duties by the state. He watched what he said and to whom. Well, he spoke disparagingly of Russia's role in this war, but only to this group, and they had made their own comments that could certainly condemn them. If they meant to trap him on that, they didn't need her as a lure. Sasha tried to rehash every conversation since the expedition began. He could think of nothing else that could convict him. Why would Mother Russia send scientists from Moscow to trap him? He couldn't be that important.

But if she came as a spy, it would be because he had offended someone on a previous trip. Yes, yes, that must be it. But whom had he offended? What had he said or done? Who sent her here to destroy him? His thoughts tortured him, crippling him.

Returning to camp, he resumed work on his kuklianka, fully resenting how Valentina invaded his every thought. Concentrating, he used a bone needle threaded with finely stripped reindeer sinews to fashion the very wide sleeves. Shortly, she also returned, fully dressed, her hair carefully braided and pinned to her head. She retrieved his balalaika, which she had stored with her belongings. He recognized the music of "Rosy Russie" (Blond Braids). He didn't know the words, but just the title caused him to think she was making a statement. He carefully avoided looking at her until he could no longer resist. Then he found her eyes upon him, and she smiled coyly. He looked away, tormented by her assurance that she would get him yet. He felt so weak. What weapon did she wield to render strong men helpless? What defense could he muster against desire when she used every opportunity to tempt, to lure him on? He packed up his materials, stowed them away, and went in search of his horse. He needed to get away to where she could not follow.

*****

Valentina watched Barbarossa gallop out of camp. That certainly had not turned out as anticipated. Oh, he wanted her, that was evident, but he ran like a startled rabbit. What made him fear her so? He was a mystery beyond solving.

Barbarossa still had not come back by the time the scientists all returned for the night. Valentina pretended total ignorance about his absence. She wondered what she should do next. Initially, she had disdained him; but the more he mocked and ignored her, the more she desired to subdue him. She harbored no doubt he felt powerless against his physical desire for her, but he also went way out of his way to avoid being ensnared. Although but two weeks remained of their expedition, confidence swelled within her that she would yet succeed.

The next morning, she rose, as usual, singing with the birds while preparing the last of the good tea. Tomorrow, they would be back to state-issued teas. Sasha came from his balagan to join Comrade Chirikov. He did not look at her nor acknowledge her in any way, not even to thank her for the salmon, onions, and potatoes she prepared yesterday afternoon as a further enticement to him. When they finished their tea and left-over breakfast and picked up their packs, Barbarossa abruptly turned to her. "You are not to come with us."

The finality with which he said this froze her, and she did not dare disobey. He definitely made this more complicated by shutting her out of his world.

When Barbarossa returned to camp, he immediately pulled out the garment on which he intermittently worked. He attached what she guessed to be a dog skin to the neck of the garment. It had the same long, white hair as the puppies'.

"Was that the father to the puppies?" Valentina asked.

Barbarossa ignored her completely and kept working. There were no surreptitious glances in her direction.

"What purpose does it serve to leave the paws attached?" Comrade Chirikov asked.

Barbarossa demonstrated how the pelt made a hood, the paws anchoring it around his face to protect it in bad weather.

"Doesn't it bother you to wear your pets?" Valentina asked.

Barbarossa didn't even send a diminishing look in her direction. She didn't exist for him.

"How did the dog die?" Comrade Chirikov asked.

"He had an unfortunate encounter with the horn of an arctic ram," Barbarossa continued to answer whatever Comrade Chirikov asked and ignore whatever Valentina said as he trimmed the edges with the long-haired, white pelt.

His very defenses, so thick against her presence, broadcast her success in penetrating to his inner core. Probably her best tactic was to let him feed on his desire for her while nurturing his imagination of what it would be like to have a woman care for him. There was yet time, and victory would be hers.

*****

Even seeing Valentina became an act of discipline. Sasha studiously tried to never glance at her. On the rare occasions when their eyes did meet, she smiled seductively at him, tormenting him with her assurance that she would get him yet. He felt so weak against this weapon that rendered strong men helpless. How could he defend himself when she was so tempting, so willing, so alluring?

Sasha could tell Valentina was doing a myriad of little thoughtful things to remind him of her constantly. She arose early every morning so he and Chirikov could have a hot cup of tea before leaving. A steaming hot breakfast waited for them when they returned. She packed food for them to eat for day-long expeditions. Except for the times in camp with her, he could keep out of her presence; but had no power whatsoever to keep her out of his thoughts. She danced through his dreams, invaded his musings, captured his heart, imprisoned his soul. If he did not find some way to end this, she would certainly destroy him.

One morning he and Chirikov left camp on horseback, planning to be gone most of the day. They came across a river full of the handsome, velvet, black-headed males that Krasheninnikov called stone ducks just a couple of miles out. Chirikov laughed at the name as he watched the rather stupid females dive into the clear water rather than flying off when he approached them. It was as easy to catch them as if they had been made of stone. Sasha drew, Chirikov observed, and together they netted some for dinner before returning to camp after just a couple of hours.

Only the puppies made any noise when they rode in. Sasha took care of the horses and then climbed to his balagan to put away his sketching materials. He sang the musical trills of the skylark, content with the morning spent with Chirikov. The door of the balagan squeaked on its leather hinges as it swung open, and the song died in his throat. He saw Valentina rifling through his pictures.

She turned and glanced at him as if she had every right to be there, doing what she was doing. "Good morning," she cheerily greeted him.

"Get your hands off my pictures. What right do you have to come into my private quarters?" His words were a subdued, measured scream.

Giving a casual shrug, she spoke with the ease of one who had planned her alibi long before the act in case she got caught. "I just came to collect your dirty laundry."

"Get out!" Sasha growled.

"You have quite a collection of books, Alexander Yuri Nikolayevich Tatischev."

Had she come to discover his name? That explained nothing. Anyone who needed to know his name knew it.

"Get out!" he bellowed, pointing to the door.

"I'm going; I'm going." She eased past him, lightly touching his arm on the way out. "Calm down. I meant no harm. Everything is in order."

He resisted striking her and reined in his desire to follow her and push her off the high platform or turn the log ladder from under her feet.

She began to descend the log ladder. When only her head showed, the sunlight dancing across the yellow in her hair, she paused and said, "Alex, you're back early. I can prepare something hot for you to eat."

"Don't bother," he muttered, helpless fury boiling within him.

He sank down on the wooden bench that circled the balagan. Fear gripped him with a force that sapped his strength. What was she really after? Could his first name, his complete name, be so important? Did she seek evidence against him? Had someone hired her to steal his pictures and notes?

He thought about asking Chirikov about her, but then Sasha remembered how the scientists glanced at each other in amusement when Valentina pestered him with questions and demands. Were they in this together? Was it somehow a goal for all of them to trap him, using her for bait? He wouldn't have to deal with them much longer. Just five more days and he would be taking them out to meet Boris, and they would be gone back to Moscow—maybe to seal his doom, but at least they would be gone.

Sasha became stiff and formal with all of the scientists. He felt he constantly needed to watch his shadow, lest it fall on them and offend them. He tried to keep himself aloof from them all, even Chirikov. He didn't think Valentina had found what she was looking for if indeed she was looking for something specific.

He checked and double-checked until certain he missed nothing in his lodging. He made sure Valentina would not get the chance to come into his lodging again by removing the log ladder whenever he was out of camp.

One evening Chirikov followed him to the fishing pond. "Has our little Valentina offended you?" he asked.

Sasha sat crouched, letting the water play idly across his fingers. "What does she really want from me?"

"Just some male companionship."

"Why did she really come on this trip?"

"*Sabeysta,*" Chirikov said. "She's suffered terrible losses in the war."

Sabeysta. To forget. That's why most men claimed they drank to excess. Could he trust Chirikov to be honest with him?

The following morning the pounding sounds of water pouring down the stove pipe announced the spring rains, which could keep them holed up for weeks. There would be no going out today. Sasha arose and pulled on his clothing. He closed the damper to prevent the stove pipe from filling up with water. Then he went to the balagan lodging the scientists and repeated the process. Finally, he double-checked the storage balagan to be certain that everything was stored well away from holes that might cause water damage.

Dripping wet, he returned to his own balagan and stripped off his clothing. He dried the water from his hair and beard and crawled back into his bearskin bed to indulge in some daydreaming. His leg touched her first. He shot back out of the bed as if shocked, pulling a blanket with him to cover himself.

"Get out! You have no right to come into my balagan without being invited."

She rested her head on her hand, her bent elbow lifting it off the bed, her golden hair falling loose and tousled. She gave a slow, lazy smile, wetting her lips with her tongue. "Why do you fight your desire for me so hard? Are you married?"

"*Nyet!*"

"Are you afraid of women?"

"*Nyet!*"

"Have you ever lain with a woman before?" Her questions never stopped. While supporting her head with one hand, she slid her other hand under Sasha's blanket to find his bare leg. She began to caress it. He lifted his leg, causing her hand to fall to the floor, and slammed his knee down on it.

"Ouch!" she exclaimed, withdrawing her hand. "You don't have to hurt me."

Sasha felt suffocated by his yearnings. He knew either he or she must get out of there, or he would succumb. He reached for his clothes.

"Alex, why are you scared of me?" She restrained him by gently grasping his hand.

"I'm not scared of you," he lied.

"You are," she contradicted.

"Why did you really come on this trip?"

She turned on her stomach, burying her face in her arms, and did not answer.

"Are you a spy?" he demanded. He reached out and turned her over, pinning her shoulders to the bed.

Her eyes were moist. "A spy?" her voice registered surprise.

"Are you trying to get me to lie with you so you can go back to Moscow and yell that I raped you, so I get thrown in a prison camp for 10 to 20 years?"

"Aluska!" she changed his name to a term of endearment, but her voice scolded, "Why would I want to do that? Let go of me. That hurts."

He released her. "I don't know why you want to frame me. Maybe I offended someone on an earlier expedition," he yelled. "Maybe they hired you to vindicate them. Maybe someone sent you to steal my pictures and notes and wants me out of the way. I don't know. Why did you come?"

She very gently laid her hand on his. When he tried to withdraw, she gave a firm but tender squeeze. "Let me explain." She sat up, the bedding falling away, revealing her bare torso. At Sasha's stare, she pulled a blanket up to her chin.

"I came to forget." Her eyes misted. Silence hung heavy as a tear trickled down her face.

"Forget what?" Sasha prompted when she didn't go on.

The tears continued. "My brothers, three of them, and my lover have all been killed in Operation Barbarossa."

"Barbarossa?"

She smiled through her tears. "In some ways, you are so isolated, so naive. Operation Barbarossa, red beard, is the name the Germans gave to their attack on Russia." She reached up and gently stroked his beard. "Not knowing your name, I've called you Barbarossa. Your beard is reddish, and winning you over has been like fighting a war."

When he did not pull back, she brought both hands to his face, letting the blanket fall from her. She kissed him at first gently and then passionately, her tongue in his mouth. No one had ever kissed him this way before.

Salt Lake City 1948

"Suffice it to say; I got my way." Valentina interrupted again. When she didn't say any more, Alex continued.

Kamchatka 1943

After she'd given him a thrill he did not know was possible in sexual fulfillment, it was a time before he regained his thoughts and voice. Finally, he said, "Now I know what kind of devil you are. Where did you learn to do that?"

"I am not a devil. I told you I had a lover."

"And he was killed?"

"He was killed."

"I'm sorry."

"Really?" she asked. "I wouldn't be here if he lived."

"Then I'm sorry for him."

She lay in his arms, and he watched a spider dangle from its thread above them. Maybe the spider that bit him the day she arrived signaled a good omen. Sasha captured the spider and offered it to Valentina. "Do you want to eat the spider?"

She withdrew, horrified, "Gross. Get that thing away from me. Why would I want to eat it?"

Her refusal surprised him, "To increase fertility, of course."

She wrinkled her nose and talked out of a scrunched-up mouth, "Thanks. I'll take my risks without it. That's not my goal anyway. In fact, since I leave in just a few days, I should take something that will prevent fertility, not cause it. Do you really believe eating a spider causes fertility? That's just superstition."

Sasha shrugged and released the spider. "It seems to work sometimes."

After a moment, she cupped his face in her hands and barely touched her lips to his. "Would you like to learn how to pleasure a woman?"

Sasha didn't know what she meant. She caught the bewilderment on his face and laughed. "You ignorant native. A woman can enjoy sex as much as a man."

More intrigued by her invitation than stung by her barb, he nodded. In his experience, he had never known a woman to seek coupling. They just seemed to submit to it like something required of them but not enjoyed. "Teach me."

With hand and voice, she guided him to touch her here with his hand, there with his lips, repeat this, oh, do that some more until she writhed breathlessly. Her eyes grew wide and wild. She moaned, and her body jerked spasmodically. She stilled his hands. "No more. Thank you." She lay quietly in his arms, her heart beating fast against his chest.

Sasha marveled at her request and response like a revelation. He always thought of coupling as something a man did to gratify himself, and women existed as the vessels of his satisfaction. But no, today, he learned that coupling was a gift to be shared between a man and a woman. A gift to be given and received, and that he could experience as much pleasure in giving as in receiving.

"Tell me again you are not a spy."

She kissed him silent. "I am not a spy."

"What do you really want from me?"

"You gave me what I want, except I want more."

She again began to caress him, but it was too soon, and his passion did not arouse.

"What will your father say?"

"Nothing. He expected me to find comfort in you."

"Are you comforted?"

"Very," she said.

Even as his fear of her drained away in the fulfillment of his desire, so did his intention to spend the rainy days with Chirikov. He knew as soon as the weather cleared, she would be leaving. He wanted the rain to continue days, nay, weeks, and he wanted to spend every second with her. And that did not include her teaching him either English or French.

Once he had looked for ways to keep her in check, but she had succeeded in putting him in checkmate. He won in losing. The tune to "Dark Eyes" ran through his mind, and he sang altered words to fit his purpose: "Blue and intense eyes, Bright as autumn skies, But a seductive flame, Caught me in your game."

She giggled, and created a verse of her own: "You turned and ran away, when I wanted you to stay, My red-bearded foe, I will not let you go." She turned and smothered him in kisses, and his desire returned.

Salt Lake City 1948

What Valentina had said when she first came in began to make sense, that she was responsible for the man in her house. Bishop Greg Bullock still had no idea how they got from Kamchatka to Salt Lake City together, but he knew exactly how Sasha had been trapped into following her to this far-off, unlikely destination.

*****

Sasha left the church first, retracing his steps. A flurry of emotions had erupted in him, rehashing all of these old memories. If only he had withstood Valentina's temptations a bit longer, she would not have trapped him, and he would not be here. 'If only' did not solve anything. The minute he succumbed to her, he fell like a comet on a starlit night. He relived in thought how he had come to give up everything he valued to follow Valentina. For him, it had become a commitment of the heart, seeking to maintain their relationship. For her, it was transitory entertainment. Because of her new religion, she didn't even want the entertainment any longer. Here they were, with conflicting desires, and he was imprisoned by language, with a death sentence should he attempt to escape. Somehow she felt this bishop could help. Now that was something to ponder.

He had never known a bishop, but somewhere in his reading, he had been led to expect embroidered robes, swinging candles, and incantations. This rather unremarkable man in a western suit and tie did not seem to possess any special powers. He reminded Sasha of Pierre in Tolstoy's *War and Peace*. Pierre had sought goodness in the Masonic Order, but never actually found it until imprisoned by the French and stripped of everything from his former life. Pierre lost his self-interest and became genuinely concerned about others. Tolstoy described Pierre as having gone to a moral bath. That described Bishop Bullock, too: a morally clean man, a fundamentally good person characterized mostly by his kindly listening. He seemed to have no agenda of his own. If listening could create solutions, Sasha felt they were in excellent hands. But how could listening create solutions? What could the bishop actually do? If nothing else, it was a diversion from his otherwise boring days. Could the bishop get him something to read?

5

Sasha bids Kamchatka Proschchai

Salt Lake City 1948

Valentina hurried home. She wanted to get there before Alex. She didn't want to talk with him and attempt to process any more of their memories independent of Bishop Bullock. She knew what she had yet to confess to Alex, and she didn't want to face his reaction alone. He had a right to know, and she knew that to repent of her sins completely, she would have to confess all to Alex. That was even harder than confessing to God or the bishop. They had not been personally harmed like Alex, and he didn't even know. Notwithstanding that, she had not anticipated being assaulted with the flurry of emotions that raged through her, least of all, desire for Alex. She would not give in. She must not give in. She must not give him any hint that she felt any stirrings of yearning. Any hope on his part could be disastrous. They would no longer be able to live in this tenuous situation.

She had barely removed her coat when she heard him open the back door. She quickly shut the bedroom door, turned off the light, and undressed in the dark.

"So you don't want to talk," he said, outside the door. "Thought as much."

She waited to see if she could hear him snore so she could get up to brush her teeth but fell asleep first.

Fortunately, she had to work the next day, so it was the following evening before he even saw her. He stood in the doorway of the kitchen, his hands in his pockets, a type of timidity she never saw on Kamchatka. "Do you want to talk about things?"

"No. I don't see any point in talking about it. What happened really doesn't matter. We're rehearsing it only because the bishop has asked. Make yourself useful. Cut up this onion."

"I see," he said as he got out the cutting board and knife. "Nothing's changed."

They fell back to their normal state of minimal communication.

*****

Sasha found himself looking forward to the next visit with Bishop Bullock. Valentina had made it perfectly clear that revealing their thoughts and feelings of times past made no difference in the present. Her only goal was to find some way to end the current dilemma. Him as part of her future was the possibility that did not even exist as an option. She obviously did not know what to do with him. The only viable option he could see, and it was the one he hoped for, was that the bishop would see some way to get him to Alaska, and then he would build a boat and make his own way back to Kamchatka. Not having her talent for languages, learning English well enough to live here un-detected was not a possibility.

Sasha admitted satisfaction when the bishop handed him a sack as he entered the office the following week. He didn't open it but hoped its contents would help pass the time. "So, what happened next?" Bishop Bullock asked.

"Valentina left Kamchatka," Sasha answered.

Bishop Bullock turned his eyes on Valentina, "Do you want to pick up the story?"

Petropavlovsk 1943

Valentina crawled back in the bed and snuggled under the covers, the taste of vomit still in her mouth. Yesterday, on the boat back from the Reserve to Petropavlovsk, she attributed it to a touch of seasickness when she threw up. Once they landed, she felt fine, but maybe she was actually sick as she threw up again this morning. Well, if she had to be sick, today was as good as any. Their train didn't leave for Moscow until tomorrow, so she could lie abed, and it wouldn't be any big deal.

Her father came in, "It's time to get up for some breakfast."

"I don't think I'll eat. I threw up again this morning."

"Would you like some tea?"

"Yes. That would be good."

Shortly her father returned, and surprisingly, she felt famished. "I'm feeling a lot better. In fact, I think I will go and eat."

"That's great! And then what do you think you'll do with your day?"

"I want to get a gift for Alex. I would like to find an art shop and get him some colored pencils or watercolors."

"That's an excellent idea. I'll go with you."

Before nighttime, she visited Boris and delivered a lovely box of 24 colored pencils and a note thanking Alex for such a memorable time. Boris promised delivery to Alex when he made his next trip to the Reserve. Valentina felt glad she had come to Kamchatka. Even though she would feel the absence of her brothers her entire life, the raw pain on hearing of their deaths had now dulled enough that she could think of life going on. Immersing her heart, soul, and even her body in another world healed her, but now she needed to put all of that behind her and move on. Despite the on-going war, her future shone brightly before her, and it would be equally diverting. It was wonderful that she could look forward to the future because of the little secret awaiting her in Moscow, rather than returning to soul-wrenching, gray memories and unfulfillable longings.

*****

In Sasha's nights and odd moments, his memories plagued him. He pined for Valentina, yearned for her, ached for her, finding neither repose nor peace from his throbbing desire. Working on the Reserve gave him boundless freedom, but now that he had surrendered that freedom to Valentina. He had fought it so long, seeing the danger of getting involved with her the day he met her, but ultimately allowed himself to become trapped through poisonous lust. He didn't want to want her, but now, try as he might, he couldn't relegate her to just a fleeting affair he could enjoy and forget. No longer content with his life as before, he wanted her alive and vibrant in his days. She danced through his dreams and took possession of his waking hours. The Reserve became its own prison, keeping him from her. He chided himself for letting this happen. If only the fear that she might be a spy had held him from involvement. Like a theme song, the tune to "Dark Eyes" played in his mind as he created new words: From the moment we met, I fought desire for you. Now I'm sad and blue. My life's tied to you.

Fortunately for Sasha, Boris not only took Valentina from him but brought another expedition to impose demands on his otherwise empty days. When he took the second expedition out, Boris brought a small package and a note from Valentina. The note said thanks but nothing more. The package contained beautiful pencils in every color Sasha could imagine. Sheer delight soared through him—such a thoughtful, perfect gift.

*****

Everywhere Valentina looked were people waiting to board the train with their cheap, cardboard suitcases and lumpy packages desperately tied together with unraveling string. String bags bulged with brown bread, cheese, fresh vegetables, cold, cooked fish, meat patties, and watery beer. It caused her stomach to lurch, and she stepped outside to disgorge the tea she had drunk that morning. They spent the better part of one day in the crowded station. The benches were all occupied with small children sleeping on blankets beneath them. She sat on the dirty floor. Her father said to Comrade Chirikov, "You stay with Valentina. I don't trust the rabble in this crowd. I'll go and secure our tickets." Comrade Ryabtsev made his way to the crowded lunch counter, promising to bring back something for the rest of them. After about five hours of this stifling station, they finally boarded the train. Since their party was small, they found themselves sharing a compartment with a grizzled old man, a plump, middle-aged woman, a frenzied young mother, her baby, young daughter, a boy of about ten, and a girl of seven. In the hot compartment of the train, Valentina shed her reindeer-skin coat for blue warm-up pajamas and idly watched as the women peeled cucumbers. Stripped to his undershirt and trousers, her father played chess with the old man, who kept laughing uproariously and slapping his knee over something Papochka said. Ryabtsev, yawning and scratching himself, read a newspaper. Chirikov showed the children the pictures of birds Alex had drawn for him.

Valentina quickly learned the return trip would not be as quick as their trip in coming. The train was shunted to a side rail numerous times to make way for higher priority troop trains. That happened three times during the first day.

That evening, she and ten-year-old Gennadi had to slip from the train searching for barley and boiled water. Ducking under the passenger cars, climbing up on platforms, and jumping down again, they tried to navigate the maze of tracks to the distribution point. Grateful for the fresh air, Valentina breathed deeply of it while she waited in line. Gennadi took the grain, leaving her to carry the water. She had to quickly jump out of the way when a train unexpectedly started up and spilled much of the water. Despite her best efforts to avoid it, both she and Gennadi had to clean human excrement from their shoes upon returning. That did nothing for the steadiness of her stomach.

The other woman eyed her speculatively when she threw up the following morning, "You sick?" Juliana, the older and rounder of the two women, asked.

"I'll be okay." Valentina gasped breaths of air, trying to quell the nausea that still gripped her. "Just some morning queasiness."

"Oh, I can diagnose your illness. It will go away after nine months. Then it turns into one of these little slave drivers." Pretty, dark-haired Gema nodded at her nursing baby.

Valentina's eyes widened. How could it be? Well, she knew how it could be; but in six months of pleasuring herself with Mikel, it had not happened. She'd only spent eight days with Alex.

"Are you married?" Gema asked.

Valentina shook her head.

"So, who's the father?" Juliana looked speculatively at the three men traveling with Valentina.

Valentina stifled a laugh. That she could not imagine. "Oh, none of them."

"He a soldier?"

"No, he's in Kamchatka."

"Then you are going the wrong way. You'd better get off at the next stop and skedaddle back to him."

This was the worst possible thing that could happen. Her plans had no place for a baby or Alex in her future. "But I can't do that. I can't have this baby. It would ruin everything."

"Oh, you've got someone in Moscow as well." Juliana nodded knowingly.

She couldn't have been more wrong. "No, not that...just, plans." Valentina glanced to see her father in an animated discussion with Comrade Chirikov. Thank goodness he had not heard this exchange.

"But what am I to do about it?" Maybe these women could give her some guidance. Her mother couldn't be consulted.

"You'll have to go visit the lady." Juliana was as quick with solutions as she was with assumptions.

"The lady?" Something seemingly known by everyone but her.

"The one who knows how to end a pregnancy."

Oh, so there was a way. "How do I find her?"

"Ask other women. I don't know Moscow."

Maybe Olga would know what she was talking about.

Salt Lake City 1948

Bishop Greg Bullock suspected Alex had not recognized the symptoms of pregnancy until it became blatantly obvious. When Valentina mentioned the lady, Alex jumped to his feet, toppling the chair. He yelled at Valentina, "You, you were pregnant with my child and killed it!"

She shrank under his glare, truly the abject, contrite sinner. Alex clenched and unclenched his fist and strode to the wall and pounded it. Greg felt grateful the wall was adobe, not drywall, although it hurt Alex significantly more. He could only guess at Alex's feelings. He couldn't imagine his wife giving him news like this because of their beliefs, so he couldn't imagine his own reaction.

"I'm going to the mountains." Alex flung the door open and hurriedly left.

Greg thought that Alex probably had no idea that Christ went to the mountains when he received distressing news, but he did know the mountains could bring a measure of peace, of healing.

Greg arose, softly closed the door, and turned his attention back to Valentina. He watched as she softly sobbed. When she eventually glanced at him, he handed her a handkerchief. She wiped her eyes and blew her nose. "You see the bear," she said in English.

"I see the caged bear. He evidently did not know of this before."

She shook her head. "There seemed to be no point in telling him. It can't be undone, and you saw what he did." She flung her hand toward the door and heaved a huge sigh. "Of all the things wrong I have done, aborting the baby is what I regret the most. I do hope and pray God can forgive me."

"Abortion is fairly common in Russia, is it not?"

She nodded.

"And you didn't know it was wrong when you did it?"

"I hadn't really been taught right and wrong about issues such as that. I had no basis to judge by. I just knew that it seemed impossible for me to carry and then care for a child under the circumstances. Although it doesn't make what I did right, the chances that that child would be alive today, considering everything, seem very slim. Now that I know how wrong it is, my heart pains. Do you think God will forgive me?"

"God knows your circumstances at that time. Of course, the child was conceived out of wedlock, but since your repentance and making covenants with God, you've not returned to sleeping with someone, have you?"

"No. I've strictly observed that commandment, much to Alex's dismay."

"God knows your heart. I trust he has forgiven you."

"Do you want me to go on?" she asked as her tears subsided.

"I don't know what is yet to be told, but it seems good, if painful, for both of you to lay it out together. Let's wait until he is ready to come back. Does he go to the mountains often?"

"Weather permitting, he practically lives there."

"Not a bad choice, under the circumstances. Don't forget the sack I brought for him. I'll see you on Sunday. Let me know if he has returned."

The next Sunday, Valentina reported that Alex had not returned, so they suspended their session for that week, but Douglas Parkins showed up on Tuesday.

He strode in; his new crew cut standing up smartly, his green linen shirt without a wrinkle, his grin showing off his perfect rack of teeth, which quickly disappeared as he launched into the purpose of his interview. "Bishop, I came to talk to you about Anita Waters."

Greg hoped his face showed only a neutral interest. Was Douglas looking to see if his expression betrayed any knowledge he had? "Yes?"

"I think she has a man living at her house."

Now Greg hoped his face did not show relief. "What makes you think that?"

"Well, I've been dating her. One evening, a few weeks back, we were sitting on her porch. I had just kissed her goodnight, and this guy shows up. I've never seen him before. She seemed a little distressed at his appearance."

"Did she introduce him?"

"She said his name was Alex. He just kind of growled at me. Kind of a surly, ill-mannered, and unkempt kind of guy. He just stood there as if he wasn't going anywhere. She didn't tell him she was busy or to come back another time or anything. I would have punched him out had she indicated she wanted me to. In fact, I suggested it, but she said, 'No, no. Leave him alone.' Finally, she told me goodnight and went into the house. He went in after her."

"I appreciate you telling me this, Douglas. I will call her in and check out what the deal is."

"Okay. I thought you would want to know." Douglas stood and extended his hand. "By the way, I'm going to be going away for a while. Did you read about the Russian spy, Nina Pavlovna?"

Greg merely nodded.

"I feel it is a calling, if you will, to help root out these Commie Russians hiding among us, spying on us. I'm going to assist Senator McCarthy in his campaign to find them. They were our allies during the war. We helped them drive out Hitler with the lend-lease program, and then they turn around and spy on us. Can you imagine?"

Proof of how dangerous a little knowledge and twisting of the facts could be. Praise the Lord he would be gone—maybe to ferret out some other victim only seeking refuge. Greg trusted Douglas did not suspect that Anita Waters was Valentina, and hopefully, she and Alex would be far from his clutches before he returned.

The following Sunday, Valentina said that Alex was back, not talking to her, but had assented to again meet with the bishop.

When Alex walked in on Wednesday, he looked more untidy than usual, with a shaggy beard growing on his previously shaved chin, an unmended tear in his shirt sleeve, and his eyes hard.

"Happy see you," Bishop Bullock said, extending his hand.

Alex did not take his hand but sat down. "You are my only hope."

Bishop Bullock did not ask what he hoped for but understood the weight of the trust being invested in him. He said a silent prayer for wisdom in guiding this troubled young man. Valentina sat ram-rod straight and chewed on her upper lip as if the tension between her and Alex strained her almost to the breaking point.

"Thank you for the pencils and bird book. I do appreciate it," Alex said somewhat stiffly.

"Welcome. Valentina left Kamchatka. What happen?"

Alex turned and looked at her for one long moment. She only briefly met his eyes and then studied her hands. He turned back to Greg and resumed his story.

Kamchatka 1943

Gradually Sasha developed a plan. After winter set in, he would visit his grandmother and then return to Petropavlovsk. After visiting the family, he would go to Moscow to sell his drawings and notes to a publisher. Chirikov had encouraged him to publish and had offered to help him. Of course, he would visit Valentina while there. He would persuade her to return to Kamchatka with him to wait out the war.

Impatient with waiting for the deep-frozen snows enabling sledge travel, Sasha kept himself busy packing and storing his personal items. Although the balagans were out of the way and not likely to be disturbed by man, the heavy snows sometimes piled high enough that an agile beast could reach the platform. However, the weather itself posed the greatest danger. The winds would tear at the balagans, leaving gaping holes for the snows and rains to enter and destroy anything susceptible to their ravages.

His first year here, he had dug an underground yurt for storing his belongings that he would not need until the next year. When he returned the following spring, the depth of the snow prevented him from digging through to the entrance, and a spring flood had destroyed his things before he could get to them.

Later he discovered a cave with a vertical, cliffside entrance. He blocked the entrance with rocks, and no beast ever disturbed it in his absence. He used it effectively for a winter storage and spring shelter upon returning each year until he could do necessary repairs to the balagans. He drove the horses to a fisherman's yurt, where food would be provided until spring.

He spent some of his brief daylight hours and many of his lantern-lit evenings drawing and redrawing, painting, and perfecting a portrait of Valentina. Finally, he achieved the glistening sunlight on her golden braids, the blush on the curve of her cheek, and the teasing in her eye he had come to love so much, and he was satisfied.

Finally, the snows swirled, piled, and froze, and the inactivity of waiting ended. Sasha found it exhilarating to lift the sledge from its storage against the balagan and begin loading it. The sledge would be loaded lightly this trip with only the remaining gifts of vodka and government-issued cigarettes from the scientists, some Circassian leaf tobacco, all of his left-over salt, sugar, tea, sarana lily bulbs, and an abundant supply of dried fish for Baba. He wrapped his pictures, notes, Valentina's gift of colored pencils, and Tolstoy's *War and Peace* very carefully in a fox skin and stowed it in the toe of the sledge, within the bearskin that encased all of his gear. Near the top of the sledge basket, he packed three extra kukliankas for the severe weather. He placed one knife in a scabbard outside the basket for easy access. He placed his other knives on top of the kukliankas and then lashed the bearskin tightly around everything.

Sasha carefully lined his knee-high, sealskin boots with a very soft grass he had stored just for this purpose, to preserve heat and keep his feet from sweating. Then he pulled the boots over heavy reindeer skin stockings. The sealskin fur covered the inside of his trousers, giving an extra measure of warmth. Next, he donned a heavy parka of deerskin and a fox skin hat. He pulled the hat over an otter fillet placed over his forehead to keep it from freezing. Around his chin, he wrapped a foxtail. He well knew that he would soon be drenched with perspiration if dressed too warmly with the constant balancing required of him on the sled. The perspiration would freeze, and then no matter how many kukliankas he piled on, he would be cold and in danger of freezing.

Ever since hunger had driven the dogs into camp from their summer foraging, Sasha had kept them leashed, and on a dried-fish-once-a-day diet, so they grew lean and ready for the hard winter work. Two of his sled dogs did not return, lost to some unknown accident or predator during the summertime. No matter. He still had eleven, and seven could easily pull the sledge as lightly as he loaded it. The pups would grow and replace those lost, as winter always exacted a toll. He harnessed the dogs in successive couples by a long central thong of sealskin to which he attached each dog by a collar and short trace. Kanalam, Little Devil, stood alone as the lead dog.

Sasha called "ha" to set Kanalam off, and they skimmed across the snow at breakneck speed. He expected to make at least 230 kilometers that day before reaching the steep mountains separating him from Baba's valley. "Tagtag, tagtag," his voice command turned Kanalam to the right, and Sasha swayed his body with the sledge to keep the balance. Though good, Kanalam, new as lead dog, still required vocal commands. If Sasha stayed and ran him all winter, he would be able to command him by simply striking the ice with his stick before spring. Maybe Boris would run the dogs in his absence.

Seeing snow hare tracks, with practiced precision Sasha threw the stick into the snow in front of the sledge and called "Ah, ah!" to stop the dogs. He lay the sledge on its side. The dogs, still harnessed, lay in a circle awaiting his return. He lashed snowshoes, made of thin boards turned up at the front, to his feet. The sea wolf skin covering the bottoms of the snowshoes gave him excellent traction.

His experienced eye picked out the white hares against the glistening snow, and he nabbed quite a few as well as some partridges. Baba would be pleased.

As Sasha saw the smoke spiraling from the volcanoes stark against the blue sky, he wondered how Kennan described riding a dog sledge. Did he thrill to the speed and skill necessary to negotiate this hazardous but beautiful landscape? And as Sasha wondered about Kennan, he thought about Valentina. Maybe one day, he would tuck her, an infant at her breast, into a closed coach sledge lined with bearskin and covered with the skin of the sea wolf and take her to meet his Baba. They would cuddle at night in the same snow bed, intertwined in each other's arms. They would talk about the legends explaining the stars or watch the splashy, brilliant green and blue displays of the Northern Lights. If Valentina agreed, they could be back here together before spring, though, of course, there would be no infant until next year. Unless, and the thought made Sasha smile, she returned home pregnant in spite of neither eating nor believing in the spider's magic.

Salt Lake City 1948

Sasha sent Valentina a brief, dastardly glare, but she would not meet his eyes, then looked at his hands and waited a bit before resuming.

Kamchatka 1943

As the day progressed, the wind howled like a woman, whipping up a blinding fury. Sasha dragged the stick in the snow and yelled, "Aha!" The team stopped. Unhitching the dogs, he threw a dried fish to each one. He put on two kukliankas and dug a shallow hollow, which he roofed with small branches. Then he slipped his feet out of his boots into some dog skin stockings so that they would soon be thoroughly dry and warm. Though he feared the ravages of frostbite, that did not deter him from his journey because of his confidence in his ability to beat this natural enemy.

The dogs slept better when fed at night, but Sasha never heard them settle until after their nightly obsequies to the gods of the moon, wind, and snow. One dog would begin a long, faint wailing cry like a human being in the last extremity of suffering. The sound swelled and deepened until the whole atmosphere trembled from its volume. It gradually died away into a low, despairing moan. Another dog picked up the howl in a high key, joined by another and another until the entire pack joined voices in a shriek destined to send the blood racing in terror through a man's veins.

Sasha waited two days before the storm blew itself out. He harnessed the dogs and pushed on over the boundless, unbroken steep. The long, wave-like ridges swept perpendicular by the north-east winds served as a compass to point him north. He reached the mountain separating him from his grandmother's yurt four hours after dark. He drove on through the bright moonlit night, impatient at the time lost because of the storm. Normally, time meant nothing to him, but he counted time as a great enemy until he could be reunited with Valentina.

Sasha made camp an hour before dawn. He was using the trick of making the dogs believe they had slept a full night if bedded down in the dark and awakened in the light. He crouched on his haunches, a snowball, completely warm in his own private snow blanket, and fell into a deep, refreshing sleep.

As dawn crept over the mountain tops, he looked from his summit into the gloomy ravines below, shaggy with larch forests and dense thickets of trailing-pine, not yet kissed awake by morning light—time to move on.

He harnessed only Kanalam for the steep descent, and off they went down the mountainside. Kanalam descended so rapidly, Sasha had to fight for balance and control. Suddenly the dog veered sharply to the left, howling after a fox dashing across the snow-covered rocks. The unexpected lurch threw Sasha from the sledge. Keeping his wits about him, he grabbed a rung on the sledge as he fell. Skipping and bumping across the snow, he exhausted his ample vocabulary of curses in both Russian and Kamchadal. The little devil charged on, heedless of Sasha's plight. Finally, Kanalam slowed and stopped his futile chase. The dog looked at Sasha quizzically as he picked himself up out of the snow. Sasha unstrapped a stick from the sledge and threatened Kanalam with it. "You'd better straighten out, or your hide will make some nice stockings for Valentina."

Until Sasha brandished the stick at him, the dog didn't even have the good graces to hang his head and tuck his tail.

Baba's yurt appeared as just another conical mound in the snow. The smoke curling out of the chimney suggested a miniature volcano. Then one noticed a number of these miniature smoking volcanoes and realized he had stumbled into a village. All the dogs, sledges, everything was kept within the yurt. The severity of the storms would either destroy or bury anything left outside. Sasha descended the pole ladder extending through the hole where the smoke escaped and caught Baba in his arms.

"I wondered if you would come." She still spoke the Kamchadal language to him.

"I always come. You know that, Baba."

"I always wonder. Someday you will not come."

As Sasha's eyes grew accustomed to the darkness illuminated only by the fire on the floor, which filled the room with blue smoke, he saw his uncle Maximov. Since returning one-legged from the Great War, Maximov had buried his sorrows in the bottle. He resigned himself to life within the yurt and only did what women's work his mother or wife coerced him to do. When Sasha wanted to play the stupid, lazy native, his uncle became his model. He epitomized everything unsavory ever said about Kamchadal natives, even down to eating the lice that inhabited his hair.

Sasha loved coming here as if coming home to the cocoon of the known. But with Valentina on his mind, he saw the yurt for the first time as Valentina might, through Muscovite eyes. He knew that she wouldn't thrill to be here. The smoke stung his eyes and burned his lungs. The pungent odors of rotten fish, dog, and fox carcasses hanging from the walls, and human and dog feces assaulted his nose, eyes, and stomach.

Sasha knew, more than saw, the recesses of the yurt where the statue carvings of the Gods reposed. One was a God with a man's torso and a seal's body, another carried a man's head on a pedestal, and a third was the cross of the Christian God. All were blackened as if offered burned offerings, but the blackening actually came from the smoke trapped in the windowless, underground dwelling. So little escaped from the small entrance in the roof, the yurt's only opening.

Wood to burn throughout the winter stuck out from under the wide bench circling the yurt. This same bench also served as beds. Winter food stored in woven baskets banked one wall. Other than some copper cooking utensils, the yurt contained no other furnishings.

Once, three families, totaling twelve people, had lived in this eight-meter square dwelling, but now only Baba, Maximov, his disgruntled wife Elvira, and assorted dogs called it home. They didn't run a sledge in the winter any longer but still kept the dogs.

Elvira had nursed Sasha at her breast as an infant after his mother left him. Maximov and Elvira's four children had been young with Sasha. He thought of them as family more intimately than his own mother, brother, and half-siblings. But, as the children received a Russian education, they abandoned the old ways. Only Sasha and Boris found some kind of bridge between the two cultures.

Sasha off-loaded his sledge into the yurt, then brought the dogs in, and finally the sledge itself. Sweating from the exertion, he gladly stripped himself to his wide leather belt with a codpiece in front and an apron in back. Last season, he had richly decorated the girdle with seal fur stained different colors. Maximov wore the same type of garment.

The women covered themselves with a *khonba* consisting of trousers tied below the knee and a camisole made of mountain sheepskin, tied at the neck. If the yurt got too hot, they would strip themselves of all clothing. Having seen these older women like this since his infancy, Sasha never responded sexually to seeing them without clothing, but the thought of Maximov's lustful eye watching Valentina naked disturbed him.

Sasha tried to quell his impatience to get everything unloaded. Accepting some tea from Baba, he acted nonchalantly. He didn't want to alert her that something unusual was in the offing. Once the excitement of his coming settled into just talking, Baba asked about his drawings. She always did. As his best teacher, she continually nourished his love of the birds. She mimicked their sounds and sang to them, and they sang back. Sasha knew the world of nature through Baba's eyes. When he went to live with his mother to attend school in his tenth year, he quickly came to love books equally with nature. He devoured any book he could get his hands on in the winter and reveled in sharing his knowledge with Baba in the summer. She, in turn, sharpened and refined his learning with her piercing observations. She eagerly awaited his every visit. Though it appeared that she lived as an ignorant, indolent native, she truly possessed keen insight.

"Are you going to study again this winter?"

"No, Baba, I'm going on a long trip."

"Trip? Where?"

"I want to publish my pictures and notes into a book."

She spat the herbal concoction she chewed. "It is no good, Sasha. Books will just bring more people here. They'll destroy what we've got. Show me your new drawings."

Pride burned in Sasha when an exclamation of surprise escaped her lips as she saw Sasha's exquisitely colored pictures. "How did you make the pretty colors?"

Sasha withdrew the colored pencils from his knapsack and handed them to his grandmother. He took a pencil and sketched her outline. Taking other pencils, he quickly colored in details. Delight showed on her wrinkled face as she saw their magic. Sasha felt an urge to give her the colored pencils. Every bit as artistic as he, what pleasure they would bring to her long winter days! Rather than break his only tangible tie with Valentina, he would buy the old lady her own set in Moscow.

"Where are you going to get your pictures published?"

"Moscow."

"No, Sasha, you stay here in these mountains. There is a war going on. You'll never return if you go."

"Baba, I'm not going to be in the war. I'm going to see a publisher. I'll be back before spring. It's only seven days by train from Nakhodka to Moscow. I could be back within a month."

"Sasha, do not go."

Sasha knew her bitterness. In the romance of the Russo-Japanese War, his grandfather left her with two sons and never returned. Her sons, in turn, left for the Great War. Maximov returned, missing a leg. He hobbled through life, emasculated.

Nicolai, Sasha's father, had returned whole, but not the same. The world he saw inflamed him with thoughts and desires he had never before entertained. He married a girl who knew not the ways of his people, and other than visiting his mother occasionally, abandoned the traditions of his birth. Caught up in establishing the new Soviet order, his father made an ill-timed criticism and found himself in a prison camp shortly after Sasha's birth.

Fearing for her children, Sasha's mother had placed her eldest son Sergei with her parents and brought Sasha as an infant to his father's mother. His mother then disappeared. Sasha remembered when she showed up in his eighth year: gaunt, tight-lipped, and disillusioned after she too suffered in a prison camp. After two years, she gathered her sons with hopes of beginning life as a family and began the heart-rending search for her husband. As weeks dragged into months and months into years, she submitted to another man's affections and bore him two children.

During that time, Sasha lived on the tightrope of what if. What if his father returned? No one voiced it except Baba. Sasha listened endlessly to her compassionless criticism of his mother. She staunchly held that once one committed to another, she should not look elsewhere for affection. In Sasha's twenty-three years, his father never returned. There was never any word of his fate. Sasha no longer remembered when

Baba finally accepted that her son would never return. She quit talking about him.

Baba put her hand on Sasha's arm. He waited for her to speak. She did not. Finally, he looked into her eyes. Then she quietly spoke. "Sasha, marry Nadia. Hide in the mountains. You don't need to go see a publisher. You do not need the money. No one else needs to know about Kamchatka. Far too many do already. As sure as you go, you will become a soldier. They don't need you to win or lose this war. If you don't remind them you are here, they'll never come looking for you. Let them waste their other young men. We've given our best far too many times. We'll be a nation of widows and orphans if they don't stop this war business."

Sasha said nothing. One never won an argument with Baba.

Baba continued to thumb through his pictures, identifying the birds and admiring the accuracy of the colors when she came upon the portrait of Valentina.

Whoops! He had meant to remove that. He hadn't intended for Baba to see it.

"Who's she?"

"Oh," he tried to act indifferent, "she came as one of the cooks on one of the expeditions."

Baba's look was piercing. "Cook, huh. You lavished a lot of work on this portrait."

"Here, you try using the pencils." Sasha wanted to divert her away from the topic of Valentina. "I'll make a gift of them to you."

Baba accepted the bait and entertained them all with her colorful drawings.

As evening drew near, Baba said, "I'll go tell Nadia you're here."

Nadia had warmed Sasha's nights on his visits to Baba the last couple of years. He knew Baba and Nadia hoped they would marry. Everyone, including himself, assumed that if he left her with child, he would marry her. He knew that she ate spiders when anticipating his visit in hopes that their fertility magic would bind him in obligation to her. Although he had lain with her in the past, he had found no excitement in her. She would be okay for a wife on the Reserve. She knew her place and worked hard, but Sasha could never imagine her meshing with his pursuit of learning in Petropavlovsk, and he could not imagine the girls he knew in Petropavlovsk on the Reserve, following the old ways. Of the modern girls he knew, only Valentina had shown any interest in the old ways.

He wondered for a fleeting moment how Nadia would react if he tried to pleasure her as Valentina had taught him. Probably with fear. He wasn't willing to risk getting her pregnant to find out. "No, Baba, I don't want Nadia tonight."

Baba's eyes bore into him. "It's the girl in the portrait, isn't it? Is she in Moscow?" Her anger showed in the way she clipped her words as she spoke.

Sasha dropped his eyes.

"Sasha!" She demanded an answer.

"Yes, Baba," Sasha mumbled the answer as if revealing something shameful.

She screeched, "And so you are going to sacrifice your life because of a girl."

"Baba, I'm not sacrificing my life!"

"You're going to give up this, all of this," she made a panoramic sweep of the yurt to indicate the beautiful snow-covered mountains surrounding her little valley and the world beyond, "for a Muscovite girl who is probably whoring with the soldiers. You'll give up all of this!"

"I'm sorry, Baba. I'm poisoned with the fever of wanting her. I'll never be content here without her."

"Oh, Sasha, Sasha." The old woman moaned. "I well remember the fervor of young love. No reasoning in the world will dissuade it. But you'll never return. Never."

She bade him farewell the next day with some of the dried fish and berries he had brought for her. Sasha gave her the colored pencils. He would buy himself a new set in Moscow. He hugged and kissed her as both of them choked on their emotions, afraid she might be right. He would never return. This goodbye could possibly be forever. He would not allow himself to think about it.

Salt Lake City 1948

"I should have listened to her. How foolish I was to think I meant anything to you." Now he glared full out at Valentina.

She slid her chair a little away from him, "You did. You do mean something to me."

"No, I don't think you've ever cared for me. You only seduced me to prove you could. One more triumph for you and then move on, not caring what you left in your wake." His volume increased.

"I was young and naive. I didn't know what would happen to either of us."

Sasha growled, "I think you wish you had never met me."

Bishop Bullock interrupted their accusations. "I don't think this is going to be productive. Let me hear the full story, and then we will see what kind of resolution we can come to that will work for both of you. What happened, Valentina, when you returned to Moscow?"

Sasha and Valentina glared at each other for another full minute before she turned to look at the bishop and resumed her tale.

6

Valentina begins Training as a Spy

Moscow 1943

Valentina lay on her bed and groaned in response to the knocking on the door. Her father opened the door as if she had said, "Come in," and entered.

"So are you just going to lie abed again today?" he asked, his voice tinged with impatience. He appeared as a bowed silhouette in the shaft of light entering the darkened room from the hallway.

"I just don't feel well."

"You've not felt well since we left Kamchatka. Maybe you should see a doctor."

"No. I'm sure that is not necessary. I'll be better soon." It had taken her over a month to learn who "the lady" in Moscow was, and then another couple of weeks before she was able to visit her. By then, her morning sickness had subsided. She had not anticipated the bleeding and general discomfort she had experienced since visiting the lady. She felt uncomfortable discussing this with her father, so she minimized her comments. If he knew she had been pregnant, he never said so. How she wished Mamochka could be here to cradle her and listen to her sob out her fears and feelings.

"Well, since you can't, I'll go get our rations. I suppose you'll be fine for a while alone. Would you like some tea before I go?"

"Yes, Father, I would. Thank you for asking."

His return with the tea jolted her back from a restless sleep. He kissed her lightly on the forehead, the ties of his *ushaka* whispering across her face, and said, "I shouldn't be too long. No one is expected, so you should be able to rest peacefully while I am gone."

So wrong, she did expect someone. She still waited and watched for the appointment to begin her training as a spy, but she desperately hoped that would happen with her father at home so she wouldn't be the one to bear the brunt of his reaction. She didn't know how she could tell him. He needed to understand it did not come from her and that she possessed no more power than he to refuse it. But she would welcome it, whereas he would violently object.

She wished she could keep her mind on this, rather than the image of the small form burned into her mind when she visited the lady. How she wished she could erase it. She preferred to think of what had been removed from her as a bloody mass of cells, not having arms and legs, and such tiny hands, not looking like a human being with an odd, over-sized head, an obvious heart stilled in the translucent chest. Until that moment, she refused to allow herself to think that a baby was growing within her, that if not interrupted, it would have grown into a person, with thoughts, feelings, ambitions, hopes, and dreams just as she. Even more startling, that was the first time she ever considered that she could have become a mother.

She never thought about that possibility as something that could happen now, although she expected to be a mother someday. She had virtually no experience with children and planned to do lots of living before committing to raising a child. Now, irrationally, a desire grew within her to become a mother. It seemed like removing the child grow-ing in her womb planted that child in her heart. She felt an urgency to go back and make right the wrong done by prematurely ending its chance at life. Of course, it would not be the same child, but confused thoughts whirled in her mind. "My baby, my baby," she murmured, hugging herself and wishing that could make it right.

Banging at the door awakened her from a deep sleep. First, she thought that Papochka would get it, and then, through the fog in her mind, she remembered he had gone to get their rations. Perhaps the rations filled Papochka's hands, and he wanted her to open the door. But, even to bang the door knocker would require him to set something down, in which case he could just unlock and open the door. So it could be a messenger bringing her appointment.

She dragged herself from the bed, felt the passing of a blood clot, and hoped her gown remained unsoiled. Valentina quickly pulled her dressing gown around herself and hurried down the stairs and hall to the door, calling, "I'm coming, I'm coming."

She heard the knocker once more before pulling the door open. There stood Mr. Fyodorovitch in the frigid air that blasted her. "Oh, miss, are you not well?"

Shivering, she passed her hand over her hair and realized it hadn't been combed in days, "I've been down but am recovering. Thank you for your concern."

"Is your father at home?"

"No. He has gone to get rations. Please come in. It is so cold."

Mr. Fyodorovitch stepped into the hallway, and the door shut out the freezing air.

"Would you care for some tea?" She didn't feel up to this level of graciousness, but her impeccable training prevented her from not offering some hospitality.

"No, my dear. I would not ask that of you, feeling as you do."

She managed a weak smile. Dear Mr. Fyodorovitch. "Thank you. Is everything all right with my mother?"

"As far as I know. Did you hear, though, that three Soviet spies were recently called back from England and executed for being traitors?"
She sucked in a quick breath, and her heart chilled at the news. "No, no. We haven't heard that. What did they do?"

"A friend of one of them confided in me that his friend spoke positively of western countries. He said their governmental systems lead to a more productive society." Mr. Fyodorovitch gave a huge sigh. "One has to be very careful what he says and to whom. I guess it is very hard for our government to have so many of our citizens in other countries. I guess one can't help but compare."

"But, my mother is all right?" Anxiety gripped her.

"I haven't heard anything to the contrary. Anyway," he pulled a packet from his satchel, "This is official government business. It is actually addressed to you, but you must realize it is not from your mother. Your father will need to know about it."

"Yes, I'm sure he will. Do you know what it concerns?" She felt the urgency and importance of the missive. She just wished her father had returned. If he would open it with Mr. Fyodorovitch here, then he wouldn't carry on as he would with just the two of them.

"I could take a wild guess, but in fact, no. I don't. Well, I must be on my way. Give my best to your father." he touched his hat in a gallant salute. "Now, you go back to your bedroom, and I'll let myself out, so I don't chill you again."

Curiosity tore at her, but she resisted opening the packet. She knew what it contained. Even though she desperately wanted to know the details, it was more important to brace herself for her father's response. He would certainly resist it, but his parental objections would not over-ride the dictates of the contents.

She desired more than anything to return to bed, but she forced herself to clean herself up, change into a dress, comb her hair. She was nibbling on a dry bun in the kitchen when she heard her father open the door. She waited for him to come in, not wanting to appear too eager, and besides, she didn't feel like helping. Father hauled two bags into the kitchen, and his eyes widened in surprise, "I didn't expect to see you up. So you're feeling better?"

"Not really. Mr. Fyodorovitch came by, so I got up. I thought it time for me to clean up and get dressed."

"I'd say." Father handed her a bag. "If you are feeling that well, help put this food away."

She didn't feel up to it but didn't dare refuse. "Aren't you curious to know why Mr. Fyodorovitch came by?"

Her father looked at her sharply. "Not really. I think I'd rather not know. I heard that three of your mother's associates have been repatriated."

Valentina pretended no knowledge of this. "Oh, why?"

"No one seems to know exactly. The best guess seems to be western sympathies."

"But the west are our allies. Isn't it them we are counting on to create a front on the west, dividing Germany's forces?"

"It is one thing to appreciate the west for what they can do for us, but entirely a different thing to appreciate them in how they differ from us. Stalin is paranoid in his fears of western influence."

"Do you think Mother is safe?" She fingered the bag on the table, feeling a need to busy her hands as if that could distract her mind.

Her father gave a weary sigh. "I don't think there is such a thing as safety, here or anywhere."

"So, you are concerned about Mother." She said it as a statement, wishing Papochka would be more forthright about what he really thought and felt.

Papochka responded by changing the subject. "What did Mr. Fyo-dorovitch want?

She handed him the envelope.

He eyed it, looking at not only her name but the return address, The Soviet Division of Foreign Intelligence. "It is addressed to you."

"I know, but I thought you would want to see it."

Father took the envelope. "I'll take care of it."

She reached for him, wondering what he planned to do with it. "But father, we don't even know what it says."

"I think we do." He eyed her sharply.

"How do you know?" She sank back to her chair.

"I'll take care of it." He tucked the envelope into his wraps and left the room.

She sat gasping after him. Papochka couldn't do a thing about it except obey. What was he thinking? What would become of him if he tried to destroy it? What would become of her?

She heard Papochka remove his wraps, and she felt quite certain she heard him go into the study. What would he do there? Open the envelope and read it? Tear it up and throw it into the fire? Storm back into the kitchen and refuse to allow her to go? Energized by her frustration, Valentina opened up a bag to find some tins labeled in English. There was something called Spam, Norwegian sardines, Swiss cheese, peaches, corn. She had heard that the west was sending aid in the form of food, vehicles, war supplies. This was the first evidence of it she had seen personally. Russians could eat the west's food but don't say anything positive about it.

She startled at the sound of shattering glass. So Papochka had read it and expressed his own frustration. Thankfully, he didn't direct it at her. She put some water on to boil, wondering how long before the kitchen door would slam open. It did not. In fact, other than the boiling water, a deathly quiet settled over the house. She placed the tea on a tray, one cup and saucer with some biscuits from the rations, and, feeling timid, carried it into the study.

Papochka sat, his head in his hands, paper littered across the floor. He did not look up as she set the tea tray on the table next to him. "Papochka?"

"Did you expect this?" he demanded bitterly.

"I....uh... Expect what?" How could she answer? Blame it on Mamochka? She poured some tea, "Here, Papochka, warm yourself up."

"I'm going to lose you too."

She dropped her pretense of ignorance of the contents of the missive. "It doesn't mean you are going to lose me."

"Of course it does," he drew her onto his lap and stroked her hair. "It is so noble and patriotic to stand by the Motherland in this war, but will the Motherland stand by you? If you go to England or France, the only route back is to be labeled a traitor. I would have preferred that you stayed on Kamchatka with Alex and bore his child."

So, maybe he had known she was pregnant. She chose not to discuss it unless he forced her to. She snuggled against Papochka's chest, feeling very much a child herself. She could not remember the last time he held her like this. They sat in silence a bit, and then she asked, "Papochka, do you think Mother is in danger?"

"If she comes back to Russia? Yes, I do."

"You think she might not come back to Russia?"

"She would be smart not to."

"But, Papochka, what will happen to us if she doesn't?"

"To me. You'll be gone too and, hopefully, much safer than you would be here. Oh, my baby, my baby," Papochka sobbed.

Salt Lake City 1948

Greg Bullock watched Sasha as he listened quietly and respectfully to Valentina's tale as if it were the first time he had heard it. Sasha only wiped his hand across his eyes as she described the aborted fetus. They sat quietly for a moment after Valentina finished speaking. Bishop Bullock prompted Sasha to pick up his side. "So, Sasha, what happened to you next?"

Kamchatka 1943

In Petropavlovsk, Sasha armed himself with flowers and vodka to visit his mother. Little six-year-old Raissa greeted him with a squeal, "It's Yuri!"

Handing the vodka and flowers to eight-year-old Andrei, who followed right behind Raissa, Sasha caught Raissa in his hands and gave her a gentle toss in the air, careful that she would not hit the low ceiling. Catching her, he gently set her down. Shaking the snow from his parka, he hung it up.

"Is Matushka home?" he asked.

"I'm here, Yuri." A voice came from behind the curtain partitioning the small house. In no other place in the world was Sasha called Yuri, the name given him at birth. When he was left at his grandmother's yurt as a baby, Maximov and Olga's toddling son Yuri also lived there. Rather than distinguish between two Yuris in the same household, Baba began to call him Sasha, the common nickname for Alexander, Sasha's grandfather's name. But, from his 10th year on, when his mother returned, she and his brother called him Yuri, and so did her subsequent family.

He had carefully timed his arrival in hopes of getting a meal and missing his older brother, Sergei. The mixed odors of cooking onions and cabbage rewarded his effort and awakened Sasha's taste buds.

"I can read now, Yuri!" Andrei jerked Sasha's hand. "I read real good."

Sasha knelt down to his level, "And, so, what does that mean?"

"A book! You promised me a book when I learned to read."

"Ah, so I did. So, what book do you want?"

"One about dogs."

"Is a puppy as good as a book?"

Raissa gently grasped Sasha's beard on either side of his face and turned him to face her. "Did you have new puppies, Yuri? Did you?"

"I did. Four. Three boys and a girl."

"When can we see them?"

"Tomorrow."

"Will you take me on the dog sledge, Yuri? Will you?"

"Sure, you bet. Those dogs need to go out a lot this winter." Sasha deliberately gave no hint of his pending trip. It would only upset his mother and cast a pall over his visit.

His mother came from behind the curtain. Stress and strain had written his mother's story on her face and framed it in hair totally gray, although her years only totaled forty-five.

Sasha greeted her with a kiss on each cheek. Andrei handed her the flowers and vodka. Tears filled her eyes. "You're so good to me, Yuri."

Sasha put his arm around her thin, stooped shoulders and squeezed her as he kissed the top of her head. Always uncomfortable with a display of emotion, she pulled away from him as he knew she would. "The soup's ready. I assume you're hungry."

"Always."

"As usual, but it doesn't look like you fared so badly this year. The expeditions must have brought some good cooks."

"Yes. The first expedition brought a spunky little gal from Moscow who cooked, and the second hired a local babushka." Sasha patted his stomach, "It made a memorable summer."

"I hear that little gal from Moscow cooked up more than food." Sasha's elder brother Sergei emerged from behind the curtain, a sneer curling his handsome lip.

Sasha sighed, not welcoming the brother he had hoped would not be here.

"Boris says you plan to go to Moscow to see her." Sergei continued to bait him.

"Moscow! No, Yuri!" The tears returned to his mother's voice.

Sasha ignored both Sergei's comment and his mother's response. He moved toward the table. "Let's eat." He didn't want to discuss Valentina with his mother this way. Sergei always sought to stir up trouble.

Emotions wound tight as a spring, Sasha forced himself to eat calmly. No one said anything. The bowls clicked on spoons, and the spoons clicked on teeth. Andrei and Sergei noisily slurped their soup. In a furtive glance at his mother, Sasha saw her eyes dart between him and Sergei. Weariness and sadness weighed her down.

Sasha peered over his spoon at Andrei. The young boy almost bounced in his chair in anticipation. His wide eyes flicked between

Sasha and Sergei. Raissa's eyes filled with fear. Sasha well knew how terrified the little girl became of the angry yelling matches he and Sergei got into, not to mention when their arguments exploded into physical violence. Sasha did not glance in Sergei's direction. He knew without looking that Sergei was leering at him, perched like a cat ready to pounce. The tension sparkled in the air, and Sasha just kept spooning the soup into his mouth.

What did Sergei want from him this time? More money? Sasha would not, under any circumstances, give him or "lend" any more money. He thought that was settled. No matter how noble the cause Sergei purported to espouse, Sasha knew it was no more than a thin disguise for women and drink. His older brother disgusted him.

"So, is she pretty?" Sergei interjected a baited question into the pregnant atmosphere.

Out of deference to his mother, Sasha didn't snap back. Looking directly at Sergei, he said totally evenly, "Very. Didn't Boris tell you?" Then he looked at his mother and saw her hands clasped and drawn up to her throat.

Sasha reached out and lightly touched her arm. "I'm going to get my pictures and notes made into a book. Chirikov, the best of all ornithologists, came on an expedition this summer. He invited me to Moscow. He said he would help me publish my pictures and notes in a book."

"Yuri, are you going to Moscow because of the girl or the book?"

Sasha dropped his eyes. He could not lie to his mother. "Both."

"The book can wait, and the girl is not worth it. Your father gave up his home for me, and then he didn't even get that. Fall for a local girl. With all the boys leaving to be soldiers, you can have your pick. Don't be so foolish. Better a dove on the plate than a wood grouse in the mating place."

"I'm going to bring her back here. It's only seven days by train from Nakhodka. I'll be back within a month."

"The trains going west only carry soldiers," Sergei spoke as he opened the vodka Sasha had brought and drank from the bottle.

Sasha reached for it. Sergei held it clasped in his hand until Sasha growled at him, "Give it, Sergei."

Sergei let go of the bottle. Sasha placed it before his mother.

"It's too risky, Yuri. You'll end up in the war."

"I love her, Mother."

"You lust for her." Sergei snickered.

"You can't possibly know what love is." His mother grasped his hand. "Stay here, hide in the mountains."

"I'll have no peace if I don't try."

"You'll have no peace if you do."

Sergei changed the subject. "Are you ready to defend your title?" He referred to the on-going chess competition which raged between them, the one place in life where they were evenly matched.

"Not now," Sasha said.

"Well, then, I'll be going." Sergei suddenly stood. He picked up the vodka and drank again. "I will catch you later for that game." He gave Sasha's shoulder a shove. Sasha clenched his fist. Sergei gave a rough laugh and slipped out the door.

Raissa climbed into Sasha's lap. "I don't like Sergei."

"What did he want?" Sasha asked his mother.

"Money, of course, but he's got something else up his sleeve as well."

"You don't know what?"

She shook her head. "I don't know what."

Sasha stood. "Where would be the best place for me to catch Boris? At Yuri Maximovitch's?"

"You don't know? Boris and Maximov's Yuri have both left for the war."

"They've turned patriotic?"

"It's war fever, and it's as contagious as measles. Even the women have it. Of Maximov's four children, only Svetlana remains. She's pregnant, and little Alina is only two, and still, Valerian went. Ludmilla is going to the munitions factories. I'm just glad they won't take you. Now is the time for the sun to shine in my yard."

The next day, Sasha went to apply for an application to travel. The clerk looked at him with bored eyes. "You want to go where?"

"Moscow."

"If you want to go west before the end of the war, there is only one way to get to Moscow. Go to Nakhodka and enlist. That's the only way. But listen, you're on the not wanted list because of your parents. Go get your papers reissued under your patronymic. Otherwise, they will stick you in a construction crew."

"Is that so bad?"

"You're out of the way of the bullets, but it is essentially like being in a prison camp. You are treated with suspicion, like a prisoner. Guards, so no one escapes. Inadequate rations. You're better off behind a gun."

Sergei lounged against the wall of the building as Sasha exited. "Well, little brother, you decided to join up yet?"

"It would break Mother's heart."

Sergei shrugged, "You'll do it anyway, you love-sick puppy. If you have to choose between pleasing mother and the possibility of never seeing that gal again, there's no question what you will do."

Sasha walked on, not commenting on this analysis by his brother. Resentment smoldered in him for Sergei's pushy involvement. No inkling suggested what prompted Sergei's goading, but he chose to worry about other things.

With Boris gone, who would he get to run his dogs? Each door he knocked on, each person he asked for, he got the same story: gone to the war. Only the old, the young, and a handful of women remained. Seeing no other options, Sasha took eight-year-old Andrei out in the sledge, not as a joy ride but as training. Sasha couldn't decide which would be worse—not to have the dogs run at all or have them run by a child. His mother lamented his choice, saying it was too dangerous for Andrei. Andrei swelled with confidence as Sasha took him out each day to train him. At the end of the week, he hugged the boy with shining eyes goodbye, tossed his small half-sister in the air one last time, tried to buy off his feelings of guilt towards his mother by giving her a substantial sum of money, and boarded the boat to Nakhodka. His only satisfaction in seeing Sergei on the boat came from knowing that Sergei would be unable to wheedle the money he had left out of their mother.

Sasha found Nakhodka crawling with soldiers and war fever. He made his way from the boat dock to the train station on streets clogged with soldiers braving the cold to strut their shining black boots and crisp olive drab military suits. Patriotic pride burned in their eyes.

At the station, young women clung to their men for one last embrace, the love in their eyes drowning in tears of fear. Wives pressed packages of food into the soldier's hands. Mothers urged them to take an extra pair of warm socks. Sasha strode right by them. He passed citizens who looked as if they were waiting for a train that never came, waiting so long that they had forgotten why they were there. None of these interested Sasha. He watched the arriving trains disgorge heavily guarded individuals on their way to prison camps and soldiers returning from the front, wounded in body and spirit.

One soldier cradled an arm in a sling. He ambled outside the train station and sat on the ground, slumped against the wall, seemingly trying to draw strength to move on. The once-smart uniform, now muddied and tattered, hung loosely on his thin body. Sasha sat down next to him and withdrew two of the good western cigarettes the scientists had given him last summer. He offered one to the soldier. The soldier's drawn and wary eyes flickered with momentary interest, and he smiled his gratitude. After a peaceful moment of smoking, Sasha asked, "How did you find it out there?"

The man took a long draw on his cigarette and exhaled slowly before answering. "Brutal. It's a butcher shop."

"I heard we drove the Germans back."

He answered with a non-sequitur. "The people welcomed the Germans as liberators. They lined the streets. The pretty young girls gave them bread and later welcomed them to their beds. Then we drove the Germans out and raped and murdered our own girls for being German whores. It could have been my wife, your sweetheart. I don't think they all slept with the Germans, and how much choice did they have in the matter?"

Sasha gulped. Valentina had referred to this last summer. "Do you think we'll win this war?"

"Who are we?" the soldier paused. "No. There are no winners in war, only losers. Maybe Stalin and Hitler think there are winners and losers, but the dead man doesn't care who thinks he is in charge once the war is over."

The man sat quietly and smoked the cigarette until finished. He ground the butt out with the heel of his scuffed boot. "Maybe I did win. At worst, I've lost an arm. At best, I came home alive, and my arm might heal."

Sasha wished the soldier luck and moved to another soldier with a bandaged leg and crude crutches hand-carved from tree branches. Sasha offered him a cigarette and let him enjoy it a minute or two before asking. "Did they treat you well in the army?"

The man shrugged, "Usually could get food and clothing. The soldiers aren't as bad off as everyone else."

"The food good?"

The soldier snorted. "Not like a feast at home, but if food could be found, we got it."

Sasha gave the soldier another cigarette and stood to leave. Another injured soldier called to him, "Hey, you. What do you want?"

Sasha saw his eyes yearning for a cigarette. He gave him one. "I want to know the quickest way to Moscow."

"Join the army," the man said without hesitation.

"Why is that quickest?"

"All other trains are diverted for the troop trains. You just sail right along. Seven days and you're there."

"The other trains?"

"Oh, maybe a month, but you've got to have a travel permit. You'd have to have a better reason than you can give to get one. You could always hide out in the coal cars. Of course, they're going full from here. Won't cost you anything except maybe your life. Food rations are hard to come by, and it's getting mighty cold out. It'll dip way below freezing through most of Siberia. You have maybe a two percent chance of survival if you're lucky."

Sasha went back into the building and saw an old man sitting on a bench. "How long have you been waiting here, comrade?"

"Off and on, over three weeks. You'd think that all the soldiers that can go have already gone, and this flood of young men would quit filling up the cars. I swear, they're importing them from China and America to ship off to war. Rarely a woman with a child has a chance in a million, but for a single man alone, it's quicker to walk."

Sasha saw the station full of people with their battered suitcases, lumpy bundles, and whiny children. Not his preference, but being a temporary soldier was a better answer than this fruitless waiting.

Sergei was sitting on the steps of the recruitment center when Sasha arrived the next morning.

"So you decided to join."

"What's your goal, Sergei? Why are you shadowing me?"

"You owe me a chess game."

"Chort! That might be your excuse. It's not your reason."

Sergei shrugged. "I thought you might need my superior survival skills in a city if you plan to go to Moscow. I'm just looking out for my inexperienced younger brother."

Sasha knew only Petropavlovsk, so even one more city made Sergei's experience more extensive than his. Granted, he might need some help finding his way around Moscow, but Sergei didn't know Moscow either. Far more likely, Sergei expected to benefit from Sasha's survival skills. Sasha would never agree that he needed Sergei's help to survive in any situation, but he well knew that Sergei did not pretend to ask if he wanted him to come. Sergei informed him he was coming. Sasha saw no choice in the matter for him, but he was glad he had left the bulk of his money with his mother once again. He'd worried that Sergei might return to Kamchatka.

Sasha didn't want to have Sergei along when he found Valentina. Would Sergei try to compete for Valentina's favor? Would Valentina find Sergei attractive? Most women did respond to his dark curls, seductive smile, and smooth manner. Could Sergei's motive somehow be tied up with Valentina? Now, that would be something to worry about.

It surprised Sasha to find the recruitment center deserted after seeing the city bustling with departing soldiers. He handed his papers to the solitary clerk. The clerk pulled out a list and compared Sasha's name against those on the list. Then he handed the papers back to Sasha. "You're not on the list."

"Of course not," Sasha said. "I'm not an enemy of the people."

The clerk's eyes hardened. "Of course not. This is a list of those we can take, not those we can't, and you're not on it." The clerk handed him a piece of paper. "This is where you sign up to be in the construction crews. You might as well volunteer for prison camp. A bullet is a much more merciful death."

"Look, I just want to get to Moscow. I'm not really interested in this war."

"How much do you want to get to Moscow?"

Sasha understood him perfectly–not how badly he wanted to get to Moscow, but how much he would pay.

"So, there is a way."

"Oh, there's always a way, but you realize, for you to go, a man who has worked for years to get in his position is selling his identity. I'll guarantee you, no one wants yours in exchange. It looks like, before this war is over, every one of our boys is going to be dredged out of the bushes. Patriotic fever doesn't burn with the same fever here as in other parts of Russia. There in Kamchatka, most of you still think of Russia as the enemy instead of the Motherland, but you'll go just the same. They are gathering up all able-bodied men from cities, villages, and farms, from streets, factories and fields. Even walking wounded are dragged back into battles. Volunteers are looked for in hospitals. Sooner or later, they will take every one of us."

Sasha didn't want to wait for sooner or later. "Okay. So I've got money. Can you arrange it?"

The clerk smiled broadly. "Of course. It will take a down payment."

Sasha reached into his pocket and pulled out a sizable sum of rubles. The clerk's eyes widened.

"How quickly can you do it?" Sasha asked.

"Oh, very quickly, I'm sure. Very quickly."

"Tomorrow?"

The clerk gulped and nodded. "Tomorrow."

Sasha handed him about half of the rubles. "I'll be back tomorrow."

He flicked the rest of the notes. The clerk did not miss his message. "I'll have it ready for you, here, tomorrow."

Salt Lake City 1948

Greg Bullock watched as Valentina also listened attentively to Alex's tale. He suspected that it was the first time she had ever heard it. They really didn't know each other at all. A seed of an idea was beginning to sprout in his mind. There just might be a resolution to this conflict between them, but he suspected that neither of them had entertained his idea. He would have to listen closely and see if it continued to grow as their stories developed. It might take some strong persuasion to convince them it would be the best route to follow. Sasha had fallen silent, so Greg turned to Valentina, "And so what happened next with you?"

"I was evaluated as a potential spy and then began my training."

"Why don't you tell us about it?"

Moscow 1944

All morning long, Comrade Zveguintsov fired questions at Valentina in English. She easily slipped into the game Mamochka had played with her for as long as she could remember, "So you think you're so smart, little English girl."

"Put this into the boot of the lorry and then lift the bonnet and put in the petrol," Comrade Zveguintsov barked.

Without batting an eye, she said, "The lorry doesn't have a boot, and though the lorry uses petrol, it's not put in the bonnet."

"Put the bonnet on the lassie," He countered.

Using the array of toys in front of her, she lifted the sunbonnet and put it on the doll. Hour after hour, it went on until the lunch break, and then it resumed, only in French, but she and her Mama had also played *"Tu es tres intelligente, petite fille."*

At the end of the day, a mere handful of prospective spies were left. They had begun the day in the large auditorium. Now they gathered in a small classroom to be issued their official appointments. As foreign intelligence officers for the great Motherland of Russia, their official training before deployment was to begin immediately.

Valentina's thoughts wrapped her like the coat she had worn in Kamchatka as she walked home from her grueling but exhilarating day. Letting herself into the house, she wished she had someone to share her excitement with. Papochka would not want to know she had passed her entry exams with high marks. Hearing voices, she removed her wraps and paused before the study door, trying to discern the voices. Did the visitor concern her or Papochka alone?

"That boy is an absolute gem. It would rob him of his beloved Kamchatka, but I wish I could have him here..." she recognized Comrade Chirikov's voice and pushed the door open. Both her father and Comrade Chirikov turned at the sound. A smile broke over Comrade Chirikov's face, and he rose, extending his hands to Valentina. "My dear, how delightful to see you."

She stood on tiptoe as he bent so she could kiss him on the cheek.

"Your father says the Motherland has required your services. I don't know whether to congratulate you or offer condolences."

"Certainly, there are both sides to it."

"Valentina, could you see if there is anything we could offer as refreshment?"

"Of course, Papochka," she stepped over and kissed him on his forehead. She felt very tender towards him since his heartbreaking response to her appointment.

She stepped into the kitchen and put some water in the teapot. Wondering if somehow the recesses of the cupboard hid something tasty she had missed in her previous searches, she began opening and closing cupboards. Denying the futility, she still did it. An unfriendly banging on the door interrupted her search. She didn't wait for her father to ask her to answer the door but stepped into the hallway. Comrade Chirikov met her there, "Go to your room, Valentina. I don't like the sound of that knock. I will get the door."

Her father stood in the doorway of the study. She saw fear written on his face. She flew into his embrace. He hugged her tightly. "Be brave, my precious, now go to your room and stay there until you know it is safe."

She did go to her room but peeked through the keyhole to see what happened.

"Citizen Mark Kaflov," a voice at the door barked.

Citizen, not comrade. Valentina's blood chilled. The title citizen was reserved for those considered disloyal to the Motherland. What had her father done to deserve such an accusation?

"I am Mark Kaflov," Papochka said, stepping forward.

Valentina bit on her knuckle to keep from crying out.

Two men stomped down the hallway and roughly grabbed his arms.

"Just a minute here," Comrade Chirikov said, "What is the accusation?"

"We have nothing to explain to you." A harsh voice responded.

Valentina could see from her keyhole that three of the four men were dressed as soldiers, but the one doing the talking was dressed in a business suit.

"Perhaps not to me, but you can't just barge into someone's home and call someone citizen and threaten them without an explanation. Mark, do you know what this about?"

"He's a traitor. He does not love the Motherland." One of the soldier men sneered.

"He served in the battle of Moscow, his three sons died as soldiers, his wife serves the Motherland full time," Comrade Chirikov said as if to explain they were mistaken.

"Yes, and with Germany still within our borders, he takes off to Kamchatka on a holiday," the suit man answered.

"That was no crime. Stalin granted that as a special dispensation because of his service in the battle of Moscow, and Moscow was no longer in danger. It had been planned long before the war broke out." Comrade Chirikov stepped closer to her father as if he sought some way to get the men to loosen their grip on Papochka's arms.

"You seem to know a lot about it," one of the soldiers said.

The tea kettle began to whistle, making it harder for Valentina to hear.

"I can get the paper giving me permission to go to Kamchatka," Papochka finally spoke.

"And I can show you the papers authorizing us to pick you up," Suit Man barked.

"Get out of our way, old man!" A young soldier pushed Comrade Chirikov, causing him to fall to his knees.

"Hey, that's Chirikov, another one that we are supposed to get. That's why he knows so much about it. Two birds with one stone." A ragged scar on the cheek distinguished the young soldier speaking. "I heard him lecture once at the University. He's a Christian."

Before she could believe what was happening, the men grabbed both Papochka and Comrade Chirikov and roughly escorted them from the house to the incessant screaming of the teapot. Valentina's heart pounded. She wanted to scream as well but didn't dare call attention to herself. She heard the motor of a truck starting, then only street traffic. She waited a bit. Then, with tears streaming down her face, she went and shut the door and locked it. She wanted to sink against it and cry but went instead to the kitchen and turned off the fire under the kettle. Then the only screeching she could hear was her own.

Would they just take Papochka and Comrade Chirikov in and question them, then realize what a foolish mistake they had made? Perhaps they would release them, and they would be back within an hour or two. Or would they mysteriously disappear as so many other people had?

So distraught by the events of the evening, Valentina paced for a while, then sat until she could stand it no longer, then paced again. Eventually, she realized the fire was no longer burning, and the room had grown cold. She got blankets from her bedroom and curled into Papochka's chair, waiting for his knock at the door. She awoke many times during the night but could hear nothing but the tick of the clock.

Finally, realizing it must be early morning, she walked to the kitchen to check the time, still wrapped in the blankets. She needed to hurry, or she would be late for her training. She didn't dare miss it, or she might be dismissed. Besides, she couldn't stand the thought of staying in the empty house, waiting and hoping for what might never happen.

Splashing cold water on her tear-swollen face, she rummaged for a piece of bread to sustain her during the day. Finding a few carrots, she nibbled on one as she walked to her training.

She entered the touch-typing room and began the warm-up. Her fingers seemed as frozen as her heart and tripped over themselves as she tried to get them to type the words. Tears continually blurred her vision, slowing her even more. After she took the five-minute test at the end of the hour, Comrade Khlebnikov looked at her score of 50 words and 12 mistakes, "This is not acceptable. If you want to stay here, you will need to do at least 65 with no more than two mistakes."

"Yes, Ma'am." Valentina willed the tears away from her voice. Once she left the room, she allowed the luxury of wiping the tear away that escaped down her cheek.

She changed into her white nurse's uniform and entered her class, where Comrade Kleinmichel taught them how to insert an IV needle. They practiced on some tubing. Valentina slipped and poked herself.

Tall, blonde Arkady Shidlovsky saw her finger fly to her mouth, "Just hope I'm far away from you when we have to practice on each other."

She managed a wry smile.

The house stood dark and cold when she returned home. She built a fire and put some water on to boil for the potatoes. Surely Papochka would be home soon, but he did not return that night, nor the next, nor the following week.

Salt Lake City 1948

Bishop Greg Bullock was not surprised when Valentina broke off in sobs. "He never did return. I don't know what happened to them. Probably prison camp and all they did was what they had been given permission to do."

Sasha sat, seemingly unmoved by her pain. Was this because she rehearsed this to him often, and he could do nothing to change things, Greg wondered. Or was it because of the recent distress Valentina had inflicted on him in divulging the abortion?

Greg rose and put a hand on Valentina's shoulder. "Bless your heart," he said. "That is a terrible burden to bear."

The more Greg heard of their story, the less he felt they were here as spies, and the more he realized why Valentina feared repatriation to the Soviet Union. "Even though this has been a short session, perhaps we should stop for tonight."

"No, it's okay," Valentina managed through her sobs, "Let Alex pick it up."

Sasha waited until Greg seated himself again before beginning.

Nakhodka 1944

Told to strip naked, Sasha was examined by a doctor who pressed a cold stethoscope against his chest and back. The doctor barraged him with questions. Had he ever had a venereal disease? Tuberculosis? It would seem easy enough for those who didn't want to go to answer yes, and those who did want to go to answer no. If the doctor couldn't tell, why would they answer against their desires? With stoic regret, Sasha saw his shoulder-length, reddish-blonde tresses fall and his beard shaved. That made him feel more naked than the absence of clothing, robbed of his identity, cloned in the garb of the soldier. But since he was playing a charade anyway, a disguise seemed appropriate. Once fitted out in his crisp suit, smart boots, greatcoat, and stylish hat, he felt like strutting himself. Inexplicably, they issued no guns but gave them advice to watch for a dead German or comrade and take his gun and ammunition. Proving himself in battle would probably be only slightly more dangerous than deserting. At least he got a return on the compulsory military tax he had paid for years as a 'suspect person'-- a ticket to Moscow.

Sasha confirmed his suspicions that Sergei had not come along just to see him off when he recognized the long lashes framing his dark eyes. Without his crown of dark curls, he looked like a plucked chicken, even with his dimple. Sasha felt a measure of calm at the idea of Valentina meeting Sergei. She would have to be blind to find the man attractive.

Sasha got his orders, pleased with the clerk's success. He would be mobilized in Moscow, where he would receive training as Artur Shulzenko.

Sasha went back to the deserted recruitment station to repack his bags for the trip. He tucked his remaining money in the bread bag and tucked his carefully wrapped pictures and notes, as well as his peasant clothing, in the backpack. He would need those things when he laid his soldier disguise aside. In the empty ammunition pouches, he stuffed the dried fish and berries Baba insisted he'd need. Then he stuffed the ammunition pouches in his army tote bag with his greatcoat, felt *valenki* boots, and one change in uniform. He put his knife and his army duffel bag in a bearskin he had made into a tote. It was heavy, but he was used to carrying it, and it might come in handy. On top, he put Tolstoy's thick *War and Peace*. He hadn't had a chance to begin reading it yet, but seven days on a train was a long time.

He fortified himself for the trip with all the vodka he could carry. Then, walking in front of the suffering, sad-eyed soldiers returning from the front and the citizens waiting for trains, he mounted the train. He felt intoxicated with the sense of power it gave him. Yesterday he had been one of those civilians, without a ghost of a chance of getting to Moscow. Today he was one of the elite, one who stepped to the front of the line and boarded the train, his trip secure. All of the troops felt heady with the power of their preferential treatment. They saluted their own importance in bottle after bottle of vodka, in jovial celebration.

Withdrawing his greatcoat to use as a blanket in the unheated train car, Sasha stowed his tote bag and backpack beneath the bench. He accepted a rough, bitter Mahavka cigarette from one of the soldiers. The air in the enclosed train grew thick with cigarette smoke before the train even began to chug its way west. One of the soldiers pulled out a bottle of vodka and passed it around. The level of joviality rose to a crescendo as more and more bottles of vodka appeared. It gradually subsided as the soldiers drank themselves into a stupor. Sasha's last coherent thought was that it would be a quick trip to Moscow if he stayed drunk most of the way.

When Sasha did awaken enough for thoughts to flow, his head throbbed. The train clacked and lurched through the dark night. The stench of vomit roiled his stomach. He removed his greatcoat and laid it on the bench and unsteadily rose and tried to make his way to the car door. The train lurched, and he slipped on some vomit on the floor. Crashing down and smearing the vile substance on his uniform and shaved head, he swore. As he tried to pick himself up, he lost the vodka-laden contents of his own stomach. He crawled back to his bench and covered his stinking, sticky, rumpled uniform with his still clean greatcoat. He eased his aching head against the blanket he used as a pillow. The rhythmic clatter of the train lulled him back to sleep.

The train stopped, and more soldiers clambered onto the train, and his bench became a shared space.

When he woke again, he watched soldiers trying to block the blinding sunlight from the train car by putting their blankets over the windows. Sasha put his greatcoat over his head. It trapped the horrible odor of his uniform and funneled it to his nose. He took the greatcoat off his head. The car smelled much the same. Looking through squinted eyes, Sasha tried to open the window but found it screwed shut. He snuggled against the still snoring bulk of the soldier next to him and tried to make himself as comfortable as possible.

Each time the train stopped, Sasha changed cars to see if he could find one with better circumstances. It seemed that all of the soldiers in all of the cars began their military service with the same sick hangover as in his original car. Finding no hope of improving his situation by moving to a different car, he settled into one chosen at random.

Sasha sobered up in more than one sense as the days wore on. Through windows on both sides of the train, again and again, he saw guard towers at the corners of barbed wire fences. Within these enclosures, guards carrying ancient rifles escorted groups of people inadequately dressed in thin, gray baggy uniforms. These emaciated prisoners marched or stood at attention. Their faces of despair haunted Sasha. By buying the identity of Shulzenko, he committed a crime which, if discovered, would surely make him a candidate for one of these places. Already, he had jeopardized his chance of ever returning to Kamchatka. His loss of Kamchatka could be realized without ever seeing Valentina. He'd very possibly cut the bough he sat on.

"Why are we stopping now?" one of the soldiers growled as the car stopped for the fourth time that morning. "At this rate, the war will be over before we get there."

It suited Sasha fine if the war ended before he got there, but he didn't intend to spend weeks, months, or years in this stinking car trying to get to Valentina.

"Inktrusk." an NKVD guard announced. "You'd better load up on vodka here. There's none available further west."

Sasha trooped off the train with the other soldiers to replenish his personal supply of the precious liquid. They searched for the bar-package stores called sheltok because their walls sported egg-yolk yellow paint, easily spotted from afar, and to a thirsty man, as teasing as a red flag to a bull. The soldiers boisterously reboarded the train, bearing their bottles like trophies. The celebration broke out anew before they even stowed the extra bottles. Sasha saw one soldier open his thick, quilted trousers and drop a bottle into either leg of the baggy pants tucked into the high boots at the knee. The soldier zipped his pants, carefully seated himself, so the bottles lay flat against his legs, and opened a third bottle as the train lurched into action. The door flipped open, and five guards entered. Two of the guards pointed guns at the soldiers, and the other three began picking up the bottles of vodka at the soldiers' feet.

"What do you think you are doing?" a soldier demanded in a slurred voice.

The NKVD officer who barked back at them was the same one who had counseled them to renew their stock of vodka. "Look at you, drinking, stinking slobs, the defenders of the Motherland!"

Sasha's foggy thoughts still registered that they'd been set up. He wondered if anyone besides himself noticed the soldier with the bottles in his pants. Stronger than the desire for more vodka, sleep claimed him.

Shouts stirred him enough to see three soldiers pantsing the vodka hider. "You've got it; you share it."

A guard pulled the fellow's pants down around his knees, and the vodka bottles disappeared like a magician's trick.

Inside the train, the stench of vomit staled enough that Sasha could eat his black bread without his stomach lurching. Sasha quickly tired of staring at the endless miles of small, snow-covered hills and tiny, straggling clumps of trees only broken up by the periodic prison camps. He played checkers and chess until that became as boring as the scenery outside the train.

Glad that he had brought the thick tome of *War and Peace*, Sasha waded into its pages. Initially, the story bombarded him with an army of characters designated not by General and Private but French-speaking Counts, Countesses, Princes, and Princesses who danced polonaises, waltzes, and cotillions, dances which Sasha had never heard of. Soon he became embroiled in intrigues involving money, titles, and love. The women seemed to fall for money, the fathers insisted on title, and the men fell for beauty. But what was love? Was what he felt for Valentina love? True, he thought her pretty when they had first met, but he had stoically resisted her advances, fearing it would only bring trouble to him. When he finally succumbed, the desire ignited in him to continually be with her resulted in this journey. Was that love? Perhaps the more pertinent question was, what did Valentina feel? Was their summer liaison a mere fleeting pleasure she sought and then moved on to something more enduring? Would she be happy to see him, or would this trip be in vain?

Salt Lake City 1948

Sasha glanced at Valentina, signaling her to pick up the tale.

7

Sasha Travels Across Russia

Moscow 1944

Valentina knew she would have to use a foreign language. She thought it would be English or French but soon found that learning the language of codes was her real task. She memorized many initials or abbreviations with some correspondence to their meaning. DM: Military Delegate, RV: rendezvous, SAS: Special Airborne Service, SI: Special Intelligence Branch, and so on endlessly. She also learned a host of English or French words with code meanings having no relationship to the real meaning. The USSR was hereafter to be referred to as Bedmaker, Moscow as Bashful, and Russians, Alibara. Baseball or BB stood for an England-to-Russia air shuttle. Everything talked about something else. Nothing was as it seemed to be. So much to remember! Enough to keep her from thinking about her sad situation until she arrived home each evening. She lived for the day and endured the night.

One evening as she approached the house, she distinctly saw smoke rising out of the chimney. A light burned in the window of the study and another in Papochka's bedroom. He had come home! Oh, glorious day! She flung the door open and rushed into the hallway, "Papochka! Papochka!"

A shapely but thin, hawk-nosed woman stepped out of the kitchen. "Who are you?"

Shocked surprise enveloped Valentina. She took a step backwards. "Who are you? What are you doing in my home?"

"Oh, no, my dear, this is not your home," the woman gave a chilling snicker, "although we can allow you to work for a room. Nikita," she called, "I think we have a hot volunteer."

Valentina backed towards the door. Her voice boarded on shrillness, "What do you mean? This is my home, granted us because of my mother's service to the Motherland."

"The Motherland has other uses for your home." A thirtyish, greasy-haired man emerged from Papochka's study. His build reminded her of Alex's, except for the way his shoulders swallowed his neck. He swirled what must be vodka in a flask, "And the Motherland can also use you, my dear."

He handed the flask to the woman, who immediately sipped from it. "Remove your wraps and join me in the study."

The lewd way he looked at her made Valentina feel he had said, "Remove your clothing and join me in the study."

"No, I, I..." Panic gripped her that mandated escape. She depressed the door handle and pulled the door open.

Nikita rushed immediately to the door, slammed it shut, wrenching the handle from her hand. "You don't have any choice in the matter. Now remove your wraps, or I shall do it for you."

Valentina rubbed her hand where the door handle scraped it. "You have no right to do this. Let me go."

Nikita pushed her against the wall and roughly kissed her, his vodka-scented, smoke-filled breath filling her with adrenaline and disgust. She freed a hand and yanked his hair. He pulled her hand free and slapped her with his free hand. "I don't mind a woman who fights. In fact, I rather enjoy it. I'll win in the end. Last chance, now take off your wraps."

Valentina stood frozen. How could this be happening? How could she stop it?

"Okay, Spitfire, I'm glad to do it for you."

The way he yanked her scarves off her head told her he would tear her coat off without any regard to the fastenings. "I'll do it, I'll do it," she said and unbuttoned the coat and hung it on the hook. She removed her boots and slipped on her slippers, still sitting on the shelf where she left them that morning.

"Okay, now in the study," he pushed her in front of himself and then pinched her arm in his grasp when she stumbled. He let out an acid laugh, and Valentina shuddered.

He threw her unceremoniously into a chair facing Papochka's desk and seated himself behind the desk as if he possessed the right to be there. "So," he sneered, "this was your home. Where is your family?"

Valentina stared at him, not knowing the best answer to give. Surely, it would not be well to admit to this man that she was alone. "My father is away on business but will be home shortly, and my mother and brothers are serving the motherland."

"Your brothers rot in graves, your mother is abroad, and your father's business will not be terminated any time soon. Admit it, my little dove, you are alone, so very alone. And you know that in our great Soviet Union, we all share-alike. This is much too much house for one little girl. But don't worry, we will take care of you, very good care," he smiled wickedly.

He knew too much about her, far too much. Who was he? How did he know these things? The KGB? Nikita was not one of the soldiers who had picked Papochka up. Comrade Chirikov had mentioned then that her brothers had been killed in the war, and her mother was serving abroad. Maybe one of them had told Nikita of the supposedly vacant house. She chose not to respond.

"Now, Valentina Markovna, I assume this generous ration card belongs to you." He tapped her ration card, which she kept in the desk against his other hand, "What is it you do for the Motherland that makes you so valuable?"

So he didn't know about her. No one had seen her the evening Papochka was picked up. She suddenly felt grateful that all her papers relating to her espionage appointment lay locked within the unbreachable walls of the Kremlin. He did not know of that. "I'm in a touch-typing course." True, just not the entire truth. She didn't know what this man would do if he knew the entire truth, but she felt a need to keep that much of herself private. It seemed nothing else would be.

"Well, this little card makes you as valuable as the other service you will render for us, maybe more so. Vera," he called out and abruptly stood, "show her to the rose room,"

The thin woman appeared in the doorway, chewing on a bun Valentina had made the night before. "What if she won't go with me?"

Nikita contemptuously laughed, "I'll enjoy giving her a spanking she won't soon forget."

Not doubting for a moment that he would, Valentina followed Vera with Nikita behind up the few steps to her own room. On the landing, they did not enter her room but proceeded to the upper story to what at one time had been Natasha's room. A scantily clad woman stood in the doorway of Mamochka and Papochka's bedroom. A soldier exited from Dmitri, Mark, and Andrei's room, fastening his belt as he went. Beyond him, she could see a woman with bare shoulders wrapped in a sheet. A sickening dread settled over her as she fully realized what her home had been transformed into during the day. Worse, she realized what she would be coerced into doing. How could she possibly escape this? It meant one thing to engage in this intimate activity by choice, totally another to engage in it by force.

"You will be entertaining valiant soldiers seeking some diversion from their difficult duty. Vera will have some water and towels sent up so you can freshen up before your first visitor."

"Please, I cannot do this," Valentina protested.

"I don't recall asking you if you wanted to," Nikita's voice would have been patronizing if not for the hard edge to it. "The soldiers don't want to do what they are required to do either. It is the very least you can do for the Motherland."

Nikita shoved her into the room. Before she could catch her balance, the door slammed behind her. Valentina heard a key turn in the lock and realized she had just been made a prisoner in her own home, except she knew of an escape that, hopefully, Nikita did not.

Before she could act on her thought, the key turned in the lock, and Vera brought not water but a somewhat inebriated soldier into the room. "Aw, baby," he caught her in a slobbery kiss. She tried to push him back, but his strength easily overpowered her. He began fumbling with the buttons on her blouse. "Too hard, I'll just tear it off."

"Let me, let me," she said, beginning to caress him. As much as she hated this, she could not allow him to destroy the only set of clothing she still possessed, or she truly would be a prisoner in this place until her body became wasted from disease. She let him have his way with her only to learn that after him came another soldier, and then another. Finally, she fell into an exhausted sleep, wondering if she would be able to awaken in time for her training the next morning.

Her internal alarm awakened her as it customarily did since she began getting up at the same time every day. She tried the door to the bedroom. Still locked. She tried the window and fortunately, it opened. There would be a way out. She cleaned herself the best she could with the water finally delivered between soldiers the night before. Then she hurriedly dressed, opened the window, swung out to the tree, and shimmied down. She wanted to scream when she saw Nikita smoking as he leaned against the house in the gray-dawn.

He languidly drew on his cigarette, "And where do you think you are going?" He obviously knew of her descent long before she reached the ground.

"I have to go to my training." She knew her only hope of survival lay in completing the training and being sent abroad. If a God lived in heaven, if he would only grant her this. Nikita continued to eye her, slowly smoking. With more confidence than she felt, she said, "They'll come looking for me if I don't show up."

Nikita ground the cigarette out. "Come and get your coat and boots and a bite to eat."

Valentina did not know if she dared enter the house with him. He might just lock her in again, but she shivered from the cold and would look silly showing up in slippers. She followed him to the door, which he opened. He went on down the hall to the kitchen while she quickly slipped on her boots and coat. She stepped outside as he returned from the kitchen with a cold, hard-boiled egg and some bread.

"Thank you," she said, realizing the irony of saying thank you to someone who has stolen everything from you and gives one small item back.

He started to walk beside her. "You do not need to come with me."

"Look, little dove, I'm not going to let you fly away so easily. We still need you tonight."

"I'm not your little dove."

Nikita gave his harsh laugh. "Maybe not, but you are my captive."

That she could not deny as he had just caught her in her escape attempt. "I cannot be up most of the night and do what I need to do each day, or I'll be dismissed." She played what she hoped was a trump card, "And if I am dismissed, I'll lose my ration card."

Nikita gave a raucous laugh, "I guess we'll have to ration your soldiers so that you can perform both services for us."

Glad her training building was nondescript, giving no clue as to what went on inside, Valentina said as they arrived, "This is it."

"What time do you finish?" Nikita asked.

Valentina knew full well that she would not be allowed the freedom to go and come at will. She would be escorted from one to the other. Maybe she could find someone in her training she could turn to for help, but she did not know who that would be. She feared it was up to her to find a resolution to this situation.

Salt Lake City 1948

Greg Bullock felt sickened by this new development in Valentina's life. Virtually everyone who participated in a war was a victim in one way or another. Alex showed no response as Valentina recounted her horrible tale. Greg didn't think him so insensitive. Perhaps he had heard it before, or perhaps he had seen enough forced prostitution that it no longer moved him. Maybe he had even visited the girls. It was so very common among the soldiers, and what teachings did Alex have to restrain him? Would his love, or lust, for Valentina have been a deterrent?

Bishop Bullock needed to let this settle a bit before hearing more of Valentina's misfortune. He turned to Alex, "You tell?"

Russian train, 1944

Rumor said that the train only stopped briefly at stations, to prevent desertions. Long stops, for what purpose Sasha could not devise, occurred between stations. Sasha failed to understand the motivation for desertion. Where would a man go in this wasteland? Sasha knew his survival skills were far superior to almost anyone else's, yet the thought of taking off in this vast wilderness gave him pause.

Gradually, kilometer after kilometer, day after day, revulsion began to build in Sasha for the filth and stench until he thought he could not stand it any longer. He didn't know how far it was to Moscow, but they had not yet crossed the Ural mountains. He wanted to be able to present himself smartly in his uniform to Valentina in Moscow. Realizing he could be captured as a deserter, he waited for a nighttime stop, with some lights indicating a village nearby.

When he left the train, he wanted to be close enough to civilization to receive the services he sought but able to hide from the scrutiny of bright lights. He pondered a full day about whether to tell Sergei his intent. On the one hand, he would be free of Sergei. On the other hand, Sergei was a blood brother and a tangible tie with home. Sergei watched him attentively as if he sensed Sasha's thoughts. Sasha decided by not deciding. He never got around to telling Sergei. He prepared his bear tote, all of his stuff stowed away for easy carrying. He moved through the train until he reached the last car and felt no surprise at finding Sergei there. He did not acknowledge Sergei's presence. Continuing the pretense that he had come to that car seeking a new challenge in chess, Sasha did not exchange names with the soldier he played.

The game was still going on as evening shadows lengthened into darkness. The men began to sleep. Sasha did not exchange names with the soldier he played. He heard the train slowing. He saw a lot of lights on the right side of the train. On the left fewer lights twinkled. He picked up his bag and climbed out the door onto the platform. He leaped into the darkness on the left side before the train came to a complete stop. Sergei followed right on his heels. Sasha heard a guard yell "Stop!" followed by the crack of pistol fire. He did not turn to see what happened but put as much distance between himself and the train as possible. His efforts to hurry made his pack seem heavier as he pushed farther and farther from the train. Finally, he reached a copse of trees, where he could set down the offending pack.

Only then did he permit himself to look back at the train. He saw Sergei struggling through the darkness, but no guards.Near the train, he could see a soldier on his knees, hands on his head, and a gun trained on him. Sasha realized this soldier had unwittingly become his scapegoat. He also knew he was safe for the moment. The guards would not discover their numbers were down until after the train chugged on.

Sergei finally caught up with him, huffing from the unusual exertion. "You could be killed for deserting," Sasha said to Sergei.

"So could you. I thought Moscow was your goal."

"It still is. And what is your goal?"

"Just looking after my younger brother."

"Your younger brother neither needs nor wants you to look after him."

Sergei shrugged.

Even though Sasha meant what he said, he found an odd comfort in Sergei's company. A new uncertainty loomed large in the darkness before them. Nothing mapped out the dangers in this uncharted territory. If they were picked up as deserters, death, or at least prison camp, would be their reward.

Sasha wanted better cover by daylight. "I'm going to look for a house."

"Why, what do you want?"

"I want to clean up, wash my clothes." Sasha shouldered his bag.

"I'll stay here, watch the bags until you find something."

Sasha debated momentarily. He could move faster, easier without his bag, but if he returned and found it gone, he'd be in a serious situation.

"Thanks. I'll just carry it."

Sergei looked around as if having his own debate. "I'll wait here. Let me know if you find anything."

This irked Sasha. He felt no obligation to do all the work and then report back to Sergei. "No promises."

Sasha made his way in the darkness, directly away from the station. He stayed within the shelter of the trees. He could hear voices and crept as quietly as possible until he could see a group of people being loaded into trucks. "Come now, come now. There is better food, the work is not as hard. You'll be glad you came." He could hear a man shouting. Only women climbed into the lorries. Not willing to risk their fate, he stayed quiet until the lorries lumbered off. He walked on in the darkness.

Within an hour, he came to a house built half into the ground. Steep steps led down to the entrance. Above the ground, the house rose only a few feet high, with two tiny windows in the front. The stairs led first into a stable where he saw a cow and a pig. Sasha knocked loudly at the door. No one answered, but Sasha knew someone was there. He had heard scuffling just before knocking. He knocked again. The light flickering in the tiny window went out. "Please," he called, "I come in peace."

"What do you want?" A woman's timid voice with an accent unfamiliar to him came through the door.

"Someone to wash my clothes."

"Why? Where are you from?"

"Petropavlovsk."

"Get someone from Petropavlovsk to wash your clothes."

"I am headed west to Moscow, and the trains going East only have deportees and prisoners of war in them. It would take weeks to get to Petropavlovsk. It's taken weeks to get here."

"The Eastern Petropavlovsk?"

"Is there another one?"

The door cracked and then slammed shut.

"You're a soldier—a deserter."

"I'm not a deserter. I'm just dirty and want to clean up. I'm catching the next troop train west."

"Why do you lie to me?"

"I'm not lying."

Sasha wasn't sure what reassured her, but she opened the door. The hut was made of straw and clay compressed into bricks, held together with more clay. He entered one large room. At the far end stood a brick-sided stove about two feet high, with a metal cooking plate across the top. The woman offered him a cup of tea. The water tasted salty.

"Are you alone?" she asked.

"My brother is hiding near the train tracks."

"If you can get him back before dawn, I'll help you. Otherwise, please don't come here. I'll not let you in, and I'll report you."

Sasha gave her some of the soldiers' tins of American spam and peaches but carried his pack and hurried back to Sergei. As he approached, he saw a girl of about fifteen leave the straggly trees where Sergei was hiding. "Who's she?" Sasha asked.

"A refugee," Sergei answered.

"What did she want?"

"Some food."

"You gave her some?"

"I told her I didn't have any. She kept begging. She said she'd do anything if I gave her some food."

"And..."

"She gave me what I wanted, and I gave her some food."

Sasha slugged him. Sergei tried to hit back, and Sasha slugged him again. "If you're traveling with me, you leave the women alone." In his vow to keep himself for Valentina, somehow, the thought that others pleasured themselves without any regard for the other person seemed fundamentally wrong.

Sasha shouldered his bag and stalked off. Sergei followed along behind. Sasha's blood boiled. Sergei had been fifteen when Sasha first met him. Full brothers, Sasha had idolized him initially. He was wise to the unknown ways of the city and willing to initiate this younger brother, who was only smart to the ways of the natives. Sasha became disgusted with Sergei's lack of values, excessive drinking, and womanizing. Baba's insistence on staying true to the one you committed yourself to had instilled a higher standard in him. He wished he'd never permitted Sergei to follow him. Sasha felt that decision would yet spell trouble.

The darkness still covered them when they arrived at the hut. The woman admitted them.

"You can sleep here," she said, pointing to plain, wooden boards arranged near the fire. "If you want to wash tomorrow, you need to fetch the water tonight," she told them. "I cannot wash for you. I work all day long."

She produced a variety of containers to hold water. Sasha and Sergei fetched water from a small well framed by wooden boards around a square hole, with a block of wood across the top.

Before leaving for her work in a bakery the next morning, she strictly instructed them. "You must stay in the house in the daytime. If you are seen, you will be arrested, and so will I. Do not even build a fire once I leave because it is known that I live alone, and the smoke coming from the chimney will be noticed."

They put as many containers as they could on the stove to absorb whatever heat they could until the fire died. They drank some tea and then used the rest of the warm water to wash their bodies. As they washed their clothes in tepid water, Sergei grumbled, "I've always hired a woman to do my washing."

"I'd rather wash than be dirty." Sasha's tolerance for being dirty had significantly diminished since he began indulging in the hot springs. He would not admit it to Sergei, but he did not want to arrive dirty on Valentina's doorstep in Moscow.

The clothes dried slowly in the small, damp hut. Sasha spent the day reading. He kept trying to see himself and Valentina in Tolstoy's characters as if he could predict their futures by what happened to those characters. Pierre was an utter fool. Prince Andrey had some admirable qualities. He was rational, not like his weak sister, Princess Mayra, who claimed everything that happened was God's will. But Sasha was no prince, and Prince Andrey preferred going off to the excitement of war to spending time in the company of his beautiful, pregnant wife. Sasha wanted only the company of a beautiful, pregnant wife. He wanted to equate Valentina with Tolstoy's vivacious, charming Natasha. He himself was probably more like the sensible Sonia but without a dowry.

When darkness fell, the woman returned with bread. Sasha took the clothes outside to hasten their drying, and they broke the bread and talked. "Where are you from?" he asked, still trying to identify the unfamiliar accent.

"Latvia."

"What are you doing here?"

"Deportees. The Germans were coming. The Russians emptied the cities and countrysides. Everyone," she said as if that explained everything.

Sasha did not understand but did not pressure her. She seemed reluctant to talk. He broke out the sole remaining bottle of vodka he had managed to hide from the guards on the train.

Once warmed by the charged liquid, she became more willing to talk. "I've been here since July of '41. I came with my three-year-old daughter, and I was pregnant. I have no idea what happened to my husband. He was so young and handsome and so good to me." She teared up and paused, sipped some more of the vodka, and continued. "They put me on one train and he on another. I was only twenty-two when I came."

The harsh conditions wore heavily on her, Sasha thought. She seemed much older than that.

"What happened to the children?"

"I lost the baby before it was ever born. They didn't feed us well, and they worked us so hard. They just herded the children together while they forced the adults to work. There was no one to watch them or care for them. They did not care if the children survived. They were just more mouths to feed. My daughter, Elsa, lived for six months but became ill and, there was nothing I could do for her. We are just a bunch of shadows living here. Even the guards know if they get harsh with us, we will just quit working. We don't care anymore."

Sasha rewarded her amply for her kindness with food, the rest of the vodka, and cigarettes she could trade for things she needed. Sasha saw Sergei look longingly at her occasionally, but Sasha's restraining glare kept him in check.

Two days and three hundred pages later, the clothes finally dried. Prince Andrey's wife died in childbirth. Prince Andrey fell in love with the beautiful Natasha but delayed the wedding for a year at his father's request. The parents had such control over their children's destinies. That was not a world Sasha knew. Did Valentina? Was she like the capricious Natasha who fell immediately in love with the handsome Anatole because of a flirtatious look and a kind word, even though she was supposedly waiting for Prince Andrey? He no longer wanted to equate Natasha with Valentina or himself with any character in the book. That fool Pierre had become a Mason in an attempt to become good. What was goodness? What was love? He knew less than ever, in Tolstoy's fiction, or in his own life.

Sasha and Sergei put their clean, though wrinkled, uniforms back on. They bid the woman good-bye and, in the dark of the night, sneaked back to the copse by the tracks. The woman assured them that troop trains passed nightly. As they crouched in the copse, the same girl who had begged from Sergei before, or another who looked just like her, came begging, "Please, sir, some food."

Sasha opened his pack and gave her a couple of tins. "I can pay you, sir."

"That is not necessary."

"Thank you."

Sergei's disgust matched her palpable relief. "Come on, aren't you a man?"

"Man enough to not take advantage of a mere kid. I bet she's not even thirteen."

Somewhere in Sasha's depths, he felt like he was making a pact with an unknown power to protect and preserve Valentina if he did not violate another woman or girl.

They heard the train across the vast steppe long before it came into sight. They heard it slow and knew it would be stopping. After the lighted engine passed their hiding place, they dashed to the tracks and swung onto a car far from the lighted station. They played chess in separate cars before the train started. The other soldiers readily accepted the Russian tobacco they offered and presumably assumed they had just moved in from different cars, seeking new chess partners. No one challenged their right to be there. When the guards came through doing their routine counting, Sasha saw them count and then recount. Too many were just as mystifying as too few. "Papers, everyone, papers."

Sasha calmly handed his papers over. He knew the guard would not find his name on the list, but they had not checked names against the list on the other train, and they did not now. The guard looked at the papers and handed them back without comment.

"Everything in order?" Sasha asked casually as if he could not possibly know the problem.

The guard mumbled. Sasha deliberately pulled out a cigarette and offered it to the guard before he could demand it. He didn't worry that his face would be recognized as new. The guards kept themselves aloof from the soldiers, never looked into their faces, never played games with them. They just counted heads and looked at papers. He trusted the guards on this train would be the same as on the previous train. They were indeed.

As soon as the guards left the car, the soldiers broke out some vodka they had somehow managed to hold onto. Sasha allowed himself one good swallow, but he relished the feeling of being clean and was unwilling to debauch himself again so soon. He surreptitiously ate some bread and a potato the woman had given him. None of the other soldiers had food as fresh. Once the other soldiers drank themselves into oblivion, he permitted himself one of his good western cigarettes. He rationed the few remaining both for his own pleasure and as currency more sought-after than money.

Three more days passed, chugging west with constant interruptions. Sasha calculated that he was now in the third week of this seven-day trip. The farther west they got, the more people they saw pouring east. The fighting zones still lay further west, but a new set of dejected humanity clogged each road and station. Other than more copious personal belongings, the refugees didn't look so different from the deportees. All of Russia seemed to be on the move, all the young men going west and all the women, children, and elderly going east. Would Valentina even be in Moscow once he got there, or would she, too, have left for some unknown destination?

At one stop, Sasha disembarked to replenish his depleted vodka supply. He saw the now-familiar cattle car open its doors, and out flowed the skin and bones of wasted young men grown old. They hardly seemed to have the power to move, but rifle butts and yells forced them to jog down the road.

"Poor devils." a man at the station commented.

"German prisoners?" Sasha asked.

The man shook his head. "Red Army prisoners of war, captured by the Germans. We retook the area. I don't know why they bring them clear back here to kill them."

"Kill them? They were prisoners of war. They are Russian. What's their crime? Why don't they free them?"

"They've met the enemy." The man mimicked Stalin's manner of speaking: 'There are no Russian prisoners of war. The Russian soldier fights on 'til death. If he chooses to become a prisoner, he is automatically excluded from the Russian community.'

"Probably most of them never got out of Russia. Their only mistake was getting captured. If you're in the Red Army, shoot the enemy, or shoot yourself. Just make sure you don't get captured."

The man's words chilled Sasha. He ached for his mountains with a yearning that nearly overrode his desire to see Valentina. His heart lay heavy in his chest with a new foreboding. He might never succeed in seeing Valentina. He might never see his beloved Kamchatka again. He just might have sacrificed everything for nothing.

The war had seemed remote from Kamchatka—like history. But here it became real, pulsing all around him. He still wanted to think of himself as a spectator, but he saw the shuffling feet, the skinny bodies, and vacant eyes, and he realized that having come this far, he would be fortunate indeed to escape with his life.

After paying his tax to the guards, Sasha still had four bottles of vodka left. He carefully placed them in his pack to not bang against each other when the pack was jostled.

The train started to climb into the Ural mountains. Sasha felt the excited anticipation of a small child. Europe, the great unknown, another continent, another world. The train continued to chug west. Sasha passed his time in a sort of daze, sleeping, interspersing chess and draughts games with his reading of Tolstoy's philosophical wrangling. He had to admit he'd never wondered if there was a God behind the actions of men, if they were motivated only by personal ambition, or if everything was random, coincidental happenings. Tolstoy declared that each view had contradictions and must be discounted. Sasha thought his personal choices dictated his own situation. But, he admitted, his being on this trip had been a reaction to Valentina's coming to Kamchatka, and that had been totally outside his will or control.

Sasha continually checked the train's direction by the sun. At some point, the train would have to turn north to end up in Moscow. He felt so on edge that he dug through his pack and pocketed his compass. Each day brought him closer to Valentina. Nothing must fail now.

One morning, he awoke to bright sunlight streaming through the windows. He opened his eyes and oriented himself. They had changed direction. The rising sun now shone on their left.

Sasha rested content. Homestretch. Suddenly his mind jolted awake. The sun should be on the right in the early morning if the train were heading north. They were traveling south, away from Moscow. Sasha caught himself before he cursed. He didn't want to alarm the others. Restless soldiers would provoke a constant watch, making desertion impossible.

"We've changed direction." He stretched and yawned.

"Headed to the Crimea," another soldier responded. "We'll be seeing battles soon."

One of the guards explained that this train would not be going to Moscow because of torn-up tracks. It had been rerouted to the Crimea, where the war was raging with greater fury at the moment.

It was time to part company. The war in Crimea was not Sasha's war and held no personal interest for him. Throughout the day, as the train approached the shifting line of the war zone, they experienced frequent delays due to torn-up tracks and bombed bridges.

The quick, seven-day trip to see Valentina had already stretched to six weeks. Impatience gnawed at Sasha. Since being on this train, he had changed cars frequently. It aroused no suspicion when he again picked up his bag and moved to another car. He wanted to be as far from the engine and lights as possible when he jumped. He shared a cigarette with Sergei and challenged him to chess as if he didn't know him at all. Though evenly matched, Sasha deliberately put his queen in danger and let Sergei win. Then Sasha bet Sergei he could not beat another soldier in a different car. Sergei took the challenge and followed Sasha to the other car. In the space between cars, Sasha said, "I'm jumping tonight. We're headed south." It wasn't an invitation for Sergei to join him. Just an announcement of his intent.

"I'm coming too," Sergei said.

"You'll follow my rules if you do." Sasha asserted.

Sergei shrugged. Sasha called the shots, and they both knew it, the big brother, little brother relationship inverted.

Salt Lake City 1948

Greg Bullock looked at them, measuring their emotions, to determine whether to wind it up for the night.

"I'm sorry, Alex, that you went through all of that to come to Moscow because of me," Valentina said, as if just fully realizing that Alex's every step after she left Kamchatka had been in search of her.

Sasha growled, "What difference does sorry make now? It doesn't put me back in Kamchatka. It doesn't bring my baby back. I'm sorry too. What a useless thing sorry is."

Bishop Bullock sensed they never talked of these feelings and resentments at home. He expected their interchanges were pretty sterile, sticking to a minimum of communication pertinent to the task at hand. He, himself, was glad to see the honor Sasha exhibited in his behavior towards women and how he showed some wrangling with philosophical issues such as goodness and cause and effect. That could affect the possible resolution to their situation.

"Shall we wind it up for tonight, or is the next part of your story long or short?" Bishop Bullock asked of Valentina.

"Short."

"We have time for a little more." He hoped what was to come was not as emotionally charged as what they had just been through.

Valentina resumed with more of her spy training.

Moscow 1944

"You are Soviet citizens leaving your Motherland. You must understand what a heavy responsibility rests on you. You are not going among others as a Soviet citizen, but as a spy, and a spy is an actor," Comrade Andolenko declared. "You should know that there are many people who will ask provocative questions. They must not pierce your facade. You are never who or what you seem to be. Great effort is being made to ensure that you are dressed exactly as a person in your situation and from the country you represent would be. If their buttons would be sewn on in a criss-cross fashion instead of two straight lines, your buttons will be sewn on in a criss-cross fashion. The fabrics, the colors are taken from the country you represent. Attention is given to every possible detail so that no one will realize you are not who you say you are."

Valentina had no idea whatsoever how people from other countries dressed. Thank goodness she would not have to worry about these details.

"You were chosen for these positions by virtue of your superior skill in certain foreign languages. Only you can be certain of your behavior. The French talk with their hands; the English do not. In whatever country you are in, you diligently study the mannerisms of the people and incorporate them. The French say "Boeuf!" as an expletive, the English, "Bloody." But before you use phrases such as this, you must carefully listen to and study the natives so that you use these and all phrases as a native would."

Mamochka had warned her from childhood not to make the mistake of making the serious, superstitious behavior so characteristic of Russians part of her behavior. Not mentioning the destination of a trip or mentioning the due date of a baby so as not to attract the evil eye were so Russian, but not characteristic of other cultures. Most of their dinnertime conversation centered on such discussions for as long as she could remember.

"You can only react emotionally in the role you've been assigned, but never, never react to anything you may hear in a personal way," Comrade Andolenko continued. "Also, you must pretend indifference to anything you hear about our great country, the United Soviet Republics. Others do not see it as we do. You must realize that all nations see the world from their own bell towers. They do not think ours is the tallest. Some may even mock us and portray their country as being the greatest. You must never, never come to the USSR's defense. Nothing will give you away quicker. For you, it is no longer *nasha luchshaya*-- ours is best.

"Here is one of your personas. Study it, digest it, become that person. We will do some role-playing to see how well you have mastered it."

Valentina took the paper and began her study, transforming herself mentally into Marie Yvette Le Moins from the city of Lille. Her father fought in the battle of Paris and was presumed dead. Early in the war, her mother and two younger sisters left France for England, where they stayed with friends. All alone in the world pretty much described herself. That would not be role-playing. She could be herself in this. Marie Yvette had remained behind as a nurse. After the fall of Paris, she continued to work under the Vichy French. Her code name, *Une Funambule*, meant tightrope walker, which seemed very appropriate. Valentina Markovna no longer existed. She buried herself in the role of a spy, thrilled at her destination. France!

"All of you are to report to the auditorium for a special presentation, important for your health and well-being." An announcement came over the loudspeaker. Valentina tucked her materials into her folder and followed the others into the auditorium.

"Brave soldiers of the Motherland," a man in military uniform boomed at the front of the room. "Often in war, you think the enemy is the guy on the other side of the lines. He is, but the women you entertain yourself with can just as surely maim you for life and give you a miserable death. A bullet would be more merciful. We are talking about the diseases you can get from having sex with an infected female."

Valentina heard a series of snickers. Would she truly be able to escape being expected to entertain soldiers in the male-dominated army? Would she be expected to entertain them just as Nikita required it of her?

"Generally, they are called venereal diseases, hereafter referred to as VD," the man continued. "One of the most prevalent diseases is syphilis. This is a slow-growing disease but ultimately can damage the internal organs, causing paralysis, gradual blindness, and dementia. It is sometimes called Cupid's disease or the French Pox. Beware, those of you going to France." He laughed, and hoots erupted throughout the auditorium. "It is not limited to France. You can get it right here. The other most prevalent one is gonorrhea, also called the clap. You'll know within a few days if you have this one. It will hurt to pee, a lot. You'll be seeking some treatment."

Valentina knew that she didn't have the clap because she did not have the symptom, but a thought had taken root in her mind. The man read from a pamphlet in a sort of gleeful way as if he expected the boisterous response he was getting from the soldiers:

1. Manhood comes from healthy sex organs.

2. It is not necessary to have sexual intercourse to keep strong and well.

3. Disease may ruin the sex organs and deprive a man of his health and happiness.

4. You have a fine healthy body now. Keep it that way.

5. Most prostitutes have venereal disease.

The man waived a pamphlet in the air. "This is excellent advice prepared by our fine American Allies for their soldiers." The soldiers greeted this with increasing catcalls and hollers. The males in the crowd were having a heyday in this unusually frank discussion of sexual issues. The military man himself laughed so hard he wiped tears from his eyes.

He could barely choke out the next statement. "They actually encourage their soldiers to practice abstinence."

As he let everyone grasp the impossibility of that, Valentina wondered if only the health officials in America gave such council, or did all Americans embrace the beliefs of the pamphlet? If they did, it would be virtually impossible for a Russian to pretend to be an American.

Regaining control over himself, the man continued, "Well, I won't expect that of you, but lucky for you, the Americans have developed cures. They have a miracle drug they call penicillin, which is administered by a needle and can cure the French Pox. The Americans also have kits for infected soldiers and aid stations. Here's a big word for you: prophylaxis. Prophylaxis means prevention. Let this be your motto: 'Defeat the Axis with Prophylaxis.' Make the Americans your allies in treating these diseases."

If only she could choose abstinence, that seemed very desirable right now. Her thought had bloomed into a full-blown plan by the end of the day. "Nikita," she said as he escorted her home, "I have tested positive for the French Pox. I am being treated for it. They told me I must completely abstain, or else I will be dismissed."

She knew she had hit the mark when his jaw clenched. "Then you are not much use to us."

"I can clean and cook, in addition to providing you with the ration card."

Valentina moved back into her own room and learned that all of her personal effects had been removed, although they did restore a little of her clothing. They kept her every bit as much occupied in cleaning and cooking as before, and she always fell into bed after midnight, but no longer did the soldiers visit her.

Salt Lake City 1948

Greg Bullock felt this was a good note to end on for the night. "Thank you for coming. Alex, it is good to see you again. Can we meet next week?"

They both nodded and thanked him for his time before leaving.

8

Sasha Finds Valentina in Moscow

Salt Lake City 1948

The following week, without any preamble, Bishop Bullock asked Alex to pick up the tale.

Enroute to Moscow 1944

Over several hours, Sasha and Sergei made their way to the end car, pausing along the way to smoke a cigarette, play a game of cards, or drink some vodka, so it appeared they were just seeking diversion. In the end car, they shared their vodka generously with the other soldiers and relaxed as the others sank into a drunken stupor. When the train made one of its inexplicable stops not near any station, Sergei and Sasha slipped into the night. As they labored along with their heavy packs, sinking with each step, bright moonlight illuminated their path across the brilliant snow. It made it easy to see their way through this waste-land, but anyone from the train could also see them and the tracks they left. The guards must all be gaming, drinking, or sleeping. No one seemed aware of their departure.

It was a good half-hour before they found a copse of birch trees. The exertion had kept them from feeling the biting cold, but when they paused, it nipped at them. Sasha left Sergei to prepare his own bed. With the seasoned experience of a Siberian, he dug a bed in the snow and lined it with the bearskin tote. He was glad he had kept it in spite of the weight. Sasha heard Sergei's snore moments after settling in. Sergei had partaken of the vodka more liberally than he had. Sasha vaguely wondered if it were the vodka that warmed Sergei or an adequate bed. His rest did not become peaceful until he heard the train chug off.

A sun high in the sky greeted Sasha the next morning when he finally stirred. He stuck his head out. A fresh blanket of snow covered everything, including their tracks. Shortly, low-hanging clouds moved in, covering the sun and limiting his vision. Sasha risked building a fire. Anyone would trip over them before they would see the smoke. He brewed some tea. It warmed him through. He chewed on some of the dried fish Baba had sent. Sergei snored on. Sasha changed out of his uniform into his peasant garb. He stowed all of his army-issue within his bearskin bag. He thought about discarding the clothes but sensed they might be useful to him. He did not dare wear them. If caught in uniform, he could be labeled a deserter, which would mean either immediate death or prison camp. As a peasant, he hoped to be seen just as a local refugee.

Sergei still had not awakened. Sasha wondered if Sergei's coming along would be a drag on him. He didn't feel he could abandon him unless Sergei suggested separating. Sasha wondered if he would have much luck limiting Sergei's alcohol consumption. Probably not. Sergei, the older brother, had never been disposed to take Sasha's advice before, and Sasha doubted he would now, despite agreeing to follow Sasha's rules.

Sasha made some of the snowshoes known as *brodovshchiki* on the peninsula. Using his hatchet, he cut a young sapling. He cut the branches off, then shaved both sides of the trunk to make it as flat as possible. He curled up the end and secured it in place with some reindeer sinew. He stripped more branches off the trees and wove a base. The laborious work gave him something to do while Sergei snored off his hangover. Sasha yearned for the deer sinews he would have used on the peninsula to make the lacings. He had but a few leather strips in his pack. He had finished his pair and began working on a pair for Sergei, long before Sergei finally stirred. Sergei reached for his bottle as soon as he emerged from his snow cave.

"Give it up, Sergei," Sasha said dryly. "We'll never make it if we have to stop for you, to wallow in that." Sergei ignored him and lifted the bottle to his lips. Sasha sighed. It would do no good to let this become a major issue between them.

After Sergei had eaten, they lashed the snowshoes on. Sasha verified his direction by his compass, and they struck out. Sasha hoped to meet someone to verify whether to go further to the east or west, but he hoped it would not be the Red Army. They might not fare too well at their hands.

They felt a certain confidence even out in the open. No one seemed about anywhere. They were clearly in an area that had previously been a war zone. They often came across abandoned military equipment. Often they saw corpses that somehow had missed the common graves, sometimes a Russian, sometimes a German, sometimes a civilian. The whole countryside reeked of war, not from odor in the frozen land, but from the sheer evidence of destruction. Sasha and Sergei each lifted a gun from one of the Russian soldiers and cleaned and dried it. Sasha picked up a significant amount of ammunition from several of the corpses along the way. He yearned to test the gun, but feared the sound could be heard from unimaginable distances and might draw the very attention they sought to avoid.

The mangled and dismembered corpses caused a revulsion in Sasha so physical that he felt like throwing up. Sergei kept swigging his bottle, but between the cold and the sights, he remained sober enough to keep going. Sasha welcomed the nights, hoping that they would be able to see the lights of a village or a farm. Three days later, he got his wish. One evening they could see the twinkle of lights in the far distance. The next morning, Sasha sought them out with his binoculars. He could see some buildings, just a cluster, clearly a farmhouse and outbuildings. It would take them a bit west of their northern track, but the necessity to talk to someone to orient themselves to Moscow required the detour. The compass told them they were going due north, but Moscow was highly unlikely to be directly north of wherever they were. They were on the fringe of a woods that stretched up to the east of the farmhouse. To the west, they could see vast distances. Sasha considered continuing on in the daytime hidden by the trees but decided to stay put when he saw movements become growing specks coming from the east. He wanted to know who they might have to confront before continuing on.

Sasha and Sergei stayed in the woods without fire through the day, watching what they soon became certain were soldiers. They were on a course where they would intercept the buildings with a slight change of direction. Sasha couldn't tell much about uniforms at this distance, so he didn't know if they were Russians or Germans. If they were captured by the Red Army, they would be treated as deserters. The Germans would treat them as prisoners of war. Either way, their plans would be thwarted.

The bright night presented too great of a risk to travel, with soldiers so close. The soldiers camped almost opposite the farmhouse, an easy reach for them the next day. Sergei drank, and Sasha wanted to smash the bottles. Sergei would soon be out of his liquid oblivion, and Sasha resolved he would take a stand before allowing Sergei to touch his own stock. He kept it not so much for himself as for barter.

The next day, a storm came up, blurring their vision but making camouflaged travel possible. Sasha anticipated the soldiers would do no more than hunkering down in the storm. He expected that the soldiers would be unlikely to return to a northern path after intercepting the buildings since they had come from the north. Therefore, if he and Sergei could get slightly north of the buildings, they would be safe from detection.

Sasha realized that this travel could be treacherous to many travelers, but the hurricanes that blew across Kamchatka had long since taught him not to be afraid of the weather. With his knowledge of the compass and survival techniques, he was often accused of being cocky, but he was actually very cautious. He never went out unless he had whatever was necessary, even if he had to burrow in for days on end. Sergei, being more of a city dweller than Sasha and not sure of his own abilities in these conditions, was confident of Sasha's. He fortified himself with more vodka, and they pressed on into the blinding, swirling snow. Sasha did not want to risk his survival to a sullied mind. He did not even permit himself to indulge when they camped. He knew well how the false warmth it induced could lead to carelessness and death in these frigid temperatures.

They traveled several hours northward. Sasha decided to make camp. He didn't want to overshoot the buildings and then have to backtrack for hours to reach them. He helped Sergei to build his snow bed and line it with blankets from his pack. Sergei pulled yet another bottle from his seemly inexhaustible supply and began to drink. Sasha turned in disgust and prepared his own bed. Although a hot cup of tea would be wonderful, Sasha decided it would be impossible to make a fire burn in this wind. He ate some dried fish and berries and contented himself with a cigarette.

Before collapsing into his own fur-lined snow bed, Sasha checked to make sure Sergei's greatcoat still covered him and that he had a breathing hole. He awoke to piercing screams of great anguish. He lay in his bed, trying to orient himself. He could hear men's voices yelling. The words wafting to him across the wind were Russian, but he caught too little of it to make sense of what he heard. He sat up. Sergei also sat up, swathed in blankets, his expression as bewildered as Sasha felt. Sasha grabbed his binoculars and crawled to the edge of the forest. In the crisp, bright, and clear day, Sasha saw they had camped much closer to the farm buildings than he had expected. With his naked eye, he could see some Red Army soldiers running randomly around. The screams had stopped. He heard hammering sounds.

Sasha and Sergei stayed hidden in their little copse of trees throughout the day. They didn't even build a fire. In no way did they want to alert the soldiers that someone was there. The soldiers seemed to be doing some plundering at the house as they became visible carrying assorted bundles. In the afternoon, the soldiers moved out, and Sasha breathed a sigh of relief when the soldiers took a southerly route. Sasha and Sergei stayed hidden until nightfall.

No more noise came from the farm. They expected to find it deserted, with no food or anything else of value left. Nevertheless, under cover of darkness that night, they crept forward, leaving their packs in the woods. As they neared the barn, they were surprised to hear soft sobbing. On the ground in front of the barn door huddled a young woman. Crucified to the door hung a naked woman, the fruit of her womb dangling from a gash in her side. Her breasts had been severed, and dried blood on her legs from her crotch attested that rape had been part of her torture also. Revulsion gripped Sasha's heart. What had this woman done to merit such treatment at the hands of the Red Army?

The young woman on the ground startled as she saw them, terror in her eyes. Sasha expected her to bolt.

"Peace," he said. "We will not hurt you."

She responded with yet more sobs. Sasha gently laid his hand on her shoulder. To Sergei, he said, "Go into the house and see if you can find something we can wrap her in," he inclined his head towards the woman on the door.

Sasha left the still sobbing younger woman and entered the barn. He found a tool that would enable him to pry out the nails holding the woman on the door and began the distasteful task. Then, he gently laid her in the cloth Sergei brought. He wrapped it around her, hiding the hideous sight from their eyes, but Sasha knew it would never be erased from his memory. He ardently wished he had stayed hidden in his mountains, ignorant of such scenes.

In the barn, Sasha and Sergei found tools that enabled them to dig a shallow grave in the frozen layers of snow. Sasha did not know of any religious ceremony to perform over the grave. The sobbing young woman, her body shuddering from the horror and the cold, allowed Sasha to lead her into the log cottage, its elaborate fretwork window shutters hanging crookedly from the smashed windows. Everything inside the house had been smashed: the table, chairs, the stovepipe dangling from the ceiling, the stove wrenched from its stand and in pieces scattered around the room. Once Sasha was able to restore the stovepipe, he deemed it safe to build a fire on the hearth and gathered some of the wood. Sergei had retrieved their packs from the woods. Sasha felt the dulling influence of some vodka would be welcome to enable them to deal with the barrage of emotions tearing at them.

"I'm Sasha. This is my brother, Sergei."

"I'm Iakova. She was my sister." Iakova choked on the vodka, obviously not an experienced drinker, but she was still a girl, maybe as young as 14.

"Why did they do this? They were the Red Army, weren't they?"

"Yes." Tears again came to Iakova's eyes. "They accused us of being German whores. The Germans did come here, but they were courteous. We gave them food, but we never slept with them. They did not rape us." Her sobs increased, "They said Katarina's baby was a German bastard. It wasn't. Its father is in the Red Army." Her sobs again overtook her. Sasha wished he could somehow ease her agony, wondering if war meant such horrific things to Valentina.

Sasha noticed that Iakova moved gingerly. "Did they hurt you also?"

She dropped her eyes.

"Rape?" Sasha asked.

She nodded.

"How many?"

"Four."

"Anything else?"

"They beat me."

Sasha groaned. This was not war. These women were not enemies to be defeated. They were not spies to be tortured until they gave out information. This was barbaric. Was this what it meant to be a soldier in the Red Army?

The next morning Sasha asked which way to Moscow. Iakova only knew that it lay north and a bit to the west. If they went west, she said, they would come to train tracks that led to Moscow. She did not know how far. She had never been there.

"What about you?" Sasha asked. 'Would you like to go with us?"

Iakova shook her head, "My mother's coming any day to help with the baby. She'll take me home."

Sasha and Sergei left Iakova with food and fixed things as much as they could for her comfort. Still dressed in their peasant garb, they waited for nightfall before heading on. They walked in a northwesterly direction. After two days of walking and hiding, they heard the rumble and the mournful wail of the trains. Train sounds always vaguely reminded Sasha of the volcanoes' roar and the wind through the trees. It took another day before they were close enough to the tracks to discern much about the trains. An occasional troop train rumbled south. None were headed north. Some trains might have been passenger trains headed north. Empty cattle cars such as he had seen carrying deportees and prisoners of war rattled their way to Moscow. Several of these wound their way south with their miserable human cargo. Full coal trains went north. Empty coal trains went south. At night time, if near a village, Sasha and Sergei could see men, women, children along the tracks searching for coal pieces dropped from the trains. Guards chased them away, yelling for them to stop stealing from Mother Russia. One group taken away by the guards for whatever punishment was reserved for these new enemies of the state would immediately be replaced by another group willing to risk their freedom, their lives for a few niggardly pieces of coal, and its treasured heat. Sasha wondered if the war made people this abject or if this were the great Soviet state propagandized in the schools and at required party meetings.

Having no idea how far south of Moscow they actually were, Sasha and Sergei decided to catch a coal train. They had kept pretty much to forests since arriving within view of the tracks or traveled only at night. Each night they eased close to the tracks. They needed to be close enough to reach the train, should it stop, but far enough away that they could not be seen from the train. One such night the train actually stopped within reach. Most of the cars were still full of coal, but some had been emptied. Sasha threw his duffel bag over the top over of one, and a voice growled. Evidently, they would not be the only occupants of the car. Sergei swung himself in, and Sasha tossed up his bearskin tote with its treasured vodka bottles carefully wrapped to avoid breaks. Then he climbed aboard, his food pack strapped to his back. Even with moonlight streaming into the car, Sasha could not see into the corners until his eyes had become accustomed to the increased darkness. He could make out the forms of at least three others. The next morning he could see there were two men and a lad, all so thickly covered with coal dust that only the whites of their eyes and occasional flashes of their teeth gave any contrast.

Sasha reached into his unflagging supply of dried fish. He and Sergei began to chew on some. The look in the men's eyes warned him that they were hungry and ruthless enough to kill for food. He reached back into the bag and tossed each of them some fish. They expertly caught it and wolfed it down like hungry dogs.

Later in the day, Sasha shared from the dwindling reserve of army tins he possessed. By silent agreement, if either he or Sasha slept, the other did not. They felt they had fallen among thieves. As dusk settled, Sasha shared a bottle of vodka with them. He offered it first to the three and then to Sergei, who only got a taste. Sasha felt glad. They might need their sharpest wits about them that night.

Somewhere in the night, the train stopped. One of the men growled, "You need to get off here. You'll be caught if you ride all the way into Moscow." One of the men clambered over the side of the car. Sasha didn't know whether this was a trick to jump them or if they were indeed nearing the city stations.

He picked up his bearskin and heaved it over the side where the man had gone. The other man climbed after it. The boy seemed to be waiting for Sasha and Sergei. Sergei climbed over the opposite side from the men. The boy lunged for Sasha's food pack. Sasha hit him, knocking him down. The boy began to yell at the men, "They're going over the other side."

Sasha threw his bags to Sergei and climbed up the side of the car as it began to move. The boy grabbed for him. Sasha kicked, catching him in the face. The boy fell, and Sasha swung down. He could hear the men cursing from the other side of the train. Before the end of the long train had passed, the darkness swallowed Sasha and Sergei, hiding them from their would-be assailants. They pushed away from the tracks until they came upon a copse of trees thick enough to hide them. They made themselves crude beds in the frozen snow and slept together since Sasha had sacrificed his bearskin. In the crisp, bright day, they took stock of their surroundings. They had camped on a high point among gently rolling hills. Three tiny communities of scattered log homes could be seen here and there. No sign of the two men from the night before could be seen. The boy undoubtedly did not make it off the train before it gained too much speed for a safe jump.

Sasha and Sergei tried washing the coal dust from them with the snow. It smeared but did not come off. Under cover of night, they crept to the nearest small village. They saw a solitary old man tapping his way through the street with a blind man's stick.

"*Dedushka*," Sasha said, "Is there some lodging? A *banya*?"

"Who are you? What do you want?"

"We are strangers on our way to Moscow."

"Soldiers?"

"No," Sasha said.

"Pity." The man said. "Then you could get me some food, and I could get you some lodging."

Yeah, thought Sasha. You'll turn me in as a deserter. They will reward you, and I will be lodged all right.

"Thanks anyway," Sasha said, turning away.

"How many are you?" the old man asked.

"Two."

"Come. We'll find you something."

The man led them to a small house full of women and children. The women poured water into containers they placed on the minuscule stove. The women eyed them as they stripped naked and washed, then dressed in their army uniforms. The coal dust so stained their peasant clothes that Sasha saw no hope of cleansing them. "Would you like these?" Sasha offered the clothes to the women. They eagerly accepted the clothing. He didn't know what they would do with it. It did not matter. Maybe they had a way to boil it clean.

"Katya's lost her husband to the war," the old man said. "She would like to please the thin one."

A very pretty young woman who had been openly flirting with Sergei with her dark eyes now dropped these eyes in false modesty, brushing her fair cheeks with long lovely lashes. Sasha would have been drawn to her had his heart not been focused on Valentina.

How the old man knew the palpable feelings in the air, Sasha did not know, but the man's inner eye seemed more perceptive than their vision when he said, "The other one doesn't want a woman tonight."

Sasha's emotions still reeled from the farm. He hoped he would be ready to take pleasure in Valentina when he reached Moscow. He had at times been indifferent to a sexual partner, but he had never been brutal to one. It seared him deeply to see women treated that way. He had seen animals kill for food, but cruelty and hate were foreign to him.

The next morning, Sasha and Sergei climbed into a cart drawn by a boney, underfed horse. Pretty Katya, the old grandfather, and a youth driving the cart accompanied them. "Did the Germans reach your village?"

"Can't you tell without asking? Our homes are not burned. We were most fortunate. We were just slightly out of the way, or we would have no horses, no young women. Already we have practically no food and no fuel. There are some completely burned out villages near here. The revenge from the Red Army is frequently worse than the German Army."

The rolling, snow-covered country they traversed in their approach to Moscow showed wartime preparation. There was an abundance of trenches. They experienced an abrupt transition from the countryside to the silent, deserted city. Paint in complicated camouflage patterns covered buildings and pavements. Boards covered many windows. Some were taped. Shop windows were vacant, except for war posters. One portrayed a beautiful young woman with eyes heavenward, a slight smile on her face. Her arms were extended with shackles around each wrist attached by a chain. Three swords were in the foreground with a flag on each sword representing the country the sword symbolized, one for Great Britain, one for the United States, and one for Russia. The poster proclaimed, "Europe will be free." It struck Sasha as odd to think of Great Britain and the United States as allies of Russia. Strange how the enemy became friends when something existed for them both to gain. Of course, that had happened in Kamchatka, too. The Russians had come there to conquer and exploit. Now, most of the natives carried Russian ancestry, and they fought alongside full-blooded Russians and other conquered peoples, but their allegiance was to Russia.

Sasha had never seen so many buildings, such big buildings, such a myriad of streets, such grayness without a hint of something growing. There were few residents about. All they saw were women and children and old men. An occasional elderly watchman bundled in a sheepskin coat with a rifle slung over his shoulder stood in a doorway. How could Sasha find one small, beloved person in all this confusion of buildings and streets? Had he come all the way to Moscow, only to be unable to find Valentina?

The old, blind grandfather seemed to know the city well. It seemed as if he had an internal map, which only he could read. He gave the youth driving the cart directions.

Women hacked at the ice on the streets. The cart rumbled past a building where the old man indicated they would be able to get their soldiers' rations, but they drove on for a short distance before stopping. Once the cart stopped, Sasha understood the old man's tactic. Katya thrust the gun Sasha had picked up into Sergei's back. "You," the old man said, speaking to Sasha, "go get your rations. You'll give us those rations in exchange for the help you've received. Your brother will be released when you return."

"Take only your ration papers and the *avos*," Katya said. Sasha noticed the string bag for carrying groceries on her lap.

Sasha dug into his pack, took out his papers, picked up the "just in case" *avos*, and walked back to the ration station. He hoped his apprehension did not show on his face. What if they could tell from his papers that he was a deserter? Would they shoot him on the spot? Would they imprison him to be shot or hung later? Or would he be sent to a prison camp? If he just took off and did not return, would the woman really shoot Sergei, or would they force Sergei to go get food, and then he also be faced with the deserter's punishment? Sasha considered just running and hiding, but all of his gear was still in the cart. All of his pictures, his notes, and his only hope of finding Valentina in this vast, brick forest was in the cart. His life would be useless anyway if he lost all purpose for living. He reluctantly decided to risk the deserter's death. A quick bullet would be immeasurably better than living a deserter's life.

Hoping his soldier's arrogance masked all trace of fear in his voice, he strode past a huge red placard on the wall of a building with the image of Josef V. Stalin, bigger than life, holding a young girl in his arms. She held a mass of field poppies as bright as her smile, as bright as her laughing eyes—flowers for the *Vozhd*, the leader. Under the image was a quotation from Stalin. "Life has become better! Life has become more joyous!" Sasha heartily hoped it was so.

He strode into the ration station and slapped down his papers. The one-armed attendant leisurely looked at the papers and called a man who limped to get Sasha his rations. The attendant casually asked Sasha to roll him a cigarette. Sasha rolled him one, using the strong, peasant tobacco the attendant indicated, and handed it to him, lighting the cigarette for him. The man asked Sasha if he'd seen any action yet.

"No. I'm just arriving from Siberia."

The man inclined his head towards the other soldier, limping back and forth, collecting the food. "Ivan and I were both injured in our very first battle—at Stalingrad. We might be cripples, but we are alive. It's a slaughterhouse out there."

The generous amount of food surprised Sasha. He placed it in the *avos* and bid Ivan and the other soldier goodbye.

The other soldier stamped his papers and told him he could obtain more rations in two weeks. Sasha was no sooner out of the building than Katya was there, carrying the gun casually at her side.

"So you came looking for me," Sasha said.

"*Dedushka* didn't trust you would return. He just wanted to make sure."

Sasha realized he could overpower her, but what was to be gained? He'd still be without that treasured pack which was far more valuable to him than this bag of food. He walked docilely back to the cart and handed the bag to the grandfather. The guard at a building next to where the cart stood, watching. His sympathy was obviously with the family. "Now you go," the old man barked to Sergei.

Sergei climbed out of the cart and headed in the direction of the ration station. "Keep the gun on him," the old man said to the young woman and pointed at Sasha. To the youth, he said, "Throw his bags out." He did.

"Now get in the cart," he said to the young woman.

"Shall I give him the gun?"

"No. He might shoot us. He is a deserter anyway. He will not need the gun."

Katya climbed into the cart, and it rambled off. Weren't they going to wait for Sergei to return? Maybe they were going to allow him and Sergei to share Sergei's food.

Sasha accused the guard, "Why did you just let them steal my food?"

The guard leveled his gun at Sasha. "The citizenry has to feed themselves somehow. Our rations are so small it is hard to keep body and soul together." Sasha bent to pick up his bags.

"No." the man said. "You'll stay here until the other returns."

"You're going to steal our food too?" Sasha asked incredulously.

"Not all of it. I've got a family to feed too, and they're mighty hungry."

Sasha squatted down, wondering whether Sergei would return. Neither loyalty nor duty bound Sergei to his side. Sergei certainly knew how to get by in a city much better than he did. Why should he stick by him now?

"He may not come back," Sasha said to the guard.

"We'll see."

Sasha felt drained. The old man's treachery did not even stir his anger. He was Katya's father, stealing from the soldiers to feed his hungry family. In every other way, they had been courteous and kind. Sasha didn't know if he would be so ethical as to not steal food from a healthy, capable soldier if he had starving women and children to care for.

He crouched on his haunches, awaiting Sergei's return, trying to figure out what compass one used to find someone in this morass of streets and buildings.

"Do you know Valentina Markovna?" he asked the guard who still had his gun trained on him.

"No. Who's her father?"

"Mark Kaflov. They live in Moscow."

"Moscow's a big place. You need an address."

"An address?" Sasha was uncomfortable with the ignorance he was being forced to show.

"Each street has a name, each building a number. That's an address. You're not from here, are you?"

"No. Kamchatka. How do you find someone if you don't have an address?"

"You don't."

He'd come all the way to Moscow to see Valentina. Now, robbed of his food, having only his soldier's uniform left for clothing, he couldn't find her because he was so ignorant he did not know her address. Evidently, all his survival skills were useless in this man-made forest.

"The traitor!" the guard suddenly exclaimed, a stream of expletives bursting from him. The guard rushed down the street to the intersection where Sasha expected Sergei to appear. Sasha grabbed his bag and followed after. He arrived at the intersection just in time to see the cart containing the old man, the youth, Katya, and Sergei before it turned down a street and out of sight.

"We've been robbed! They took all your food, and the other soldier's gone with them. Are you part of this treachery?" The guard swung his gun at Sasha, but Sasha dodged its blow.

"Thief!" the man yelled. "Give me your bag. I'm not watching over you for nothing."

Sasha handed his bag over. The man again had the gun pointed at him. He struggled with the ties on the bag while trying to keep his gun and eye on Sasha. Sasha was well aware he could easily overpower the guard, but he was not inclined to do so. Nothing would be gained by it. The guard's blustering pretense of power amused Sasha, but still, he had a real gun. Finally, the guard shoved the yet unopened bag towards Sasha and more firmly fixed his eye and gun on him. "You open it."

Sasha obeyed and withdrew the items one at a time—*War and Peace*, the blankets, the mess kit, the package containing his pictures and notes. The man asked him to unwrap it.

Sasha said, "Not in this snow. It will be ruined. It's just papers."

The man palpated the package. "You'll come home with me, and you will open it." Sasha repacked the things and walked where the man told him to go. They passed many streets. Some had been bombed. There were buildings with roofs missing, walls missing, rubble still lying all around. The old man's shelter was a basement. Two women and three children huddled near a square tin box the size of a big book, radiating heat. The stovepipe led out through a small hinged pane such as Sasha had seen in Petropavlovsk to air the room in the winter. A mustard-colored, mushroom-shaped lamp gave scant illumination, and dirty lace curtains were swept up to avoid touching the stove pipe. Sasha was not offered a seat or a drink. He stood, shifting his weight from one foot to the other.

"Keep this gun on him," the guard said, handing the gun to the older woman.

"And what has he done?" asked the younger woman.

"Robbed us."

"Robbed us of what?"

"The food we might have had."

The man emptied the bag and unwrapped Sasha's package. The young woman gasped and reached for the pictures as the guard carelessly rustled through the pages, "Nothing here. Nothing! We shall starve. At least we can burn the paper for heat."

"Father!" the young woman protested. "These are exquisite pictures. You'll not burn them. The heat they bring will last for minutes only. This war has made you into a despicable person. Burn the book."

"We have our own books we can burn. I guess it has come to that."

The old woman had put down the gun. She pointed to a chair. "Sit. Have some tea with us."

Sasha accepted her offer.

The man dropped his hostility. "I'm sorry. Our rations are so meager. They feed the soldiers much better than the rest of us. And the children, we can't get rations for the children. They are *besprizhorniki*. Their parents were Jewish, picked up, and sent off because they have supposedly committed some crime, and the children are left, orphans. Anyone that helps the children will face the same fate as the parents. The girls quickly learn men will give them a crust if they give the only thing they have to give. You see them out there, five, ten, fifteen years old, lifting their skirts and begging 'Little Uncle, for just a crust.' I do believe I'll yet stand before a God and account for my choices in this life.

I'd rather tell him I robbed you to feed them than I turned them out to that horrible fate. They'll be dead within months of disease, abuse, hunger, or cold."

"Shh," the old woman admonished. "You don't know our secret is safe with this man."

"He doesn't know the territory. He's from Kamchatka."

"There's some dried fish and berries and some sarana lily bulbs that can be pounded into flour sewn under the false bottom of the bag," Sasha told them.

"Bless you." The older woman said as he retrieved the food.

"You have an address on this paper," the man said, holding up the note Valentina had written him when she sent the colored pencils. Tomorrow Masha will show you where to find it."

Masha, the younger woman, picked up the paper and examined it. "I can lead you there."

Sasha huddled on the floor in his greatcoat and tried to sleep. The external cold did not trouble him, but his spirit chilled. Why had he not listened to Baba, to his mother? Tomorrow he might find his trip was totally wasted. Would he find Valentina? Would he be able to find Chirikov from his name only?

The next morning he accepted a meager meal of his own dried fish, sarana lily flour bread, and some dried berries, the last of his food. A few pieces of green had been clipped from the scallions growing in the window were scattered over the bread to ward off the dreaded scurvy.

Then Masha led him through twisted streets and alleys. He knew how to find his way on an unmarked, snow-covered steppe, but now he felt hopelessly lost. He had inwardly mocked the Muscovites for their ineptness in Kamchatka. He now realized that he was just as unsuited to the territory they handled with ease. He was glad for Masha's guidance.

They walked through a section of the city where many buildings had been bombed before approaching a house much bigger and grander than Sasha would have expected. Masha rapped with the door knocker.

"Your friend must come from an important family. This is a grand house in a grand neighborhood."

He had not associated nobility with Valentina and her father. He remembered the importance of title in Tolstoy's story, and it rankled him. Would he not be worthy of Valentina because of her ancestral roots? Had that all been swept away in the revolution, or did it still color Valentina's evaluation of others?

"We're looking for Valentina Markovna," Masha said as a pinched-face woman opened the door.

The eyes in the face narrowed, "Who wants to find her? You or the soldier boy?"

"The soldier."

"She's dead," the face disappeared in the closing door.

"She's lying," Masha said.

"How do you know she's lying?"

"Because it mattered which one of us wanted to know. The soldiers haven't always treated the women well. Some of them move so soldiers who have mistreated them can no longer find them. Or the woman may be just hoping for a bribe. Too bad you don't have some vodka to pry her tongue loose."

"Now, what do I do?" Sasha asked.

"Hide nearby. Watch who goes and comes. I'm confident the woman knows her. Maybe she will lead you to her. Maybe you can get her to relay a message for you."

Sasha left the street, glancing back to see the woman watching him through the window. Masha left him, and he walked to the back of the block and back through the rubble of a building. The building facing the one with the woman in it was bombed out. It had lost its roof and one wall, but the front facade stood and obscured his hiding place. The woman still stood at the window looking after where he had gone. He was confident she did not realize where he was.

He watched. Eventually, the woman left the window. Some soldiers came and went in and out of the house that was supposed to be Valentina's. He waited and watched.

His stomach growled. Even his dogs had it better than this. They could count on him tossing them a dried fish each night. One year they had run out of food, and the dogs had eaten their leather traces in their crazed hunger. He wasn't that hungry yet. If he didn't get some clue how to find Valentina soon, he would make his way back to the coal trains. Hopefully, they traveled really fast on their way east to the coal fields. He watched. He yawned. It was getting dark. The woman came out of the building. Silently, like tracking a deer, he followed along after her. Should he follow at a distance, hoping she would lead him to Valentina, or should he try to catch her and get information? It was getting darker and darker. There were no lights on the streets. He was going to lose her. He hurried. She hurried in proportion. He ran. She ran, but he gained on her. She screamed as he grabbed her arm. "I'm not going to hurt you. You don't have to be frightened."

"What do you want?"

"Tell me how to find Valentina Markovna. I've come a long way to see her."

"That's what they all say. Do you have food?"

"No."

"Vodka?"

"No."

"She'll not give it to you for nothing. Besides, she is diseased. There are others you should consider."

Sasha's heart sickened. This woman thought he wanted to use Valentina as a common prostitute. Surely she had not been reduced to that.

"That's not what I want."

"You expect me to believe that? That's what you all want."

"Valentina and I are old friends."

"What kind of friends?"

"Just friends."

"Sure. Lovers."

"Do you even know who Valentina is?"

"No. I've never heard of her."

Contradictions, contradictions. Did she really know Valentina, or was she just drumming up customers for the business she obviously conducted?

Sasha felt she would be useless to him. He dropped his hand. "I'm sorry. I didn't mean to bother you.

He turned away into the darkness. He had crossed the continent for nothing. Valentina could not be found. He was without food, without money, officially a deserter from the army. He would be more than fortunate to get home alive.

More people were on the streets now. Sasha guessed they were returning from work. He moved towards a street that was still lighted and watched, staying in the shadows. The people were sullen, heads down, quietly hurrying along in the cold. Very few cars or trucks passed on the streets, an occasional trolley. The passersby trickled to nothing. He squatted into a ball, only sleep easing the gnawing in his stomach. The muffled noise of the workers flowing in the other direction awoke him the next morning. It was still dark. If by some miracle, Valentina were to walk right past him, he would never know. He had been so foolish to think he could come to the city and find her. He slept again until an increase in noise awakened him. Stretching to ease the cramp in his muscles, he tried to think about what to do about his stomach. Was he going to be reduced to the same thieving as others just to keep alive? He moved along the street until he was out of the residential area and into a business district. There were more hustle and bustle here, of people and cars. Still, he saw no options for food. A city was really a horrid place. Maybe he should focus on trying to sell his pictures, but where to start? Who to ask?

Sasha asked the first person he saw. No, he did not know of a publishing house. He asked another and another. He read the signs on the buildings. He passed a large poster of Lenin with troops beneath. The banner read, *Forward to Victory!* No victory for him. Sasha's hunger grew with his despair. Fewer people were on the streets now, as they were all entering various buildings. Occasionally some would come or go from the buildings. Would any be generous to him in his hunger, or were they all victims too, all as hungry as he? He was not yet hungry enough to reduce himself to begging.

That coat! That coat! It was like the one Valentina had worn in Kamchatka. Could it be her or just another woman with a similar coat? She was about the right size and hurrying along on the other side of the street, a man at her side. Sasha dodged a trolley and hurried after her. She was too far ahead. "Wait," he called. She glanced at him. It was her! It was! She turned and started to run away from him. "Wait, Valentina, wait!" he called, but his voice wafted away on the wind. She disappeared inside a building. He ran up the stairs after her into the foyer. She was nowhere in sight, but a uniformed guard with a gun stopped his advance. "You cannot enter here without a pass."

"I need to speak to the young lady who just came in here."

"You're not permitted to enter without a pass."

Sasha tried to catch his breath. Sometime she would have to come out. He would wait in front. He sat down on the steps, praying to an unknown god that the guard would not chase him away. God was powerless against the power of the guard. Sasha went across the street and sat on the stairs of an unguarded, bombed-out building, hunger and tiredness threatening his vigilance.

Salt Lake City 1948

Sasha nodded at Valentina, and she picked up the tale.

Moscow 1944

Valentina paused just inside the door and tried to catch her breath. Who was this soldier chasing her? She was quite certain she heard him call her name just before she slipped into the building. She didn't recognize him from the soldiers who had visited her when forced to entertain them by Nikita and Vera. His build vaguely reminded her of Nikita, but Nikita had been escorting her as he habitually did every morning. What in the world did this soldier think he was going to do with her here in the daytime in the middle of the city with Nikita at her side? Well, she was safe from him here. He wouldn't be permitted to enter this fortress.

All thoughts of the soldier flew from her mind as she was issued her travel orders in her final nursing class. In two days, she was to report and change into a newly issued light-yellow skirt with flecks of other colors in it that swirled around her knees and a smartly-fitting, square-shouldered jacket reminiscent of a soldier's uniform. She would then report at the train station, travel to a port, and board a ship to England. There she would receive further instruction in preparation for the anticipated Allied invasion of France. Would she be able to see Mamochka? She could not ask, but she couldn't help hoping.

As the day ended, Valentina left the building much later than usual, her mind itemizing what she needed to do before she departed from Russia, perhaps forever. She would likely never know what had happened to her father. She wished Nikita and Vera had not taken over their home, and all mementos of her family went who knew where. But it was probably just as well. Anything that could identify her as a Russian could be dangerous to her. All that remained of her brothers, her father, her childhood now existed only in her memory and that she could carry with her wherever she went. It was better to look forward than back. Even though she would undoubtedly see the horrors of war, she thrilled with the anticipation of seeing England and France, of playing her role. It seemed like such an adventure.

Filled with such thoughts, she was astonished to see the soldier from that morning at the bottom of the steps as she exited the building. She glanced around—no, Nikita, but then she was late today. What was with this soldier? Had he waited all day for her? What did he expect of her? She hurried down the stairs, ignoring him, hoping she wasn't his target.

Then she heard his plea, "Valentina, please, wait. Talk to me."

Alex? Could it be Alex? What was he doing here, in a soldier's uniform? A wash of emotions swept over her. She felt dismay and anger, but at the same time, she was so glad to see someone she knew. Why had he followed her here, clear from Kamchatka? She hoped that he hadn't. She was leaving Russia in just two days. What would become of him? She could not, would not let his unexpected arrival derail her.

She stopped and turned and peered at him. "Alex! Is that you?"

"Yes, Valentina." He moved towards her, stretching his hands out.

She stepped forward and primly kissed him on either cheek in the distinctive French greeting. She then stepped away with none of the lavish kissing and hugging he would expect of her both as a former lover and from just simply being a Russian greeting someone after an absence.

"Oh, Alex. I didn't recognize you in the soldier's uniform. It's so good to see you. You really should not have come. It's very dangerous for you."

He opened his arms to her, bewilderment showing on his face, but she didn't go to him.

"Who were you afraid I was?" He asked.

"A soldier." She gave a vague answer.

"I am a soldier. Who do you fear? Has someone hurt you?"

She didn't know how to answer, but tears came unbidden to her eyes. She had felt so alone, so defenseless since her father had been taken. Now here was someone who wanted to protect and care for her, and she was going to leave him disappointed and to who knew what fate.

Now Alex did draw her into his arms and gently kissed her forehead. "Have the soldiers mistreated you?"

The tears freely cascaded down her cheeks. "I've been required to uh—entertain them." She didn't know if he would realize what she meant by that. He certainly would once they got back to the house. He tried to walk, his arm wrapped around her to protect, comfort, but they couldn't walk rapidly through the cold that way. He settled for holding her hand. Finally, in coats covered in frozen snow, they arrived back at the house.

Vera opened the door at their sound on the doorstep. "You're late! You should have been..." She trailed off when she saw Sasha.

"Liar!" Sasha hissed at her.

"You talked to her?" Valentina asked.

"Yes. I came here from the address you gave me and asked if she knew you. She said no."

"You must not have had any vodka or food," Valentina said ruefully.

"No, I was robbed."

After removing their snow-plastered wraps, Sasha followed Valentina into the kitchen, where she handed him a knife and some cabbage to chop as she began washing potatoes.

"What's your role here? What's going on?" He asked.

"It's complex at best. They give me board and room in exchange for cooking and cleaning."

"But where is your father? Is this not your home?"

When she didn't answer, she saw Sasha look up from his chopping.

She bit her lip as tears rolled down her cheeks, unable to talk. After gaining some control, she said, "My father was taken." After more tears, more time, "This was my home." Another sniffling pause. "They took it over. I have nowhere else to go."

"Chirikov?"

She shook her head. Eventually, she choked out, "He was taken with my father."

"Taken? Where? Why?"

"A trumped up charge. Supposedly it was a lack of patriotism for them to go to Kamchatka with the Germans still on Russian soil, but Stalin granted them that trip in gratitude for their role in the defense of Moscow. Stalin has a short memory and more fear than loyalty."

They worked side by side preparing food and then did some laundry, not only hers but piles brought down from the upper story of the house. "And, are you not one that the soldiers visit because I am here?"

Valentina hesitated, weighing her answer. She did not doubt as to where Alex hoped this evening was going. In one sense, she felt she owed him at least that, but he had made her pregnant once. She feared that even more than disease. The Americans had magic to combat disease, but it would be foolish and risky to find herself in France and pregnant. That she could not risk.

"I became diseased." She watched her hands wring the linen and avoided Alex's eyes.

"So you did earlier." His eyes cast upward indicating, that she must have been there before.

"Not because I wanted to."

"The woman forced you?"

"More the man that escorted me this morning."

"A prisoner in your own home."

"My food ration is more generous than theirs, so they let me stay here."

Vera kept a sharp eye on her throughout the evening. Nikita never did show up. Valentina felt a certain courage, knowing Alex would stand between her and any demand Vera might attempt to inflict upon her. Valentina always insisted on stopping whatever work was demanded of her by midnight. As that time approached, she said to Vera, "My friend will share my room. I need a blanket and pillow for him."

Vera snorted. "I thought you said you were diseased."

"I didn't say we were going to share that way."

She sniffed in an expression of disbelief. "This is not a hotel, you know. I don't have blankets and pillows for your guests."

Valentina sighed and rolled her eyes. "Come," she said to Alex.

"I'll get my greatcoat," he said and retrieved it from the rack in the hall.

Valentina led him into her small room with the narrow cot, shut the door, and lit some candles.

He immediately took her into his arms. "Come back to Kamchatka with me."

She allowed him to draw her tightly against his chest.

"Oh, Alex, I would. I would if I thought we could. Nobody travels east unless they are being sent to the prison camps." Trying to make her decision seem less heartless, she declared, "All the residents who evacuated two years ago are now returning."

"But what will happen to you?"

"I'm leaving, but they must not know." Her head indicated the door where they had last seen Vera.

"You're leaving. Where?" He stepped back, alarm registering in his voice and on his face.

Valentina spoke very quietly, not certain that Vera was not listening on the other side of the door. "I'm going to France as a spy. Remember when I told you I could be a spy? Now I really am going to be one. If they find out and prevent me from leaving, I may never get out. I must act as if nothing is different until I go."

"Please, Valentina, come back to Kamchatka with me."

"I can't, Alex. Not only do Vera and Nikita watch me, but the KGB is also watching me too. Now that they have decided I am valuable as a spy, they will not let me go."

"Don't make excuses, Valentina. We'll disguise you. We'll trick them. We'll get out together."

His raw, desperate hope grated on her resistance. Her eyes filled with tears. "Alex, I am so sorry to hurt you. I don't think we could make it safely back to Kamchatka. I want to go to France. I want to leave this horrid country behind. I don't ever want to come back."

"But, Valentina, what about me?" A fire of anger had ignited in his eyes. "I didn't come all this way for nothing."

She sat on the cot, unable to look at him. "I never expected you to follow me here. I feel bad about that. I really do. Find a way to get out of the country. Come to France, too."

"I don't want to go to France. I want to go back to Kamchatka." He turned from her and banged his fist against the wall.

She came and tentatively touched his back. "I will come to Kamchatka after the war."

He moved away from her and turned and yelled at her. "That's an empty promise. Why do you even make it? I am a deserter without money. Only a bullet waits for me. You seduced me. Made me want you and then told me to come to Moscow."

She grabbed his arms. "Shh! Alex, shh. The walls have ears."

"I came, and it wasn't easy. I found you, and now you are leaving." He grabbed her by the shoulders and forced her to look at him, mimicking her in a high-pitched voice. "I'm sorry. I'm going to France."

She saw the anger drain from him. He turned, punched the wall again, and sank to the cot, his head in his hands. She wrestled with what to do.

"Well, at least we have tonight, for old time's sake." He spoke his remaining hope.

She would not look at him. She gave a deep sigh.

"You're going to deny me even that?"

"I am diseased. I am being treated." She lied, but his anguish tore at her. She came and pulled his head to her chest, her hands caressing his hair. "I am so sorry, Sasha. Sudba has not been good to you."

No, fate had not been good to him but, as unhappy as that was, she could not, would not give him what he desired. They pleasured each other short of intercourse, but a pallor of despair diluted any joy they felt.

Part II

Moscow, *Proshchai*

Farewell, my Moscow, my home
Farewell, you cupolas of the Kremlin
Alas, it may well be that never again
I shall hear the tinkling of your bells
    Theodore Bikel's translation
    of *"Proshchai"*

9

Valentina Leaves Moscow

Moscow 1944

The ache in Sasha was far worse than hunger, far worse than sexual desire. His whole life had been snatched from him, and yet he had to go on, without hope, without plans.

Valentina left in the dark for work. Sasha spent a restless, miserable day wandering the city. He came across a statue of a youth in Young Pioneer costume, holding his hat in one hand and with the other hand, clinging to the pole holding the Soviet state flag whipped by the wind. The statue stood on a white pedestal. Sasha didn't have to read the inscription to know it represented Pavlik Morozov, the thirteen-year-old who had denounced his own father to the GPU.

Sasha had been required to attend the opera depicting the story and was well-schooled in the songs extolling the glorious young martyr. The school he attended in Petropavlovsk was renamed after Morozov was murdered, supposedly by his uncle, grandfather, grandmother, a cousin, and his younger brother. Supposedly, thousands of telegrams from all over the Soviet Union urged the judge to show no mercy for Pavlik's killers. All of them except the uncle were rounded up by the GPU and sentenced to the highest measure of social defense, execution by a firing squad. The stories differed as to what the crime Pavlik's father, Trofim, had been. In one version, he was the Chairman of the Village Soviet and had been forging documents and selling them to the bandits and enemies of the Soviet State. In another, he had stolen potatoes or was hoarding grain from the *kolkhoz* to feed his starving family. The elder Morozov was sentenced to ten years in a labor camp and later executed. Where did loyalty to family end when it clashed with loyalty to state? Did the state always trump the family? Was it the state's prerogative to destroy the family? Sasha didn't know if he were willing to declare Pavlik an exemplary hero in this conflicted story with various versions. How would it be, feeling you could not trust even your own children as they, too, acted as puppets of the state?

Sasha also saw multiple statues and posters of Lenin and Stalin and a variety of posters with war themes papering the sides of buildings. One featured a sailor in uniform holding a gun, ammunition strapped to his chest, with a red star and the iconic hammer and sickle on a white field in the background behind him. The poster urged, "Forward! Westward! To meet the invaders." He knew sailors figured prominently in posters promoting the war because the mutinies on czarist ships in 1917 had sparked the Bolshevik Revolution. Another poster had a line of modern-day soldiers holding their guns pointing forward, red stars on their helmets, a tank blasting before them with ghosted figures above them of Chapayev, a World War I partisan general who led Communist soldiers against the forces of the Czar, Suvorov who routed Napoleon's army in Italy, and a third general from yet an earlier era, the history behind whom he did not know. The inscription was an appeal to the grandsons of Suvorov, the children of Chapayev, to join in the battle to preserve the freedom that these earlier generals had fought for.

Finally, as the day drew to an end, Sasha went back to meet Valentina at her work. She came down the stairs, beaming, and kissed him. "I have a bottle of vodka. Tonight we celebrate."

"What is there to celebrate?"

"Being together. That you arrived before I leave."

He accepted what he had, enjoying the midnight celebration after the cooking and washing chores were accomplished. He kissed her lips, sweet with vodka. He wanted to drink cup after cup, bottle after bottle into mindless oblivion.

The next morning he lay in solitary darkness. Through his drowsiness, awareness penetrated that she must not have drunk much for him to have drunk enough to have little memory of the previous evening. Had he dredged it out of his morbid thoughts, or had she really said she was leaving tomorrow? Was tomorrow today or tomorrow?

When Valentina returned, Sasha looked through his pictures by candlelight. She came and rubbed his shoulders, quietly looking with him. She was so willing to touch, caress, and leave him.

"I make a gift of my pictures to you."

Tears came to her eyes, "Oh, Alex."

"Of what worth are they to me?"

"I will find a publisher for you."

"It doesn't make any difference to me."

"I will give my gift of you to the world."

"All I want is you. The birds will still be there. They can be drawn again, but you..."

"We will find a way. We will get back together. *Sudba* will be good to us. It was a miracle we got together this time. We are meant to be together. It will happen. Believe! And next time, I will be healed." She kissed him hard. She kissed his eyes, his mouth as if she could drill her words into his melancholy and empower them. Instead, they were empty promises bouncing off the vacuum of his hopes.

The next morning Sasha was surprised that Valentina took nothing with her from her home for her trip to England. When he commented that she was not even taking a change of underwear, she said, "All the clothing is provided. Neither the English nor the French dress as we do. There must be nothing on me or about me which would suggest that I am Russian. I will leave on the train dressed as an English woman, and then when the Allies invade France, I will be dressed as a French nurse."

Sasha carried his pictures and gave them to Valentina when she entered the gray, brick building where he had found her originally. He waited across the street, still barred by the formidable guard. After a couple of hours, Valentina, but not Valentina, emerged. Gone was the Russian coat, replaced by a coat of fabric which suggested a gray, woolen blanket. Gone, the Russian scarves covering her crown of braids. In fact, gone were the braids, with her hair cut just below the ears. She carried a black valise. It was discordant to hear Valentina's voice coming out of this stranger and see Valentina's eyes in her face. At the station, it didn't seem so odd that she just gave him a quick peck of a kiss and said, "I hope everything turns out well for you, Alex. I truly do," and then boarded the train. The Valentina he had known and loved in Kamchatka was gone; he knew not where. It didn't seem like he was saying good-bye to her but to a stranger.

Sasha wished he had some vodka to drown his miseries in. He sought *sabeysta*, but there was no possibility of forgetting. He returned to Valentina's house to retrieve his few belongings. Maybe, with luck, he could take the bedding from Valentina's room, some useful items from the kitchen, and some food. He trusted his ability to overpower the woman, Vera if she were the only one there.

Vera watched him as he entered. She followed him into Valentina's room. He saw no one else. He ignored her as he pulled the blanket off of Valentina's cot and stuffed it into his bag. She stood in the doorway, her arms folded. "Where is Valentina?"

"Wouldn't she be at work now?"

"Liar. You just put her on a train."

"Then why do you ask, if you already know?"

"I just want you to know I know more than you think." She moved towards him, her eyes and voice growing seductive, "It's okay. She was diseased. We can use men too. Take off your soldier's suit."

He grabbed her arm and twisted it behind her. "Get out! Leave me alone. I could kill you for what you did to Valentina."

She gasped, "Let me go. That hurts."

He twisted tighter, and she stood on tip-toe. "It better hurt. It's only a hint of what's going to happen if you bother either Valentina or me again." He shoved her towards the only chair in the room. "You sit there until I am out of here."

She sat on the chair, unconcerned, too unconcerned. He packed bedding, clothing Valentina had left behind, anything he might be able to trade for food en route. He was ready to move to the kitchen to look for a knife and any other utensils which might prove useful when suddenly the door burst open. Sasha turned to see the man who had escorted Valentina the day he first saw her, the one she called Nikita, with a gun leveled at him.

Vera said, "Our little bird has flown, but I trapped us a deserter."

"Does he have his food pass?"

"I assume."

"You hold the gun. I'll search him."

"It's in the shirt pocket," Sasha said. It was not going to serve him at all where he was going. If it would get them off his case, he had nothing to lose.

Vera removed the food permit and unfolded it. "He received food just four days ago. We cannot get more until the end of next week."

"It's okay. We'll need the uniform too. Take it off, soldier."

"I have no other clothing."

"That's no concern of ours."

"It's a concern of mine."

"Do you want to teach him to obey, or shall I?"

"I would like to," said Vera, "he's been too free with me."

Though Sasha saw what was coming, he didn't know how to protect himself from the blow in the groin with the gun pointed at him. He doubled over in pain, and Nikita stripped him. While Vera held the gun on Sasha, Nikita stripped himself and put on the uniform. Sasha grabbed Nikita's clothing and put it on. Neither Vera nor Nikita moved to stop him. So this was the kind of treatment Valentina received if she refused to cooperate. No wonder she felt so powerless. But *sudba* was good. Going east, Nikita's civilian garb would serve him much better than the soldier's uniform. Sasha needed to hold onto his greatcoat, having left the bear rug behind. The man's coat did not look as warm.

Sasha had just finished dressing when there was a great commotion in the hall. Nikita stepped into the hallway, followed by Vera and Sasha.

'"There he is, the deserter!" Four men stood in the hallway. Each had a gun trained on the trio.

"March, soldier boy." One of the four moved to Nikita and jabbed him in the ribs with the gun.

"But, but…," Nikita sputtered.

"Shut up, or you get the gun now."

Two of the soldiers marched him out the front door. A third, the one who had been doing all the talking, turned to Sasha.

"Well, peasant boy, I don't know what was going on here, but the army's going to be down one soldier once that dunce receives his due. Mother Russia needs you. Come, I'll show you where to enlist. You get to do your patriotic duty. Mother Russia is proud of you, son. It's your lucky day."

He had his gun trained on Sasha. "March."

Sasha marched. He heard the fourth soldier say, "And the woman?"

"It's your turn, my boy. Do with her as you like."

"Oh, no, please no," whimpered Vera.

"Well, the Red Army could use you too, but I think I would rather use you first. After the Red Army's done with you, maybe Germany would have some use for you."

This was more than justice. There probably would be nothing left of her after the Red Army was done. Women at home in Kamchatka suffered only heartache and hardship as their men marched off to war. On the front lines, women fought the battles as victims to be exploited. How glad he was that Valentina was on the train, speeding away from this madness. Was there a God in France who would see to her safety?

Aboard ship from Russia to England, 1944

Valentina, now schooled in thinking of herself as Marie Yvette, stood at the stern of the ship, the last tangible vestiges of her Russianness clutched to her chest. She picked up a paper showing a brownish bird with a red patch under its beak and black eye patches with white borders. Alex identified the bird as a Siberian Rubythroat in his condemning Cyrillic script. Valentina let the wind whip it out of her hand. She watched as it fluttered for a long time before finally descending to rest upon the water, but by that time the papers depicting the marbled murrelet, rufous turtle dove, three-toed woodpecker, and Swinhoe's red-tailed robin had all flown after it, each twirling, fluttering in flight, before coming to rest upon the water, perhaps ending as fish bait. The living birds might once have consumed fish; now fish consumed their representations and their damning Russian names. She picked up the next sheet and almost released it without looking at it but saw just in time it was a portrait of herself—beautiful, beautiful. More beautiful than she was, obviously the way Alex saw her.

Valentina found tears upon her cheeks. She wasn't sure if it was from this manifestation of Alex's desire for her, destroying something as beautiful as his other pictures, or tears shed for Alex, whose life she had ruined by her lust. Whatever happened to him after she left, she would never know. Or was it because she might never see her homeland again? She could pretend to be French or English, but she was Russian. It tore at her that her beloved brothers and her friend Mikel had lost their lives driving the Germans from their homeland. She loved Russia, but she had a compartment in her heart that hated Russia. It was the Russia that could break into one's home and take a man and disappear him without any further comment. Her father did not deserve whatever had happened to him. She hated that that could happen, and somehow, it was okay because it wasn't. Now, she had to fear for her mother and herself. She was thrilled to participate in the war effort in espionage, but would she ever dare return? Would she always be suspect? The Russia that would turn its back on her and destroy her for serving it, that Russia she hated.

Salt Lake City 1948

Valentina became choked in her storytelling and broke off. Sasha saw her glance at him. He didn't say anything. She had destroyed his baby, his pictures, and she realized she had destroyed his life through her lust. Although the destruction of his pictures tore at him, would he have wanted her to keep them with the power they had to destroy her? No, he admitted. He did value her ever so much more than the pictures, even if she didn't want him now. Pictures could be redrawn, but a human life? Each was unique and precious in itself. He cleared his throat and picked up the story.

Western Russia 1944

After what seemed extremely brief training, Sasha and the other new recruits climbed onto open trucks from the American lend-lease program, and the Studebaker trucks headed west, carrying the soldiers to drive the Germans from Russia. "You have to wonder why they train us at all," Volodya, from central Siberia, grumbled as he tried to burrow his face in his coat. "We're just targets to absorb German bullets. Let's hope that Germany runs out of bullets before Russia runs out of men."

"It looks to me like they will freeze us to death before giving us a chance to catch a bullet," a burly soldier Sasha knew as Vladimir observed. All of the soldiers frantically dug in their packs for something more to wrap around their heads to protect their ears, cheeks, and noses from the battle with General Winter. The scientists in Kamchatka had claimed that General Winter defeated the Germans in their effort to take Moscow. Just because General Winter fought on Russian soil, he evidently didn't favor the Russian people with any mercy.

When their frigid transport finally halted, Sasha battled the frozen ground, trying to dig a snow bed with an entrenching shovel and knife. Neither was adequate, but the exertion briefly warmed him. He piled on every item of clothing in the pack and then the pack itself, wondering if he would survive the night. The next morning, the soldiers gathered around a fire to heat some liquid to warm their insides. One extended his hand he had inadequately protected through the night. It looked to be ice. The fire heated it, and soon the soldier hopped around, yelping in pain. With a crazed look, he grabbed his gun and shot the offending limb off. He was taken into a tent, still whimpering. One way or another, the war was over for him.

"I'll give you a biscuit for five pages." Kirill requested. Sasha had not anticipated that *War and Peace* would be a valuable commodity. The soldiers, officers, even generals sought him out for a page they could roll into a cigarette filled with the bitter-tasting Russian tobacco. They all had so little they could trade, but their smokes were more important to them than virtually anything else. Sasha was a rich man with his thick book in the midst of their poverty.

One morning, their driver poured warm water over the engine block of the American truck to dissolve some of the ice caking it. Once the ice diminished, he swore, "It's cracked!" Sasha saw this as a distinct advantage. Not only would this mean that by walking, they could generate some heat, but also it might delay meeting enemy number two, the "Fritz." Could the Germans be any more fearsome or dangerous than a Russian winter?

The long walks gave time to reflect on the craziness of war. Why didn't they just all go home to their bit of land, build their homes, father their children, do their work? Wasn't there enough land in Germany for the Fritz? Sasha had never met a Fritz who wanted his little spot on earth in Kamchatka. Not even most Kamchadals wanted it. He could be content there. What was he doing here, freezing to death, fighting someone else's quarrel? True, he had never met a German at all, but he couldn't imagine they were here because they wanted to be. Surely, they just wanted to go home to what was familiar and comfortable, just as he did.

One morning, Vladimir did not join the others, stamping their feet and flexing their hands around the fire. Though certainly familiar with death, Sasha had never before awoken to see someone he had walked and conversed with the day before cold and unresponsive. It seemed so quick, so arbitrary. Had Vladimir sensed that his life was leaving him? Had it been more painful than the cold and hunger? Was he truly nothing more than this frozen corpse, just like an extinguished fire?

England 1944

Once they landed in England, Valentina was transported to London in the back of a lorry with canvas sides. She rued the entire way that she could see nothing. Excitement built in her heart. She was taken to a building where nurses readying for deployment were billeted. The building was clean, and everything seemed so precise, a place for everything and everything in its place. She wondered if this were because it was the English way or the military way. She marveled that in the washroom, warm water was available by merely turning a tap. Did the normal English have such things in their homes, or was this special for the soldiers? Also, the toilet, incredible! No need to go outside to an outhouse. In any weather, any time day or night, she could privately and comfortably relieve herself. Why had she never seen such a thing in the great country of Russia?

Valentina was told to report to a building where she would be issued her gear. After checking in, she was issued a bicycle, a bedroll, olive drab trousers, beige shirts and neckties, blue nurse's dresses, white caps, and a heavy, navy blue cape. She was also issued guns they called a "carbine" and a ".45 calibre Colt automatic".

She looked at the things in panic and amazement. She had never ridden a bicycle. She didn't know how. She had never touched a gun. She was confident there would be some training on that. Surely she wouldn't be the only one not knowing how to use a gun, but did all of these other soldiers know how to bicycle? She decided to take her gear to her barracks and return to retrieve the bicycle. She was passed by a multitude of cyclists carrying gear, going both to and from the barracks. She hoped they all would be finished with their trips before she fetched her machine. Most were, but there were a few stragglers when she began pushing hers to the barracks. She was not the only one. All of the others had been in training in Moscow with her. Not one of them seemed to have learned to ride a bicycle previously. How did everyone else know how to do this? She felt that "Russian" was stamped on their foreheads, even though none of them muttered to each other in Russian or spoke in their slightly accented English. She was mortified to make a display of her ineptitude in front of those who expertly sped by. "Hey, luv!" A young man with a strong British accent slowed to a stop next to her. "Somethin' de matta wi' yer bike?"

"Uh, no, I don't think so," Valentina answered, blushing furiously, just wanting to disappear. Others in the parade stopped also. The first young man parked his cycle and came to inspect hers. "'Ere, lemme take a gob at it. This is not a casualty department," he said, waving an arm at other cyclists who had stopped. "No need'n a tailgate. Just because you see a crumpet thrown in the cart don't mean you need to chip in. Skedaddle! Do I need a bobby to get the rest of ya to rescue those soldier boys?" He tossed his head at the others, pushing their machines.

The riders rode on or offered assistance to the others, and she was left with the young man whose English she hardly understood. "I don' see nothin' de matta wi' it."

"I, uh, I don't know how to ride a bicycle." She confessed.

"Blimey!" He said, pushing his hat back on his head. "Guess we betta remedy that. Follow me." Wheeling his own bicycle, he fell into step with Valentina until they came to a spot where there was no vehicle traffic. Again the young man parked his bicycle. "I'm Liam," he said, extending his hand.

Valentina wavered. Should she give her real name or alias? She extended her hand. "I'm Marie Yvette."

"Or at least, pretendin' to be. Headin' to France in espionage, are ya? Well, jump on yer bike. I'll hold ya steady."

She obeyed, not knowing what else to do.

"Now, you peddle, keep yer handlebars steady. You'll get the hang quick enough."

He ran along behind, holding her steady as she peddled, trying to follow his instructions for balancing. A new audience formed. "Dead heavy!" Someone yelled as she peddled on her own a moment before crashing. Fortunately, she got her foot down before the machine fell on top of her. "Got to peddle a mite faster, but you're getting it," another young man rushed forward to help her stand it back up.

Liam came running up, panting. "Don't need a gooseberry. I can handle this."

"Didn't know she was your gal," the second young man said, backing off. "Cheerio!" he said, waving to Valentina.

She didn't know she was Liam's gal either. Caught between the embarrassment of exposing her inability and the possessiveness Liam exhibited, Valentina didn't know how to extricate herself from this situation.

All of the other Russian non-riders were far too proud to accept any help, but it was at once awkward and reassuring for Valentina. None of the onlookers mocked her or made fun in any way. It was just goodhearted cheering on. Valentina got over her mortification and realized these were going to be really good guys to work with, willing to help. "Thanks, chaps," she said, trying out some of the English lingo she had overheard.

Liam stayed with her until there were just some wobbles and no crashes. "You'll get it," he said. "It will be easy fer ya in a couple of days. See you about."

She was told that she was to dress in her prettiest dress for a tea with the other women serving in espionage the next afternoon. Now her stomach was all aflutter. If there were a chance to see Mamochka, this would be it.

She put the English, gaily printed, pink, floral dress on, cinching the matching belt, and delighted herself with a little twirl to see the skirt flare out. She didn't know if she had ever had such a pretty dress. Her little bob of a hair-do was so quick and easy to style. She liked the Marie Yvette she had become. She tucked the portrait Alex had drawn of her into a folder she had been given. Perhaps she would give it to Mamochka.

Squarish, black taxis transported her and other girls also dressed up. Some wore more alluring styles. She suspected their task ahead would be different from her own. She had a hard time not appearing a gawking tourist, seeing sights she had heard of, such as Buckingham Palace and Big Ben, and many things she had never heard of. Most of the buildings were old but not as gray as in Moscow. Evidence of the bombing by the Germans was everywhere. Buildings were in rubble. Walls were missing; roofs missing. The bombing had been more minimal in Moscow, but the very sight of all the devastation again reminded her that war was not a vacation. Terrible times would certainly be ahead.

They were transported into the countryside to a large, stately home. Its curving drive wound through a green field of cut grass. What was that English word for this? Ah, yes, lawn. She must be very careful to never reveal her ignorance if she were stumbling for a word that would be commonplace to everyone else around her.

A butler dressed in black with a crisp, white shirt greeted them at the door. He escorted them into a lavish room full of reds, browns, and greens in carpets, curtains, and upholstered chairs. One by one, the girls curtsied and introduced themselves by their assigned name to a tiny woman named Miss Cleveland. She had a tremendous mass of red hair all fluffed up. Miss Cleveland was seated royally upon the biggest upholstered chair in the room and held the stem of eye-glasses upon a handle to see them better. In her charming English accent, she welcomed them to her home and invited them to be seated until the others could join them. She then began riffling newspapers and said in her fussy, excited way, "Now, where did I put that?" She eventually located some scissors and began clipping articles out of the newspapers, leaving the girls to watch her in amazement and to mingle among themselves.

Valentina sipped daintily on the offered tea, barely registering the distinct flavor of sugar. Her nerves felt frayed as she tried to school herself into acting nonchalant. The thought of seeing Mamochka choked her. And then Mamochka stood before her, introducing herself as Vivian and speaking English with exactly the same lilting accent as Miss Cleveland. She did a perfect job of acting like her heart was not doing flip-flops as she was introduced to her daughter posing as Marie Yvette. She just shook Valentina's hand with a slight squeeze, "So pleased to meet you." And then she moved on to the next girl. They sipped their tea and ate the sweet bread the English called biscuits, chatting about inconsequentials such as the shortage of nylons and cosmetics. Miss Cleveland interrupted this chatter by saying, "Girls, you may not think this is important, but this is the very kind of thing that is superlatively important. Citizens in France have been without these items for a long time. The girls do the best they can. For instance, in place of nylons, they draw a line up the back of their leg with an eyeliner pencil to simulate the seam of the nylon. You must pick up on these things. You must pick up on every little thing."

Valentina allowed her eyes occasionally to stray to Mamochka as she casually looked around the room. Once Mamochka's eyes met hers, and Mamochka gave a slight smile and a barely discernible wink.

The tea ended, and the black taxis came back to fetch them. Valentina had had no opportunity to talk to Mamochka in private. She was, however, able to slip the folder containing her portrait to Mamochka as she brushed by her on the way out of the room.

Western Russia 1944

Each day became a blur of sameness, a battle for survival, a fight for sanity. Sasha tramped up hills, down ravines, stripping socks or gloves from dead comrades in an effort to keep himself warm and dry, shutting his mind down to their ravaged bodies and vacant looks. He spent his days looking for the enemy and hoping not to find him, but new enemies had sprung up among the troops. Exhaustion stalked them, gums began to swell and bleed, making eating the meager food difficult and painful. Sasha knew some fresh greens could help combat this devastating condition, but nothing green broke through the graying snow. Spring—why was spring delaying its arrival?

One day as they carelessly traipsed through yet another field, Sasha heard someone yell, "Tank!" Immediately he dived with the others into ditches as the shape of a tank loomed out of the fog before them. He kept his eyes trained on the approaching tank but saw only one soldier marching alongside. Surely the soldier had seen them but seemed unconcerned about his exposure. Sasha wondered about the troops that must be backing him and felt some of the exhilaration Tolstoy had talked about when the soldiers went into battle. There was an excitement, a break to the monotony, an anticipation of the unknown and dangerous. He positioned his gun, his heart beating wildly, waiting for the signal to fire. Then he sheepishly lowered his gun as he realized the tank was but a peasant's wagon piled high with manure. The laughter that rippled through the ranks brought welcome release from the tension.

As the soldiers became more accustomed to dealing with the unrelenting cold, hunger became the greatest enemy, claiming many victims every day. Many days, Sasha's food rations consisted of one dried crust and a soup-like liquid in which floated a few beets and potatoes. After eating, he often doubled over from the pain in his abdomen. Then he would have to run to relieve himself.

One morning they were issued a couple of biscuits to eat for their midday meal. By the time they were allowed to eat them, the biscuits had turned brick hard. Sasha put some snow in his can and built a fire beneath to soak the biscuit in the water. The wind carried a spark to the biscuit. The sawdust in the biscuit immediately sprang to life with more energy than the struggling flames licking the sticks provided. Sasha quickly threw snow on the biscuit, extinguishing the fire. If possible, he was hungrier than he was cold, and the heat would satisfy for much less time than the small nourishment the biscuit gave.

Abominable weather with freezing temperatures limited the soldier's advances. They spent as much time cutting crude patterns from blankets and sewing them together for makeshift mittens and foot warmers as they did marching. Even the sick kept marching. Stopping meant certain death. As it became commonplace, Sasha no longer entertained thoughts about what an odd thing a human death was except to wonder what would it be like not to wake up some morning-- just nothingness, nonexistence?

They also saw many dead Germans—dead from cold, dead from hunger, dead from fatigue, and the only fighting that was going on was with General Winter. Why did the Russians even bother? Why didn't they just stay home until spring and then come in and mop up what General Winter left unfinished?

Sasha had seen a lifetime full of desolate landscapes, burned-out villages, eyes of civilians devoid of hope for relief from the cold, the hunger, the senseless destruction before they found the sought-for enemy. Then one day, the bullets flew, and any excitement at the prospect of battle quickly melted away. He would not have applied the adjective of merrily as Tolstoy had to the bullets buzzing around his head. Why did these men want to kill him? He had never done anything to them, and yet one of their bullets could make Baba's prophecy come true. He would never come home. One sharpened branch converted into a deadly weapon from an exploding tree hitting him, and he would have a ticket home to limp around Baba's hut like Maximov, marry Nadia, and live out life in bitterness. Why had he not listened to Baba? Why had he not believed her?

England 1944

Valentina dressed in her men's trousers with six buttons on the fly and wondered how anyone got in and out of the contraption in a hurry. She retrieved her bike and, still shaky, peddled after the others. She gathered with many others in a large auditorium, not only with the women from her barracks but also a large contingent of men. A man in the green, creased, woolen military uniform of an officer addressed them. "You are all here for one reason and one reason only. We are united from several different countries against tyranny, specifically in the European theater against the Jerries in France. You see around you the great devastation they have wrought upon England, and their goal is to spread this evil throughout the world. We must defeat them. We will defeat them with you great young men and women gathered here for an assault not far in the future." It was a lot of the rah, rah they had heard before. Valentina could tell that the feeling among the soldiers was one of excitement, even though they saw the rubble in England, even though the vague scent of death was in the air where bodies had not been removed from buildings. They just wanted to get on with it, not hear more of this seemingly endless buildup. "All of you here in this building have assignments in medical support to the soldiers putting their lives on the line. Some of you may end up giving your own lives in this great cause, even as many of the soldiers will. Some of you will finish the war maimed in various ways. The enemy is indiscriminate, and even though, supposedly, the medical teams are off-limits, you are not out of danger. Those of you who do survive will see things that may torment you the rest of your lives." Finally, he concluded, and all who had not been inducted before were asked to stand and take an oath of allegiance to the Allies. Valentina was sworn in as a second lieutenant.

There were just seven other individuals. She recognized only one who had been in her training in Moscow. It was Pascal, with broad shoulders and an eye for pretty women. A tall blond man with a great build flashed a welcome smile at them. He stood and shuffled papers as they seated themselves. "*Bonjour,*" he spoke to them in French, "You will know me as Etienne. I have been asked to head up our team. Our code name is Cartouche. We have a unique position because we are all medically trained, but our actual responsibility is espionage. We will work behind enemy lines, posing as a German/French medical team. All of us are fluent in French. Dietrich," Etienne signaled to a slim man with curly, black hair, who nodded back, "and Gretel." A very pretty brunette with a heart-shaped face waved her dainty hand at them. "Both are fluent in German as well. They have been given German names as aliases. They will work, especially with the injured Germans who are brought in. We will all work with the French-speakers. We will not see those so severely injured that they cannot communicate. They will be separated before they arrive at our site. Our job is to extract any information which might be pertinent to the Allied war effort. Mostly we are to be compassionate. Injured men are more apt to open up to us if we are kind. Because they think we are really on their side, the expectation is that they will divulge information they would be reluctant to reveal if they perceived themselves as prisoners. After we have extracted all the information we are able, they will, in fact, be sent to prison camps. We will capture some French ambulances. A team we will meet later will pick up the injured at the front, sort them, and deliver them to us. This same team will remove those no longer of value to us and take them to the prison camps.

"Now there are a couple of individuals with other unique language skills among us, Marie Yvette and Pascal. They both speak Russian." Now it was Valentina and Pascal's turn to wave and smile at the others. "You may not know this, but intelligence tells us that the Germans have conscripted Russian prisoners to fight with them, promising to liberate Russia from the government that calls them traitors, after they successfully win the war on this front. These Russians are not necessarily loyal to Germany. Our goal is to capture them, injured or not, and persuade them to infiltrate back into the German army. They probably have limited access to intelligence, but they can persuade other Russians to join them in sabotaging the German effort in any way possible. We will reward those willing to help with false identities so that they can remain in an Allied country after the war."

That was news. It seemed to corroborate what Papochka had said about it being dangerous for them to return to Russia. Surely what was just said was not for Stalin's ears. And what about herself? Would she be returning to her Russian homeland branded a traitor just for serving?

The other nurses were each introduced: Monique, with dimples and a black fringe. Hélène, a plumpish girl with red curls and a ready laugh, Annick, a petite girl with dark brown eyes who seemed very young. And Giselle, whose eyebrows formed a half-square shape. She constantly crossed and uncrossed her legs and swung her foot.

"All of you who have been trained in touch typing will type up reports of any information that might be of interest. It is imperative you do this as quickly as possible. Take notes as you speak to the injured in such a way that they think you are noting their medical condition."

"Until you are deployed, you will work as a team in the hospitals here, where we are treating the pilots and other crewmen doing bombing missions over Germany. There are a lot coming back injured. You will be speaking English in the hospitals, as these injured are primarily British or American. In theater-- that means operating room for those of you not familiar with English medical vernacular-- we will speak French, as only our team will be there. Whenever you see each other and are not talking directly to these soldiers, you are to speak French, to accustom yourselves to using that language when addressing each other."

Valentina and the other nurses on her team all bunked together and quickly fell into speaking French with each other. She couldn't distinguish a thing about their origins when speaking French, but if she heard them speaking English to others, distinctions quickly became apparent. Monique spoke the same distinct English dialect as Liam, heavily littered with idioms and cropped words. Valentina suspected Giselle and Annick were American, as their English was vastly different than the others. She decided to begin modeling her own English after theirs. Maybe she would relocate in the United States after the war.

Western Russia 1944

Terrorized by the day-in, day-out battles, Sasha's frustration with the senselessness of the war grew. Why did the government not care enough to make sure the army had the food, clothing, and equipment necessary to win a war? If a war was worth fighting, wasn't it worth winning? Why the endless marches, the guns that jammed; why fight in the extreme cold? Why did they not just send all the soldiers home for the winter, let them father a child to replace them if the war took them, and then come back in force and drive the Germans home for good? Who had planned this war? What was the crazy motive?

After one triumphant battle, their thinning troops were reinforced with prisoners liberated from the Germans. They entered the previously occupied village and met a gruesome sight: village leaders suspended by spikes in the village center. The soldiers respectfully took care of the bodies, and the grateful villagers established a soup kitchen. A long queue stood, waiting patiently to enter for their portion. As Sasha entered, an elderly *babushka* with a toothless smile, her head wrapped in two scarves, handed him a tin spoon, "Give me your cap, sonny." She tossed it onto the growing mountain of caps behind her. Soon Sasha noticed a number of the soldiers left bare-headed, forfeiting their caps. He did the same. There was a spare cap in his kit, and caps were continually available from the dead, but spoons were indispensable. The next time he visited the kitchen, the old grandma was not smiling. "Two *roubles*," she demanded. Word had preceded his visit, and he handed over the money for the superior rations. Volodya made the mistake of turning his head when he appreciated the pretty girls dishing up the soup. One of the gals swooped in and removed his plate with his spoon. "Wait! Wait!" I'm not done."

His cries and pleas fell on deaf ears. "No spoon. Ten *roubles*," demanded the *babushka* at the only exit. She was more fearsome than a German general.

"It's not my fault. She took my plate before I was finished."

"Spoon or ten *roubles*. No exceptions, now pay up or move aside."

He paid up and never looked at the pretty girls again.

England 1944

Valentina faced her first day in the hospital with anticipation and trepidation. What would it be like to work with really injured men? Would it be awful to see the disfigured faces? Would it be terrible to assist in cutting off limbs and mending torn bodies? She approached her first day in kind of a breathless horror. The hospital smells assaulted her nose. She braced herself and soon learned there were others in command, willing to tell her what to do. The first day, she and the other nurses on her team were initially assigned to work under a brisk nurse named Agnes. "Clean up that puddle of sick," she barked, pointing to some vomit on the floor. "Change the plaster on the arm of the chap in bed four." "Give the soldier in bed eight an additional rug. 'E's shivering." "Get a flannel, wet it, and wipe down the brow of the bloke in ten. 'E's burning up." "Grab a jar for the American in bed seven. 'E's about ta slash." "Empty the rubbish."

Monique grumbled, "Her never-ending chunter. You'd think we're her dogsbody." Eventually, it seemed all of the garbage had been emptied, the bedpans filled and poured out, the brows wiped, and all other menial tasks accomplished, and Valentina could take a moment to speak to the soldiers. She found a young man, his head swathed in bandages. "Hi," she said, touching his arm, "My name is Marie Yvette. I will be your nurse today."

"Oh, God bless you," he said in a lazy drawl. "I'm Jeffrey Smith. Could you please get me a drink of water?"

She met his need, plumped his pillow, and moved on.

The next had a chart identifying him as Brian Jarvis. He had no apparent injury but just stared. "Hi, I'm Marie Yvette," she said. There was no response from him. "Is there anything I can do to help you?"

Still no response. She looked at his file: Battle shock.

She got a glass of water for him and held it to his lips, "Here, Brian, you need to drink. You're safe now."

He drank rather mechanically but with no other response.

In the next bed lay Peter Lunt, the bandage on his leg ending where the knee should have been. "Just let me hold your soft hand a moment. Do you think the girls back home will want anything to do with me, one-legged?"

"Of course, with your quick smile and twinkling eyes, you're going to have to fight them off."

Soon each one was like Dmitri, Andrei, Mark, or Mikel. She teased them, she flirted with them, met their needs, and was completely at ease. Only a few hours had passed.

She wondered if Dmitri, Andrei, Mark, or Mikel had been privileged to be under the kind administrations of a nurse before death took them. Or had they died on the battlefield? She nursed these boys she had come to think of as brothers or a dear friend as if that could somehow make up for what they had not received. She found her patience was boundless, and her energy renewed.

10

D-Day

Western Russia 1944

Even though dug into a foxhole, terror seized Sasha as he saw the first of the German Tiger tanks rolling towards him. He ducked, wondering if its fearsome tracks would crush him. He saw some soldiers attempt to crawl out of the foxhole and run, but they were quickly cut down with the brrrp of the German burp gun. He tried to roll himself into a ball as the clanking tank approached. The trench collapsed to the right, but his position remained untouched. A soldier down the trench began crying. Blood gushed from an amputated arm. Sasha offered him his canteen of vodka to ease the pain. The dying soldier choked out, "I'm not crying from pain. I am crying because I promised myself not to die until I had killed five fascists."

Volodya assured him, "You killed fifty with that machine gun. I saw them falling under your bursts." Sasha knew and was equally sure the dying soldier knew that there was no way that any of them could know such a thing. What lies one would say to give some comfort! Such empty words.

In the flying dirt, screams, and stench of fresh blood, Sasha stayed huddled in the trench until the sounds of the tanks receded. He gingerly stuck his head out and saw several other soldiers doing the same. Seeing the Germans going beyond them, they grabbed their packs, scrambled out of their holes, and ran in the opposite direction. Generalissimo

Stalin's mantra, "Not one foot backward," had no power over the flee-ing men. They did not slow until they came upon a screaming horse, writhing in pain. They quickly put him out of his misery. Sasha and a couple of the other soldiers pulled their knives and joyfully set to carving up their find. Other soldiers busied themselves finding wood and searching for something to boil some water in but found nothing but their helmets. As the meat roasted on a hastily constructed spit, Sasha took advantage of the fire to heat some stones in a can to drop into his boots and socks to dry them out. This had become a luxury never to be wasted. The twelve soldiers had become isolated from their unit but slept with more contented stomachs than they'd had in a long time. Their bowels punished them the next day. Still, they ignored the rebellion of their intestines and roasted the rest of the horse meat. They spent most of their day scavenging among the dead Germans for anything serviceable. The soldiers pocketed all ammunition. Food was either eaten on the spot or saved for later.

Sasha rummaged in the pockets of a well-decorated officer, hoping the findings might be more valuable than those found on the privates. A picture in the man's wallet showed six men harnessed like oxen to a cart. Two German boys, about 12 years of age, drove them with whips. Adult German men stood nearby with guns. There was no way for him to be sure, but in Sasha's mind, the six men being treated like beasts of burden were Russians. He picked up the dead German's gun and shot him six times, once for each of the abused prisoners.

The German socks and boots were better than the Red Army's when they weren't too worn, but Sasha didn't dare touch them. The story was told that some Russian soldiers had replaced their socks and boots with German socks and boots. They had been captured by the Germans, who cut their feet off as retribution. The footless soldiers were left for their comrades to find, so word would be passed among the Russians never to touch a fallen German.

Sasha briefly contemplated working the horse's hide to preserve it, but it would take too long. While a welcome protection against the cold, it would be heavy to carry. Spring could not be too far off with its less severe cold and more abundant food.

One day, as the meat began to run out, one of the soldiers found a good-sized cauldron. Repeatedly filling it with snow until they had a sizable amount of water boiling in it, the soldiers threw in the bones and head of the horse for their last meal before reluctantly heading out to find another food source. Sasha found an eye in his portion of the broth. It was a bit rubbery, but he gobbled it down. It was meat, and tomorrow there would be no more. Then they refilled their cauldron and boiled the hide, taking turns overnight to keep the fire going, and the water replenished with new snow. Come morning, they scraped off all of the hair they could, then cut the hide in strips, stored it in their packs, and headed out.

"Where are we going?" Volodya asked.

"To find another food source," a soldier named Gleb answered. "Remember, men, we are not deserters. We were the only survivors of a battle, looking for our units. Same story whether it is the army we meet, or we run into a farm or a village."

They were without a commander. They didn't know where they were or where they should go. They lacked the manpower, the desire, or the weapons to make an effective front against the Germans, so they wandered in the woods, focusing on survival.

Two days later, they happened upon a village.

"Ah, women," Gleb sighed, "I need that more than food or a decent bed. I wonder where I can find one to do her patriotic duty."

Sasha felt punched in the stomach. That's what Valentina had been pressured to do, against her will. With the shifting of the front line, any woman could find herself with the fruit of the enemy in her womb, to suffer the cruel fate of the young woman on the barn door. He could not contemplate pleasuring himself at the risk of such terrible consequences to the young woman. Nevertheless, he was pleased they found a shop with a good supply of vodka, and he soused himself as he had not since the train from Nakhodka.

England 1944

One morning as Valentina arrived at the hospital, she was told she would be in the operating theater. She scrubbed herself as she had been instructed and donned the mask and gown provided. Etienne, Pascal, and Giselle were all doing the same.

Pascal took the lead in removing a bullet from a soldier's arm. It was a self-inflicted wound. He gruffly barked out orders for the others. "Knife." "No! Over here. Can't you see what I need?" "Wake up! You're supposed to be helping me. Injection." Although the whole operation took less than an hour, Valentina felt bruised by his abrasiveness before it was done.

Immediately after, they had a leg amputation. Again, Pascal took the lead, acting as if the nurses were working against him instead of with him. Valentina knew she would dread surgery days. They had a brief rest, a bite to eat, and they scrubbed up again to operate on a soldier with a crushed skull. Etienne took the lead this time. Even though they were tired and the surgery both delicate and long, he respectfully made his requests. "Scalpel, please. Thanks. Tongs. Thanks. Put pressure here with clean gauze." On it went, but his politeness and efficiency made her feel a part of a valued team doing something essential. She would have feared for the soldier's life, but she knew Etienne had given him an excellent chance to recover.

"That was awesome. Thanks," she whispered to Etienne as they cleaned up.

"It was a privilege working with you," he said.

"Want to grab some beers with me?" Pascal asked, splashing clean water on his face and putting on his most charming smile. He directed his comment to Giselle.

"I'm dead. I need to rest."

"I need a woman," Pascal said. "Marie Yvette?"

Valentina shook her head. She had rebuffed his advances in Moscow, and she had no desire whatsoever to respond to them now. He held no attraction for her.

"You're back in surgery tomorrow. You need to keep your head clear," Etienne gave a gentle reminder.

"And I don't need you telling me what to do!" Pascal flung a towel down and stomped out.

The next day, Valentina was back in the ward. Monique joined her as they bicycled back to their barracks, "Wow! Did you hear what happened in surgery today? Pascal and Etienne were doing an appendectomy. Pascal was a bit drunk. He is such a sod. Anyway, he was chief doctor. Suddenly, Etienne says, 'You're botching it.' I guess Pascal dropped a clanger. 'I'm taking over,' Etienne says. This big kerfuffle broke out, and even though Etienne seems small compared to Pascal, he hit Pascal, and Pascal just dropped. Etienne continued with the surgery. We were cleaning up when Pascal revived, and he just pounced off."

Valentina didn't see Pascal again, nor did any rumors reach her about what had happened to him. She wasn't truly sorry since he had been so unpleasant. But then, he was a countryman, and now she was the only Russian on the team.

Valentina received notice that she was to report to 70 Grosvenor Street, W1. Any out-of-the-ordinary communication she received left her a little unnerved. What could it mean? She settled on the most formal of her wardrobe, the woolen trousers, jacket, and hat. She asked Monique, who knew London, how to find the place.

"Blimey, whatcha doin' there?"

"I don't know."

"Um. That's the OSS headquarters," Monique raised her eyebrows and gave Valentina directions.

Valentina now expertly pedaled off through the gray, drizzling day, her mind a flurry of questions. She presented her credentials and waited briefly before being escorted into a room. Shortly her mother entered, shut the door, and extended her arms for a hug. Valentina rushed into the embrace, savoring the moment of intimacy. Her mother began to talk, "Oh, my dear, my dear. Very shortly, an Allied invasion of France is going to occur. You will be sent in at that time. I do hope and pray that you will be safe. War is gruesome, and not only will you be in danger from combat, but also, you could be discovered as a spy, and who knows what would happen then. But your greatest danger will be after the war if you go back to Russia. You must not go back. Everyone who has been called back who served in espionage has been executed. I have a false ID and plan to emigrate to the United States. For this reason, I cannot keep your beautiful portrait. It might endanger you. It is in the folder, as well as a couple of IDs you can use if you also can emigrate to the United States. Do not carry these on you, and be careful how you store them. Their very possession could also endanger you. I do hope we meet again. Goodbye, my precious."

She kissed Valentina on the head and was out the door. Valentina managed to choke out, *"Ya tui lyublyu, Mamochka,"* just as the door closed.

Her mother quickly opened the door again, *"Ah, moya malen'kaya ptitsa. Ya tui lyublyu."*

Valentina had thought herself nervous when she came, but she wobbled on her ride back to the barracks, her mother's words playing over and over in her mind. "My Little Bird, I love you." She wondered if Mamochka knew that Papochka and Comrade Chirikov had been taken.

Western Russia 1944

Not feeling welcome in the village, nine of the soldiers moved out in a couple of days. They knew they were approaching the front as they saw new evidence of a recent battle. That night, a show of heavy shellfire lit up the whole sky as if it were attempting to tear the heavens wide open. Slender fingers of intense light pointed perfectly still toward a little cloud in the sky. All of a sudden, each light would start roving across the sky as if unleashed by some magical power until it lit upon a plane. It kept the plane bathed in its light until the ack-ack guns began spurting their tracer bullets at the hapless plane. Many planes tumbled like shot birds from the skies in a spiral of fire, but Sasha found himself cheering one that managed to escape until he heard the whistle of a falling bomb. A nearby tree exploded, sending spear-sharp splinters into the trench he and Volodya were hiding in. When the noise subsided, he whispered, "Volodya, you okay?" No answer. "Volodya! Volodya!" In horror, Sasha waited for another burst of light, which confirmed his fear. Volodya was pierced through. Sasha spent the rest of the night in shocked numbness.

As daylight came, he gingerly lifted his eyes over the top of the trench. He couldn't see any sign of the other men. The only soldiers nearby wore the mustard-colored uniforms of the Germans. He slunk back into the trench. At first, he avoided looking at Volodya's vacant eyes staring at him, at the tree branch which stuck out of his chest and the gush of dried blood around it. Volodya had been with him since Moscow. Another tie to his past had been severed. Finally, late in the day, Sasha allowed himself to rummage through Volodya's sack. He removed a couple of pieces of the boiled horsehide and stuffed them in his own pack. He couldn't bring himself to remove Volodya's boots even though they were substantially better than his own. When darkness fell, he crept to another trench, only to find Kirill's body there. Kirill was the only other soldier he had any kind of real friendship with.

Sasha moved on to yet another trench and hunched down. Maybe the Germans would just think they had killed them all and leave. He listened to the diminishing sounds of battle until it erupted into a volley of unintelligible gibberish. Wham! Something hit his helmet and bounced off. He crouched, ducking his head. Bang! Again he was hit. Any minute, any second, he would either know nothing or what death was all about. Splat! Right in his chest. This wasn't bullets. It was snowballs. He looked up to see a German laughing at him. The German picked up his gun and barked, *"Für Sie ist der Krieg vorbei!"* as he swung the gun in an upward motion. Sasha instantly understood, climbed out of the pit, and put his hands up. Several others, none of whom he knew, stood with hands on their heads, surrounded by only three Germans.

One German kept a gun trained on him, a second covered the other prisoners, and the third German yanked off Sasha's helmet, demonstrating that Sasha was to put his hands on his head. Then he patted Sasha's pockets, found some ammunition and some of the horsehide strips, which he immediately pocketed himself. He then went through Sasha's pack. Sasha was glad *War and Peace* had long since been depleted in supplying paper for crude cigarettes or fuel to get a recalcitrant fire going. He had heard that the Germans would shoot a Russian who looked like he could read or write. That could be just about all of them. They were not as illiterate as the Germans thought.

The Russians could probably overpower the Germans and only lose a couple of men. Sasha looked at the other prisoners. No one met his eyes. No one met anyone's eyes. Two of them were wounded. Silent tears coursed down the cheeks of one as the blood oozed between his gloved fingers. One of the Germans barked a command, and, in the international language of war, they marched and marched and marched. Hour after torturous hour. They came at last to some kind of station where one by one, they were taken before a German who spoke excellent Russian. He barked many questions at Sasha: "How many men are in your unit?" "How many tanks do you have?" "Do you have any maps? Letters from home? Diaries?" "What is the Russian plan to win this war? Did the men believe they could?" "What is your profession?" The questioner alternated between being very kind and then striking him with a truncheon. Sasha remembered being told to say that his profession was a cook or a farmer. That way, you would be useful to the Germans; but he was given no special consideration in spite of insisting he could cook.

For many days, they marched, some dropping in their tracks when they could no longer go on, other prisoners joining their ranks as the time passed. Their meager food consisted of an occasional crust of bread, or sometimes, hot water with a potato floating in it. Sasha had no chance to replace his boots or, more importantly, his socks, which were soaked alternately with sweat and melting snow. He worried about frostbite and trench foot. The German soldiers were not even taking care of their own feet.

The wounded soldiers received no medical attention. And despite the strictly enforced silence among the prisoners, one screamed in agony. A threatening gun silenced him the first few times, and then a bullet did the last time. The compassion Sasha felt was more of a relief that the poor guy didn't have to endure the pain any longer. He wondered if his future was so bleak that he would prefer a bullet to another day. They finally boarded a truck, which took them, shaking with cold, to a train. There were maybe fifty to seventy boxcars on the train, but each was so crowded that they couldn't lie down to sleep. Still, the crowded car offered little shared heat. The prisoners stomped their feet and tried to move their limbs in any way they could to generate a little warmth. Eventually, neither the cold, the hunger, nor the stench from the large latrine box could keep Sasha awake. At each train stop, the dead were thrown out, and more men crowded in. Sometimes they would hear the drone of a plane and then a zipping ping of bullets strafing the train. The screams and hollering of the men did nothing to stop the bullets. Some of the shots penetrated the boxcar, and more men died. More prisoners joined them along the way, all with the same wary eyes, sometimes with different uniforms.

The train chugged west and met spring on its crawl east. The warmer air eased their days and nights, but the stench from unclean bodies, human waste, and bodies beginning to decompose, became overpowering. For respite, they had only whatever diversion they could muster in their individual thoughts. The singing birds cheered Sasha's heart, but he did not know their dialects. These birds spoke a foreign tongue as surely as did the earth-bound men in this strange country. Sasha wondered if he would recognize any of them as the distant cousins of those birds he knew so well.

Finally, they arrived wherever they were going, and Sasha didn't know where he was. In Germany? Poland? Maybe still in German-occupied Russia, but he didn't think so. They had traveled too far. His life was safe—for the moment, but his future was not. Stalin had said, "There is no such thing as prisoners of war. Only traitors." If he ever got back to Russia, a bullet, hanging, or prison camp awaited him. Just like his parents, except he hadn't even left a son behind as proof that he had existed. If only he had planted his seed deep within Valentina, and she brought forth a sturdy boy. On dark nights she would sit and hold their little one, telling him of his father she had known in far off Kamchatka. She would tell him how beautiful it was there and how this hellish war had separated them and left only him as evidence of their love. She would show their child the pictures he had drawn and instill in him the urge to know the birds as his father had. Kamchatka would draw him like a powerful magnet until he came home to find his roots for himself. Valentina would read him Kennan's poetry and Kreshennikov's facts and that French guy's adventures. Maybe their child would be a pretty little girl like Valentina. No! A first child needed to be a boy. But even if it was a girl, she needed to know who her father was, what her roots were.

Salt Lake City 1948

Sasha glanced at Valentina, knowing he was deliberately torturing her, but she refused to meet his eyes, so he resumed his tale.

Germany 1944

When they arrived at some kind of camp encased with barbed-wires and gun-toting guards, initially, they were treated with a measure of humanity and allowed a shower. Albeit cold, it was the first time Sasha had been able to clean himself in ever so long. Then he had to put back on the same dirty, lice-infested clothes and wondered what the point was. He was herded out with the other prisoners, and through pantomime and translation, they all understood that they were to form lines. There were now a good number of women in the group. Sasha had been unaware that the numbers of female prisoners were growing, but they must have put all of the women in the same boxcars, probably a good move with the bestiality the men had been reduced to.

The noise of approaching vehicles caused the guards to snap into stiff poses. The prisoners looked at a string of large, sleek, black cars followed by trucks. As the automobiles stopped, drivers jumped out and opened the doors with a flourish. Portly, middle-aged, cigar-smoking men wearing leather breeches that went only to their knees climbed out. In a multilingual translation, Sasha came to understand that these men were to be their owners, and he thought of the picture of the men being driven like dumb beasts. He would die fighting before he would succumb to that.

The men brazenly stepped up to the captives and felt their wasted muscles and subjected the women to pinched breasts and buttocks, the self-important Germans obviously enjoying the women's distress at this indignity. They opened their mouths as if they were inspecting horses. The affront of it was too much for one man, who vociferously objected in a language Sasha did not understand. The crack of a bullet cut off his protest, and the rest of the prisoners cooperated with whatever the arrogant men subjected them to. One of the prospective owners took delight in the appearance of a full-breasted young woman who had obviously not seen the level of deprivation virtually all of the men and some of the women had suffered. He lewdly caressed her breast and then opened her mouth and turned away in visual disgust when her upper teeth revealed gold caps.

One man signaled at Sasha and indicated a truck he was to climb into. The truck was soon filled with men, and it drove them to a barbed-wire enclosure that had minimal barracks with wooden slabs to sleep on. The next morning, yet another boxcar transported them to work. After a couple of hours swinging heavy hammers, breaking large rocks into small ones for building a road, morning rations were delivered in a big oil drum filled with tea. This was accompanied by a dark brown bread which tasted good in spite of the inevitable sawdust.

Sometimes they would be loaded onto the train, then just sit there for an hour or more before departing. After hours of work in the warming sun, a lunchtime soup of water with some cabbage in it was served. A third meal composed of a soup with a couple of small cooked potatoes finished their meals for the day. These rations were better than any he'd had in the army before his capture. Imagining a child with Valentina filled the eternal days, distracted his grumbling stomach, and soothed his aching muscles. As he rhythmically swung the sledgehammer, the rock exploded in pieces, chips, and dust. The days and weeks passed-- how many had gone by? It was warmer now, late spring, maybe early summer. The birds he now knew, if not by name, at least by sight and sound. They answered his calls and came and sat near him. They spoke in dialects, just as the men babbled in English, Italian, German, Russian, Polish, and only God knew what else. Sasha made little effort to talk to the men. His dream world offered much more than the harsh reality.

But there had been no child. He had not lain with Valentina in Moscow, and it was obvious she was not in the last months of pregnancy from her visit to Kamchatka. She would marry some Frenchman, destroy his pictures so her husband would not imagine she was unfaithful even in thought, and his memory would go up with the smoke of his efforts, ashes to be scattered by uncaring winds. Valentina would soothe her children with French songs and words, never telling them of the wild man she had known and loved in Kamchatka. That was enough to make his heart break. Valentina would never know what became of him. She would never know when to shed a tear for him. Baba probably shed tears daily. She'd known he'd never come back. She'd never know when to stop shedding tears. Maybe if he ended up in a prison camp, he could one day make it home—probably too late to ever see Baba again, but maybe not too late to father a child and warn him to never chase after love into a war.

Salt Lake City 1948

After these final jabs, Sasha knew he had milked the issue of a child to its ultimate and fell silent, allowing Valentina to pick up her story.

England 1944

It seemed almost nightly that, just as Valentina fell exhausted into her bunk and had drifted into a troubled sleep, she would be jerked from her dream by a piercing siren. "Air raid! Air raid!" She rushed outside with the others. In the road, women carried howling children while they screamed at others, "Hurry!" "Move along!" "What! You didn't get your shoes? You're going to cut your feet to shreds."

One night, Valentina scooped a little boy into her arms whose mother carried a wailing baby and followed her down the stairs into the dusty, smelly underground shelter. The mothers tried to quiet and comfort their screaming offspring. Some babies quieted when put to the breast, but explosions rocked the shelter, and dust fell around them. Trying to comfort the little boy, Valentina realized she didn't know any of the little soothing songs or fingerplays in English. She heard Giselle saying to a young child, "One little, two little, three little Indians." Gretel crooned to a different child, "Jack and Jill went up the hill to fetch a pail of water." Eventually, the night quieted, many of the children slept, and they made their way out into a dusky twilight to see the building topping the shelter reduced to complete rubble. The nurses helped carry the sleeping children back to their homes, and some of them returned to bed while others quickly dressed for another day in the hospital.

Valentina passed an unexploded bomb in the roadway as she bicycled to the hospital. Though others called them duds, it didn't reassure her that they would not just inexplicably explode at some time later. She was always happier when she passed by again to see they had been removed.

Germany 1944

The Germans worked the men hard until their bodies became wasted, and newer, fresher prisoners replaced them. Then the skeletal prisoners going through the motions of work disappeared, to what fate no one knew. One day Sasha was not taken out with the work gang. He feared a bullet would be his fate; but he was surprised when he and the other barely mobile skeletons were walked to yet another train and then taken to a truck, and after driving for some hours, taken to a brick building with a now-familiar high fence around it. Each of these buildings had a name written on it, but in the Roman alphabet, he could not read. They stopped at one building, and something was yelled that Sasha understood as English, and one group of soldiers got out. The soldiers lounging inside that fence appeared well-fed. They were smoking and jovial. Were they going to get special treatment? Why had they been brought here? At another building, another group of prisoners got out. Prisoners inside that compound kicked a ball around. This did not look like a prison, except for the fences. Why treat prisoners so well? He did not understand it, but nothing about war made any sense. At the next compound, no men lolled around in the bright sunshine. He was ordered in Russian to get out. Inside it was dark and the men listlessly laid on slabs. One of the other skeletons asked, "Why are the Russians treated so rotten?"

"You haven't heard? Stalin, our fearless leader, has declared, 'There are no Russian prisoners of war. The Russian soldier fights on until death. If he chooses to become a prisoner, he is automatically excluded from the Russian community,'" Bitterness dripped from his mocking of Stalin's speech.

"Do we work?" another new arrival asked.

"No. We are sent here because we are too weak to work," someone answered.

"What do we do?" the same man asked again.

"Wait to die of starvation." A different man answered.

"No food at all?" Apprehension was strong in the questioner's voice.

"Very little." A third man answered.

Sasha now understood the Germans had sent them here to die. They were not even worth wasting a bullet on. So they would die slowly, tortuously. The new arrivals soon learned that the English to their right would throw them foodstuffs and cigarettes over the fence, but a Russian daring to pick them up often met with the coveted bullet. Each day death diminished their numbers, but occupants of new trucks swelled their numbers to new highs, and Sasha yearned for the work of the rock mine. At least there, a man could die of fatigue.

"But why do the Germans treat the others so well and signal us out for this despicable treatment?" One of the men asked in bewilderment.

"It's something called Red Cross," One of the old-timers explained. "Each country is permitted to provide for their own prisoners of war. Since Russia doesn't have any, we don't exist."

"True enough. We won't exist soon."

Hunger gnawed. Sasha thought he had been hungry before. Now he knew real hunger. Each morning there were new dead. The barely mobile skeletons would remove the bodies to a hole dug in the ground. They watched for the early afternoon when the guards grew drowsy and bored; the Russians who could move would parade on the ground just to feel the warmth of the sun. There were no trees they could strip the bark from or pull the new spring leaves from to eat as they had in times of hunger in the past, but there was the hope that the Italians on one side would pitch some potatoes to them or the English on the other side would risk attaching a tin can to a pole and push the food-laden can through the double-wire fence. When that hope was exhausted, they would sneak to the dump, carefully scraping out the remnants of each can with their index fingers and then licking whatever was found from the bony digit. Sometimes even a German would call "Kriegie" or "Cossack" and toss one of the Red Army prisoners a piece of bread or a morsel of potato.

One day a group of soldiers entered bearing cauldrons of steaming food and trays of meats and breads. One smartly dressed soldier in a German uniform raised his hand in a clenched fist salute: *"Zdrasti, tovarich!"* (Greetings, comrade.) Some of the skeletons returned a half-hearted salute.

"Eat up," the soldier indicated the food. The salutes became more numerous and sharper. The soldiers cautiously eased toward the food, wondering what kind of trick this was. The soldiers stood with their hands crossed behind their backs, allowing the skeletons to fill and refill their plates until they had eaten themselves into a stupor. "Your day of liberation has come. Anyone willing to put on this uniform and fight to conquer the Allies will have the German backing to invade Russia and free our countrymen from the oppression of Stalin and the Soviet Union. We will bring freedom to our own land under the inspired guidance of General Vlasov."

The food spoke louder than the words. Every skeleton that could move was soon dressed in the uniform of the Russian Liberation Army. Only a handful of the men seemed hesitant to join the traitorous German Army. Others stepped right up, Sasha included. It was salvation. It was life. Already a traitor's reward awaited him in Russia. By joining the Germans, he would guarantee that should Germany win, he might make it back to Kamchatka, might see Baba again, might, by some miracle, track Valentina down after this war. These Germans were offering hope. It was more than Russia was willing to do. It was no surprise the men turned against the Motherland, which had thoroughly abandoned them.

Sasha's stomach rebelled against the food, but his hope was nourished and healed. As the train chugged off with skeleton soldiers newly decked out in the Russian Liberation Army's uniform, Sasha realized they were going west, not east.

"I thought we were going to liberate Russia," he said to one of the commanders.

"We have to fight for Germany in the west first. Once we crush the allies, we'll have the manpower and lack of threat to attack Russia. We will be victorious. We will rule the world."

Sasha let others spin their imperialistic dreams. He was not going home. He would not be able to slip away from this army once on Russian soil. More bullets, more walks, more wounded, more dead. How had he not realized that? But still, a bullet was a more merciful death than starvation.

"Where are we headed?"

"France."

France. That was where Valentina had gone. Would a miracle enable him to see her? What god could he favor to make it happen? Surely it would happen. *Sudba* had brought him here. *Sudba* would be good to him.

Sasha was part of the 243rd division made up of the emaciated Russian recruits, old German men over 60, and youths of 14 to 16. They did not seem a fearsome army who could conquer the world. It was obvious the Germans disdained the Russians, calling them Hiwis. Sasha did not know what that meant, but the sneer that went with it made the insult obvious. He and the other Russian vagabonds didn't care. They had food. Only the Germans were issued arms. "Hilter declared not the Slav, not the Czech, not the Ukrainian, and not the Cossack was to be trusted," one of the Germans who spoke Russian explained. Sasha did not mind helping behind the scenes, running supplies back and forth. The Germans spouted patriotic rhetoric frequently translated for them that was supposed to inflame them to do their duty, but only the food spoke Sasha's language.

One day their German captain announced, "Worthless swine, a gun for you. America. England. Come. Pow! Pow!" So, the long-awaited invasion of France by the Allies was going to happen.

England, D-Day 1944

They had been intense anticipation for weeks when the word finally came that tomorrow was D-day. Operation Overlord was on. There was an intoxicating thrill at finally having arrived at the point that all of the preparation had been building towards. "I'm so excited. I can't get to the loo in time!" Gretel grabbed her helmet and used it as a bedpan. In the darkness of early morning, broken only by lantern light, Valentina's fingers trembled as she tried to button the six buttons on the woolen trousers even the women had to wear. Their dress was to disguise the fact that they were women. That might work for a few minutes from a distance. She wasn't quite sure what protection it afforded them.

They clambered aboard lorries. The heavy, olive drab canvas sides provided little warmth in the unusually cold June morning but obscured their view of the English countryside. Chattering like a gaggle of geese, the nurses huddled together, gathering what warmth they could from each other. When the lorry lurched to a stop, they jumped off one at a time and then turned to catch their duffel bag as their mates lowered them.

Valentina was unable to stifle her open-mouthed amazement at the uncountable ships all moored in the harbor. Each one had an odd balloon anchored over it, adding its flapping to the incessant waves, the continual roar of the lorries rumbling past, and the nervous excitement in the voices all around. Each time Valentina felt she had a grasp of this operation's awesome bigness, something happened that multiplied its size exponentially. She, a relative nobody, felt she was participating in something of infinite importance. Surely this was one of those moments the annals of time would record as significant.

"Guess what! Now that we are here, we're not going anywhere." Valentina turned at Hélène's voice. "The weather is so bad; the invasion has been postponed." Valentina picked up her pack and trooped after the others into an ancient stone building, feeling like they too had been inflated like the balloons over the ships but had just been popped. "Welcome to Tortworth Castle," Annick greeted them. "It's as warm as the stones it is built from."

"At least we can build a fire, and it won't burn."

The next morning, again dressed in full battle gear, with red crosses on white armbands identifying them as medical, the nurses loaded into yet another lorry, and were transported down to the edge of the water. Amphibious loaders called "ducks" waited to carry them out to the ships. The nurses lined up, each listening for her name to be called as part of the 128th evacuation hospital. Operation Neptune, the code name for the medical side of the invasion, was underway. Valentina shouldered her heavy pack on her back and grasped the net hanging down from the ship with both hands. The net continually shook as others climbed at her side, above and then below. Valentina steeled herself to keep climbing. Up, up, up until two hands finally reached over the top and pulled her over the railing. Once she was settled on board, she glanced across the ocean at the myriad of ships. It truly looked like a bridge of ships which one could, with giant hops, leap from one to the other all of the way to France. She wondered how they could sail without bumping into each other.

"What are the balloons for?" She heard someone ask. She paused to listen to the answer, glancing up at the tethered balloon. From this angle, it looked like she looked up at a monstrous gray fish suspended in the air.

"They are all painted blue on top. Supposedly, hopefully, to a plane flying over, the ships just appear as unending water."

So far, Valentina had escaped the ravages of the planes. If only it would continue! She could hear a constant drone of planes which suggested the skies were as full as the ocean, but they were completely obscured from view by the balloons. It was cloudy enough that they probably couldn't see them even without the balloons, which meant the enemy planes would not be able to see them either.

A strong gale lifted the boat on a large wave and then dropped it into a deep trough. Her stomach was just out of step with the ship. Rushing to the railing, she pitched her breakfast over the side. All the others did the same, and there was continual pushing to get a place at the railing for their turn to feed the fish.

All morning the bridge of ships labored toward France. What was left of their holiday spirit evaporated when the piercing scream of a bomb flew into an adjacent ship. It burst into flames, and horror seized Valentina as she watched the soldiers on that ship fall into the water as the ship sank. It was war they were going to, not a party, and the seriousness of the specter gripped her. The explosions increased, and the air became thick with smoke, screams, bursts, and blasts. What had seemed an invincible armada suddenly became so vulnerable. They expected them to go in under these conditions? Evidently, they did. Would any survive?

Instructions were yelled at them. "Make your packs lighter. Take out everything you will not need." Valentina went through her pack, itemizing the contents, reading labels, and trying to imagine their use. Three sets of underwear, two skirts, two blouses, a change of shoes, three pairs of socks, a nurse's cape, a helmet, boots, gloves, a rifle, a pistol, three different kinds of knives she had been taught were a trench, jump, and hunting knife, a machete, a cartridge belt, two bandoliers, two cans of machine-gun ammo, a round of .45 ammo, a Hawkins mine capable of blowing the track off of a tank, according to the label, four blocks of TNT, one entrenching tool, two blasting caps, three first-aid kits, two morphine needles, a gas mask, a canteen of water, three days' supply of K rations, two days supply of D rations, hard tropical chocolate bars, six fragmentation grenades, one Gammon grenade, two smoke grenades, one orange and one red, an orange panel, a blanket, a raincoat, two cartons of cigarettes, and a few other odds and ends. She couldn't imagine using much of it. She removed everything that was a duplicate or she didn't know how to use.

"Disembark, disembark!" And it was her turn to climb down the swinging net. She felt like they were target practice in a circus arcade. Bullets popped and burped around them. Suddenly Giselle fell from beside her. Valentina couldn't look, she couldn't think, she could only move mechanically to the calls, "Move, Move." Finally, her foot hit a bouncing amphibious duck as it rose on the crest of a wave, aware that Monique had missed it as it fell into a trough. 'Don't think, don't think," she commanded herself. She knew she would be paralyzed by fear if she let her thoughts process what was going on around her. After she had a firm hold on the railing, she glanced in the water and saw it was full of jellyfish about the size of a hand. In the center of each of them was a green design exactly like a four-leaf clover. Other sights quickly pushed the jellyfish aside. Bodies of dead soldiers bobbed up and down like corks, submerging and reappearing. Empty life rafts and soldiers' packs and ration boxes floated in the water, with sightless eyes looking up, bodies face down, arms, legs. Unable to stand the sight, Valentina looked back at a huge cargo ship. Its hull opened like closet doors and belched forth jeeps, lorries, tanks, and cannons. The duck came to a stop, "Jump off," they were commanded. At the slightest hesitation, a man pointing a gun at them yelled, "Move, or I'll shoot!" Valentina jumped into water mid-way up her chest with the others, speeding their descent as a bullet from the shore toppled one of them. Valentina struggled in the water with her heavy pack. Finally, she shrugged it off, keeping only the satchel with one change of clothes, a day's worth of rations, the IDs her mother had given her, and the portrait Alex had drawn. Gaining her foothold, she turned to see the Duck move back out towards another ship, just as an explosion demolished it in smoke and flame.

France 1944

Another train ride, more marching, and they were on a beach called Dunkirk. From behind what the Germans called a pillbox, Sasha could see the unending stream of ships, thick as mosquitoes on a summer eve in Kamchatka, approaching the French shore. The sheer numbers were staggering, but each was filled with untold numbers of soldiers and equipment with the power to kill and destroy. That was not to mention the sky full of planes overhead strafing the beach to minimize the German attack when these allied ships made their landing. It seemed impossible that the Germans still had enough men and equipment to repulse such an invasion. In a pep talk before they took up their position, a blustering German general had his speech translated into Russian, "I want all my soldiers to fight hard and without pity. The battle must be fought with brutality, and all resistance must be broken in a wave of terror. The enemy must be beaten, now or never! Thus lives our Germany! Soldiers of the Western Front! Your great hour has come. We gamble everything! You carry with you the holy obligation to give all to achieve superhuman objectives for our Fatherland and our Fuhrer." It didn't have any power to motivate Sasha.

Soon their hiding position was strafed by planes overhead. The ships drew nearer the shore. Land mines exploded. The din, the bursts of fire, the sight of the planes, and the ubiquitous boats both exhilarated and terrified Sasha. It appeared to him that maybe he was fighting on the wrong side. How could the depleted, rabble soldiers of the Germans conquer this awesome enemy? Previously, the Germans had been his enemy; now, he was fighting with them against the new enemy: England and America. Who knew, but what he would be fighting for them next? Would the Germans then again be his enemy?

Once the ships had pulled in as close as possible, men began to climb overboard on rope ladders. Jeeps and tanks drove their way onto the beach. The German counter-offensive began in earnest. "Fire!" Sasha heard the command. His finger clicked on the trigger of the German Rapid-firing burp gun. Again and again the ripping b-r-r-p of the shots rang in his ears, until the thought struck him that Valentina could actually be climbing down the side of one of those ships. Now his gun aimed high or too low to hit anyone. He would give his life before he would take hers.

*****

Now that she was here, what was she to do? Valentina followed others as they ran further inland, wondering where safety might be in the beehive of bullets buzzing all around. She didn't know if she had seconds or moments to live, as someone to her left and then to her right would fall. Would any of them survive to fight this war? She ran across the littered shore, dodging crumpled bodies, shot-off arms, a leg, a disembodied head, pictures of sweethearts, scattered apples, tins of Spam, not knowing her destination. She passed a tank burned to dull gray and still smoking. A single shell turned what the soldiers called half-tracks carrying office equipment into shambles, their interiors still holding smashed typewriters, telephones, office files. Two boats stacked on top of each other, with sides caved in, and their suspension doors knocked off, blocked her path. Abandoned rolls of barbed-wire and smashed bulldozers, and big stacks of thrown-away lifebelts littered her path. Valentina's mind cataloged the random items as she continued her dash inland: socks, shoe polish, sewing kits, diaries, Bibles, and hand grenades. There were toothbrushes and razors and snapshots of families back home staring up at her from the sand. She tripped over pocket-books, metal mirrors, extra trousers, and bloody, abandoned shoes. She stepped around broken-handled stoves, portable radios smashed almost beyond recognition, and mine detectors twisted and ruined.

"Climb aboard, climb aboard." A duck that had come up on land paused to take up those fleeing across the dreadful shore. Hands reached down and pulled her up. When crowded to capacity, the duck dashed off, running roughshod over anything in its way. It bounced over a burned jeep, tipping dangerously to the side, and crashed on. Valentina clung to the railing, thinking she might live to be of some use if she managed not to get bounced off this crazy, careening vehicle.

At last, they seemed to be beyond the shooting, cannons, and explosions peppering the shore, and for a moment, Valentina breathed easier. She didn't know where the duck driver was taking them, but it hardly mattered. Anywhere was better than where they had been. The duck climbed a high bluff and halted before a row of white tents with the familiar Red Cross designating them as medical. Evidently, the duck's course hadn't been as random as it seemed. The soldiers jumped out and then reached up and lifted down the nurses dressed in their manly trousers. Among the whole duck load, only two of the soldiers still had their duffel bags, and a few others clutched satchels or had them strapped to their backs.

Valentina took a moment to glance around. She looked up and down the littered beach and far out to sea. The gigantic collection of ships went on as far as the eye could see. Those that had disgorged their cargo tried to move out of the way to allow other ships in. Cannons boomed, explosions flashed, and the nightmare continued. Not far from where she stood, she could see a barbed-wire enclosure. American soldiers, called "doughboys," sporting tommy guns, herded what must be German soldiers into the prison cage.

"Come, you've got to get out of those clothes. The water was full of gas. Someone strikes a match, and you'll be a living torch," someone called to them. She followed the other women into one tent while the men went into another.

"I lost my pack in the water. I have no other clothing," echoed all around.

"No matter. There is some here."

Redressed, Valentina strapped her satchel to her back with her few personal items and immediately began bandaging wounded soldiers after the surgeons did what they could to repair the torn and shredded bodies. She offered what words of comfort she could as she wrapped each limb, chest, or head, her heart revolting at the idea that not two hours before, every one of these young men had been whole, with his life full before him, filled with excitement at the prospect of going to war. So many already were out of the war. Each tent held 300 patients, and she had seen dozens of tents. That didn't even count the dead or injured still on the beaches. It just sickened her. Such a senseless waste of human life. Her brothers and Mikel had been slaughtered for the same useless cause.

They worked until darkness enfolded them. "Follow us," nurses who seemed to know where they were to sleep told Valentina. She tried, but immediately lost them in the dark. "Where am I supposed to sleep? I can't find you."

"We're over here, in a foxhole." The answer drifted back to her. She walked in its direction "What foxhole? I don't see anything."

"We're here by the fence."

She altered her direction to follow the sound and bumped into a pup tent. "Anyone here?" she asked.

No answer. "I found a pup tent. Goodnight." She called to the others and crawled in and fell into an exhausted sleep.

*****

When, finally, no more ships disgorged their contents onto the gory, littered beach, Sasha fell back with the ragtag German division. They counted their losses as they ate a meager meal of bread and tea. The Germans took the guns and ammunition from the Russians as abruptly as they had been given. Sasha fell into his tent, grateful he would not be asked to shoot others tomorrow but wondering what his new task would be.

The next morning, he followed a Panther tank preceding his division along a narrow road canopied by trees on either side, growing in the hedgerows. After issuing him an ax, the Germans pantomimed chopping down the shrubs and trees on either side of the entrance into the field the hedgerow surrounded. German soldiers stood around and smoked while the Russians labored. Sasha felt the Germans valued the Russians just slightly above the Jews. Once the entrance permitted the Panther to enter, it slipped through, followed by three howitzers. Sasha and the other Russians swept away the tracks and the freshly chopped trunks. When they too entered the field, bushes completely covered the tank and howitzers. Sasha found a spot to hide with his newly reissued gun, waiting with the others for an unsuspecting enemy to enter. The day seemed calm and peaceful. Sasha could hear bird songs. He strained to get a glimpse of the birds and wished he had been issued binoculars. He looked around for an officer, who might have a pair, but they were all so well hidden, he couldn't tell who did and didn't have them.

It was the next day before they heard the sounds of an unfortunate unit approaching. Quiet as a wolverine waiting for its prey, their unit made no move until the field was full of soldiers and a tank had rumbled into the field. Suddenly, the German Panther tank, the howitzers, and the guns let loose at once. Howls, screams, and blasts filled the air until the dissipating smoke revealed that all of the Allies lay motionless in the field. The Allied soldiers had managed to disable one of the howitzers with a blast from their own tank, but only two of the old Germans had caught a bullet. All of the Russians miraculously survived. They hadn't shot much, thereby not calling attention to their hiding places. The tank blasted the trees and shrubs on the side where it had hidden and bumped back to the narrow road. It trundled along some time with soldiers investigating intact fields for evidence of the enemy. The whole ruse was repeated days later, in another field many kilometers down the road.

11

Sasha is Captured by the Americans

France, 1944

After a few days, in a reassignment to the 42nd field hospital, Valentina saw Etienne, Hélène, Dietrich, Gretel, and others of her espionage/medical team who had survived the horrific landing. The positions of Monique and Giselle were filled by people she had never met. The work remained the same: cleaning mud-caked wounds, dusting them with sulfa powder, applying airtight bandages to sucking chest wounds, and helping to set and splint broken and torn limbs. While emptying the urinals and bedpans, she discovered one soldier dead in his bed. The IV had run out on another. As quick as she could, she met their needs to the extent possible or alerted others if the needs were beyond her training. Outside the crowded tent, wounded men waited for surgery on litters on the ground near the entrance to the OR tent. Medics brought in one badly wounded GI whom the Germans had diabolically booby-trapped. He had lain motionless for 72 hours in the combat zone, fighting pain, delirium, and unconsciousness so that he could tell his rescuers about the bomb. Finally, medics discovered him and, on his warning, disconnected the booby trap before administering first aid.

Valentina toiled, exhausted, with the others, trying to stem this endless flood of wounded young men, catching only moments of sleep intermittently, until one day, Etienne said, "Tomorrow, we move out. Get some sleep tonight. There is water in the stream. You can clean yourself up a bit. Be ready to head out at 0600. Wear this uniform." Valentina picked up the newly issued pack. It looked to be recycled, but the differences indicated French origins as opposed to English or American.

She followed instructions, cleaning herself as best she could and tried to erase the exhaustion with some sleep. She put on the blue striped dress in her bag, with its white pinafore and cute little white cap. She took only the IDs her mother had issued her and the portrait Alex had drawn as personal items. Dawn lighted the sky as her medical/espionage team mounted their captured German battle cars or ambulances. The now-familiar, large Red Cross designating it as medical transport marked the ambulances. These vehicles were definitely older than the ones brought by the Americans and English, and the driver sat on the left side of the vehicle as opposed to the English right. Valentina's fearful heart choked her breathing. She feared they might hit a mine as they bounced down the torn-up roads. They were behind enemy lines on a spy mission, under the guise of medical personnel.

They passed an old man trying to drag a plow behind him while an old woman held the handles and plowed. A couple of children followed behind, one dropping seeds in the furrow and the other covering them. The ambulance traveled through dark green tunnels. Trees planted at the edge of the fields like fences met in an overhead canopy. Their driver called them hedgerows.

Glad when the ambulance finally jerked to a stop after the long, dusty, bumpy trip, Valentina climbed out and stretched before collecting her new bag of French issue clothing. Then she followed the others into the tent, also with the Red Cross on it. The familiar odors of blood, rotting flesh, and quinine, mixed with the screams and moans of the suffering, assaulted their noses and ears. The equally familiar calls, "Please nurse, some water." "Why me, why me?" "Hey, babe, over here." only in French and unintelligible German instead of English, fell on their ears. Valentina decided that injured soldiers of whatever nationality were all the same—wanting comfort, wanting respite from the pain, wanting to go home, wanting this nightmare to be over.

The astonished German and French doctors and nurses serving in the tent hospital were relieved at the unexpected news that they merited some R and R in Paris, happily gathered their things. They excitedly chattered as they boarded the battle cars and ambulances, totally unsuspecting that their R and R would be in a prison camp, perhaps in the environs of a soon-to-be liberated Paris. They might even be pressed into medical service with the other prisoners after they had been thoroughly interrogated. Their future promised to be more secure than the future of the Allied team replacing them.

Valentina fell into her routine, meeting the injured soldiers' needs, changing dressings, uttering soothing words, replacing drip bottles. No one seemed to question her team's French or German. Hours passed and fatigue began to take a toll when Dietrich pushed a bucket into her hands. "See if you can find a stream or other water source."

Glad for the chance to relieve herself, she went into the cluster of trees behind the tents to seek some privacy in the fading light. The smell of death assaulted her nose much more forcefully than in the hospital tent. She relieved herself and started to search for a stream when she came upon a boy's slightly bloated body about nine years old. What caused his death? She knelt and did a quick examination. No bullet hole tore his body, no trace of blood bore witness to violence, just tell-tale needle marks in the crook of his arm. She stood, suddenly sickened by what she feared had happened, and spied a young girl of maybe eight, a few paces away, her sweater pushed up to her upper arm, revealing the same needle mark. Biting her knuckle, Valenina glanced around and did a quick count of six more children. She rushed back into the surgery, "Etienne, can you come with me?"

He didn't question the importance of her mission, perhaps because of the urgency in her voice, possibly because of her totally white, blood-drained face. Etienne turned over the bandage he was wrapping around a wound to Hélène and followed after Valentina. She led him into the trees to the first child she had come upon. Etienne examined the child as she had, and when he stood, she gestured to another, "There are many more here."

Etienne carefully examined each one. "*O, mon Dieu!*" he said. "*Les diables!* It would have been better for them if a millstone had been hung around their necks and they were drowned in the depths of the sea."

Sometimes he said the strangest things. "The children?"

"No, the devils who did this to the children. Some people seem to think they will never have to account for the crimes they commit in a war. They have no conception of the hell they are creating for themselves. Bleeding a child to death to use their blood for transfusions is not acceptable. I am going to find the priest in the village."

"The priest? Why? Won't the villagers come after us in retaliation?"

"We have to take that chance. What if it were your brother or sister or child? Get some clean sheets and wrap each child in one. Wash their faces, make them look as presentable as possible. Get the others to help you."

Etienne returned with the priest and a cart before they had finished their gruesome work. Eventually, they collected twenty children to be transported to the church. Etienne organized three nurses to accompany him, including Valentina. They placed the bodies on the cart, and Etienne led the bony cart horse back to the church. The priest rang the bell, calling the villagers, as Etienne and the nurses laid out the little bodies in the cemetery behind the church. Once they finished, they entered the cold, stone church, now virtually full. There were a few old men, many anxious women, and a scattering of children. A question marked the face of each of them as to the meaning of this gathering. The nurses sat on the wooden benches at the back of the church, and Etienne went up front with the priest. The priest rose, made the sign of the cross over his body, and said, "The good doctor has news for us." Etienne rose and spoke to the thin, darkly-wrapped villagers with sunken eyes.

Valentina shuddered, knowing the news wouldn't be anything the villagers would want to hear. It was bad news, but necessary. Their hearts must already be breaking, wondering where their children had gone.

"Mes cheres, fr..." Etienne began and hesitated a long time before continuing, his Adam's apple bobbing up and down as he obviously sought control of his emotions, *"Meres et peres."*

My dear fr... What had he been about to call them? Not friends, because he wasn't speaking English. Hmm.

"We just replaced the doctors and nurses at the military hospital and learned some most disheartening news. We learned the whereabouts of many of the missing children from this village, and we have brought them back to you." Only the break in his voice and the muffled sob changed the momentary look of joy on the villager's faces, which would have undoubtedly erupted into a cheer, into a look of horror. "The doctors before us committed a gross war crime against you, your children, and this village. They used the blood from your children's veins to replace the blood lost by the injured soldiers, and did not stop until they drained them dry." Again his voice broke and the sobs and cries of the villagers filled the silence. After a moment, he spoke again. "It is scant comfort to you, but this crime will not go unpunished nor will it be repeated as along as we are here."

Valentina breathed a mite easier, certain now that the villagers would not retaliate against them.

"As long as my team is in the service at the hospital established here, you are all welcome to come for whatever medical needs you have, and we will do our utmost to assist you in any way possible. Further, if you do not find your child among those brought in, please notify us, and we will join with you in a search. It is with my greatest regrets that I have to be the messenger of such sorrowful news."

He sat down, unashamedly wiping tears from his eyes.

The priest spoke briefly about the nobility of this good doctor and then led the villagers out to the bodies. Etienne stayed right with them, offering words of comfort and holding sobbing parents. *"Mon Alain."* *"Marie, voila ton Denis."* "Pascal, has anyone found my Pascal?" *"Ma belle Antoinette!"* and shrieks and cries tore the air and their hearts. At the end, all of the children brought in had been identified and taken to be prepared for burial. Three children remained missing. Etienne told the parents to come to the hospital at daybreak, and he would provide help for them in their search, a search that would continue until all were accounted for.

Two days later, Etienne, Valentina, and as many of the other medical personnel who could be spared attended the funeral. Etienne spoke with great fervency about how a loving God had welcomed their little ones into his arms, and they were at peace, and he promised them they would all be reunited with their precious children. Valentina was having a hard time buying this. If such a loving God existed, why hadn't he stopped the Germans from doing this horrible deed? Was he powerless? Did he not care? Etienne spoke with such conviction that she couldn't doubt that he believed it. How could he? He didn't seem to be a naïve man.

*****

Sent ahead on a scouting mission to discover yet another field where they might trap the Allies, Sasha heard a moan coming from a tree. Not being one of the bird calls his ears were trained to hear, his eyes did not begin to search for a bird. This sounded like a human in agony. The moan came again. Sasha looked around for a parachutist. Many times he had seen these unlucky airmen snagged by one of the trees in descent from the silver birds. The unfortunate men hung there, either killed in the fall or helpless until a friend cut his strings or an enemy cut him down with machine gun fire. Birds pecked at bodies left hanging in the trees until little remained unless soldiers of the same army happened by and rescued the body.

Sasha did not see anyone hanging from a tree, but a yellow parachute billowed from the branches of a tree in the field to his left where the moan came from. Moving closer to the tree, Sasha called and heard the agonized voice again. He looked up and could see a boot. Sasha looked for a way to climb the tree, knowing the Germans would be on them shortly. By extending his gun as high as he could reach, Sasha looped the strap of his gun over a sturdy stub of a branch. He climbed into the tree by pulling himself up the gun stock. Before assisting the soldier, he quickly found the strings tethering the parachute and cut them. The breeze caught the filmy material and carried it away. Sasha breathed much easier. Germans riddled trees with machine gun fire if they saw a parachute blowing from a tree. Those random bullets most certainly would find their mark, and the unlucky parachutist who had survived the fall would become the victim of enemy fire.

Moments later, the German unit passed below, unaware that their scout was hiding in the branches above them. Sasha held his breath, hoping the soldier would not moan until the Germans had passed far beyond. He did moan quietly, but the hustle, bustle of the marching unit completely masked the noise. Once the last of the Germans had passed, Sasha turned his attention to the soldier. One trapped arm fell in an unnatural position, most assuredly broken. Sasha freed the soldier's limbs, and holding to the parachute straps, lowered him down as far as he could reach, and then dropped him, not knowing if the soldier were conscious enough to break his fall. Apparently, he was. He began a roll, but screamed in pain. Sasha dropped down from the tree. The soldier now lay unconscious. His uniform bore the flag with white stars on a blue field and red and white stripes, which he knew to be the American flag. Sasha originally thought the soldier had black skin but then realized his face was blackened. Sasha straightened the soldier's limbs, but he suspected that the left shoulder was dislocated and the right arm broken. Sasha shook the canteen strapped to the soldier's chest. Sounded full. He smelled it. Water. The soldier could certainly use something stronger than that in his condition. A Russian with any choice carried vodka.

Waiting for the soldier to revive, Sasha helped himself to some wafers and a tinned meat from the soldier's pack. The soldier stirred, and Sasha held his head and gave him a drink. He chose to conserve the water rather than wipe the blackened face. Sasha then offered him some of the tinned meat from his pack, but the soldier shook his head and said something. The soldier kept looking at him expectantly and said something again. Not knowing what the soldier wanted, Sasha offered him a wafer. When the soldier did not reach for it, Sasha held it to the soldier's mouth. He took a couple of bites and shook his head and said the word again. Sasha dove into the pack and held up a different tin. Again the soldier shook his head, then Sasha pulled out another, and the soldier vigorously nodded. Sasha opened the tin and found a golden half globe of fruit in liquid. He used a spoon in the soldier's mess kit and cut it into smaller pieces. Each time he offered the soldier another bite, the soldier ate it, and Sasha understood the dehydrated soldier sought the moisture and sugar of the fruit.

For two days, the soldier and Sasha hid in the overgrowth. Sasha tucked a white handkerchief from the American's pack into his pocket. He took up a point of observation if he heard tanks or soldiers on the canopied road. As soon as he identified them as German, Sasha crawled deeper into the thicket of bushes. Two days later, a tank with a star on it instead of the German cross, followed by troops, came down the road. Sasha tied the handkerchief to a branch he had selected for this purpose, stuck it out, and then flattened himself to the ground. He knew the Germans would shoot first and then investigate later. He didn't know what the Allies would do with someone who sought to surrender.

The tank stopped, and he heard a command barked. Realizing he might be giving his life for the American, Sasha crawled from his hiding place and stepped into the clearing, hands up. All of the soldiers near him trained their guns on him. Sasha yelled, pointing with his head, "Amerikana, ja." The soldier with the gun on him looked puzzled. Sasha repeated himself. These soldiers carried a flag with a red leaf on a white field. Sasha didn't know which Allied country it represented. The soldier yelled something into the bushes in English. Sasha heard a faint response from the injured soldier. One soldier kept his gun trained on Sasha while two others crashed through the bushes in search of the faint voice. Soon they were calling back and forth, and a flurry of activity began. Marched into the field at gunpoint, Sasha saw a man with a red cross on a white armband going over the American. The American bit his lip, eyes filled with tears as he tried to cope with the pain. The medic positioned the American on his stomach and requested assistance from a couple of others. They pushed and pulled on the American's shoulder. He gave a scream and then painful grunt followed by a groan of relief as Sasha heard the shoulder snap back into place. The medic then set about examining the splint Sasha had made, while another soldier started to tie Sasha's hands. The American said something, and the soldier dropped the rope. A huge soldier pulled a device out of his backpack and began tapping a code on a device in transmitting some kind message to some other place. While the medic attended the American, other soldiers held a quick conference. The tank and all but one of the soldiers then headed on down the road.

The soldier who stayed behind sat against a tree smoking, his gun at his side. He offered Sasha a cigarette, and they smoked companionably. Being in the hands of the Allies might not be so bad. His American conversed with the soldier. Eventually, they heard the whine of an engine. The soldier jumped to attention. He moved out of the hedgerow and flagged down a two-seated, roofless vehicle like Sasha had seen come off the ships in Dunkirk. They strapped Sasha's American to the back bench so he couldn't roll off, and motioned for Sasha to sit on the floor in front of him. The vehicle sped back in the direction from which it had come, Sasha's American occasionally wincing as they bounced over the road. Eventually they arrived at a sizable house. They carted his American away on a stretcher and...

Salt Lake City, 1948

Sasha paused in the recital as he noticed tears streaming down Bishop Bullock's face. After a moment, the bishop said, "You. You my Russian. You save me. I so grateful. I hug you?"

He stood and offered an embrace to Sasha, and Sasha walked awkwardly into it, trying to piece this unexpected news together. This was the very man he had rescued? It was not surprising they did not recognize each other. He had never seen the poor soldier standing, and, though he realized the soldier was tall, he didn't know how tall. The soldier's hair had been buzz cut, and his face was blackened. The soldier had been in such a delirium the entire time they were together, it wasn't surprising he had never formed a clear idea of Sasha's appearance.

"I sorry, I did not plan to stop you," Bishop Bullock said as he resumed his seat. "Our stories being the same, I had to thank you. Thank you, thank you. Where you go next?"

Sasha took a moment, realizing the unlikeliness of their meeting again, and feeling amazement that they had. It took him a moment to remember where he had left off.

France, 1944

Once at the American compound, a soldier indicated Sasha was to follow him into a room with a tub of water. Through pantomime, the soldier instructed Sasha to clean himself. Such luxury! Sasha wondered how much better being in American custody would get. After he washed himself, Sasha discovered his ROA uniform had disappeared. In its place, he found a shirt with large red dot painted on the back and some trousers with six buttons on the fly. He stepped into a hallway where the soldier waited, who had allowed him privacy as he bathed. He led Sasha into a room with food spread on a counter before him— stew with savory meat, potatoes, onions, and carrots. He hadn't eaten so well since he left Kamchatka. A handful of the good cigarettes like the soldier in the field smoked lay on the tray. Whoever would have imagined good fortune in war? Then he joined a group of men dressed in the same shirts with large red dots on the back and the button-fly trousers, all of them speaking Russian. "What's going on?"

No one had an answer. No one complained about their good fortune, grateful they no longer had to fight for the Germans.

*****

On a rare day with no new causalities, Valentina joined other medical personnel who had escaped the rush for a brief lunch away from the hospital, so they could indulge in English, the only language they all had in common. Some of the new recruits spoke English and German, but not French.

"I don't know why they call these tins 'English 48'. It is bloody graveyard food. Wouldn't feed a year old corpse," Dietrich grumbled. "I wish they would capture some American tinned chicken, tomato, juice, or bully beef. You can tell I'm hungry when that sounds good."

"The driver said they were dropping these 'English 48' by small silk scarves. That is why they are available for us. He wore one of the orange parachutes around his neck. I understand the Allies are dropping medical supplies also. We could use some of that," Gretel responded.

"We surely could. It is so primitive, what we can do for the men with the limited supply we have," Hélène chimed in.

Etienne read from a dark blue book as he often did when he had a stolen moment from the incessant demands of the surgery.

In a treasured moment in the early July sunlight, one could momentarily forget the horrors of war.. The others drifted off one at a time until just Valentina and Etienne remained. She took the opportunity to talk to him about something he had said the night they found the children in the woods.

"Can I ask you what you meant the night we found the children, when you said that the doctors who bled those children to death are creating their own hell?"

"Are you Christian?"

"By Christian you mean...?"

"Believing in Jesus Christ. Believing that he came to earth to show us the way to return to God and to offer himself as a sacrifice in payment of our sins."

"No, I don't know anything about Jesus Christ except that some people worship him, claim he was divine."

"Well, it is a deep and involved subject. In a nutshell, I believe that we lived before this life in another existence, and we were sent to dwell on this earth, to choose between that which is good and that which is evil. When we choose evil, we are creating a hell for ourselves in the life after this life. I fully believe that unless we repent of the evil we have done in this life, we will suffer for each and every suffering we have caused others. Those doctors and nurses who did this great horror will suffer not only as the children suffered, but as their loved ones suffered in discovering their children had been killed, in suffering as the other villagers in knowing such a terrible thing has been visited upon their village. They will suffer what you and I have suffered in nightmares, in tortured thoughts on behalf of those children. They will suffer what anguished feelings anyone we tell of these horrendous experiences feels. In other words, it is like the ripples in a pond. The extent of suffering from one evil act goes on and on. The only way to end it is to allow Jesus Christ to heal all of the suffering any act creates, to ask him to forgive you for any suffering you have caused. Here, take this book and read it. It will tell you about the life and mission of Jesus Christ and why he is so important to me." He handed her the book he was always reading, Jesus the Christ. Pray about it as you read."

"Pray? To whom? I don't know how to pray."

"Simply address God. It doesn't hurt to thank him for blessings in your life, and then ask him if the things you are reading come from him. Close your prayer in the name of Jesus Christ. Then listen more to your heart than your mind. I testify to you that God will speak to your heart."

"But how can I do that? I don't even believe there is a God. I would feel foolish trying to talk with a God I don't believe even exists."

"Ask him if he is there. I testify that he is, that he is real, and that he cares about you. He is not going to force himself on you. You are here to choose for yourself what you believe. You will find him if you seek him. Take the book, try to read it with an open mind, not overshadowed with all of the atheistic doctrines of communism. Just ask God if he is there, if what you are reading is of him."

"Okay. I'll try. Thank you," Valentina accepted the book only because she esteemed Etienne so highly. "Is being Christian what makes you different from the others?"

Etienne smiled. "Possibly."

*****

After a few days, Sasha's ROA uniform was returned to him dirty and stinking as before. Everything he had had before: his socks, boots, pack, and gun were returned. Inside the pack, were German cheeses and biscuits. He was evidently going back into the German army—but why would the Allies want him to do this? Would the Allies recapture him and then forcibly recruit him to fight against the Japanese and then the Japanese would capture him and use him to fight the Chinese, and the Chinese would capture him to fight against the Russians, and he would pass from enemy to enemy and end up home again?

Once again dressed in their repulsive ROA uniforms, a soldier dressed in a clean and pressed green uniform of the Germans came before them speaking Russian. "So sorry we couldn't wash your uniforms, but we fear it might give you away. We trust none of you have a particular love for the Germans."

There was a mummer of assent among the prisoners.

"In view of that, we want to recruit you to work for the Allies in two ways, recruiting other Russians away from the Germans. If you have a chance to talk to them, please do so. There are also fliers for you to drop in secrecy, written in Russian, and encouraging desertion. Also, seek any opportunity you see to sabotage the German effort. You are welcome to surrender to the Allies once you have done what you can. You will be well-treated. When you surrender, the password to tell the Allies you are part of us is Dogpatch." He made them say the English word many times, and Sasha wondered how he would ever remember the strange sounding word.

That night Sasha and the other recruits were escorted back into the German army by a German-speaking Allied soldier as well as the Russian dressed in the German uniform. They came to a bridge guarded by the Germans. The Russians lined up in formation as they had been instructed to do, and the Allied soldier shouted commands in German. They marched across the bridge under the noses of the unsuspecting guards. Two by two, they dropped out in the darkness to be absorbed back into the German army. Sasha's pockets were stuffed with fliers written in Russian, urging the Russians to sabotage the Germans. He didn't worry about coming across a German who could read Russian. That would certainly be a death sentence considering what the flier said. He did worry that the Germans would wonder how they had come across something written in Russian. Would they attempt to find someone who could translate the condemning words? Under the cover of darkness, Sasha quickly dropped the fliers for other Russians to find and marched far beyond where he dropped them.

*****

The villagers became frequent visitors at the field hospital, seeking help with a laceration, a broken limb, a toothache. Etienne and the other doctors and nurses treated them with as much diffidence as they did the soldiers, knowing that the soldiers were actually the enemy, and the Frenchmen their friends. They grilled the Frenchmen in an off-handed, friendly way, as much as the soldiers, and gained as much information from them as from the soldiers. Even though posing as enemies, the Frenchmen recognized them as friends and poured food and invitations upon them.

One day Etienne and a number of the nurses followed behind a wedding party to celebrate with the villagers. The young groom made his way on crutches, half a leg amputated due to a war injury. The young bride's happiness that her fiance was still alive showed in her dancing gait. As they made their way down the road, a group of six American soldiers broke from the bushes and surrounded the wedding party, guns pointed. Valentina's heart caught in her throat. What did these soldiers want from the villagers? They had suffered so much. Couldn't they just leave them alone? They were not the enemy.

One of the soldiers grabbed the young bride and pushed her to the ground, saying in English, "Want some pre-wedding night fun? Maybe we can give you a little memory to grow in you to remember the war by?"

He laughed rapaciously. Valentina strangled a scream. In a flash, Etienne was at the soldier, grabbed him by the collar like a cat grabbing a mouse, yanked him off the young woman, and flung him to the side. Etienne growled in a menacing way, and said in perfect English, "You leave these people alone, you scum." He reached to lift the young woman to her feet. "*Je suis tres desollee.* Go on ahead. We will meet you shortly."

"Who are you?" The soldier sneered at Etienne while still lying on the ground, his pals standing with their guns now pointed at Etienne. "We could shoot you and take our pleasure with your nurses. Doesn't matter to us."

"Yes, and you've already done enough to get court-martialed. You should be filled with shame and self-loathing. I suggest you skedaddle back to your company. You had better treat the Frenchmen with the utmost respect or I guarantee I will hunt you down after this war, and you will pay to the uttermost." Unarmed, Etienne stood and glared at them like a lion, staring down five armed soldiers.

Etienne never took his eyes off the one on the ground, but the others lowered their guns. "Come on, Hansen, let's get out of here, before we get in some real trouble," one of the five said.

Etienne picked up the helmet of the soldier on the ground, "Put in a little gift for a wedding present." His eyes snapped in a way that the soldier did not offer a protest. He emptied his pockets, as did the other soldiers. Etienne scooped the cash into a satchel he carried and tossed the helmet back to the soldier. He continued to glare at the soldiers until they had disappeared. Valentina felt amazement at the power Etienne's indignation and demands had over these low-life soldiers. If it was his religion which made him into this kind of man, it would be worth her time to learn about it. She started reading his book and attempting prayers, although she felt like she was talking to herself.

As the front line shifted, so did their field hospital. Soon they bid these villagers good-bye and were in a new village. Etienne soon won the friendship of these villagers as well, and houses were offered for both their hospital and lodgings. Valentina often sought out Etienne out to ask questions about this Jesus Christ she was learning about in his book. She wished she had unlimited time to sit at Etienne's feet and be taught, instead of the fleeting moments she caught him eating or cleaning up after one surgery or preparing for another. Whenever they were alone, he prayed with her. She felt a peculiar warmth whenever they did this, and it seemed less strange to try to talk to this unknown God on her own.

One night Valentina sequestered herself in the building they used as an office to type up her report of the German movements she and other medical personnel had garnered from the most recent causalities. It was due for transport with the ambulance driver in a couple of hours. A smart rap sounded on the door. She pulled her paper from the typewriter and buried it in a pile of German documents before going to the door. Valentina was immediately on guard when she saw the green uniform of the Germans. She relaxed when she recognized the visiting official as someone in the spy unit from England. "Fetch your head doctor," he demanded.

She found Etienne washing up after surgery. "Someone from command is here. He wants to speak to you."

Etienne gave a huge sigh. "Okay. Could you see if you can find something to offer him for refreshment?"

The villagers had been generous with their chewy breads and cheeses. Valentina spread them on a plate, adding slices of the American spam and the tinned apricots, which formed the foundation of so many of their meals. She poured cups for each, the apricot juice for Etienne and coffee for the General, placed everything on a tray, and went to the door. She paused at the loud voice of the visitor insisting, "We could probably gain a lot of information if the nurses were to sleep with German officers."

"Some information is not worth the price one pays to get it." Etienne answered in a much softer voice.

"They don't have to worry about VD. We have penicillin. For pregnancy, the girls could insist the officers use rubbers."

"It's against God's law."

"And killing is not? Where does God's law fit into a war?"

"We still have choices we must make and account for once the war is over. Would you ask this of your girl? Your sister? Your mother?"

"No, of course not. That's different."

"And how is it different? Each of our nurses have family who care about them. They might have a husband, a fiancé, a boyfriend waiting for their return from the war. There is no way I would ever ask any of them to subject themselves to sleeping with an officer in hopes of getting information."

"And what if it is an order?"

"I would defy the order before I would require it of the nurses. I have to live with myself after this war. The expediency of the moment does not make right what is inherently wrong."

"Why you arrogant young...."

Valentina rapped at the door. Etienne opened it. He picked up some bread and cheese off the tray, "I'm wanted in surgery."

At least, Valentina was sure he wanted out of there. He paused and looked at the visitor. "Dismissed," the visitor growled at him. Etienne snapped his feet together and saluted. Valentina set the tray down before the visitor.

"Would you be willing to sleep with the Germans as part of your espionage?"

"I don't speak German. Only French, English, and Russian."

"Then you are not so much use to us here. We do need help recruiting Russians to our side. I guess that is why you're here."

"Yes. I am involved in that effort."

Valentina found herself praising God she had escaped that degradation before reminding herself she still wasn't sure there was a God.

*****

Sasha quickly learned that the hedgerows were as effective as General Winter and fought equally impartially. They could completely conceal a division waiting to ambush a hapless enemy, but just as likely, the enemy could be waiting to ambush you. The first time the young Germans were sent into a field and caught enemy fire. After that, the expendable Russians were always sent in first. Sasha didn't see what difference it made since the enemy could easily wait until the whole unit was in the field before letting loose with the gunfire.

Nevertheless, he always approached the entrance to a field cautiously, wondering why he was bothering to try to prolong his life. Wouldn't a bullet be just as welcome today as tomorrow or next week? Either he would know nothing, no pain, no hunger, no fatigue, no yearning, or he would know what came after death. Surely, if there were something after death, it couldn't be any worse than the life he was now living. Maybe it would even be better. There was one way to find out. Only the thought that there would be no return made him avoid that deliberate bullet.

Sasha was not more than a few steps into the field before he was certain the enemy hid there. "Amerikans!" The soldier next to him screamed just before a bullet took him down. Sasha felt a burning pain in his shoulder as he stumbled and fell. More shots swirled around him, and the pain burning in Sasha's shoulder made him regret he had not gotten a quick death with a bullet in his heart. Would he lie here, abandoned by the Germans, until he bled or starved to death? Maybe he could expedite it with his own gun, but still, he didn't raise up to find it. Maybe the Allies would finish him off. He felt so weak.

He must be dead. He was warm, he was dry. A pungent smell. Death smelled like this? Female voices but not speaking Russian. Death must be good. A cool hand ran across his brow, and a voice prattled in an unknown tongue. It was Valentina's voice. Now his imagination was truly running wild. His eyes flew open. It was Valentina's face, a little white cap posed on the hair cut he had seen off on the train in Moscow. Her voice prattled again but not in Russian. Had they both died, and she somehow cared for him? Then why didn't she speak Russian? He tried to speak but could not. She saw his struggle and held a glass for him to drink. He sipped and fell back on the bed, and looked at her. "Valentina."

She looked at him with uncomprehending eyes, but they were Valentina's eyes. They were! He spoke. "Valentina. I know its you. Where am I? What has happened?"

She turned and spoke to others in this other language. Why would she doing this? Why was she here? What was going on?

Each day she came. She fed him, she bathed him, she changed his linens. Oh, how he relished her touch! But she did not speak to him in Russian or acknowledge in any way she knew him. He came to realize he was in some kind of hospital tent. They fed him, treated him with dignity, saw to his needs. Nice dream. He realized he was hearing a lot of German among the nurses, doctors, and patients, but Valentina spoke differently. It must be French. A couple of the other nurses, a doctor, and a few of the patients also spoke the language Valentina was speaking. Other patients spoke Russian. He could hear them call out, but none of the medical personnel responded in Russian. What was Valentina doing here? Weren't they the enemy? Was she somehow spying, or had she too been captured and forced to work for them? But she could be part of the Allied effort even as he had been.

Sasha became stronger, and when he could walk again, a truck took him to another fenced-in prison camp. It was an Allied camp, confirming for him that Valentina was working for the Allies as she posed to be French. How he yearned to speak with her! But she hadn't once broken her mask of nonrecognition. Sasha was given cigarettes and slept in a western-style cot, ate good food, played cards and chess, and once again wondered that the Allies called this a prison. He hoped he could stay here until the war ended.

A radio played incessantly during the day. Sasha heard the same songs sung by a seductive female voice so often that he could sing them himself, though he had no idea what the words meant. *Bei der Laterne wollen wir steh'n Wie einst Lili Marleen.* The radio played the song in German, but the guard sang to the same tune in English. He could hear the words, "Lili Marlene" in both languages. He realized more fully than ever that music was a universal language.

*****

Valentina found herself looking for excuses to talk to Etienne. She liked being in his presence. She liked the deference he showed her, really the respectfulness he showed everyone. She liked the feeling of calm that Etienne communicated that in spite of the craziness of this war, there was a God in control and that he cared about the individuals suffering from the injustices of others. Never wanting to say or ask something which would blow their cover, she waited for the rare times they were alone. Because of her interest in Jesus Christ, he seemed to seek opportunities to speak with her. She said when they were alone, "You seem very fond of the French."

"I served here as a missionary for my church."

"Here? In this village?"

"No I was in the south of France, but I came to know the French people and to love them dearly. I almost addressed the parents of the children in the church as my dear brothers and sisters, as I would have as a missionary."

"What church is that?"

"The Church of Jesus Christ of Latter-day Saints."

"I've never heard of it."

"I'll get you a pamphlet about it."

She read the pamphlet that very night about a young man named Joseph Smith seeking to know which church to join. He prayed in a grove of trees, and the very God Etienne spoke of and Jesus Christ appeared to him. That was rather fantastical. Would they appear to her? She would have to ask Etienne. If they did, then she would certainly know they existed.

Valentina waited in the farmhouse for her new recruits to arrive. She knew Alex would be among them. What a total shock it had been to see him when he was brought in injured. She had fully expected that in some manner he would find his way back to Kamchatka when she left him in Moscow. Still, his very presence here in the ROA uniform meant that somehow he had ended up in the Red Army, had been captured, and then practically starved to death before being shipped to France to fight for the Germans. How incredibly peculiar that they should both end up here, both outwardly supporting the German cause. And now, tonight, she would recruit him to work for the Allies even as she was. All coincidences were strange, but this was probably the strangest in her life. She fully expected Alex and the other recruits to join the Allied cause. She had never had a Russian refuse yet.

The group of newly healed ROA soldiers entered the room, obviously full of curiosity about what this new deviation meant. They had just come from an Allied prison camp where they were treated very well. Alex entered and recognition showed on his face. Poor guy. Surely nothing made sense to him. He didn't attempt to speak to her. All the time she had nursed him in the hospital, he had attempted to talk to her, and she had continually refused to acknowledge that she understood him. "Comrades," she greeted them in Russian. The expression on Alex's face was priceless. If possible, she would give him the satisfaction of speaking with her before the evening was over. "We understand the circumstances under which you are wearing the uniform of the ROA. You have been screened for your loyalty to the German army, and none of you exhibit any kind of loyalty. You have been captured and in some cases nursed back to health by the Allies. For many of you, it appeared that you were under German care while you were hospitalized. The doctors and nurses who cared for you are actually enlisted in the Allied cause, working in espionage. You were brought here this evening to be recruited for the same cause. We want you to go back into the German army and recruit all the Russians in the units where you are, to do whatever they can to sabotage the German efforts. Here are fliers you can scatter among the Russians in the ROA, urging them to surrender to the Allies. They will be treated well, even as you have been. When you have done all you can, you may also surrender to the Allies. Tell them "hot-diggety-dog." That is the password for any ROA soldiers who have been recruited by the Allies." She had them repeat the phrase many times until they could say it reasonably well.

*****

A different password than he had been issued before, but it was basically the same task. Under the cloak of darkness, the Russians were incorporated back into the German army. When daylight came, the unit Sasha was now associated with headed into a French city as dead as a Roman ruin. During the march, he saw a flier identical to the ones he was supposed to be scattering. He picked it up, glanced at it as if he had never seen it before, and then let it float back to the ground as the lead Panzer tank hit a mine and the explosion sent everyone scrambling for shelter. Soon it seemed all of their tanks were disabled. Burst sewers, broken gas mains, dead animals raised an almost overpowering smell. Shattered glass paved the streets. Wires hanging from poles and trolley cables dangled and twisted together everywhere, some of them live with electricity. Wrecked trucks, armored vehicles, and guns littered the streets. Sasha half expected snipers to begin shooting at them, but only carefully placed mines seemed to be in the city to obstruct their efforts. Nevertheless, he was glad when they pushed beyond the city and settled down for the night. In the darkness, he heard the soldiers whistling the plaintive 'Lili Marlene' and vowed to find someone who could explain the words to him.

*****

Valentina's days and nights were filled with bandaging wounds, giving morphine shots, administering sulfa and plasma. While they did not function as medics at the battlefront, they were one of the forward stations where, as Etienne said, "We are not trying to get them ready to play a piano, we are just trying to get them to larger institutions for better care." Life-saving surgery was performed before sending them off to those ambulances which in fact delivered the Germans, Russians, and French to prison camps where they either became prisoners of war or were recruited for the Allied cause. The German ambulance drivers were instructed to bring them only the injured deemed capable of recovery and returning to battle. In their hospital tent, a radio station called Soldatensender West played eight times a week, broadcasting in German. Many of the songs had no propaganda content but attracted and held listeners for the news segments. Others had a nostalgic appeal promoting war-weariness and defection. Still, others were hard-hitting satirical songs attacking Nazi leaders or relating to the discomforts and disillusionment of war. In addition to straight musical programs, there were also fifteen-minute variety shows in the best tradition of the political cabaret so popular in Europe. One day a loyal Nazi grabbed the radio as a hard-hitting satirical song attacking Nazi leaders blared from the radio and tuned it to a station called "Axis Sally"--threatening the Allies, taunting that German victory was imminent. The announcer addressed hospital personnel-- nurses in particular, and described what would happen to them if captured. "All of you nurses will soon serve the German soldiers in the most intimate of ways." Valentina knew she, as a supposed German ally, should be rejoicing in these threats to the Allies, but in fact, they terrified her. She just hoped it was empty propaganda and "The krauts are in the bag," as the Allies affirmed.

Etienne told her that, while he fully expected God to answer her prayers, it was unlikely that she would have a visit of God, the father, and Jesus Christ. Joseph Smith needed such a strong witness, Etienne explained, because he was tasked with the great responsibility of re-establishing the Church of Jesus Christ upon the earth. He had suffered much persecution and, in the end, was martyred for his beliefs. Her task, Etienne said, was to come to know God and Jesus Christ through study and prayer and then to decide if this Church of Jesus Christ of Latter-day Saints was indeed the actual church of God upon the earth. With this focused task, Valentina spent much of her minimal free time reading about Etienne's religion. She joined other worshipers when she could, where soldiers made trays for the Lord's Supper out of shell casings. She found the teachings there resonated deep within her. She didn't know if it were true as Etienne claimed, but she wanted it to be true. She wanted to associate with people like Etienne and the few others she had met with the same beliefs. She began to consider taking the step of baptism seriously. Etienne assured her that her desire to believe was sufficient.

*****

When the Germans swarmed from the forest into the village like ants, Sasha thought they would surely be victorious. He hoped not. He desperately wanted to surrender to the Allies again, but it had been some time since he had had an opportunity, and they always quickly sent him back out to the Germans. Once again, the village they had seized was in turn besieged by the Allies. They were beaten back, but there was no opportunity for surrender. The Germans surged forward again, hitting the American tanks and setting them afire. Flames spread throughout the wooden houses of the village. With a blinded soldier hanging onto his belt, Sasha led the way up a steel ladder leaning against a steep cliff behind the hotel. At the top, he flopped to the ground panting, then turned to look down at the ground below. It was an inferno of burning buildings. American bazookas shot their rockets, which bounced harmlessly off the heavily armored Panzer tanks. Panzer tanks rumbled through the rubble-filled streets, firing their cannons point-blank at houses where GIs still held out. Overhanging everything was a pall of oily smoke, pierced here and there by the white fingers of German searchlights bouncing off the clouds to illuminate the attack. One by one, the last pockets of resistance were eliminated, and the shooting ceased. Lost in yet another German victory, Sasha moved away from the burning city, seeking darkness in which to lose himself. He heard the incongruous sound of piano music floating through the night. The sound emanated from a grand mansion, somehow still standing. Curious, he crept toward it. Tiptoeing and darting until he came to a baronial hall deep in the chateau, he saw a lone American seated at a massive piano, playing Rimsky-Korsakov's *Flight of the Bumble Bee* while rubble sifted down over him. It probably wouldn't do any good to surrender to one solitary soldier, and there was no heart in him to shoot the pianist for the Germans. As the soldier finished with a flourish, Sasha applauded. The soldier jumped, startled.

"Diggity dogpatch." Sasha tried to remember the English words he had been told to use as passwords.

The American laughed good-naturedly and signaled him over. They shared a meal from the tins in their respective packs and eventually bedded down in the palatial hall. The American was soon snoring loudly, and Sasha wondered sleepily if the noise would attract the Germans.

German shouting startled him awake. He opened his eyes to daylight and no American. Discovering the piano, one of the Germans sat down and began playing a skillful and complicated piece Sasha did not recognize. After the German had played a bit, and over his strenuous objections, a number of his fellow soldiers took their hatchets and, in vicious merrymaking, hacked the piano to pieces. Sasha had no idea what had happened to the American but realized he was again back on the German side.

*****

Valentina continually wondered how long this war could go on. It seemed with all of the men killed, all of the prisoners taken, all of the tanks and equipment destroyed, that one side's ability to keep fighting must soon be over-extended, but the war dragged on and on. The injured soldiers talked about the Germans running out of gas for the tanks, but somehow, there was a battle another day and then another and another. Valentina fervently hoped the Germans would lose this war. From what she had seen, she feared life otherwise might not be worth living. She didn't know what the Germans would do with Russia, with the Russians, with her. She only knew that she didn't want to find out.

One day, Valentina assisted Etienne in an amputation of a leg. It was rare that they did this type of surgery. It was a Russian soldier, who would not be going back into the battle. But Etienne felt he would not survive if he were transported to the next station before receiving help. Etienne continually amazed her. Though it was a war with defined enemies, and they were officially incognito in an enemy camp, no one was Etienne's enemy. He did his utmost to repair, comfort, and assist any soldier of any nationality who fell into his care.

Valentina quickly took the soldier's blood pressure and then returned the cuff to the wooden supplies box sitting on two sawhorses between the two laced-together hospital tents. Supplies had become so scarce that all of the nurses shared only two blood pressure cuffs. Oxygen tanks were equally scarce. As Etienne began the gruesome task of cutting through the flesh and bone, Valentina monitored the patient's pulse by placing her fingertips over an artery. She suddenly felt an increase in the pulse. Quickly she rushed to the supply box. The coveted cuff was fortunately there. She took the blood pressure, increased the anesthesia, and returned the cuff to the box. Etienne finished his ghastly task. He picked up the severed leg as she began bandaging the stump. "I need to speak to you. Meet me at two if possible," he whispered.

He didn't have to specify where. They always met in the woods so they wouldn't be overheard. She knew that the injured soldiers and the rest of the medical staff all thought they had a romance going on. She wouldn't mind it. She found Etienne very attractive. She had never met a man like him. She yearned for that association, for that special feeling that life meant ever so much more than the horrors of the day. She had asked him to explain what happened after death. Where were the spirits of these soldiers who slipped from their grasp every day? Where were her brothers? Where was Mikel? For that matter, where were her grandparents? What a grand idea, that they still lived. What was their life like, free of pain, free of the mortal body? Were they individual consciousness as they had been when embodied? Were they aware of what was going on with those they had left behind? She was bursting with questions, and Etienne seemed to be the only one who had answers. He claimed that his teachings were the truth, but why were others not seeking such comforting truths? One would think people would join his religion in droves.

Just before two, she had to assist a soldier with a bullet in his shoulder. The soldier flirted with her the entire time, "You're sure pretty. It's worth being injured to see a pretty face. What are you doing tonight, Babe? I think I'll be up to some fun."

When he tried to touch her breasts, she said, "Whoa, boy. Flirting is okay, but you're getting out of bounds." Virtually every soldier assumed that the few females they met welcomed their advances. Only Etienne and very few others, mostly those she had met at church services, restrained themselves.

"Sorry, sorry," the soldier apologized. "Do you know any place I can find a gal?"

"There's lots of demand and short supply," She put him off as she did every soldier. "I'll get you a drink of water and then I really need to be running."

She was so glad Etienne was still waiting when she dashed into the woods with her crust of bread and hunk of cheese for her lunch. "Thanks for waiting. There was a soldier who just came in who needed attention."

He smiled. "There always is. Actually, I just got here myself." He handed her an apple, a gift from the villagers. He always made friends wherever he went, and they always gifted him in whatever way they could.

She allowed him a moment to eat his meager meal before beginning to speak. "So, do you have time to tell me about life after death?"

"Not right now. A nephew of the Prophet Joseph Smith who later became a prophet himself has recorded a most remarkable vision he had of the afterlife. I'll hope to get that to you after the war. I asked to speak to you because they are disbanding our espionage unit. They need our expertise more as medical personnel on the Allied side. We expect that it will be but a few months until the war is over."

"Thank God," she breathed.

"And more personally for you, they feel you have already recruited nearly all the ROA Russians that we are going to be able to reach. Your special expertise in that area is no longer required. You are aware of the danger that poses for you."

"Yes, I am quite aware." It had been foremost in her mind, knowing there was no way she would be permitted to return to Russia without being branded a traitor.

"Being on the Allied side will enable you to craft an identity you can maintain after the end of the war. You could go to the United States, England, or stay here in France. Get your belongings together. Transportation will be here at 1800. If we become separated, here is my real name and contact information in the US. I would be glad to help you in any way. I want to know what happens to you after the war."

She choked back tears. "Thank you."

He gave her a quick hug and was gone.

12

Salt Lake City

France 1944

Weary of never-ending war, Sasha wondered why another destroyed village, another thousand dead men, would enable someone to declare a winner to this madness. He looked for opportunities to be recaptured by the Americans. He saw fewer and fewer Russians he could recruit, and he just wanted to be done with this mission while his life and body were still intact.

Summer moved into fall, and mud clogged the roads, trapping the tanks in the rich goo. Passing planes dropped fliers in the Cyrillic alphabet as well as the Roman, encouraging the soldiers and citizens to rebel against the German army. Three times Sasha's German unit surrendered. Each time he was given a few days respite and then sent out again to recruit yet more Russian captives. He looked for the day when they would no longer send him back.

Winter trapped them with its cold, and they chased from one battle to another, looking for respite from the cold. Snows seemed to fall early. Then it warmed up, and continual mud again prevented progress. Then the temperatures dropped again, and it became extremely cold. Sasha welcomed the occasional newspaper, which could be wrapped under his greatcoat, to block the wind that seemed to reach to the very bone. He wrapped his feet with as many layers as he could and still be able to put his boots on. Steam poured out of his nose and mouth, and icicles formed on his growing mustache and beard. When he tried to breathe through his nostrils, they stuck together as if they were glued. His teeth were so sensitive, he had to cover them with a scarf. He jumped, moved constantly, threw his arms out, and then thumped them on his chest. He rubbed his forehead, nose, and cheeks. Through diligent effort, he managed to avoid frostbite, but he feared the cold, which took so many soldiers around him. It was a daily battle not to surrender and just succumb to it.

Some of the soldiers cadged bed sheets from civilians and made capes to camouflage themselves against the snow. Others, not lucky enough to get bedsheets, put their white long johns over their standard combat clothing. Sasha and the other Russians were assigned to apply white paint to the tanks. At nighttime, the white sheets hung over their green tents. Sasha participated willingly in all of this because Allied planes or soldiers could not tell he was working for the Allies. He was just as vulnerable as any of them.

Tactics changed as different leaders replaced those lost in battle. To muffle the sound of traffic, they padded wagon wheels and horses' hooves with straw. Low-flying aircraft zoomed over the assembly areas to drown out engine noises. They burned charcoal when they could get it, so that wood smoke would not betray their location. Guns and howitzers were moved into position five miles behind the lines. To cut down on noise and conserve gasoline, they moved ammunition for the opening barrage by hand.

Yet another village was taken, and soon the Allies were upon them. Sasha realized the Americans had surrounded the large brick building where he and the German unit he was currently attached to were hiding. He could step out and surrender, but he had no white flag and feared a bullet would find him before they realized he was surrendering. Their food ran short. The Allies knew they were there. Gunfire had been exchanged. Did the Allies have a plan for eliminating them? They couldn't even sneak outside to melt snow for water. He didn't know what the hundreds of German soldiers planned to do. He and the three other Russians tried to figure how to surrender to the Americans without being shot in the back by the Germans. The Germans did not share their meager rations with them. Once, Sasha succeeded in trapping a rat. Even its blood provided nourishment.

One night the battle intensified, and another flight of planes flew overhead. Sasha didn't know if they were German or Allied planes. It hardly mattered. The troops were so close that any bomb dropped had equal chances of harming either side. After all of these years of suffering yet surviving, would his life be suddenly snuffed out now? So many of those around him had died. Why was he more lucky, more important than they? Or were they the lucky ones, released from this continual deprivation? To what fate, he didn't know, but he couldn't imagine it could be any worse than this daily hell.

Sasha watched out a glassless window. German tanks were hit and bled flaming fuel, lighting up the darkness and aiding the marksmanship of the planes and artillery. In the garish light, grapeshot and bombs pounded the German weapons. Shells screamed among the pines surrounding his building, exploding trunks and branches and spraying a rain of splintery, blazing death through the windows.

Sasha rushed down the stairs, fighting for the exit with all the other trapped and panicked soldiers. Dazed and exhausted, hands in the air, the Russians and Germans poured through the exit. Sasha's every hope was on avoiding the falling fire from the tree bursts before the building erupted in a conflagration.

"Ruskie, friend. Hot diggety dogpatch." Sasha said to the Allies as they sorted through the prisoners. "Ruskie," he said, pointing to the other two Russian recruits. The three Russians breathed easier as they were ushered into a jeep, separated from the German prisoners. Sasha didn't know what the Germans faced. Certainly interrogation, perhaps torture. He would be spared that.

Belgium 1945

On the Allied side near Wallonia in Belgium, Valentina no longer worked in espionage but was still in disguise. She transitioned from Marie Yvette to Rachel, a more English-sounding name. The war also changed complexion as bitter winter weather fell over the countryside. In Kamchatka, the men had spoken of the impartiality of General Winter. It seemed he had declared war against both the Allies and the Axis powers, determined to annihilate both sides.

With temperatures well below freezing, three inches of mud had frozen on the bottom of the tent used for the casualty department. Valentina, like the other medics, carried syringes in her armpits to keep the liquid medicine from freezing as she darted from one injured soldier to another. Ursula, the commanding nurse, barked orders right and left, "Clean up that puddle of sick! Grab a plaster for this chap. This cold is making a hash of everything. This bloke's drip bottle is frozen. Give the fella in bed four a jab o' morphine."

And, finally, a personal order for her, "Rachel, throw on your mackintosh straight away. I want to see if they've dropped us any bits and bobs. Crack on, meet me outside."

"Who needs some penicillin?" Valentina asked and handed the syringes from under her arm to the nurse who answered, "Me."

She slipped the yellow mackintosh over her already heavily wrapped body and placed her helmet with the prominent Red Cross over the knit caps on her head. The mac added little warmth, but the snow would slip from its slick surface rather than clinging to the wraps she wore day and night. The little pot-belly stoves used in the tents never generated enough warmth. Even rushing about, one would not feel too hot to wear coats, hats, and gloves.

While waiting for Ursula, Valentina watched how busy everyone was throughout the camp. Engineers were drilling holes through the frozen snow in order to drive another tent peg. Three off-duty nurses were working together to get some laundry done in the difficult circumstances. A teapot on a rack over an open fire melted snow and heated the water. One nurse poured the water into a helmet and immediately began washing clothing items in the quickly cooling water; another immediately refilled the teapot with fresh snow. A third hung the washed clothes on a line strung between trees. The clothing immediately froze and did a stiff ghostly dance in the breeze.

Ursula joined Valentina, and they strode through the Ardennes forest. They could hear the boom of cannon and bursts of artillery shells, reminding them that they were not far from the fighting. They carefully picked their way along a path marked with white tape by combat engineers to show it had been cleared of all mines. Exhausted stretcher-bearers carrying the wounded through hip-deep snowdrifts passed them, going the opposite direction. Some pulled improvised sleds along the icy roads, which was much safer for the injured. The walking wounded formed part of this parade to the battalion aid station. Valentina and Ursula greeted them all with, "You're not far now. Another ten minutes."

They reached the field that was their destination and watched for either Allies shooting blood to them in artillery shells or planes dropping supplies by parachute. The German medics had caught on, and they equally watched the skies and scrambled on the ground to collect these precious commodities. "It is so beastly being surrounded by the Krauts. They get half of our stuff that we desperately need." Ursula voiced the sentiment shared by their entire unit. They prayed daily for a breakthrough to restore a direct line to their supplies.

Valentina watched surgeons she recognized speeding on gliders to the scene of the battle. Whenever she saw surgeons on these errands, she fruitlessly watched for Etienne. What would she do if she survived the war and he did not? He was her only American contact who knew she was actually Russian. If she ended up going to America and was unable to contact him, would she be able to make her way on her own?

"I like you, mate," Ursula interrupted her thoughts. "You don't chunter like so many of the girls."

Valentina was surprised that anyone would talk non-stop in Ursula's presence. Her demeanor certainly did not encourage idle chit-chat.

"By the way, they have found a farmhouse with an undamaged wing where we're moving to as soon as we can get some petrol for our old irons. All the lorries are such bangers, I don't know if they can get us through, but it will be a sight better than trying to move all the injured on foot. However, you are not going with us. As soon as we can get you out, you're being transferred as medical personal for those causalities being evacuated to the Zone Interior of the United States. I think they've assigned you a plane".

"Really?" Valentina had never been on a plane in her life. She didn't know if the butterflies erupting in her stomach were from excitement or nervousness.

"Some doctor, Russell George, requested your transfer. I'd guess he has clout."

Etienne! Russell George was the name on the address he had given her, and she suspected it was his real name. Now she positively felt like doing somersaults.

They heard the waited-for drone of a plane in the air as they watched a jeep rigged for carrying stretchers lumbering its way across the field. Suddenly the jeep exploded, its occupants flung into the air like rag dolls and the flying debris of tires and metal barely missing them. Ursula and Valentina scurried to the victims, quickly assessing living and dead. Finding two less injured, they dragged them under the trees. A surgeon arrived on a glider just as the planes began their drop of supplies.

"Leave these," Ursula commanded. "We can't let those Jerries get all of our supplies."

Valentina did as she was told and scurried about, gathering up as many of the little orange parachutes and their precious attachments as she could. Germans swarmed the field also, picking up the coveted commodities.

Rejoining Ursula, Valentina removed her mackintosh and helped her slide one of the injured soldiers onto it. She pulled on it, and it slid behind her as a sled as she retraced her steps back to the camp. The soldier lay unconscious and bleeding as they bumped across the ground. Although still horrified by the brutality of war, these incidents no longer tortured Valentina as they had in the past. It was not only that they had become so commonplace, but more that she now knew the lives just lost actually did still exist, free of pain, free of suffering, free of the horrors of war. Many were welcomed into the loving embrace of their Maker, and others would have the opportunity to learn of Him away from the war's desolation. Yes, their loved ones would mourn them, as they should, but their lives would go on as they accomplished the work they had been sent to do. They had not just been snuffed out.

Valentina just had to prepare herself to meet the Maker she had come to fervently believe in, should she step on a mine or meet a bullet and be dispatched into eternity in a blink of an eye. She had decided to accept baptism in the Church of Jesus Christ of Latter-day Saints, believing that was truly His church upon the earth, possessing the authority and power of salvation. Before taking the step of baptism, she was told she must repent of her past sins and try to make restitution where possible. She pleaded with God to forgive her for the abortion. She hadn't known it was wrong, as she now did. She vowed to follow the law of chastity, with no sexual relationships outside of marriage. She didn't know what she could do about having indulged with Mikel except to promise to never do that again. She had discussed with Russell how she had been forced to service the soldiers, and he assured her God would see her as the victim there, not choosing to participate. She did feel burdened with tremendous guilt towards Alex. If she had not seduced him, he would not be here, fighting this war, risking his life, with virtually no hope of returning to his beloved Kamchatka. She finally decided that, though totally inadequate because it didn't change anything, she at least needed to write him a letter of apology. She would seek baptism as soon as she was in a position to do so.

France 1945

Sasha reveled in the regular, if sometimes boring food, the adequate blankets, the non-demanding days of the Allied prison camp. The Americans didn't seem inclined to send him back out into the German army, and he passed his days indulging in two universal pleasures known the world around: chess and music, this time on a stringed instrument the Americans called a guitar. He drew the birds he could call into camp on the paper provided for writing letters. One day in a heated game of chess, his opponent stopped when the blast signaling mail call came. Sasha didn't trouble himself with hope at mail call. No one knew where he was, and no one would write to him. He startled with surprise when the American handing out the mail sought him out and tossed him a sealed envelope, "Alex, of Kamchatka."

Only Valentina called him Alex or knew he came from Kamchatka. Did she know he was here? Did she care?

He opened the letter. He verified Valentina's signature before indulging in reading her Russian words.

Alex,

I am sorry I have not seen you since recruiting you to work for the Allies. As I am sure you are aware, I was the nurse in the hospital. Since I was posing as a French woman, I could not reveal that I spoke Russian. We worked as an espionage unit, and we had to strenuously keep our false identities up. I know this frustrated you.

First, though, I want you to know that it was so good to see you and such a surprise. I don't know how you ever ended up in France. Well, I do, in that, you obviously ended up in the Red Army, then were captured by the Germans, and finally recruited into the ROA. So that all makes sense, but I know you intended to return to Kamchatka. Our miracle continues. I saw you. Maybe someday yet, I'll hear your story.

I owe you an apology. I feel so badly that I enticed you to want me in Kamchatka. I never suspected what consequences it would bring to us. I know how dearly you loved Kamchatka. I regret that you will probably never be able to return there. The war will soon be over. The Allies definitely have the upper hand, and Germany will not be able to hold out much longer. At the end of the war, all people from other lands are to be repatriated. That word means be sent back, in case you don't know, to their homeland. This is especially dangerous for any Russians. Since you fought for the ROA, you unquestionably would either face death upon returning to Russia or life in a hard labor camp. I don't know how to ask your forgiveness for enticing you into this mess. I don't see how I can make it right for you. I am so sorry.

Now, this is the important part. I plan to emigrate to the United States under a false identity. Enclosed is a piece of paper with a contact address for me in the United States. Destroy the rest of this letter but keep the address. Please do not try to write to me as all letters are censored. Once the war is over, please do try to contact me using this address. I would like to know what happens to you.

I pray that God will be good to you.

Valentina.

Praying and God? Sasha didn't know this side of Valentina. Did war do this to one's psyche? He saw no way to escape his inevitable fate of repatriation. He saw no way to disguise himself as non-Russian, no way of going to the US, and no way of knowing how long it would be before the war ended.

Daily the prisoners passed the rumor that the end of the war was near. Each day Sasha looked for one day to be different than the others. This day looked like rain, it felt like rain, but it did not rain. Sasha felt restless. He played a game of chess against a German prisoner. but he became bored and did poorly. He didn't care if he lost. He walked aimlessly in the yard, smoking. In spite of the fine treatment, being caged made this a prison, more of a prison to him than the others who could talk, read the books, understand. He heard airplanes droning overhead. He glanced up--a US plane, not a threat. No sirens announced its presence. Just the drone overhead. Sasha felt the explosion before he heard the bomb searing through the morning air. The crazy plane had bombed them! Didn't they know they were bombing an Allied prison camp?

Oh, oh. His leg burned painfully. Sasha looked around. The bunkhouse was flattened. A few painful voices called out in agony. Flames shot from the mess hall. The guard tower lay crumbled, the guard thrown lifeless to the ground, just a few feet away. The dust, the smoke choked him. His eyes watered, his nose stung. He tried standing but could not endure the pain. He crawled to the dead American, dragging his injured leg. He went through the American's pockets, looking for a handkerchief to stem the flow of blood. Finding one in the back pocket, he folded it lengthwise and wrapped it around the calf of his leg. The blood soaked his pant leg.

The American was about his size, a little more robust. Sasha saw no blood. He must have broken his neck or something when he fell. Alex tugged the American's pants off. He paused and then took the underwear, too. He saw his chance to get an American uniform. Sasha worked feverishly. He felt so weak. His hands trembled. Rolling the heavy American back and forth to undress him took all the strength Sasha possessed. The blood continued to flow from his leg, the wound pounded, seared. He managed to get the American's clothes on. Should he take the ID tags? Yes, he'd better. Now he was American, but who was he? The blood seeped through the American's uniform. Sasha didn't feel right leaving the poor American naked He struggled to get his clothes on the American. Turn him over, button buttons. Each effort was so hard. He felt tired. So tired. Valentina's letter. He must get the letter. No— not the letter. He'd better not have anything written in Russian on him if he were an American. But her address! He must have her address. He fumbled for the letter, withdrew the address. He wanted to toss the letter into the fire, but he could not drag himself that far. He could not. He stuffed the letter back into the American's ROA uniform pocket. His leg was still bleeding. Soon he would be dead from loss of blood in an American uniform. Would he be buried in France, or would he be sent to America and the American to Russia? Wouldn't his American mother be surprised when she saw her dead son's body and realized it wasn't him? Sadly, that would probably give her the hope that her son lived.

Rocking. Gentle rocking. Death felt like this? The pain in his leg erased that idea. Surely one did not feel pain after death. So if he wasn't dead, where was he? On a boat, a ship? Where was it taking him? What had happened? He couldn't think clearly. He couldn't think at all.

Days or weeks passed. Sasha felt the pain throbbing continually in his left leg. It was bandaged. Oh yes, the bomb, the explosion. He'd been found before he bled to death. So he was in a hospital. On a ship? Going to Russia? No, they would put him on a train from France to Russia.

Waking again, Sasha felt drugged. Why could he not stay awake? Voices. English! Was he in England? He no longer felt rocking, so he must be on land.

Tubes in his nose, in his arms, in his penis. Couldn't they find any other places to stick tubes in? He felt good. So much better. He wanted to open his eyes and see if the face that belonged to the hand that was washing him was pretty. Her voice sounded young. He opened his eyes to see lovely brown eyes and long, dark hair held back by a red ribbon. She clapped her hands and called at the door. Two others, a man in a white doctor's coat, and an older, plumper woman, with a pleasant smile, with one of those heart listening instruments around her neck, came into the room. They all talked at him eagerly, and he realized his tactical error. They thought he was American. They expected him to understand and respond to them. Surely his ruse would be discovered soon. Then what would happen?

He closed his eyes. All of this for nothing. All this pain, all this suffering, all this incredible good sudba, he was alive in America, and soon he would be discovered and sent back to Russia to a traitor's death. How could he bear it?

The gentle hands wiped across his face, and the gentle voice soothed him. He pretended to sleep. What could he do? To get out of here, he would have to get clothes. He could not just walk out of the hospital onto the streets of America in this skimpy thing they covered him with. It didn't even cover his backside, but how would he get clothes?

And once he got on the street, if he magically found clothes, how would he communicate? What could he pretend was wrong with him that would convince them he couldn't hear them? Pretending deafness would not be that hard. Uncle Maximov served as a role model for this. He could mimic his behavior.

He needed to get rid of these tubes. Through pantomime, he could tell the nurse he wanted them out. The one in his arm must be feeding him. He had no question as to what the one in his penis did.

Sasha opened his eyes and saw nothing but brightness in the room and another bed. Soon a heavy nurse with a beautiful face and dark eyes and dark hair bustled into the room. She saw his eyes open and gave him a big smile revealing a perfect rack of white teeth. He smiled back. She began to talk. He pantomimed drinking. Her eyes became puzzled. She pointed to her ears. He shook his head. She moaned, and a look of pity came to her face. She left the room and came back with a man in a white coat. The man looked at him, shined a light in his eyes, in his ears, in his throat, talking to him the whole time. The doctor shrugged and turned and talked to the nurse. She picked up a piece of paper and wrote on it, and handed it to him. He closed his eyes.

No! This wouldn't work either. Of course, she would expect him to read English. Ol' Maximov could not read at all, so no one ever tried to write him notes. They just pantomimed in an effort to communicate.

What now? He couldn't pretend he was blind as well as deaf. They had seen his eyes respond to them. Maybe they would think he suffered some kind of mental derangement that left him unable to speak or read or write. Since he couldn't just sneak out of the hospital onto the streets of America wearing only this skimpy hospital shirt that didn't even button and with no shoes; he saw no hope of being inconspicuous on the streets of America in this, especially since he didn't know the language. He'd take his chances right here. In this hospital. With his eyes open. Totally incommunicado. Sasha opened his eyes.

Holding the piece of paper, he shook his head. The doctor wrote again. Sasha shrugged and put the paper down. The doctor's eyes shadowed, his face reddened, and he yelled. Sasha looked at him, amazed at how easy it was to pretend he didn't hear when he didn't understand.

The nurse pantomimed eating. Sasha vigorously nodded his head. She turned, and the inflection in her voice asked a question. The doctor shook his head and left the room. The nurse held up a finger and left the room. She returned with flavored broth and a yellow crescent. She held the crescent, broke the top, and peeled it down, revealing a pale yellow phallus. I am American, Sasha reminded himself. I have seen this before. I know what it is. He picked up the broken piece she offered him. He ate the mushy fruit with a mild flavor. He could smell other, more enticing odors. He pantomimed eating again when the nurse returned. She shook her head. He twisted his face into pleading. She grabbed her stomach and expressed pain on her face and in her voice. He knew she hoped to tell him his stomach would cramp if he tried to eat more. He knew that cramp. How many days until they gave him more?

He pantomimed removing the tube in his arm. She shook her head. He indicated the tube going into his penis. She nodded. He suffered the indignity of her handling him there, not wanting to react sexually, but still, he did.

The days passed. They removed the tube from his arm, and he was given better food and more of it. He learned where the bathroom was, but his leg ached too much for him to get up. They gave him a metal bottle to fill up with urine. He had to place it on his bedside table when he needed a nurse to empty it. It was the same table they put his food tray on. That disgusted him, but there was nowhere else to put it. He supposed it was alright since neither the bottle nor the food ever actually touched the table.

He slept. He wondered what would happen next. What could he do when he felt well enough to attempt an escape? He would have to steal some clothes. He noticed that when his roommate left, they opened up a closet and handed him a bag of clothes. When he could get up, Sasha looked in his closet. Nothing. He hoped for a new roommate. Two more days, and he got one, a man much taller and much wider than himself. Even if he got clothes, what would he do once he got out of the hospital? Where would he get food or money or work? How would he survive in the city, unable to talk? He only knew Valentina in the United States. Where was she? He no longer knew where the little paper with her address had gone, and the hope of ever finding her was gone with it. Surely his pretense would be discovered, but he would not help them discover him. In the meantime, the food wasn't bad, and the bed was comfortable.

Sasha felt the sun warm on his skin through the window. His room-mate listened to a radio. Sahsa dozed. The boredom of doing nothing gnawed at him. His leg began to heal some, and the doctor urged him to try walking. He was limping, slow, and painful, but walking.

One day he hobbled back to his room on crutches, exhausted from having forced himself up and down the hall, waiting for the shot that alleviated pain and brought sleep. When he entered his room, he saw a smartly dressed woman in a purple suit. Still shapely but not young, her hair slightly gray but expertly coiffed on top of her head. She turned to him, tears running down her face. She murmured something, then her face turned to stone, and she began screaming and ran from the room.

Dread sat in Sasha's stomach. Something had happened. He didn't know what. The heavy nurse came in and looked at him with worry on her face. She left, and Valentina walked through the door. He stared at her in astonishment. Where had she come from? She was pushing a chair on wheels. She motioned for him to get into the chair. She opened his empty closet and withdrew two suitcases and a bag. She tucked the blanket around him, hung the bag on the handles of the cart, and put the suitcases in his lap.

She whisked him down the hall into a small room containing brooms and mops. She shut the door. Her first words to him, "Quickly. Into these clothes. That was your mother, or at least the mother of the soldier whose uniform you wore. She was screaming that you are not her son."

Valentina took a dress out of the bag, pulled it over the top of her nurse's dress, pulled the cap from her head, and slipped her feet into some shoes with skinny heels.

"How did you know I was here?"

"A nurse on the boat that brought you to the United States found my address. She sent me a telegram telling me you were injured and where you were being sent."

"How long have you been here?"

"About a week."

"Why did I not see you before?"

"I needed to learn what would be required for your care, get you some clothing, and some medicine."

"Why didn't you let me know you were here?"

"The risk of betrayal is extreme. Let's go. Do not talk to me at all, except when we are absolutely alone."

She stuffed his hospital pajamas in the bag. Once back in the hall, she pushed him out of the building. A brassy yellow car was parked at the end of the driveway. The man in the driver's seat put the wheelchair, bags, and suitcase in the trunk. The car drove away as the doctor and nurse came running from the building, waving their arms and yelling.

Sasha's leg throbbed. He moaned. He felt hot, so hot. Valentina pulled his head onto her lap and spoke soothing sounds to him, running her fingers through his hair. He was finally safe, finally with someone who knew the territory. The car stopped at a train station. Back into the chair, screaming from pain. Valentina shushed him. "Don't talk." She bought tickets while sweat streamed down his face. She opened a suit-case and shot something into his arm. The pain subsided, and he slept.

Clickety-clack, clickety-clack. The train, the pain. He opened his eyes. Valentina put her finger to her lips. She gave him a drink and two slices of bread with meat in between. He wanted to see this American landscape whizzing by the train window, but the pain consumed him. He moaned. Valentina gave him another shot that sent him into oblivion.

A fever raged in his throat and eyes, blinding, burning. Valentina gave him water and put damp cloths on his forehead. His fever dried them out in no time.

Salt Lake City 1945

Valentina sighed, wondering for the millionth time why she got mixed up in this. Obviously, Alex was still suffering from a considerable infection. When she saw him on crutches, she thought him well on the way to being healed. She would have to get something soon to combat the infection.

They had dodged one bullet in escaping the hospital, only to be in the path of dozens of others. When would the war end for her? When was her day of armistice? She foolishly thought it was her day of peace when she boarded the big C-47 plane flying to the United States. Terrified at the noise of lift-off, she had calmed herself enough to help attend to the injured soldiers strapped into the eighteen litter cases, nine on each side of the plane. It had been non-stop feeding, getting drinks, checking IV drip bottles, emptying urine bottles, continually pressing herself flat against the litter cases so someone else could pass in the narrow aisle. Only sheer exhaustion overruled her terror of flying when her turn came to sleep. She didn't have time to think she was high in the air until the plane descended for landing. Her ears felt like they were going to explode, and the plane shuddered and rocked, and they had landed in Long Island, New York.

No one was allowed off the plane. Only fuel was taken on, plus a gal with a pad of paper and a typewriter, who began interviewing the soldiers, even before the huge metal bird again lifted in the air for the trip to Moline, Illinois.

As soon as their plane landed, Valentina, the other nurses, and one doctor boarded another just emptied plane for the return trip to France, while others boarded their plane to carry off the litter cases. Looking out the window, she watched another of the huge C-47 planes landing and saw yet another circling as her plane waited for clearance to take off.

After a few trips across the ocean on the gigantic metal birds, Valentina saw an opportunity to become the preliminary interviewer. Now she went up and down the rows of soldiers. Name? Home? Parents living? Wife? Children? Civilian occupation? Military history? She then seated herself at a small, bolted-down metal table and typed out the information on a form.

On the ground, the first chance she got, she telegraphed Etienne, or rather Russell George. Or was it George Russell? She couldn't keep his name straight, but to her, he would always be Etienne. She told him that she had arrived in the United States.

When Etienne told her that he was currently serving at Schick Hospital in Clinton, Iowa, she requested yet another transfer. She rode one of the ambulances up from Moline, Illinois to Clinton, Iowa, and soon involved herself in the stateside mop-up of the Battle of the Bulge.

One day Etienne handed her the telegram that would force yet another transfer. She opened it and read that a Henry Davidson was soon to arrive at Fitzsimmons Army Hospital in Aurora, Colorado. "I don't know a Henry Davidson," she said.

"Could it be someone under an assumed name? Did you give my address with your," Etienne paused and then just said, "your name, to anyone in France?" Her US name had not been her French name, and her French name was not her Russian name. Even Etienne didn't know what her Russian name was.

"Yes, one of the recruits I knew previously." Alex. It had to be Alex. She knew that even here, she must not ever indicate she was Russian. The zealots of Russian repatriation were all around. Senator Joseph McCarthy claimed Russians were infiltrating the US as Communist spies and must be routed out. She was not any safer here than she had been on Utah beach on D-Day, with bullets flying all around her, except to the extent that she could remain invisible. And now, here was Alex. He couldn't be hidden in plain sight with his language deficiencies and total cluelessness about American culture.

"Well, somebody called Henry Davidson had the name of Rachel Hamilton and my home address. He is being transferred to Fitzsimmons Hospital in Aurora, Colorado. We have a plane headed there later today. I'll cover the paperwork for you if you want to go."

So she had had to say an abrupt good-bye to Etienne yet again, this time for Alex. Surely if she hadn't rescued him, he would be repatriated and would face a traitor's death or hard labor for the rest of his life, all because she had seduced him in Kamchatka. Why in the world had she done that? Initially, her goal had been to make him submissive to her, to knock off his air of superiority, but by the time she had succeeded, she had grown to respect him, and she had enjoyed their little liaison. But she had never imagined he would actually follow her to Moscow and then end up in France, and now the US. Alex had told her *proshchai* in Kamchatka, in Moscow, in France. It was like that one verse of the song was coming true:

Perhaps we'll meet in San Francisco, in Paris,
Hong Kong, or New York
The world is small and growing smaller every single day
You'll meet tomorrow, the friends you leave today
You'll see us all and ere the dust has settled in our tracks
You'll turn around, and you will see us coming back

Was he destined to be part of her future here or the cause of her downfall? She had learned that she could pass in the US with her English. When questioned where she was from, as Americans seemed inclined to do, she would say she was originally from England but now a US citizen. That's what her falsified passport claimed, and that ended the questions. But Alex was another matter. He could not even open his mouth and say anything at all, or they would both be condemned.

Etienne had given her what could be their passport to survival, the key to his grandmother's home in Salt Lake City. The grandmother died recently, and Etienne inherited the home but had no immediate use for it. So she and Alex had a place to live for the time being. Etienne told her there was a Veteran's Hospital in Salt Lake City and had written her a letter of recommendation for employment. Alex would just have to be a house prisoner until they sorted this all out.

That alone could be problematic. Valentina had promised God and herself that she would not drink coffee, tea, or alcohol or use tobacco. That did not sound like a Russian man. Except for the coffee, all of that had been part of her early relationship with Alex. Compound that with no sex outside of marriage, and she couldn't imagine what it would be like trying to live with him. She didn't think he would force her, but he had every right in the world to be completely unhappy with her.

An active man like Alex would be incredibly bored with nothing to do all day but stay in the house. She couldn't have anything written in Russian in the house on the off chance that someone should come into the home. Perhaps she could get him some paper and pencils, so he could draw. It probably would not be enough, but it would be something to alleviate the boredom. What future was there for them?

Having come this far, she was not going to compromise her goal of being married someday in God's temple to a man such as Etienne. Where did Alex fit in with this? Nowhere at all! And now he was her responsibility, not to mention he still had a raging fever. That was its own problem, but at least it kept him quiet on the train, so it could be counted at least as a temporary blessing.

Salt Lake City 1945

The screech of a seagull. Was he home? Was he dreaming? Where was he? Sasha opened his eyes. He was in a room of white, the same type of flat surface as in the hospital where his supposed mother came in screaming. Sunlight streaming through a clear glass window illuminated the room in brightness. Pink, green, and yellow floral print curtains obscured most of the view out of the window. The seagull screamed again. Between the curtains, he could see blue sky, puffy white clouds, treetops, the steep slope of a roof, and black lines that ran between poles and buildings. The last he remembered, he was on the train with Valentina. She nursed him but forbade him to speak. He remembered fading in and out of consciousness and the fever burning so hot. He must still be in America.

His mouth felt dry, but his head did not burn with fever any longer. He tried to sit up. So weak, so very weak. He pushed himself up, using his elbows to lift but a few inches off the bed, and then collapsed again. He lay in a western-style bed. He felt the sheets against his body. Other than the bed, he could see a dresser with a mirror over it, a wooden chair, and a small table next to the bed. There were two doors in the room, both closed. The room did not seem like a hospital, compared with that other hospital.

Where was Valentina? He wondered if it were safe to call her name. Could he speak in Russian here? She had cautioned him that others discovering they were Russian could mean instant repatriation. He'd better not say anything. He had no idea who was here with him or even if he were alone. One of those bottle gadgets that had dripped liquid into his vein in the hospital was attached to his arm with some tubing. Maybe this was a hospital. His penis was also attached to some kind of collector.

Sleep overtook him again. The squeak of a drawer opening yanked him into consciousness. Through eyes barely slit, he peered at the individual in the room with him. Valentina. Relief flooded over him. He opened his eyes fully and cleared his throat. It was so dry. Valentina turned. "Are you awake, Alex?" She asked in Russian.

"Can I speak Russian?" Sasha heard the gravelly quality of his voice.

Valentina nodded and moved next to the bed. She felt his brow with the back of her hand.

"Where are we?" he rasped. "I heard a seagull."

"We're in the rocky mountains in the western part of the United States. There is a large lake nearby."

"I can't see any mountains out the window."

"The clouds are covering them."

Seagulls, mountains. Some things from home. Maybe he could survive.

"Are there any volcanoes?"

"No. No, I don't think so. I have never seen any smoke from any of the mountains nor heard any thunder from their bowels. The people neither talk about volcanoes nor fear the mountains. I don't think the city would be this close to the mountains if there were volcanoes. Besides, it doesn't smell right. How do you feel?" Valentina finished her physical assessment of him.

"Thirsty as a bird in winter."

"I'll bet. I'll get you something to drink."

He didn't realize he had fallen back asleep until Valentina shook him. "You need to eat, Alex."

She propped pillows behind his back until he was in a semi-reclining position. "You are so weak. Let me feed you."

She brought a spoonful of a thick broth to his lips. "Come on, open your mouth." At his resistance, she added, "You can enjoy the attention while hating the necessity for it."

This reminded him of when she had cared for him in France, but now at least, she would speak to him. He opened his mouth and allowed her to feed him. She wiped his mouth with a cloth and patted his hand.

"You are getting better. It is just a matter of time." She stood and walked to the door, "I need to get some things done before I go back to work tonight."

"You can't spend time talking with me?" Sasha asked, already bored.

"Not now, maybe tomorrow."

*****

Alex was now fully awake. Valentina'd had no idea he was still so ill when she kidnapped him from the hospital. Now she knew she would not come home from work to find a dead body. It was a huge relief that he wasn't going to die on her. How did one go about disposing of the body of someone who supposedly didn't even exist? To the extent she had formulated a plan, she would have told Bishop Bullock that a visiting relative had died. It would have been difficult to fabricate all of the lies necessary to get it taken care of, but that was not the issue now. He was not dead and apparently not going to die. Now she had to deal with the fact that he was going to live.

The taxi driver had helped move him into the house from the car. She had tucked him in the only bedroom in the small house, and she herself slept on the couch. What a blessing the fully furnished small house was. She had sent a brief thank you to Etienne but didn't dare involve him in regular correspondence since that could prove a danger to him too if they were discovered. She felt so isolated. She knew people at work and was beginning to know people at church, but she didn't dare become friends with any of them. If it were just herself, she could pretend, but with Alex? Any relationship she developed had to be kept far from her home.

Well, now that he was awake, she had to orient herself to that. She managed to remove the catheter while he slept. She didn't want to have anything to do with that sensitive part of his body when he was awake. It would definitely be a thorny issue between them.

*****

Sasha lay in the bed, restlessness beating in his chest. He had survived the war, prison camp, deportation, injury, and disease. Now it was time to live, if he could just get out of this bed. He pushed to a sitting position and breathed. Sweat broke out on his brow. His own body had become his enemy, and he would defeat it. He would stand victor, tomorrow. He slumped back on the bed. He would have to prepare for this battle and resolve alone was not a sufficient weapon. His robust, physically demanding life was being spent in a bed. He had mocked Valentina's ineptness in Kamchatka, but he was no better than a baby here, totally dependent on her. He couldn't even take care of his most basic needs. He couldn't get to the bathroom to relieve himself. He couldn't clean himself, he couldn't feed himself.

He let himself daydream about Valentina. They were here together, but did she care about him? Did she love him? She had met his needs in an objective, professional way, just like the other nurses, but there hadn't been any tender touching, no kiss to the cheek. Was it because he was still so weak, or was it because this was the way it was going to be?

The penis collector was gone. How was he supposed to meet that need when it became urgent? He looked for a bottle. He didn't know if he could walk to take care of it.

*****

Having stopped smoking, Valentina hated the way so many of the soldiers, nurses, and doctors in the hospital smoked constantly. It was so obvious who was Mormon and who was not. Non-smoker, Mormon. Smoker, maybe Mormon, maybe not. Evidently, a lot of good Mormon boys had embraced the ways of the world while away at war. Mormons or not, they all assumed she was just waiting for a little romance in her life.

Now that Alex was feeling better, he certainly was going to make the same assumption. He had more claim than any of them, and her professional skill in batting down the soldiers in the hospital was not going to work on Alex. Well, she'd known they'd have to cross this bridge sooner or later. She didn't intend to give him any false hope. She said a silent prayer that she might be wise in what she said. She didn't know how it would go down but was sure it could not end pleasantly. She quietly opened the door to the bedroom and glanced in. He slept. She slipped in. She needed to move her clothing out of this room, but there wasn't another chest in the small house. Alex didn't have any clothing to speak off, just what she had grabbed at the hospital in Denver and a few things she had picked up that had been left behind at the Veterans' Hospital where she worked. The chest and closet were actually perfectly adequate for both of them, but only one of them could sleep in the bedroom. She liked the safety of having herself between the bedroom and front door, should anyone unexpected appear.

She pulled the drawer of the chest open and it made the inevitable creak. She didn't turn to see if he had awakened.

"Valentina?"

"Oh," she turned, "I thought you were asleep."

"Your noise woke me up."

So now he was turning into a light sleeper. Great. "How do you feel today?"

"Thirsty. Hungry."

The hunger she saw in his eyes was not for food. She was afraid of that. "I'll get you a drink now. Then I want to shower and change, and I'll get you some food."

She brought him a glass of water and retrieved her clothing. She had temporarily stored the portrait Alex had drawn of her beneath her underwear. It was better he did not see it. She slipped it underneath the paper lining the drawer.

Valentina loved this ready hot water. It was her favorite luxury of this American life. It must cost money, but Etienne hadn't charged her for a thing. He must be covering all of the expenses, the electricity as well. She didn't dare inquire about it. Everything might require revelations she couldn't reveal. Bless Etienne for covering her bases. She nevertheless saved from her wages to be able to reimburse him some day. It wasn't fair to expect him to do that.

She made Alex some toast and a soft boiled egg. She planned to remove his IV bottle today. Fortunately, she had sponge bathed him the day before he awoke. The next time that boy was getting a bath, he was giving it to himself. If only each solution did not create another problem. When would she be able to live without feeling like she had to hold her breath?

She ate her own breakfast as she watched Alex eat his. Then she picked up his plate and went to leave the room. "Do you need to relieve yourself?"

"Not yet. You told me last night that we needed to talk. I'm ready."

"Can we talk later? I just worked all night and I am tired." It wasn't tiredness that made her put him off. She just didn't know how to approach this.

"Do you want to sleep here?" Alex tapped the space next to him on the double bed.

"No." She shook her head emphatically. "I'll sleep better in the other room. It is darker."

"Do you have a cigarette I can have?"

Although he didn't keep pushing on the sleeping issue, he turned to another issue they needed to address. Valentina shook her head. "You can't have cigarettes here."

"Why? You do."

"No. No, I don't."

"I smelled it on your nurse's dress both last night and this morning. Why are you lying to me?"

"Alex, listen. I am not lying to you. I have no cigarettes. I do not smoke anymore. People smoke at the hospital and the odor clings to my dress."

"So, get me some cigarettes."

She put the plates on the dresser. She could avoid it or face it. They might as well get this over now. She sat in the chair, but not close enough for him to touch her.

"Etienne, the owner of this house, does not smoke. He would not want his house to smell like smoke. The curtains, the rugs, everything absorbs the smoke odor. We will not smoke here."

"Why? Everybody smokes. What nonsense is this?"

"Alex, everyone does not smoke. Have you ever heard of the Mormons?"

Alex shook his head.

Of course, he hadn't. When would he have? "Salt Lake City?"

Again Alex shook his head.

"The Mormons are a group of people who believe in a living prophet who talks to God. One thing that prophet has said is that it is bad for us to smoke. Salt Lake City is the headquarters for the Mormons."

"And we are in Salt Lake City?"

She nodded.

"Why did we come to Salt Lake City?"

"Mainly because a friend gave me access to this house, but you need to know, I have joined the Mormons. I now follow their beliefs. I wanted to be among them."

"And you brought me here." It was an accusation.

"I'm sorry. You don't have to stay here. There are plenty of other places in the United States where people smoke. You can even smoke in Salt Lake City. Just not in this house, and, please, not in my presence."

"And how am I supposed to go to other places?"

"I'll give you some money initially, but you've got to learn the language. The accent should come easy for you since you can mimic bird sounds so well. Once you get the vocabulary and grammar down, you can go anywhere and pass for an American." Was this a pipe dream, because she had no other viable option?

"Valentina, I have followed you to be with you. I don't want to be in this place. I would have stayed in Kamchatka if it weren't for you. I would have been happy there, but I left Kamchatka because of you."

Guilty as charged, but did that condemn her? What was she supposed to say? "I know, Sasha, I'm sorry." She had never called him Sasha, even though she knew he called himself that. She needed the distance of calling him Alex.

"Why won't you sleep with me or at least by me? Why won't you touch me or let me touch you? Did you take a pledge of celibacy when you became a Mormon?" Alex's words were angry.

"No, Sasha, not complete celibacy, just celibacy until marriage. It's wrong before God for a man and woman to sleep together like we did in Kamchatka. The only time it is right is when they are married."

"So, let's get married."

Well, to him that would seem like a solution, but it would solve nothing. "It's not that simple, Sasha. I don't know if I want to marry you. I don't know if you would want to marry me."

"Of course I want to marry you. That's why I'm here. What difference does making the commitment make? I've given up my whole life for you anyway. I might as well be married to you."

"Sasha, there's more to it than that. I don't want to just marry so I can have sex and not offend God. I want to marry a man who loves God, who follows his commandments, who will teach our children both by example and precept to live lives of righteousness."

"And I don't qualify?"

He needed to ask? "I can't imagine you embracing Mormonism. Your happiness is as important as mine. You need to do what will make you happy."

"What will make me happy? I can't have what would make me happy. You dangle yourself before me, give me a kind of love I never had, never even imagined, never would have missed having; and when I give up everything so I can have you, you tell me 'Sorry. I've changed my mind. I don't want you anymore.'" He was yelling as much as his yet weak voice would allow. "I was content before I met you and now I can never again have the happy life I had then. Thanks a lot. I need to do what will make me happy!" He mimicked her as he said this and then his voice slid into despair. "What's left for me?"

She sighed deeply. There were tears in her eyes. Her sorrow was genuine but her determination was too. "Alex, we can't change the past. I did come into your life. I did seduce you. You followed me. From chance, from fate, from design, whatever, we are here together now but that doesn't mean we need to continue together. We can look at things, take a stand. We don't need to just let the winds of fate continue to blow us about. We can make choices about our lives."

"So what does your God ask besides no smoking and no sex outside of marriage?" He probably didn't realize he was baiting her.

"Well, the rest of the health code says no drinking of alcohol or tea or coffee."

"What! Not even tea or coffee? What do you Mormons drink?"

"Water, milk."

"So you won't marry a man who doesn't drink anything but baby food and who doesn't smoke?" Alex's voice was thick with sarcasm.

"No, I won't." Valentina's voice was equally sincere.

"Well, you can count me out. It doesn't seem to me that it is a man you want to marry. What kind of weak-kneed women are these Mormon men?"

This had actually gone better than she had hoped. Valentina stood. "The Mormon men are magnificent. I knew you wouldn't understand." She left the room, shutting the door behind her.

Part III

Discovered

How do I talk to my children?
About the place that I call home
To them it's just a story
that I tell when I feel alone.
-- from Self-Imposed Exile,
   by Joe Murphy

13

Bishop Bullock's Soution

Sasha lay there seething, tethered to the bed by the IV. Valentina had brought him here, enticing him with her touch, her words, her shape, his memories. Now he wasn't good enough. She didn't want a real man. She wanted a sissy, and she wouldn't take him because he wouldn't castrate himself. Well, he'd show her. He didn't need her either. He didn't need her to support him. He didn't need her to teach him English. He didn't need her to be a woman for him. He was a survivor. He knew how to survive in the harshest of climates with a minimum of resources.

He yanked the needle out of his arm with such a jerk that the bottle fell off its hook on the wall and crashed to the floor, breaking. The tape securing the needle in place tore the hair off his arm. Sasha caught his breath and winced and swore. Valentina appeared at the door, clutching her garment around her.

"What's going on?" she demanded.

"Go away," Sasha barked. "Get out. Leave me alone. I don't need you."

"Alex, you do need me. Right now, you do need me." She moved within reach of the bed.

He grabbed her wrist and attempted to pull her to him. "If you touch me, I'll lie with you by force."

"You're so weak right now you couldn't make that happen if your life depended upon it." She easily wrenched away from him. She cleaned up the mess from the broken bottle on the floor and slammed the door when she left the room.

He massaged his arm. Blood oozed from his inner elbow where the needle had been. His leg throbbed. He'd forgotten all about his leg. She really did have him in a corner, a helpless, dependent corner.

*****

Well, she should have known it hadn't gone as well as it initially seemed. She couldn't blame Alex for his anger and frustration, but that didn't change anything. If he were going to survive, he would have to play by her rules. She could survive here. She could disappear, become someone else. She had some other IDs in her folder. Although it might come back unpleasantly on Etienne if she were to abandon Alex here, she would do that before she would give in to his demands or permit him to reveal her. Would he try to do something to her in her sleep? She lay on the couch, wondering if she would be able to sleep with the anxiety in her mind. She was sure Alex was too weak to force her, but she slept in a dress, leaving her coat, shoes, all of her IDs, and money by the door. She slept lightly with one ear cocked.

Valentina awakened from a deep sleep. The sun was now on the east side of the house. It was morning, and Alex had left her alone. She relieved herself and then thought he might have the same need. She tapped on the bedroom door, "Do you need to go to the bathroom?" she called through the door.

"Can you bring me a pot?" He didn't sound angry any longer.

She laughed gently and cracked the door.

"Welcome to civilization. There's a bathroom just across the hall. You did see flushing toilets in Europe, didn't you?"

"Yes."

"Can you stand by yourself?"

"I don't need your help," he growled.

If he behaved like a soldier in a hospital, who knew he had better respect her limits, she would allow him to put his arm over her shoulder for support as he shuffled to the bathroom. He had to be frightfully weak. It had been weeks since he had used his body. She pushed the chair to him. "Use this as a support."

He looked at her from under his bushy eyebrows and muttered, "Don't you dare get too close to me."

Exactly. "I'll find a bottle for you to pee into if you can't get to the bathroom." Reinserting the catheter might be an option, but that wasn't going to happen. She would not touch him there unless he were unconscious.

Sasha slipped his feet to the floor. He looked as if his legs were going to buckle under him. She took a step towards him, but his glare stopped her. He steadied himself by clinging to the bed. She pushed the chair closer, and Sasha shifted first one hand and then the other to the back of the chair. Sweat beaded on his forehead.

"I think you better get back in bed. I don't think you're ready for this," she said.

"Move those rugs and get out of my way. I will do this."

She kicked the throw rugs out of the way but still held her breath as he slowly shuffled across the room, into the hallway and then into the small bathroom, using the chair as support.

"You probably should sit on the toilet."

"I'm not one of your Mormon sissies. I don't need a woman to tell me how to pee. Get out of here. You don't have to watch me while I do it."

And she'd thought he wasn't still angry. Raging anger roared in him, and they were confined together in this small house. He was a virtual prisoner, she the warden, but also the prey. She could escape whenever she chose, but each time she came back, she would have to face him. What would he be like when he regained his strength? What solution was there to this? She wiped a stinging tear from her cheek. There truly was no safety for her anywhere. Not willing to give in to her despair, she banged the frying pan onto the stove, and the handle snapped in her hand. She stared at it for a stunned moment and then flung it into the garbage. Rather than give Alex the satisfaction of hearing her sobs, she grabbed her coat and slammed out the door. Stuffing her hands in her pockets, she set off at a brisk walk.

*****

What right did she have to be angry? Sasha fumed. She was here because she wanted to be. She didn't have to rescue him. Didn't she think through what that would mean when she came to that hospital and took him away? What was he to do now? Evidently, he had been totally foolish to think that she loved him. What did she think was going to happen next? He had but one goal. Get back to Kamchatka if possible, but if not, at least get out of here.

He sat on the toilet for a long time before grasping the chair. Pulling up with his hands, leg by leg, he got back into a standing position. He would not be going anywhere soon; maybe he would never heal enough to get out of here. He should have died when he had a chance. If he couldn't have managed to get in the path of a bullet, he should have used one on himself. Maybe there was a knife in the kitchen. Butchering oneself was so repulsive. He would have to accept her food, but this would end as soon as he could make it happen.

He wanted to push the chair to the window but was afraid he would fall asleep, and fall off it if he did. He pushed it to the bed, flung his torso over the bed and tried to lift his leg. It wasn't going to work. He didn't have the strength in his arms to lift his leg. He was so tired. He would rest awhile and then try again.

*****

Valentina found his upper torso lying across the bed, deeply asleep but fortunately, far enough across the bed not to slip back into a heap on the floor. She was able to pick up his legs and slide them onto the bed. He stirred but did not resist nor fully awaken. Should she put the catheter back in now that she had a chance? No, she would have to remove it again later. They would manage, somehow. He was still asleep when she left for work that night. The next morning as she fixed some breakfast, she heard the sounds of the chair being pushed across the bedroom. She waited attentively to see if she would hear a body fall. She did not, nor did she hear the bedroom door open. She took a bowl of oatmeal with a splash of milk to the door and tapped.

"What?" Alex growled.

"I have breakfast for you." She tried to sound cheerful. He said nothing more, and she opened the door. He sat at the window looking out at a winter scene: a fruit tree piercing the sky with its naked limbs, snow on the ground, on the backs of houses, garages, and sheds within his view. Clouds still hid the mountains.

"How close are we to that lake?"

"I don't know. I haven't actually seen it."

"Does the city live off the fish in the lake? Is that their industry?" Maybe he could get a job working with the fish somehow.

"No, Alex. The lake is very salty."

"So is the ocean, and it has fish."

"Salt Lake is so salty that not even fish can live in it. It is compared to the Dead Sea in Palestine. The only industry is the salt."

"Do you expect me to work in the salt mine?"

"You will have to learn English to work any place at all. Russians cannot be here legally."

He growled and grabbed the bowl and wolfed down the oatmeal and then slammed it down on the table and turned back to the window in obvious dismissal, without saying another word.

Salt Lake City 1948

"Well, that's about it," Alex said as Valentina finished talking.

Bishop Greg Bullock looked at them in astonishment. "How long you here?"

Alex and Valentina looked at each other as if measuring the time. Valentina answered, "Close to two and a half years."

Greg addressed Alex, "You live with her for two years and not touch her?"

Alex glanced at Valentina as if seeking permission to tell. She nodded, "Once I came into the living room. She had begun undressing for bed and did not hear me coming. I guess I thought that I could entice her to want it as bad as I did. I came behind her and slipped my arms around her, cupping her, uh--" he did another quick glance at Valentina, and she nodded again, "—uh, breasts in my hands."

Greg restrained his smile. Alex had definitely learned that there were things Valentina did not want him to discuss. "Then what happen?"

"I felt like I had been attacked by a windmill. Her arms flew in every direction, throwing me off. She had on one of those shoes with skinny heels, and she stomped on my foot. While I'm hopping around, yelping, and holding my foot, she dashed into the bedroom, threw my clothes out, and locked the door. That was when I decided it was time to leave again."

"You left other time?" Greg asked.

"I attempted to. After I became strong enough, I decided I was going to go back to Kamchatka—mind you, I had no map or compass. I only knew that Kamchatka must be north and west of Salt Lake. Initially, I thought I would walk there. I headed west, taking what food and water I could carry and what tools I could muster from the house. A knife. A small ax. I had lived a survivalist life. I had endured great deprivation in the army and prison camps. I thought I would be up to it. I did find the Great Salt Lake and did verify it was very salty and not a source for food or water. There was no source at all for food or water, or even shelter, anywhere west of here within feasible walking distance. I gave up and came back before dehydration killed me."

"Only time you leave?"

"No. I went back, again recovered my health, and tried a different plan. This time, I hid in a train, much as I had on my way to Moscow. The problem with this was that I didn't know where the trains were going. I could not read the names of the towns I came to. I didn't dare go into the stations to see if there were some sort of map. This still might be an option to get me out of here. With someone to tell me which trains to take, if I can make it to Alaska, I'm sure I could find a way to get back to Kamchatka."

"Valentina not help?"

"She said it was dishonest to go that way, and she didn't have the money to buy me a ticket."

"What you do?"

"You mean, besides swear, and yell and scream? That time I went to the mountains. I thought that even though it would not be Kamchatka, there must be animals there that I could eat and water I could drink. I could live there."

"Like a--" Greg looked at Valentina and asked in English, "How do you say hermit in Russian?"

She supplied the word, and Sasha answered, "I've been a hermit most of my life. I'm not afraid of living like that. It's better than living with people who do not want you around."

Greg could well understand how Alex had come to this conclusion. "Why you come back?"

"I needed more tools, more resources. I wanted to draw the animals, the plants, but I didn't have pencils and paper. I hoped for some matches or flint to make building fires easier. You know, things like that. Also, my shoes were practically worn out, and even though I know how to tan a hide and make my own, it is time-consuming."

"When he come back, what happen?" Greg addressed this question to Valentina.

"Well, let me answer that by backing up a bit. He had been gone for over two months. I didn't know where he was or what his intentions were. I didn't know if he were ever coming back. I had started to relax my vigilance and began to form friendships with those around me. I had begun dating Douglas Parkins. The night he came back, Douglas and I were talking as we sat on the porch swing of my house. It had just been announced that my mother had been picked up. I was a bit jumpy inside, of course, but trying to keep a calm exterior. Because of my mother's arrest, the whole Russian spy thing was foremost in Doug's mind, and it was this night that he proclaimed that he was going to do whatever he could to root out those Russian spies hiding in America. I did my best not to react. It may have been my finest moment of acting. I was totally torn apart, but I realized that he had no idea I was Russian, and while I am not a spy, did it matter? I would be repatriated. I had to keep totally calm, unruffled. I had to finish out the evening as if he hadn't said anything that upset me. Our relationship had progressed to the point that I allowed him a goodnight kiss. He began to kiss me, and all of sudden, he shrieked, 'Who is that wild man? You want me to punch him out?'

Alex had come up to the porch. His hair and beard were long and shaggy, and he had not bathed. I tried to show no surprise. I told Douglas that he was my cousin visiting from Europe, and he had been camping in the mountains. They just glared at each other, but neither said anything. Douglas left, and it was then I decided I had better find some kind of a solution to our situation, so I made the appointment to come and see you."

"Only time you feel danger?"

"Well there was another time. I doubt it was really a serious threat, but I felt threatened at the time. After Alex first began to recover, he started to notice the birds. He wanted to know what the bird with a red breast and cheery song was called. He asked me to ask about it at work. I asked during a break at the VA. There were about five of us chatting at a table. They just looked at me and said, 'You're not from around here, are you?' I just said, 'No, I'm from England.' I hadn't thought about the danger of revealing my ignorance of common knowledge to anyone from here. I refused to ever ask such questions again. What if the robin is a common bird in England too, and one of them had known that?"

Greg was continually amazed at the delicate balancing act their lives had been and how it could all tumble so easily over the smallest thing, like the proverbial house of cards. There was no place where there was security. Everyone and everything could be a threat.

"So that is our story. What do you think we should do?"

Greg hesitated only a moment, measuring their anticipation for an acceptable resolution among the few options. They could turn themselves in, they would face interrogation, perhaps torture to determine if they were spies. He had no idea what would happen if the authorities decided they were spies, probably imprisonment. Of course, they would eventually come to the conclusion they were not spies since there was no evidence. So, they would be repatriated sooner or later if they turned themselves in, and would most certainly face either death or a hard labor camp for the rest of their lives. He could not feel good about encouraging that course. He had to live with himself after this was over. Another option, of course, would be somehow to get Alex to some remote part of Alaska and then he could use his vast skills to survive until he found a way back to Kamchatka. Valentina would make her way in American society, always under the guise that she was someone she wasn't. They could probably pull this off. Greg knew that was the answer they anticipated, but there was a third answer. He knew they would not like his answer, but still, he knew it was the right one. "I think you marry." Just as he expected, they both looked at him in stunned amazement.

"But that doesn't solve anything," Valentina protested. "Well, it does solve one thing. Alex gets sex, but he still doesn't speak the language; he still cannot get a job; he is still a house prisoner or on the run."

"True. But if marry, husband need to know you Russian. No problem with Alex."

"Does even a married couple ever really know each other? In observing others, I don't think so, but it doesn't matter. I'll just stay single. That is not a good reason to get married."

"Not said good. You ask what I think. I think God want you together." So much more he wanted to say, but his Russian wasn't up to it. Although he was certain God did not condone their relationship, beginning with Alex's seduction, he didn't think it was just happenstance they managed to see each other in Moscow, then France, and now, here. He didn't add how much it astonished him that Sasha was his own Russian rescuer, now sitting in his office seeking help. God had his hand in this; of this, he was fully confident.

"But Alex doesn't know the Lord."

"The Lord know Alex. That can happen. You not always know Lord." That seemed to stop her protests, momentarily.

"But how does that solve the other problems?" It was obvious that Valentina was struggling with this, not so sure she wanted to accept it as an answer.

"God know. He can work out. You okay ask Him?" Greg wished he could slip into English. It was so clumsy trying to explain his thoughts in his limited Russian, but it was vital to include Alex in this decision.

Valentina's answer was not immediate. She looked at her hands, looked at Alex, who alternately stared at the floor and glared at him. Alex never gave Valentina a glance. Finally, after several minutes of struggle, she said, "How can I know his will?"

"Saturday I take kids to temple. You come too. Maybe baptize for your brothers. Their names?

"Dmitri, Andrei, and Markov."

"Dmitri and Markov sound Russian. Better not. But spirit of Lord strong at temple. We all go without food and water to know will of God." That was a clumsy way to try and explain fasting to Alex, who would certainly see no relevance. Greg said to Valentina, "You explain fasting to Alex later. We pray. If you get no answer from God, we talk again, make new plan. Okay?"

She still paused and then said, "I will fast and pray about it and join you for the temple trip, but I will not marry him unless I know it is the Lord's will."

"I not ask. Alex, you okay marry Valentina?"

He growled, showing more of his inner feelings than his words, "She doesn't want me."

"If she do?"

"She doesn't." There was no quibbling on his part, and it seemed to come down to this.

Well, this would need the Lord's intervention if it were to happen, but Greg believed in a God of miracles. "Alex, I need speak Valentina alone." His Russian was way too rudimentary to try and explain what a temple recommend interview was.

*****

Sasha felt a roiling fury boiling within. He had expected more of the man who owed him his life. Why did he have to hide behind his God, blaming Valentina's rejection of him on God's will, instead of just stating it was what it was. She didn't want him. Well, fair enough. It would end up the same anyway. After their God said she was free of any obligation to this heathen, then hopefully, Bishop Bullock would come up with a plan to get him to Alaska. He could manage it himself from there. Surely that would be how it would end, and that was what he wanted, wasn't it? Why was this little charade over asking God so important? Maybe to assuage their moral sense when they looked back on this later. Perhaps he should not begrudge them that, but he did. They were playing games with him, and it infuriated him.

He did not wait for Valentina to come out of Bishop Bullock's office. He didn't know what this little private interview was about. Maybe to make their plans to get him out of their lives. He stomped out the door and tried to slam it. A mechanism closed it softly, not allowing it to be slammed shut, as a sort of an exclamation point at the end of the evening.

*****

Valentina left Bishop Bullock's office, clutching her temple recommend. She still hadn't caught her equilibrium since Bishop Bullock had suggested that she and Alex marry. Of all the admittedly limited options that seemed to exist to resolve their dilemma, this had not even been on the list. Was Bishop Bullock really suggesting it as a result of inspiration? It made no sense even to contemplate it from any other point of view. If it were inspiration she needed to know for herself that this was what

God wanted her to do, because she couldn't imagine it. It would not solve any problems. Sure, Alex would have the sex he wanted, but that made babies, not a marriage. What kind of marriage could they possibly have? It would seem to be a marriage that could go nowhere. She felt she was just spinning her wheels trying to figure this out.

Alex's expression and ill-tempered departure from Bishop Bullock's office made it quite clear that he was not happy with this turn of events either. The next couple of days, he was more morose and irritable than usual. She tried to be happy and upbeat, but it just made him more glum. What hope was there for a blissful marriage when he just clammed up? He had no problem-solving skills at all for interpersonal relationships. In a moment of honesty, she realized she was hoping God would say that they shouldn't marry. What would she be condemning herself to if she did marry Alex? She would try her best to really hear God's will in this matter. It would be the biggest act of faith she had ever done.

Friday night, Alex ate the meal listlessly, as a man eating his last meal before facing his executioner. He mechanically helped Valentina clean up.

"Well," she said, "we need to begin our fast. I need to explain what that is. Going without food and water is symbolic of being hungry and thirsty to know God's will. It makes one more humble, more receptive to His answer."

He looked at her dumbly.

"Come, Alex. Don't be afraid. God loves you. He wants your happiness. You can trust Him. We kneel like this to talk to God." She demonstrated by kneeling on the floor next to the couch. He knelt next to her. She clasped her hands and leaned her forearms on the couch. Alex did the same.

"I'll begin the prayer. You can add anything at the end if you want to." She closed her eyes and lowered her head. "Heavenly Father. We kneel before thee to know thy will regarding the most important decision in our lives—whether to marry each other. For reasons unknown to us, thou hast brought us together. First on Kamchatka," Could she blame that on God? "Then in Moscow, again in France, and now, here."

There were explanations of their own choice and circumstances, making all of that happen, apart from God and his directing hand. "It almost seems we have a mission together, but only thou knowest." Bishop Bullock has suggested this.

"Perhaps it has been fulfilled. We know that we are not without sin, even the hideous sin of aborting our own innocent unborn child conceived in lust. We do not know if Thy Son's atonement can ransom us from our wicked ways." Her voice caught. Tears overtook her, and she quit speaking. She was sure Alex's eyes were on her. She found his hand, squeezed it, and then kept it in her grasp. Eventually, she resumed. "Please, dear Father, guide us. Speak to us that we might know thy will in our lives. Let us know if it is good for us to marry each other. In the name of Jesus Christ, Amen."

Valentina had not expected to become emotional when she prayed, but, really, so much did ride on this decision. She opened her eyes and looked at Alex. He looked at her with an expression of open curiosity, much softer than the sour glares he had bestowed on her the last few days.

"Do you want to add anything?"

He shook his head. She gave his hand another squeeze. "Do you want to come down to Temple Square with me? It's beautiful. Lots of flowers and grass, a peaceful place. After I finish there, I may go to City Creek Canyon to pray. It's a nature place. Do you want to come?"

Sasha shook his head again.

"Don't be so negative. Have a little faith. Whether the answer's yes or no, you will feel at peace about it."

She arose and went to the bedroom.

The next morning, she did not disturb Alex in his cocoon on the couch as she dressed in her Sunday best. She prayed again for God's guidance before leaving to catch a ride to the temple. She was glad he had declined to come with her. How would she ever struggle with making this decision and listening for the quiet voice of God's spirit with his negative flow of emotions?

*****

Sasha lay motionless in his sleeping bag as he heard Valentina prepare to leave. He had spent a sleepless night. Who was this God Valentina wanted to give power over their lives? Was there really such a being? What did He have to do with them? Did He know them in any sense? What difference did it make? Sasha knew the story of the Christian God Jesus, who had been crucified by his own people and then supposedly came alive from the dead. Did that have anything to do with this? Valentina had closed her prayer in his name. Did that God still live and talk to people? What did he care who they married, except to keep Valentina from marrying a non-believer? Then he would say no to their marriage. Why couldn't she just say no? Sasha's mind was a whirlwind of thoughts, all of it biting, stinging, hurting. None of it was comforting.

He had to refuse her invitation to come along. A restlessness already gripped him. He did not feel he could contain it if he were around Valentina all day as she tried to decide how to tell him that her God rejected their marriage. She had seemed amused by his lack of belief. Her amusement cut him like a knife. She seemed outwardly very considerate, but she held all the cards. He had no power in this situation.

As soon as she left, he tried to go back to sleep. The room was too bright, and thoughts plagued him like mosquitoes. He tried to work on his drawings and notes but was unable to concentrate. He paced, then went out the back door and looked to see if anyone was in the alleyway before slipping into the street, his mind in a prison. Valentina would return, all happy that her God had said no. She would be free of him, free of the burden he represented to her. She could marry one of her fine men who did not smoke or drink.

At best, somehow he would end up in Alaska and maybe someday be able to make his way back to Kamchatka. At worst, his tongue would betray him because he did not know the language, and he would be repatriated to the Motherland. He would be cheered as a returning hero who saw the superiority of the Soviet System and then taken out and shot because he had defected to the decadent West.

Why had he not listened to Baba? Why had he ever left the security of Kamchatka? Why had he not stood firm in resisting Valentina's charms? He'd known they were poison to him the minute he met her. Why was she so important to him now? Why wait for Valentina to declare his fate? Maybe he should just disappear into these mountains for good. He could live off the land. That's what he would do! He'd go back, pack his gear and just disappear. If he did not survive, what would it matter? It would be better than being shot in Russia.

He returned to the house and began packing his things. Hunger gnawed at him. He was tempted to eat but felt honor required him to wait, to see this fast through as she had stipulated. It would be the last thing he ever did for her. He lay on the couch, and eventually, sleep did come. He dreamed of looking for her. His desire was not sexually driven, but the desire to see her, talk to her, be with her. Finally, he awoke and paced, wondering when she would return. He wanted her so badly. How could he just walk out of her life permanently? Because she would tell him it would make them both happy. Happiness was what it was all about. He would never be happy again.

*****

Valentina followed the others down a long yellow hallway in the temple to the baptistry. Here she was issued white clothing and waited and watched while the girls in their group were baptized. Bishop Bullock baptized each girl for and in behalf of someone who was dead, whom he called by name. And then they were baptized for someone else. Each girl was baptized for about fifteen individuals. When her turn came, Valentina stepped into the font of warm water and felt Bishop Bullock's benevolent smile on her. She felt such a feeling of peace and joy.

After she was dressed, she met the others at the entrance of the temple and declined their offer of a ride back home. It was a couple of miles, but she felt she needed to be encircled by this peace as she sought to hear God's voice. She didn't quite know even how to approach the issue. If she felt it were God's will that she not marry Alex, then it would be pretty much up to Bishop Bullock what happened to him. Alex would no longer be her responsibility and she could craft her life the best she could under the circumstances. But if it were God's will that she marry Alex, everything would still be her problem even as it was today. He could not work. Maybe he would feel a need to learn the language, but that would be a long, slow process. He had made no effort so far. There would eventually be children. How would they keep them safe? Sooner or later, the children would speak, and the whole torrid secret would spill out. She and Alex would be repatriated, but what would happen to the children?

It wasn't that she didn't like Alex. She had liked him fine in Kamchatka. The man he had been there was not the man she lived with day-to-day. Basically, they didn't have a relationship now. They only had history. A sexual relationship would not be a sufficient base for a happy marriage. She just couldn't see what their lives could be together here. She wanted to believe in Bishop Bullock, to believe he had received inspiration. But she didn't see how even God could solve this situation. There was no magic wand that would suddenly make everything all right.

She alternately prayed, rehearsed all of the aspects in her mind, cried that she didn't know how to recognize God's voice. She couldn't do something as irrational as marrying Alex unless she absolutely knew it was God's will. Late in the afternoon, she offered one last prayer and then began her trek home. If the answer wasn't yes, then it must be no. That thought had no sooner passed through her mind than she saw the answer with a clarity that astounded her and laid all doubts to rest. It left her so breathless that she sat for a moment on a bus bench.

It seemed that she saw Alex in a flash, a glimpse for just a moment, but it was years down the road. He was talking to a young man who looked very much as Alex did now but taller. Alex told the young man that nothing mattered as much as his family and his testimony in the restored gospel. That was all she saw, but it was like a vision of the future, and it was enough. It felt so real that she was reassured. It told her that somehow they would escape repatriation, that they would have children who would reach adulthood, that someday Alex would come to know the Lord. Accompanying the brief vision was an overwhelming feeling of love for Alex. She sat on the bench and pondered this. A bus came by, and she waved it on, then said a prayer of thanksgiving and continued on her way.

*****

Valentina slipped in so quietly that Sasha didn't notice until she sat on the couch next to him. Her face glowed as if God's glory shone through her. Peace and serenity emanated from her.

"You got your answer from your God," he said.

"I did." She smiled at him. "Did you?"

"I don't know how to talk to your God." He braced himself, told himself that he needed to accept her rejection graciously. It would do no good to lash out at her, though he felt like it.

"Let's say a prayer of thanksgiving." She fell to her knees and grasped Sasha's hand. He knelt beside her, his heart as heavy as hers seemed light.

"Father in Heaven, thank you for answering our prayers and communing with us. We will strive with all our hearts to do thy will and seek thy guidance in our lives. In the name of Jesus Christ. Amen.

She was in his arms, kissing him. He was dumbfounded, his sluggish mind not quite understanding what had happened.

She stroked his face with her fingertips. "Alex, I do know that it is God's will that we marry. I don't know how we are going to solve all the problems. I do know we will solve them, and everything will be all right. We will be happy."

She kissed him again.

"So you're going to marry me?" That much had finally registered.

"I'm no longer afraid. Our troubles are just temporary."

"Do you love me?"

"I will, with a love I can't even imagine right now."

Now Sasha kissed her. He hugged her, but he kept his hands from touching any part of her body to which she might object.

"I think we should be married as soon as possible."

"How soon?"

"Well, it won't be like where you have to be a slave to my father for two years and all my female relatives try to keep you from me."

"Thank goodness." Joy welled in Sasha. This was for real. She really was going to marry him.

"Will we be married in your temple?"

"No, not now." A shadow passed over her face. "Maybe someday. I'll have to talk to Bishop Bullock to see what we must do to get married."

Monday Valentina was late in coming home.

"Well, I know what we have to do to get married. I will make application for the marriage license tomorrow. This is your story. Your name is Alexander Darke. You were born on June 24, 1919 in Des Moines, Iowa. This is your birth certificate." She handed him an official-looking paper.

"Where did you get this?"

"I got it in France shortly before I left. There was a group fabricating passports to get people like us or Jews out of Europe. They had a bunch of them. We chose ones born about the same year we were born. I had just seen you in France when I saw this one for Alexander Darke. I didn't know if you would ever need it, but I took it just in case. You at least get the same first name. In order to apply for the wedding license, you've got to be able to sign your name in American cursive." Valentina wrote on a paper. "You've got a middle name of Joseph, but most Americans would just use the first initial. You have to practice writing this again and again until you can do it without looking. You need to begin practicing. As soon as you can write your name, we can get married."

"That quick?"

"That quick."

Sasha took the pen and paper and began practicing. Valentina gave him some hints for forming the letters. He was able to write it to her satisfaction before the evening was over.

"Okay. So now we can get married?"

"We will be getting some special clothes to get married in."

She took Sasha to a store marked with the letters ZCMI. She told him he would be wearing a western suit and tie. The closest Sasha had ever come to wearing a western suit was his army uniform. He wanted to protest. He would never wear this, but Valentina had insisted all he could say in the store was okay when she nodded her head at him. When he protested at home, she said, "You can wear it to church."

"I've not agreed to go to church."

She put her hands on his shoulders and kissed him. "I know. I can hope."

He kissed her long. "Don't get your hopes too high."

Valentina had bought herself a silky pink dress. Sasha liked the way she looked and felt in it. Beautiful enough to be a bride.

"I am going by the name of Anita. You need to learn to say it. After marriage, my last name will be the same as yours."

"That wasn't the name on the envelope you gave me in France."

"No. I came to the states under the name of Rachel Hamilton. That's the name I worked under at the hospital where I rescued you. In case the hospital has traced your disappearance to her, she had to disappear.

"We will be married by a justice of the peace, a sort of a minor judge who specializes in weddings. We will be in a courtroom, but do not be frightened. This judge has only the power to marry us. He cannot send anyone to prison. Bishop Bullock also has authority to marry us, but he says there would have to be witnesses, and that would mean involving other people who know me. It will be more routine before the justice of the peace. He does so many weddings, he probably will not even remember us later."

Valentina went to the court and observed some marriages, then scheduled their own. She warned Alex what to expect in the ceremony. He had to practice saying, "I do" until he could do it to her satisfaction. They went to the court at what Valentina said was the busiest time, so they could watch others getting married while they waited their turn. Sasha was able to say "I do" with no more clue than the justice looking at him and pausing. They accepted the offer to have a wedding photo taken. Sasha carried a small suitcase that Valentina had prepared. They walked the few blocks from the City-County Building to the Hotel Utah. They ate in the hotel's fancy dining room-- white walls, white table cloth, white napkins, white-clothed waiters and waitresses, and brightly colored carrots, green beans, with a steak and white mashed potatoes on a white plate.

Sasha was surprised when Valentina led him up the broad, red-carpeted marble stairs of the hotel. She unlocked the door to a room with a bed. Valentina locked the door behind them and jumped into Sasha's arms, kissing him passionately as he stood looking around the room, still holding the suitcase. The intent of her passionate kisses was unmistakable. "Why are we here?"

"It's our honeymoon."

"What's a honeymoon?"

"It's how a couple celebrates their marriage."

"Why didn't we just go home?"

"This is our wedding day. It needs to be different, to be memorable. You talk too much." She kissed him passionately and began to caress him. He quit talking.

14

Escape Into Hiding

They returned to their house, and life was much as it had been before their marriage, except the nights were warm and sweet as they slept in each other's arms. Valentina began a determined effort to teach Sasha English.

"Listen more carefully, Alex. You've got to get the accent exactly right, or it will be the quickest thing to betray you. This sound does not exist in Russian. Try to imitate exactly what I am saying: "Ah."

"Aw"

"No. Listen to the difference: Kawmchawtkaw, Russian, Kahm-chahtkuh, English. Now you say it."

"Kawmchawtkaw."

"No. Not the Russian way. The English way."

"Kahmchawtkaw."

"You only got one of the three right. I don't think you're trying very hard."

"I'm sick of this. I don't even want to learn English."

"You're going to be a prisoner in this house until you stop fighting it."

Sasha could tell Valentina was exasperated, but so was he. "I don't care."

"You'd better care. I don't plan to spend the rest of my life supporting you. This is ridiculous. You can imitate bird sounds so accurately the birds think you're a bird, but you can't imitate human sounds at all."

"I learned to imitate the birds as young as I learned to talk. I can't help it that English is so hard."

"You're not trying. You don't want to learn English."

"You're right. I don't want to." He debated whether to stay and argue with her or get up and leave.

"You need to learn English to survive here."

"I know how to survive in Kamchatka."

"But you're not in Kamchatka. It doesn't do you much good to know how to make sarana lily flour without any sarana lilies.

"Quit rubbing it in."

"Cooperate. Say it--Kahmchahtkah."

"No. Leave me alone." He got up and walked to the door.

"Alex, we're married now. Just leaving you alone is not an option. English is your ticket to survival."

Sasha wanted to be with Valentina each night, but soon the mountains began to call. He resisted for a while, but the magnetism of the call became so strong that he told Valentina he was sorry, but he had to go. With tears in her eyes, she bade him good-bye, "I'll miss you."

He went for only three days and returned.

After she lovingly greeted him and fed him, she said, "Alex, we've got to talk."

He sat on the couch and put his arm around her. "About what?"

"It's not right that I should do all the work, and you spend your time in the mountains."

He removed his arm from around her shoulders, "I work in the mountains—same as I did in Kamchatka."

"Yes, but you're not getting paid for it."

"The only work that counts is the work that you get paid for?"

"Of course not, but you don't do any work around here either." Her hand swept a semi-circle encompassing the house.

"Work around here?" he echoed, not really comprehending.

"The cooking, the cleaning, the dishwashing, the washing of the clothes.

"That's woman's work." Sasha protested.

Valentina's eyes snapped at him. "You did it for yourself in Kamchatka."

"I didn't have a woman to do it for me."

"Then it's men's work to provide for the financial needs of a family. I coddled you as a child for a long time. I can't do it indefinitely. You've married me. You need to take a role in providing for this family's needs. I can't do it all. It's not fair." She began to cry. Sasha stood and moved to the window.

"So you want me to cook and clean."

She cried some more, angrily wiping the tears from her cheeks. "What I really want you to do is get a job, and I'll stay home and cook and clean."

"But you said it's dangerous for me to get a job until I learn the language.

"That's the point. You make no effort to learn the language."

"It's a crazy language. It sounds so...so garbled. I already feel like a child, but when you're constantly telling me to say this, to say that, it's worse. 'No, that's not right, say it this way.'" He mimicked her voice, but it was heavy with his anger. "I can't take it. I'm sorry."

He finally came to her and pulled her sobbing into his arms. "Maybe I shouldn't have married you. It isn't fair to you."

"Don't say that. Alexska! I know it is right that we be married. I want to be married to you."

He kissed her and tasted her tears. Her words warmed him. He was glad she still wanted to be married to him even though neither of them saw their way out of this bind.

"I'm only going to talk English to you." She said.

"Oh. That's really nice of you. I can't smoke. I can't drink. I can't go anywhere except for the mountains. Now I can't talk. You spend all your days with people you can talk to, and I have to spend mine in solitude, and you won't talk to me. Maybe they could use you as a guard at a prison camp."

"Quit yelling."

"I'm not yelling."

With pantomime and repetition, she succeeded in communicating with him, but only as long as they talked about things. Ideas were impossible, and he always answered back in Russian. She wouldn't respond to him unless he tried to say it in English. She'd model for him.

"Tay-ble. Say it."

"*Nyet*."

"Table, sink. fridge, chair, man, woman," she pointed as she talked. "This is a table. This table is big. That table is small. Which table is big? Show me the big table."

"I don't want to play these children's games."

"Well, there's no way to serve English up to you on a platter. Haven't you ever had to learn something hard? You've got to work at it--all the time."

He felt a mild triumph. She had slipped into Russian. "Leave me alone."

"I'm beginning to think that is an excellent idea."

"So you are going to leave me to be sent back to Russia to be executed. You think your God will be happy about that?"

"You think my God is happy about you just sponging off me? You are going to have to ask for your food by name. Bread, butter. Pass the butter."

If he refused to use English words, she'd ignore his requests. Finally, in frustration or anger, Sasha would comply and spit out the words as near as he remembered. She never corrected him, but once she murmured, "You can make bird sounds well enough that the birds can't tell you're not a bird. You're just not trying."

Her words angered him because of the sting of truth. Sasha returned to the mountains and stayed for two weeks, but he missed her, and his feelings mellowed. It was an issue they would have to face. He knew the issue was much bigger than the language. In fact, refusing to learn the language kept him from having to face the real issue. Valentina had said the type of job he could probably get once he learned the language was a daily job working eight hours or more in a factory five or six days a week. He'd virtually have to give up his mountains with such a job. He'd only have one or two days a week free. It took him that long to hike into the places where he was researching. Two days a week would never give him that opportunity. As much as he cared for Valentina and wanted her to be happy, it was in the mountains he got in touch with himself. He felt he would lose himself if he gave up the mountains.

He hiked down the mountain to within an hour of home, caught some trout, and cleaned them. When he got them home, Valentina was asleep, even though it was only late afternoon. Sasha rummaged through the cupboards and fridge looking for things he knew how to cook. He liked rice with fish, but he had never noticed how Valentina cooked it. He realized instructions were written on the box, but he had made no progress in learning to read English. He settled on potatoes. He knew how to cook them. When he was rummaging for pans, Valentina came to the kitchen. He stopped his work and offered his arms to her. She came willingly into his embrace. He hugged her and kissed her.

"I miss you so much when you're gone."

He traced her facial features with his fingertips. "I miss you too. I just need the mountains."

"I know," she said.

He didn't know if she did know or not. She seemed weary, unwilling to make a fight. She was not even speaking English.

"What pan do you cook the fish in?"

She got a pan out. "Cook the potatoes first. They take longer."

"I'd rather have rice, but I don't know how to cook it."

"I'll teach you."

He took no offense. He knew that it wasn't criticism that prompted her to help. They worked together to put the meal on the table. After they had eaten, he began clearing the table.

"I'll do it. You must be tired after walking home."

He kissed the top of her head, "It rejuvenates me to walk home. I know you'll be here when I get back."

She followed him to the sink and dried the dishes as he washed.

"Thank you," she said as they finished cleaning up.

"I try learn English. Use bird book give Bishop Bullock. Okay?"

She smiled at his fumbling attempt to speak English and richly rewarded him with kisses.

The next morning she slept in, longer than she ever had before. Sasha rummaged in the kitchen to find what he knew how to cook. Relying on the hints she had given on using the stove the night before, he cooked some eggs and made some toast. He set the table and tiptoed into the bedroom and kissed her awake.

"Food on table."

She came and sat at the table and ate. "Sasha." She never called him Sasha, "I don't want to anger you about learning English. What if I say it in English and if you can't understand me, tell me, and I'll say it in Russian and then repeat it in English."

"I need a time, a place where we can really communicate without English being an issue between us."

She sat there and pondered a moment. "Okay. Suppose we call our bed the peninsula. When there, we speak Russian."

"I want to lie with you in bed, not talk with you."

"We can do both." Suddenly she leaped from her chair and ran to the bathroom. Sasha heard her retching. He went to the door of the bathroom and led her to the bedroom after she washed her mouth out. He tucked her in bed. "Are you sick? You're sleeping so much, and you're throwing up."

"I'm pregnant, Alex."

Sasha paused. Pregnancy. This was not a particularly good time for her to get pregnant. Although he certainly realized that sex led to pregnancy, he had chosen not to think of that consequence when pleasuring himself with Valentina. "So you are going to have a baby."

She took his hand and squeezed it. "We are going to have a baby."

"We are going to have a baby." he echoed. In Kamchatka, men had virtually nothing to do with babies. Sasha sighed. What was she trying to stress with the "we." What were her expectations of him?

"When?"

"In the fall."

That would give them time. Something could happen. Maybe she would miscarry. He knew she would not abort, not with the distress her other abortion caused her. Maybe he would give up and learn English. Maybe he would surrender and take a factory job. Why had he been so foolish to get her pregnant? He could end up a prisoner of a factory job for the rest of his life.

He let her give him an English lesson, but it ended in angry yelling over this inconsistent language. He was supposed to know that in the word 'throat,' he said the 'oa' as an 'o', but in 'broad,' he was to say the 'oa' as an 'aw.' In mourning, he was to say the 'ou' as an 'o', in Rufous, 'ou' was to be said as 'uh,' and in mountain, 'ou' was to be said as 'ow.' There was no rhyme or reason to this craziness, and there was no way that he would ever be able to master it.

He redoubled his efforts not to learn English. He spent more and more time in the mountains. It may be his last opportunity. Each time he expected Valentina to rant at him for his refusal to take the bull by the horns and be responsible for the inevitable future. She was strangely calm and peaceful. She seemed to enjoy this pregnancy. As she grew, she would smile and rub her enlarging stomach. "Alex, feeling a child grow within is the most amazing experience. It's in me, it's of me, but it's not me." She grabbed his hand and placed it on her protruding stomach until he felt pressure, "That's a kick. Don't you love it?"

No, he didn't love it. It panicked him. This child was going to cost them their lives. Time ticked with every heartbeat. He understood more and more English, but he could not speak it without a heavy accent and constant grammar errors. He could not go into the workforce and pretend he was American. He would fool no one. Why was Valentina so unconcerned? Couldn't she see the problem? They did not talk about it, and the panic grew in Sasha proportionate to the growth of the child in Valentina. Finally, he decided that the only solution would be for him to disappear into the mountains, to either survive or die and let Valentina make it with the baby as best as she could. Maybe she could find a wet nurse to keep it while she worked. Maybe she could find a job where she could keep the baby with her. He debated about whether to tell her of his plan or just simply disappear into the mountains and leave her to figure out he was not returning. He found it tore him apart to think of just leaving her and her thinking he had abandoned her. He did really care about her. He did appreciate all of the many sacrifices she had made for him. She needed to know he left her because he loved her because he wanted to give her every chance to survive, to make her bid for freedom good.

Aching for the loss of her, he decided to make their last days together as sweet and memorable as he possibly could. She was at work when he arrived at the house. Though she kept it pretty tidy in spite of the pregnancy, he could tell that either her bulk or tiredness was taking its toll. He cleaned himself up and began scrubbing the house. He had done a top to bottom cleaning of the bathroom and bedroom before she returned. He was pleased with himself as he took her tenderly into his arms and kissed her. Her protruding abdomen pushed against him, and he felt the child kick. Tears came to his eyes. This child, his child, would never know its father just as he had never known his father. Were children destined to always be raised by women without a man to guide, protect, and inspire them?

Valentina saw the tears and gently wiped them from his eyes. "What's the matter?"

"I love you so much." He did not dare add 'I'll miss you.'

It was so good to hold her. It was so empty, so lonely to think of life without her. Birds, flowers, trees. What was that without her to come home to? At least in a factory job, he could be with her in the evenings and on weekends. Why had he not valued that enough when there was yet time to learn English well? Now it was too late. Everlastingly too late. Too late for him. Too late for Valentina. Too late for their child. Tears threatened to overwhelm him. She must not see him like this. She must enjoy these last days together without the shadow of him leaving. He went to the kitchen and busied himself preparing dinner.

She came out of the bedroom, amusement in her eyes, "What's the matter? Do you have nesting instinct?"

"Nesting instinct?" He did not understand, although he knew what each word meant in English.

"Just before a mother gives birth, she gets nesting instinct. She prepares the nest for her little bird by cleaning everything."

"Yes. I guess I have it." He drew her to him, hungry to hold her, to feel the baby's kick again, to feel her hair, her cheek, her lips against his. Let her think it was nesting instinct that prompted him to clean. He did want to leave the nest the best he could for her and their little one. How had he ever been so foolish to not anticipate how he would feel at the inevitable moment?

They sat to eat. She blessed the food. He treasured her every movement and stored it as a memory to comfort himself with later.

"Alex," she said, taking his hand, drawing him back to the present, "Please don't go to the mountains again until after the birth of the baby. I've never seen a baby born before. I'm scared. I don't want to be alone."

Another thing he had not thought of. In Kamchatka, tribal women just took care of these things themselves—with the other women. Very little fuss or bother surrounded a birth. The women just dealt with it.

"We can't afford for me to go to a hospital. I have no one to attend me."

He only vaguely knew of hospitals as a place for a birth. He couldn't understand a hospital for a birth. After all, a birth was not a sickness.

"I'll stay with you," he promised. He had been present at human births as a child in the yurt, but he had been young, and he had not paid much attention. He remembered the women screaming in pain. He had seen numerous animals give birth. In these births, the mother seemed much calmer. He knew the process. At least he could be with her at the birth, help her through it, and know whether their child was a boy or girl.

"I've saved some money so I can stay home a couple of weeks after the birth. After that, you'll have to care for the baby in the daytime. I know it will restrict your trips to the mountains, but I don't know what else we can do. You can still go to the mountains on my days off."

Sasha finally subdued the astonishment that had silenced his tongue, "But Valentina, I can't care for a baby. I'm not a woman."

Her eyes snapped at him, "Don't give me that men's work, women's work nonsense. You have to. There is no other way for us to manage since I'm working."

"But Valentina. I can't feed a baby."

She looked at him as if he had just said something ludicrous. "You use a bottle," she said, her brow furrowed in confusion.

"A bottle?" The only bottles Sasha knew about contained liquor, other than those occasional root beers Valentina brought home.

"A baby bottle. Haven't you ever seen one?"

Valentina went and brought a box he'd assumed contained baby stuff from the blankets on top and withdrew a clear glass bottle with a nipple screwed on top.

"That's how they feed babies in America?" Sasha took the bottle in amazement. "What do you put in the bottle?"

"Milk. It's a special milk. Babies often get sick if they drink cow's milk when they're tiny. I still want to nurse the baby as much as possible," Valentina paused and looked at him. "How did you think we were going to manage?"

Sasha couldn't meet her eyes.

"You have a plan, Alex. Don't you?" He didn't answer. Of course, she had thought about the problem. She would have recognized the need for the care of the baby, and someone would have to work. It was as if she had resigned herself that he would not be the one to work. It tore at him to realize the sacrifice she was making. How selfish he had been to refuse to learn English.

"What was your plan, Alex?"

"I didn't realize I could feed the baby. I knew my English is not good enough to work without exposing us." Alex's words became hesitant. "I thought to protect you, I would have to just disappear into the mountains and leave you to pose as an American since you can do it."

"Abandon me?"

"Only because I love you."

"You've never said that to me before."

"I never before realized what love is. When I first met you, I was afraid of you. Then I was driven by sexual desire. That's what brought me to Moscow to see you. It was the same sexual desire plus jealousy, plus a panic of trying to live without you that made me want to marry you. Now I want your happiness, your safety for you, even if it means I have to give you up."

"That makes me want to cry."

"Anita," he said in English, "I still learn English. I work hard. I get job, so you stay home care for baby."

She did begin to cry, "Oh, Alex," she said in Russian, "I'm so happy. I do love you. I, too, am learning what love means."

He did stay by her until the birth. She struggled and cried through the labor, and neither of them knew how to ease the pain. Eventually, the baby was born in spite of their ignorance. Sasha held his red-faced, squalling daughter in his hands, surprised by the strength of her voice for her tiny size. He placed her at Valentina's side, and she quieted as she began to suckle. Sasha cleaned up after the birth, acutely aware that they had taken a terrible risk in not having someone more knowledgeable about births attend Valentina. If something had gone wrong, he would not have known what to do.

"What are we going to call her?"

Sasha hadn't even thought about names. "Natasha," That was the name of Tolstoy's darling.

"No, that is a Russian name. We will call her Nancy. Think of it as a nickname for Natasha. If we are ever safe from this threat of repatriation, you can call her Natasha."

The days went by, and Valentina returned to work. Sasha's days were consumed with caring for the infant. She cried all the time. She fought taking the bottle. She needed to be changed and bathed. Sasha dozed when she dozed. In her few happy moments, Sasha tried to clean or do laundry, but it seemed he could only catch a moment here or there. Valentina returned from work and cared for the infant, but that meant Sasha had to fix the evening meal. The house felt unkempt. Each evening both Sasha and Valentina fell into bed exhausted, only to be awakened by the screeches of their unhappy daughter.

Valentina took the baby to a doctor and was told she had colic. The doctor made some suggestions to ease the pain, but none seemed to work. The doctor told them time was the only cure. Valentina tried taking Nancy to church to give Sasha some respite, but she disturbed the meetings so much that Valentina gave up and stayed home. Sasha urged Valentina to go to church without the baby. Church renewed her. Valentina reciprocated by urging him to go to the mountains when she was off duty. He did but found Valentina hopelessly behind in laundry, shopping, and housekeeping when he returned. He decided babies were a time-consuming, energy-wasting nuisance and wondered why anyone wanted children.

The days, weeks, and months crawled by. Sasha's English got no attention. He felt like a prisoner with no release date. Even a factory job sounded like a good alternative.

One cold winter day when Sasha picked Nancy up to feed her, she gooed and smiled at him instead of screaming. She drank her bottle without fighting and burped without crying. She played in her bath and lay peacefully on her blanket after being dressed. Sasha cleaned the bathroom and then checked on her. She slept. He covered her and lay on the bed. Soon he slept too. He awoke feeling rested and checked on Nancy. She still slept. He washed up the dishes in the kitchen, waiting for her wail. It did not come. He checked back on her. She lay, watching her hands as she batted them in and out of focus. He quickly fixed a bottle. Still, cries had not shattered the silence. He risked changing her before feeding her.

"What's the matter?" he said to her, "Did you decide to surrender and join the human race?"

She smiled and laughed as if he had said something witty. He continued talking to her, enjoying how her whole body wiggled in joy as she responded to him.

He fed her. She placed a tiny hand over his and solemnly watched him with eyes so wise. He burped her, liking the feel of her downy head under his chin.

She slept again, and he cleaned. The house looked tidier than it had since her birth. The happy baby stayed, and Sasha began an intense study of English. The grammar began to come together slowly, but the accent eluded him. Valentina brought books from the library for him--bird books, flower books, geology books, tree books. Because he was genuinely motivated to understand the books, he quickly learned to read, each day making lists and lists of words for Valentina to define for him in the evening. As his prowess with the language increased, his desire to get a job diminished. He enjoyed this baby now. Valentina surprised him with a bicycle for Christmas. When the roads were clean enough, he wrapped Nancy in a blanket and made it into a sling, and they biked around the city. On Valentina's days off, he went to the mountains. Valentina could now take the pleasant little Nancy to church, giving him more free time.

Soon he was fighting the learning of English again. He watched for Valentina's eyes to accuse him of being too slow in mastering this crazy language. He had become a fluent reader of English. The books nourished him, and he read ravenously, but he pretended less ability than he actually had.

Spring was close. The mountains were so beautiful, pulling him like a magnet. He knew he would smother if he took a factory job. Maybe next winter, if Valentina would just give him the summer and fall. He felt guilty, but unless she confronted him, he was not going to bring it up. Even if she did confront him, he would probably still make the selfish choice.

As spring broke, Sasha biked every day as far as the road would take him into the mountains. Then he would hike in as far as he could go and still return by night time. He bound Nancy to him with a blanket sling. She was a content and cheerful baby, and she charmed him. He looked for the accusation in Valentina's eyes, but he saw there only weariness and despair. That twisted him even more than accusations would have. He could defend himself against accusations, but not against her vulnerability. He felt so torn. He felt driven to do his self-appointed work in the mountains as if there were an important, inevitable deadline to meet, but he did not know what it was, and he did know that Valentina needed him.

Reluctantly, he asked Valentina if he might stay overnight in the mountains. He expected her to protest since she still nursed Nancy at night. She paused, sighed, and agreed. Sasha felt guilty in his victory. He stayed overnight Thursday but spent the weekend at home. He had not gone any deeper into the mountains. He needed more days in a row without having to return home.

Many times he tried to get up the courage to ask, or really to tell Valentina that he was going to spend a week in the mountains. He would clean the house, fix the meal, and sit down with Valentina to eat the meal, hoping the mood would be right to lay his request on her.

"Valentina." She looked at him with those sad, tired eyes. He knew she saw through him. He backed down and did not make his request. The drive was so strong in him to go to the mountains that he knew he would do it, but at what cost to Valentina and his relationship with her? Time and again, he tried to approach her and then backed down.

One night as they lay in bed just snuggling together, she said, "Why don't you just say it and get it over with?"

"Say what?" He feigned ignorance.

"You know what." She turned over and pulled away from him.

He drew her back to him. "I don't want to hurt you, Valentina."

She didn't say anything for a long time. He could imagine her in the dark, biting her lip and swallowing hard to keep from crying. When she did speak, tears were in her voice. She spoke hesitantly and slowly, "I am going to be hurt, and you are going to go anyway, so we might as well get it over with."

"I'm sorry, Valentina."

"Not sorry enough." She cried quietly in his arms.

"I promise I'll get a job next winter."

"We'll see."

Sasha knew she didn't believe him.

He found preparing for a week in the mountains with an infant was considerably more complex than it would have been just for himself. His problem was diapers and food. He decided it would be easier to wash diapers daily in the mountains than try and bring back a week's worth of dirty ones. The canned milk was heavy, and he would need a lot.

Valentina watched his preparations silently, with pained eyes. He kissed her good-bye at 5 a.m. one Monday, promising to be back by Saturday morning at the latest. He peddled off, Nancy asleep in her blanket pouch, the bike heavily laden with the paraphernalia of a baby's needs. When he came to where he could no longer continue by bike, he hid the bike, loaded himself, and continued his hike.

Sasha quickly realized he was not up to packing all this stuff as far as he had planned. He decided to go as far as he could in one day and make camp there. It was slow going. Stopping to make a bottle for Nancy, build a fire to warm it, change a diaper, and clean up took a long, long time. This was not a good idea. In fact, it was foolishness to think he could get done what he had planned with a baby. She cooed and smiled for him, rewarding his efforts, but he got that from her at home. He didn't have to hike all the way up here just to enjoy his baby.

By nightfall, he was only half as far as he had hoped to be. If he hiked on tomorrow, it would take him two days to hike back out. That would leave him only a day and a half to work. Frustration gripped him. This trip was futile. Combined with Valentina's pain, it was not worth it, but what option was there for him? He decided he would spend his week, do what he could, go home, give this up, and get a factory job. His English was now good enough that if he did not have to talk much, he could probably pull off the illusion he was American. Who was he kidding? Nice words, but how did one convince himself to do what he did not want to do but felt that he had to?

The next morning Sasha awoke early. Nancy still slept. He heard the early morning bird songs he had come to hear. One was new to him. He listened carefully to catch the trills and pauses. He gathered his drawing and writing materials. He mimicked the call. Not close enough. The bird did not respond by flying into view. He listened more carefully and refined his mimic of the trill. A bird flew into sight. A startling bright blue, smallish bird perched on a tree just above him. He began sketching it, grateful for the colored pencils Greg Bullock had provided him. He could get the color's shades just right. The bird flew out of sight. Sasha chirped again, and the bird chirped again and settled on a nearby limb. He began to make notes.

"It's a lazuli bunting," a voice startled him. "Do you speak English?"

A man stood right next to Sasha, looking at the picture he had drawn and his notes in Russian. Sasha felt burned, seared through and through. How had he not heard this man coming? How had he concentrated so much he shut out all sounds of his approach? Sasha rarely saw anyone on his hikes into the mountains, so rarely that he didn't even take any precautions. They left him alone, and he left them alone. Now this man had walked right into his camp and caught him writing in Russian. All of Valentina's carefully executed plans, and he had blown it.

"I'm Marvin Savage." While Sasha's thoughts raced, the man extended his hand.

Sasha shook his hand but did not say anything. Maybe the man would just leave.

The man stood between him and Nancy. Could he get to the baby and disappear without the man following him? The man knew he was Russian and that he was with the baby. If it were just him, the man wouldn't have to know about Valentina, but the baby would need to go back to Valentina if he were to be repatriated, and so she would be discovered too. Would the baby, the innocent baby, be repatriated with them? Would she also be executed, or would she be sent into hard labor to perish like the children of the woman he had met from Latvia? How had he been so foolish to place them in this vulnerable position?

"That's a beautiful drawing, so accurate. You've got an incredible talent."

Sasha said nothing. Could he kill the man? He had killed in the war, but this would be murder. He had no weapon except a knife. How grisly. Could he do it? To protect Valentina and the baby, he would.

"You called the bird too. I thought it was the bird itself. That's how I found you."

Still, Sasha said nothing.

"Do you understand what I am saying?"

Maybe the man would just leave if he didn't speak. Sasha held his tongue. Why wouldn't the man give up and go away?

The man spoke very slowly. "I am the head ornithologist at the University of Utah. Do you know the word ornithologist?"

Sasha thought of tearing up the picture. If he did not speak to the man, did not allow him to follow him, gave him no evidence, maybe he could get away safely. But then he would never be able to come again because the man might be looking for him.

"You are afraid of me." The man seemed puzzled.

Nancy began to fuss. Sasha stuffed the picture into his pocket. He turned his back on the man, hoping he would leave.

"You have a baby with you." The man was surprised. "What a little doll."

Couldn't this man take a hint? Sasha didn't know how to be more inhospitable.

"Do you work for someone?"

If it were possible, he would grab Nancy and run.

"I would pay you for your picture. I would pay you well to draw pictures and make notes. We have a large amount of money and no one really skilled to do the job. Oh, yes, a lot of us can identify the birds and their songs and calls, but none of us can draw them, and we certainly cannot call them to us. Finding you is finding a gold mine." The man withdrew his wallet and pulled out some money. He held out the money and pointed to the picture. The man pantomimed drawing another picture, and he added money to his first pile, another picture, more money.

Sasha got his message clearly. This man meant him no harm. He wanted his skills, not to repatriate him. Evidently, just like Greg Bullock, the man did not believe he was a spy just because he was Russian.

Sasha offered the man breakfast. They identified various bird sounds they heard as they ate. "How do you know their names in English?"

"My wife gets me books. She is fluent in English. She answers my questions, helps me with pronunciation."

Marvin pulled out a list of birds. Sasha indicated which ones he had previously drawn. "I'm impressed. Where are your pictures?"

"Home."

"Do you write English?"

"Very little." Sasha shook his head.

"Then, we'll have to find someone to translate."

"My wife can," Sasha volunteered.

"Is she American?"

Sasha chose not to answer that question. "She reads Russian and can write English."

"Then this is perfect. When are you returning to the city?"

"I'll go as soon as I can break camp. This will be good news to my wife."

Sasha caught some trout on his way out. When Valentina returned from work, his gear was all put-away and dinner was nearly ready. She walked in and stopped in amazement. The table was set with flowers. He wanted to make this evening as memorable as she had made their wedding night.

"That was a short week," she said. "What's all of this about?"

"It is about how much I love you."

She came into his arms and returned his kiss. She seemed wary even though Sasha could tell she was genuinely happy that he was home. After dinner, he cleaned up while she met Nancy's needs. Then he led her to the bedroom for a leisurely lovemaking session. She was submissive but lacked enthusiasm. He was fluttering with the anticipation of how his news would put the spark back in her eyes. He drew her to him and kissed her long and passionately. He began to remove her clothing. Most of the time, their lovemaking was a quick session in the dark of the night just before falling into an exhausted sleep. He loved being able to see her body, her face in their lovemaking. He was glad for the early hours still giving daylight through the window. He ran his fingers over her naked body as she stood before him. Her eyes told him before his hands. Her lower abdomen protruded. Pregnant! No wonder she was so tired. He looked into her eyes and found fear.

"Why didn't you tell me?"

She sank onto the bed. "How are you going to care for two babies?"

"But it is so soon after Nancy. I thought they would be farther apart."

"Nursing only spaces them if the baby isn't taking a bottle most of the time. Otherwise, the mother can get pregnant shortly after the birth of the first baby."

"When will it be born?"

"September."

Sasha pulled her to him. So many concerns were weighing her down. He lifted her face and gently kissed her. He pulled her nightgown out from under the pillow and slipped it over her head. He would not ask her for sex tonight. He'd let her rest.

"Are you angry with me?" she asked.

"No. I'm not angry with you. I'm concerned about you."

"I think you really will have to get a job. Your English is getting pretty good. I don't see how you can possibly continue your research in the mountains and care for two babies."

"How about you stay home and care for the babies?

"Dream on, Sasha! Somebody's got to work. You've got to get a job."

"I did."

She looked at him blankly, not comprehending. He loved this moment.

"I have a job."

"Not a paying job!" She reacted just as he anticipated she would.

"Yes, Valuska, I have a paying job."

"Since when?" Doubt saturated her words.

"This morning."

"Doing what?" She wasn't an easy sell.

"Drawing pictures of birds."

"And who's going to pay you to do that?" She still wasn't buying it.

"Marvin Savage."

The name obviously caught her up short. Her entire tone changed to curiosity, "Who's that?"

"The head ornithologist at the university."

"When do you start?"

"I started today. Tomorrow I take him all of the drawings I've done so far, and he will pay me for them. Then I just continue to work for him."

"You're serious, aren't you! Oh, Sasha!" She hugged him and kissed him. "And you get to do what you love. God is helping us."

Maybe he was, and maybe he wasn't, but that wasn't all the good news, "Marvin wants to hire you to type my notes in English."

A shadow crossed Valentina's face. "He knows we're Russian?"

Sasha nodded. "He knows I am. He saw my notes. But don't worry. He's not interested in sending us back. He wants my talents. He wants my abilities."

"Did you talk to him about repatriation?"

"Yes. He called it a...a, he used a big word,...travesty. He's going to help me with my English. He wants me to be able to lecture someday."

She kissed him again. "So you get to do what you love, and I get to stay home and take care of my babies. I'm sorry I've been angry at you."

"I deserved it. I was being selfish at your expense."

"But if you'd gotten a factory job, you'd always have been unhappy, and I'd have felt guilty."

He kissed her, and she aroused him, and they had sex after all.

*****

Valentina realized she shouldn't be surprised at the huge difference employment made in Alex's life and, consequently, in their life together. Especially employment doing something he loved and was good at. He exuded happiness. He played with Nancy, fixed meals, cleaned house, constantly whistling, singing, chirping bird songs. He was tender, kind, and considerate of her in every way. He was fun to be around, and she felt her love deepening for him. She gratefully gave up working at the VA and became a full-time homemaker, mother to Nancy, and typist of Alex's notes. She carefully burned each sheet he wrote in Russian as soon as she finished typing so that no physical evidence of their Russianness remained in their little house. Alex completely gave up his resistance to learning English. Finally, Valentina felt ready to present him to her church without the gnawing anxiety of being discovered. Valentina had known these people for four years now. She had claimed for two of those years that she was married. Her pregnancies eloquently attested that there was a man in her life, but no one besides Bishop Bullock had ever met him.

"Sasha, would you like to go with me to a campout with my church group?"

"Yeah, I want to meet these men you claim are so magnificent, who don't smoke, drink, or swear."

Had she said that? Probably implied it. "You've seen it in Greg Bullock and Marvin Savage."

"I can imagine a few saints, but a whole congregation like that? I can hardly believe it."

Even though Alex now earned the money, he had not tried to justify spending it on alcohol or cigarettes. He occasionally swore in Russian, but he didn't know the swear words in English, and no one was teaching him.

"Well, you don't either. Does that make you a saint?"

"Hardly," but his eyes twinkled in a way that she had come to love. She stood on tiptoe to reach around her distended stomach and gave him a kiss on the cheek.

"Hey, I deserve more than that." He pulled her into a full embrace and enjoyed a lengthy kiss.

The birth certificate which supposedly gave Alex legitimacy said he was from Illinois, but no one they would meet would see that or know that, so they decided to say he was from Bulgaria. He didn't struggle with English any longer, but his r's did not sound American, and he couldn't always find the right word. He still could not pass for a native.

"Alex! So good to see you," Greg Bullock pulled Alex into a hug. Obviously, he was not going to pretend they had never met before.

"And it is good to see you," Alex said, slapping him on the back. Bishop Bullock had not found a natural way for Alex to have contact with him since their marriage.

"I hear you are doing very well." Bishop Bullock always asked Valentina about Alex. He had responded enthusiastically to the news that Alex was employed but had cut her off before she could tell for whom or what he did, just saying, 'I think it is better I do not know too much.' Valentina wasn't sure that knowledge might make them more vulnerable, but she never disclosed any details anyone might overhear and wonder about.

Valentina introduced Alex to a number of the other couples. He was becoming an acute observer of human behavior in his attempt to make sure no unAmerican gestures or attitudes betrayed him. She was glad he tended to be taciturn in public, listening much more than he spoke.

Valentina was pleased that Alex pitched in and helped. He set up the tent Marv Savage had provided for him and laid out the sleeping bags, his purchased by Marv and hers purchased by themselves. He then concerned himself with caring for Nancy. He would never have done that in Kamchatka, but here, with the months he had spent as Nancy's primary caretaker, it seemed natural for him to respond to Nancy's needs. He held her, fed her a bottle, and watched her while Valentina visited with the other women.

Most of the men had gone off to play an American game with a bat and ball. They invited Alex along. He declined, but then Bishop Bullock came and got him, "Come on, you'll do great." Alex gave her a glance as if seeking permission, and at her nod, he handed Nancy to her and followed the Bishop. There were situations he had avoided, especially those that revealed his ignorance of something every American had known from childhood. But, since they were not portraying him as American, it was okay if he came across as a little clumsy.

Valentina realized as she laughed and visited; it was as if the shackles of fear had fallen away. The fear and pain of the war were gone, the weariness and mounting frustration that had plagued them since their marriage was gone. She felt as free as she had been in Kamchatka. She was happy, and Alex seemed happy too. Their future was hopeful.

She joined the other women in setting out a communal meal. She sliced the tomatoes for the American hamburger. Just as she was arranging them on a plate, she heard a man's voice call, "Anita?"

She looked up to see Douglas Parkins, and her heart constricted. No, they weren't safe. "Hi, I didn't know you were back."

"Been back for a while. I'm not in the ward. An old friend invited me to the campout. You're married." It wasn't a question but a statement as he looked at her distended stomach.

"This is actually my second child. Are you married?"

"Uh, no. I actually was hoping to see you again, to see if we might..., well, you know. I didn't know you were married."

He drifted off, but a cloud covered Valentina's happiness. She didn't want Douglas to meet Alex, to talk to him. Would he recognize him as the wild man at her doorstep so long ago? Alex was much better groomed and dressed now. Still, would Douglas ask too many questions? Mormons were prone to do so: "Where are you from? Do I discern an accent?" "How long have you been here?" Surely, since he had deliberately gone in search of so-called Russian spies, he would be alert, and he would ask and push for answers.

"Sister Shupe, did you say you were returning to Salt Lake this evening?"

"Just my husband. He has to work tomorrow morning. He's in charge of the campfire program, and then I want him to help put the children to bed before he leaves."

"So, he would have room for some passengers? We had planned to stay, but the baby is a bit feverish, so I think we'd better go back." She had to come up with a reason for them to leave abruptly, one they had not anticipated. She wanted to get Alex away from Douglas before he could be revealed. Hopefully, no one would check Nancy's head or come with some wonderful home remedy, aborting their need to go home.

"I'm sure it will be fine."

Alex came back from his baseball game, triumphant that he had hit the ball a good whack and caught three balls. He was one of the guys. Valentina watched carefully during the meal, but Douglas didn't seem to be paying any observable attention to them. If Douglas showed up at church on Sunday, they would have to leave Salt Lake, or at least this area. She couldn't deal with worrying every minute that they might be exposed.

Valentina wanted to talk with Alex before they had to make their abrupt departure but couldn't find a good time. If they discussed the problem in English, others could hear what they were saying, and Alex was bound to ask questions. It would be hard to answer without disclosing too much. He knew that Nancy wasn't sick and would argue with her if she told him that was why they had to leave. She couldn't talk to him in Russian. That would be even worse if someone overheard.

Alex was right in the middle of building the campground fire. Valentina was happy that he felt so at ease with her people, but she felt so threatened. Douglas was also there, and Alex didn't even know the danger. Did Douglas realize Alex was her husband?

*****

Sasha took Nancy wrapped in her blanket as Valentina came to the campfire. He didn't know why Valentina was suddenly apprehensive. He had just realized he was truly happy here. He no longer mourned for Kamchatka. Utah was not Kamchatka. Too dry, much too dry. There was not the comfortable rumble of the volcanoes, the odor of the burning ash in the air, the predictable shaking of the earth. This had never spoken terror to his heart but the warming comfort of being home. He dearly missed it, but he realized he could be happy in this desert wasteland with its mountains, snow, birds, and vegetation. He was happy in his work for Marvin Savage. Valentina seemed happy too. The day had gone extremely well. He felt comfortable around these people. Sasha sat on a log bench, Nancy alert in his arms, Valentina tense beside him. Sasha listened to the campground singing songs he did not know, many words he could not understand.

Some people started to drift back to their tents, and the rest began talking, telling jokes, with punch lines he couldn't comprehend. He lay the sleeping Nancy gently on the ground and leaned over and gently kissed Valentina.

She said, "Not now," and pulled back.

Not understanding why she resisted except that they were in public, he decided to express his feelings of contentment through music and asked the man next to him if he might play his guitar.

As he pondered how to express his emotions in English, he idly strummed the chords to *"Proshchai."* The only English song he knew was "Lili Marlene," which he now knew told the story of a soldier's unfaithful lover. Not the sentiment he wanted today. "I am so happy to be here with you," he sang, to the tune of "Dark Eyes." Valentina picked up the sleeping baby, and suddenly. Nancy began to wail at the top of her lungs. Sasha stopped his strumming and stared, "Is she all right?"

"I think she got stung. I'm taking her to the tent."

Sasha put down the guitar and followed her, "I didn't see any insects."

"Shhh!"

Inside the tent, Valentina handed him the screaming infant and said, "Stay here until I come back."

*****

Valentina went in search of Brother Shupe. How could Alex have been so idiotic! Strumming *"Proshchai"* and then singing to the tune of "Dark Eyes," Russian tunes, with Douglas Parkins sitting there staring at them. He knew, She was sure he knew. She could see it in his eyes. Did he realize that Nancy's sudden tears were because her mother had pinched her? She'd had to stop Sasha anyway she could. Why didn't he think? Of course, he hadn't been introduced to Douglas; she had made sure of that. So he had no idea there was a snake in their midst, though one always had to assume there might be. Most Americans wouldn't recognize the Russian tunes, but she had heard *"Proshchai"* played in Europe, so it seemed to be known outside of Russia. Then Alex clinched it by playing a second Russian tune, and a very well-known one at that. She didn't know what Douglas had done to help him spot hiding Russian spies, but he had evidently acquainted himself with Russian music. Now their fate was sealed.

She found Brother Shupe and verified he was ready to leave. "The car is the blue Buick. It is unlocked, so you can just get in."

She went back to their tent and picked up a now calm Nancy, and the bag with her things in it. She said to Sasha, "Go out as if you are going to pee in the woods, and then meet me at the cars in about five minutes."

"What's going on?"

"We're leaving."

"Why?"

She whispered, "Just come."

*****

Soon they were in the car. The driver had been the pitcher in the game, and he complemented Sasha on his baseball game. Sasha didn't dare say much. He didn't know what had gone wrong, but he feared that somehow he had revealed them.

"What about our tent, our sleeping bags?"

"Bishop Bullock will get them,"

Sasha marveled at how quickly their contented happiness had been snatched from them. Soon the talking subsided, and the driver found a radio station. Sasha felt Valentina's stiffness and still wondered what had happened that was dangerous. She instructed the driver to drop them at their house. As soon as they were inside, she said, "Go through the alley to the gas station. Call Marvin Savage and tell him to please come to our house immediately. We have an emergency."

"We do? What's going on?"

"We've been discovered."

"We have?"

"Yes. Please, just go and call Marvin. We have to disappear."

He went.

15

Bishop Bullock on Trial

Greg Bullock threw some kindling on the crumpled newspaper before placing crisscross logs on top. He struck a match as he heard footsteps approach.

"Bishop, where did Anita Waters go?"

Greg looked up to see Doug Parkins standing before him. "Go? I think their tent is over behind the Peters' tent, the small gray one."

"Yeah, well, they are not there."

"Maybe they've just gone to the outhouse."

"All three of them, at this time in the morning? No, they are gone, gone. Bishop, I am not going to play games about this because I think you know more about it than you are willing to confess. Anita's husband is Russian. I am sure of it. In fact, she may also be. You know as well as I do what that means. They are spies. They are here because they are communist spies. I think you know that. I don't know what your involvement is, but we will get to the bottom of this." Douglas shook his finger threateningly in Greg's face and stomped back to his tent.

Greg slowly expelled his breath. So it had come to a head. He glanced towards the Drake's tent. Would it be somehow confessing involvement if he went over to investigate? No, as their bishop, he was involved with them. True, he did know they were Russian, but he was convinced heart and soul that they were not spies. But were they really gone? That he did not know, and that was probably good. If somehow they had been discovered and managed to escape, the less he knew, the better.

He walked over and knocked on the tent post. When noone answered, he peeked in. The sleeping bags were there, laid out as if someone had intended to sleep there, but with none of the rumples of a recently slept-in bag. No personal items. It would appear they were, in fact, gone. He had no idea where and was so glad.

"Come on; we've got to hurry," Greg heard Doug say to Dan Jones as he walked back to his now flaming fire.

"What's the rush?" Dan asked. "I'm going to have some breakfast, enjoy myself a bit. Find another ride back if you are in such a hurry."

Although most people had not even emerged from their tents, Douglas went through the campground, calling, "Is anyone going back to Salt Lake right away? I need to go now."

Greg Bullock chose not to hurry Gayle and the children. Hurrying would neither help nor hurt Anita and Alex, and it probably wouldn't protect Greg either.

He debated all the way home whether to say anything to Gayle. Douglas Parkins was hot on the trail. What would that mean to him? Surely he would be questioned. Jailed? Imprisoned? What happened to someone who was suspected of having information considered damaging to national security but was withholding it?

It was obvious from Gayle's glances that she knew he was preoccupied. Since Greg frequently was, and his preoccupations were confidential, she didn't pry. He tried to keep the conversation light, on things that mattered to Gayle, but a debate raged in his heart. Should he tell her anything? He worried until they were in sight of the house. A car was parked there, not a police car. But would they send the police at a time like this? He doubted it. Probably the FBI. The black Chevy was what he might expect of them. He drove around the block.

"Dear, where are you going?" Gayle asked as they passed their home.

"I've got some business at the church." An identical black Chevy was parked there. He kept driving.

"Greg?"

"I need to tell you something, someplace where we can be private."

"Private? Isn't our home private?"

"Without black cars."

He drove to the park. The kids quizzically got out but were soon swinging and climbing. "Daddy, push me," Emma cried.

"I need to talk to Mommy. Kathy, would you please push her?"

After they talked, after Gayle cried and he comforted her, they loaded the kids back up. The black Chevy in the Church parking lot had not moved. They had no sooner pulled into their driveway than two black-suited men exited the Chevy. They were at his side as soon as he stepped out of the car.

"Greg Bullock?" one asked.

Greg nodded.

"FBI agent Halbert Norton." The taller of the two flipped open a black leather wallet, revealing his identification.

Greg took a deep breath. "Yes?"

"We need to question you."

It would probably be best to feel his way slowly. "And what about?"

"Do you know anything about Anita and Alex Waters?"

Evidently, Doug Parkins did not know Anita's married name. Just as well. It would make it even harder to trace them. "Yes. They are members, well, at least Anita is a member of the ward of the Church of Jesus Christ of Latter-day Saints, of which I am a bishop."

"Do you know that they are Russian?"

Okay. Already push had come to shove, and easy, direct answers were no longer appropriate. "I do not know the rules about how the FBI operates or what a citizen's rights are in being questioned. Do I have the right to representation?"

"Is that an admission of guilt?"

"That is not an admission of anything."

"Well, if you are not willing to answer that question directly, we are forced to assume you know something. We will have to take you in to be interrogated."

"May I at least shower, change my clothes? I've been camping."

The men looked at each other. The short one with the goatee shrugged. "All right," Norton said.

"Is Daddy in trouble?" Kathy whimpered.

"Shhh. Daddy'll be fine." The tears evident in Gayle's voice betrayed her confidence in her words.

Greg reached to unstrap the tent from the top of the car.

"A shower we agreed to. Nothing else."

"Sorry, dear," Greg said, heartsick that he was leaving the whole task of unloading the car and caring for the children to Gayle, not to mention the emotional burden he had dumped on her.

"It's okay," she managed, but the tears now fell freely down her cheeks.

Norton spoke to the second agent, "You stay here. You can see both the front door and the side door in case he tries to bolt. Don't hesitate to shoot him in the leg if necessary."

Greg felt the temptation to roll his eyes. This was unnecessary. If he had planned to bolt, he would have bolted the minute he saw their cars and never showed up for their capture at all.

Norton followed him into the house and up the stairs. He stayed in the hall as Greg gathered clean clothes from the chest in the bedroom. Norton didn't follow him into the bathroom.

When Greg returned refreshed, he asked, "Am I going to be gone overnight?"

Norton shrugged, "Could be."

"Am I permitted to take a bag of toiletries?

"I suppose it won't hurt. I will need to inspect what you put in the bag. No knives or anything that could be used as a weapon."

Greg removed his pocket knife from his pants, packed a change of clothes and some toiletries as Norton watched.

They descended the stairs. Greg took a still tearful Gayle in his arms, "Be strong for the kid's sake. I'll be okay. This is the United States."

Gayle eyed the suitcase. "How long will he be gone?" She addressed Norton.

"Maybe a couple of hours, maybe a day or so."

"Where will he be? Is there a way I can contact him?"

"If he's gone overnight, you'll be notified."

"But you don't even know our phone number.

"He does." The FBI man inclined his head toward Greg.

Greg wondered if they would put handcuffs on him and roughly push him into the car, but they were courteous in every way. He was even more relieved for Gayle and the kids' sakes than his own. He didn't want them to experience more fear than they already were. They passed by the church. Norton pulled up by the Chevy parked there, rolled down his window, and called, "We've got him."

As they wove through the streets toward downtown, Greg was totally uncertain about what was going to happen. He couldn't help contrasting this with when Valentina's father was taken in Russia. Her father had never returned as long as she was there. Greg did not fear either hard labor or death, not in the United States. Gayle would never wonder if he were going to return. While she might not know how long he would be gone, she could be assured she would have contact with him and that he would one day return.

Would they torture him to extract info? Did they do that in the US? Maybe in novels, but he didn't think they did in real life. He hoped not. In fact, he had to confess to a certain curiosity as to what was going to happen. His only concern was for Gayle and the children and, of course, Alex and Anita. He truly did not know where they had gone or exactly what had happened that precipitated their departure.

He was driven to a nondescript, mustard-yellow, brick building without a sign. Norton walked on one side of him, and Goatee, as Greg had mentally tagged him, carried his suitcase and walked on the other side. In the lobby of the building, a thin, bespectacled woman with frizzy hair sat behind the desk with a telephone and a typewriter. A couple of wooden chairs faced it.

"Is Crowther in?" Norton asked.

"Yes, but he is with someone right now."

"Please inform him as soon as he is free that we have brought Greg Bullock in for questioning concerning the Waters case."

"Okay. Put him in room two."

Greg was escorted down a hallway to a small room completely empty except for two chairs. There were bars over the windows. Goatee set down his suitcase, and Greg heard the key turn in the door as he was left alone with his thoughts. He had been debating how much to reveal. What was his personal responsibility to report anyone of Russian nationality living in the United States? Would he be tried? What would the charge be? He didn't feel he had endangered the security of the United States by not reporting Anita and Alex. He believed with every fiber of his being that they were as they presented themselves—refugees, not spies. Equally powerfully, he knew that their lives would be in danger should they be returned to the Soviet Union. He was grateful that he didn't know more than he did.

He hadn't yet formulated what he should do when the door opened again, and three men entered. One wore what seemed to be a uniform black suit such as Norton and Goatee had worn. The other two were burly fellows dressed casually. Guns were prominently displayed at their waists and sticks stuck through a holder in their belt loops. They carried an air that proclaimed, "We are not to be messed with."

The man in the suit pulled one of the chairs to face Greg. The other two stood directly across from him on either side of the door. "I'm Agent Crowther, chief investigator for the FBI, Salt Lake Division." He extended his hand. Greg shook it.

"I understand you have information about Anita and Alex Waters."

"I know them," Greg said.

"And what do you know about them?"

"Evidently, this is very important if the FBI is involved."

"Yes, it is, for them and for you."

"Because of its significance, I would like to be informed of a citizen's right to representation in being questioned."

"Let's just say, Mr. Bullock, if you have information you refuse to divulge because this case concerns national security, it would be a felony for you personally, with a prison term of," he pursed his lips, "probably ten to twenty-five years. I am inclined to be lenient with you at this time if you share all that you know with us."

"What I don't know is where they are now. They disappeared from a church campout without a word to me. I have no idea where they are now."

"Did you know they are Russian?"

"I am Anita's bishop. Anything she may have divulged to me about her private life was in confidence. As her clergyman, I am not free to discuss anything she has told me in that context."

"I take that as an admission that you did know."

"As a clergyman and citizen, am I entitled to representation? Because this case seems to carry such significant consequences, it would seem that I should."

"So, you are refusing to cooperate?"

"I did not say that. I only asked for representation."

"You realize that will force this to a trial, and you are the one that will be on trial, for treason. A conviction will be a sure prison term. Is that what you want for yourself? For your family? Is it worth protecting a couple of spies at that price?"

Treason! Surely the man used that word as intimidation. No way could having not disclosed the whereabouts of Russian nationals be classified as treason. "I have no information that will help the FBI in the case. I only ask for representation if you continue to insist I cooperate with you." They already suspected Anita and Alex to be Russian, enough to work from that assumption as if it were true. And it was true. Who they had been in Russia, in Europe made very little difference. The fact that they were Russian was enough to condemn them. It wouldn't matter that Valentina had spied for the Allies, that Alex joined the ROA to avoid starvation, that they had come to the US under false identities to save their lives. If they were caught, they would be summarily sent back to Russia. No trial for them. Probably even little Nancy would be sent back—an outcast because her parents were enemies of the people just as Alex's parents had been. Would Valentina's unborn infant face a horrendous death such as the infant of the woman Alex had seen crucified to the barn door? No, he could not be part of this witch hunt. How dared the US condemn Hitler while sending such innocents to their deaths?

"All right," Crowther said. "If you make that choice, you'll face the full consequences for it. What a legacy to leave for your children. A traitor to your country. What's your church going to think?"

This man laid it on thick but Greg's only thought was that Anita and Alex's best and probably only chance was through public sentiment. He could think of no other way to make that happen than through a publicized trial.

"Take him to a cell," Crowther said to the burly men behind him. One of them grabbed Greg roughly by the arm. Mr. Nice Guy was over. Greg wondered how horrendous it was going to get.

He bent to pick up his suitcase on the way out.

"Leave it," the man growled and shoved Greg through the door.

As he was locked in a cell containing only a cot with a blanket, Greg said, "I was told I could call my wife if I was kept overnight."

"She'll figure it out," the burly man said. He turned, his footsteps echoing down the hall.

Upon request, Greg was escorted to a room at the end of the hall to use the bathroom. He had not had to ask permission to use the restroom since high school. That made his freedom seem as restricted as the cell did. He received his suitcase when a dinner of pork and beans and a greasy toasted cheese sandwich was delivered to him.

The hours dragged by, and he wished he had put in his scriptures or something else to read. Maybe they didn't torture him here—at least not yet—but having nothing to do but think was a torture in its own way. Greg slept fitfully, his mind mostly on Gayle, and the unexpectedness of being treated like this in the United States. Had they even called her? Would she be permitted to visit him? Tomorrow he would miss church. What would be said there? Gayle could tell his counselors he would not be there. It would certainly be best for the congregation not to know where he was.

He was given an adequate breakfast of eggs and toast, and he asked if they had a Doctrine and Covenants he could read. He wanted to read of Joseph Smith's imprisonment in Liberty Jail.

"I don't think we have one."

"A Bible?"

"Probably. I'll look. Most prisoners are not interested in reading such stuff."

Sometime later a Bible was brought to him. He found himself too restless to concentrate on it and finally set it aside, preferring to let his thoughts turn to prayer. "Heavenly Father, I believe that good could come out of this. Guide me in what to say and what not to say. Protect Alex and Anita from danger. Comfort and provide for my…"

"You have a visitor." His prayer was interrupted by the jingle of keys as his cell was unlocked.

The unnamed burly from yesterday escorted him back to the same room where he had been interrogated the day before. Stake President Hansen sat there. Greg could have hugged him. Finally, a contact with the outside world, his world.

"How are you?"

"Okay. As well as can be expected, under the circumstances. How did you learn I was here?"

President Hansen handed him the Tribune. Large letters on the front page announced:

MORMON BISHOP SUSPECTED OF SHIELDING COMMUNIST SPIES

Greg skimmed the article: "Douglas Parkins, a trained expert in identifying Communist spies, recognized that Alex, last name unknown, was Russian from his accent and from the Russian songs which he played on the guitar. It is not known if Alex's wife, the former Anita Waters, is also Russian. Alex and Anita have disappeared, and a search has been initiated nationwide to discover their whereabouts. Anita Waters' bishop, Greg Bullock, of the Eastgate Ward of the Church of Jesus Christ of Latter-Day Saints, is suspected of having protected the two for some time. Bullock is currently in the custody of the FBI. Anyone having any information concerning this case should immediately contact the FBI."

"Well, I was wondering what my ward would be told," Greg said.

"You do know this Alex and Anita?" President Hansen asked.

"I do."

"Are they Russian?"

"Is it private to talk here? Are we being monitored?"

"I don't know."

"I would like representation. Do you know a good lawyer?"

"How are you going to afford one? You don't have that kind of money."

"I'm going to have to trust that justice will be done. Before God, I don't feel that I have done anything wrong."

"But before the US government?"

"If you had lived in Germany or any of its occupied nations during World War II, would you have turned Jews in because it was the law, or would you have done what you could do to protect them?"

"It's not the same. These people are spies. They undermine our national security."

"I don't believe they are spies, any more than the Japanese we interred during the war were spies."

"So you do know something."

"Not much. Nothing that will really help. I don't know where they are."

*****

While it was still dark, Marv Savage woke them up. "I don't know exactly how this will unroll, but I want to get you out of the city before local authorities are notified that you are Russian. They may set up roadblocks to prevent your escape."

"Where are we going?" Valentina asked.

"The mountains above Manti, Utah. I have an uncle who runs sheep there, and he just lost a sheepherder to a heart attack. He himself is laid up with arthritis. The timing is perfect. I used to herd for him when I was in my late teens. I told him I had found a replacement and will see to your training. He is thrilled."

"Does he know we are Russian?"

"No, but because he is laid up, he will never come around. Another herder has been covering until we got someone. I think you will be as safe there as you could be anywhere. I will come every couple of weeks or so and bring you food. You will be able to eat all of the mutton you desire. I cannot drive you myself, though. I have arranged for a friend to drive you down."

Valentina realized she and Alex were as trusting as small children. How did they know that those pretending to help them were not, in fact, those trying to trap them? Still, they went, placing their lives at the mercy of the ones they had trusted before. Marv bid them goodbye with the admonition to Alex, "Keep drawing the birds you see there. Have Anita translate your notes into English. I'll see you in a couple of weeks."

He introduced them to their driver, Aaron Dickenson. Aaron threw their belongings into the back of a ratty, red pick-up truck. Helen, Marv's wife, came out carrying a folded wooden drying rack. "Marv, go get the playpen. They are going to need it to keep the baby safe from the stove." Soon Marv returned with a folded-up structure that had wooden railings and a solid bottom. Helen hugged Valentina, wished them the best, and they all climbed in the cab and set off.

Valentina felt like she was caught in a whirlwind gale, a torrent of words and actions carrying her without her desire or assent. Alex sat by the window and held Nancy. Valentina tried to doze against him but found herself listening to the conversation. Aaron asked Alex if he had ever herded sheep before. Alex said, "No."

"Are you familiar with using horses and dogs?"

"Yes." Were sheepdogs of the same dog mentality as sled dogs? It hardly mattered; they would find a way to make it work because they had to. Aaron indicated Alex was to ride around the sheep twice a day to keep them from wandering too far. He was to watch out for coyotes, bears, and wolves or any other predator which might attack the sheep. He was to give them salt to lick as a necessary part of their diet; and, when told, he was to move camp to specified places so the sheep would have fresh grazing areas.

"That's it?" Sasha asked.

"That's it. It is pretty easy. Your food and housing are provided, so even though you are not paid much, the money is all yours."

They bounced through small towns with stretches of country in between. As daylight broke, Aaron stopped for gas. Valentina changed Nancy's sodden bottom and served the boiled eggs, bread, and canned peaches from a hamper of food Marv had given them. She gave Nancy a bottle without heating the milk. Then she handed the baby to Alex with a crust of bread to chew on. Nancy looked at Alex out of big, adoring eyes. Valentina wondered if it ever occurred to a baby that her parents could be scared. Once Aaron had exhausted his instructions concerning the sheep camp, Valentina kept him engaged in a lively conversation about the drought Utah was experiencing and skiing. This did not feel like a trap. If they were being trapped, she suspected that they would have been turned over to authorities immediately in the city. Evidently, Greg Bullock and Marvin Savage weren't the only ones who didn't label every Russian a spy. She didn't know if Aaron even knew they were Russian. Alex no longer participated in the conversation. Valentina expected he found it too hard to concentrate on their rapid English. He looked out the window, taking in whatever there was to see.

As they headed south, the mountains became smaller. Alex commented on a red-winged black bird and red tailed hawk. As they came out of one small town, they saw a large white castle glistening in the distance.

"Do they have a king here?" Alex asked.

"No." Valentina laughed, "That's the Manti Temple. That's where we are headed."

"To the temple? They are going to hide us in the temple?"

"Of course not. The temple is in Manti. We're going to the hills above Manti." She wished he had not said hide. That might have triggered something in Aaron, but he seemed unconcerned.

Once they arrived at the sheep camp, Aaron set up the playpen. Valentina kept Nancy's jacket on against the chill and put her in to play with some toys Helen had thoughtfully provided. While Aaron showed Alex the horses and gear, Valentina became acquainted with the small trailer that would become their home. It was only slightly bigger than the bathroom of the house they had lived in. There was a wood-burning stove, a tiny coat closet, and every other vertical surface was either drawers or cupboards. Benches long enough to comfortably seat two adults ran along each side, with more little cupboards underneath. Every drawer and cupboard was crammed with canned food or cooking supplies. A double bed spanned the entire width of the trailer. It concealed a board, which could be pulled out to form a table. Outside, in the back of the trailer, another door opened to reveal a slab of meat she assumed to be mutton, with more space to put belongings that would not fit inside the trailer.

Aaron returned, showed her how to build a fire in the stove with wood and a few pieces of coal to keep it burning long in the evening. He used a saw to cut up the mutton and cooked a delicious meal, supplemented with white, fluffy bread. There were canned beans and canned peaches from Helen's provisions. As Aaron left, he said, "Don't worry, ma'am. I'll not say anything about you to anyone. I was at Ft. Dix."

Valentina didn't know what he meant by that, but was reassured that he felt there was a need to reassure them. She worried no more about him revealing them. Alex lit the lantern, giving light to the little space as night fell. After Nancy was settled in bed, Valentina read from her scriptures, then pulled some newspapers from the drawer, "Do you want to read in English tonight?"

She and Alex read a couple of articles out loud together. Then she thumbed through the newspaper for anything of interest. She saw an advertisement for Samoyed puppies. It showed a dog sled being pulled by the dogs. She tore it out and slipped it into an envelope she found in a drawer, resolved to buy a breeding pair for Alex. She felt she would always be trying to make up to him for the life he had left in Kamchatka.

*****

Gayle was permitted to visit Greg on Monday. She brought a newspaper. Her eyes were red-rimmed from crying.

"I'm so sorry dear, to have created this burden for you."

"It's okay. I think you are doing what is right." She thrust the Tribune into his hands.

As anxious as he was to read any update on his case since yesterday, he put it aside to read after she left. "How did the ward take the news?"

"I don't think anyone looked at the newspaper until after Sunday School. I didn't go back for Sacrament Meeting. I'm sorry. I guess I'm a coward."

"Lambs to the wolves. I don't blame you."

"Reporters are trying to talk to me. They call, and one came to the house."

"You don't have to talk to them."

"And I am not going to."

"President Hansen came yesterday. He said they will be releasing me as bishop, hoping to keep the church from being dragged through the muck."

"The reporters are already doing that, making a big issue about how Mormons are supposed to sustain the government."

"It's hard, but I do appreciate your support."

"They are asking $100,000 bail for you."

"No one will pay that. No one can. I guess I'll be here for a while."

"Have you been formally charged?"

"Accused but not charged. I keep asking for representation, but I don't know who to ask to represent me or where we will get the money."

Gayle ran her hand through her already tousled hair. "I don't either. I'm just praying. I'll ask around about a lawyer, make some phone calls."

He kissed her tenderly, "I'm so blessed to have a wife who will stand by me at a time like this."

Once Gayle had gone, Greg opened the newspaper to see a beautiful, hand-drawn picture of Anita. It must be the picture Alex had drawn of her in Kamchatka. She was younger, with lustrous braids wrapped around her head. Whether it was because the picture was drawn by the man who loved her or that she had a tender, youthful softness that did not show so much anymore, it was gorgeous. Greg wished he could see the picture in color.

The article said that Ronald Schupe was the one who drove Anita and Alex back to Salt Lake. He dropped them at their house. Their clothing and anything personal was gone from the house, but this picture had somehow been overlooked. Janet Hardin from the church had identified the picture as being Anita. The artist was unknown. That might be important, Greg thought, to not reveal that Alex had artistic skills. The less the investigators knew, the better. He would not tell about Alex's particular interest and skill in calling birds and drawing them. He would tell them nothing they didn't already know, and it was unlikely anyone knew that. The article went on to say that Anita had worked as a nurse at the VA hospital. The home they lived in had previously been owned by Maggie George and was currently owned by her grandson, Russell George of Indiana. He was being contacted to see..."

Greg looked up at the rattle of keys in the door. Mr. Burly was back. "Get your suitcase, Bullock. You're free to go."

"But the bail?"

"It's been paid."

Greg believed in a God of miracles, but he followed Burly in stupefied amazement. Who was the angel of deliverance?

A very tall man stood in the lobby, immaculate in a gray, tailored, pin-stripe suit, with every wave in his black hair precisely in place. He extended his hand, "I am Scott Hadley. I am pleased to meet you."

Greg grasped his firm handshake, wondering who in the world Scott Hadley was, and how he had gotten involved in this, but refrained from asking.

Scott escorted him from the building into blinding sunlight.

"Did you pay my bail?"

"I did."

"Thank you. That was good of you, but I don't even know you. Why did you pay my bail?"

"I needed to get you some place I can be assured no one will overhear us."

A man equal in stature to the burly guards in the FBI building jumped from a slick black Cadillac limo and held the door for them to enter. Greg slid in, wondering if somehow he were dreaming.

Greg felt that calling his rescuer "Scott" might be a bit overly familiar under the circumstances. "Mr. Hadley...." he began.

Mr. Hadley held up a hand and addressed the driver, "Sam, take us to the Hotel Utah." Then he turned back to Greg, obviously ready to give him his full attention.

"Excuse me, Mr. Hadley, who are you? What is your interest in my case?"

Amusement tinged Hadley's crisp answer. "I am your lawyer."

Greg swallowed hard. "I don't think I can afford you."

Hadley smiled broadly, his dark eyes twinkling, "You can't. I'm doing this pro bono."

"But who contacted you? Who asked you to come?"

"You are certainly full of questions, Mr. Bullock. I learned about it from the newspaper and came at my own initiative. I am from Chicago. Now, are you hungry?"

"Well, actually, I am."

"Great. We'll get some food, and then I need to do a preliminary gathering of information before taking you home to your family."

*****

Valentina stroked Nancy's brow and sang to her in Russian:

"Where the dreamy Volga flows
There's a lonely Russian Rose
Gazing tenderly
Down upon her knee
Where a baby's blue eyes glisten
Listen
Ev'ry night you'll hear her croon
A Russian lullaby
Just a little plaintive tune
When baby starts to cry
Rock-a-bye my baby
Somewhere there may be
A land that's free for you and me
And a Russian lullaby."

Valentina was choked with tears by the end of the song. She'd had such hopes that the United States would be a land that would be free for her and her future children. Now they were hunted like animals. Only the protection of God and a few good men would keep them from being discovered. She needed to shift her thoughts from this endless, frightful circling. No good ever came of it.

Spokoynoy nochi , moya malen'kaya, she whispered to the sleeping babe. She usually followed her rule, which Alex constantly violated, that no Russian was to be spoken to Nancy. But the Russian lullabies came more readily to her mind than the English or French ones her grandmothers and mother had sung to her in her own infancy. Maybe they had only sung the Russian ones. Nancy's eyes drooped and the thumb slipped from her mouth. Valentina stepped from the small trailer. Alex fussed with his horse tack.

"Will you listen for Nancy?"

"Sure. Don't go far."

"I'll be back in plenty of time for you to bed down the sheep."

"Okay. You've got about an hour for your walk."

Valentina headed for the copse of trees growing along a little stream. She loved the sound of the water skipping across the rocks. The miniature, pink flowers that looked like the ears and trunk of an elephant enchanted her. Nature was lovely. She had imbibed more of it since coming to this mountain than ever before, except in those days in Kamchatka before she had succeeded in seducing Alex. She hadn't been as appreciative then except for starlit nights which were exquisite here. She enjoyed the buzzing and chirping sounds of the insects, the few birds who sang in the drowsy afternoon, and the faint bleating of the sheep and the bell on the horse before uttering a word of prayer and opening her Book of Mormon—the only book in her possession.

Her thoughts were not on reading today. She continually marveled at how happy Alex was here. He was in his element. He had been much happier since being hired by Marvin Savage, but that was but a shadow of the happiness he exhibited living in the mountains full time. She didn't miss the irony that what for him was freedom from the isolation of the city was imprisonment for her. She was safe, at least seemed so for the moment, but she couldn't talk to anyone but Alex, just the opposite of what it had been when he had been housebound in Salt Lake. Now he talked to his birds, his dogs, his horses, and yes, her and Nancy. Try as she might, there was a lot more Russian than English. She sighed and opened the book again. Since her days were full with the care of Nancy, her time alone was limited and she needed to maximize it.

She had just begun reading when she heard the sound of a car. That in itself was unusual. Marv Savage had said that periodically someone would bring food, but they hadn't seen anyone yet. Who would it be? Could Alex handle talking to whoever was in the car without revealing them? She crept to the edge of the copse and watched the road. The car drove right up to the camp. Her breath caught as she waited to see who stepped out. Marvin Savage bounded from the vehicle and opened the door for his wife, Helen. Valentina ran from the copse, so happy to see them she could have hugged them. "It's so good to see you. Thank you for coming."

Helen didn't hesitate to hug her. "And how are you doing?"

"Well." Valentina hoped her word didn't convey all of the loneliness she felt.

Helen brushed her cheek as if she had shed a tear, "I can't imagine living so isolated up here with only Alex and the baby to talk to. I brought you some books and handwork. I don't know your tastes, but maybe that will help pass the time."

"Oh, thank you, thank you." Now real tears had escaped to her cheeks, and she wiped them herself, unashamed, so grateful that her need had been met without even the need of expressing it and then waiting to have it met."Could you see if you could get me a book about the constellations? They are so beautiful here. I want to learn their names in English."

"I will do that for you," Helen promised.

"About ready to ride around the sheep?" Marv asked Alex.

"Just need to saddle up the horses." It was a bit earlier than Alex normally rode around them.

"We brought a tent to sleep in tonight. It's too far to come from Salt Lake and go back the same day. Let's set it up and then we can ride around the sheep while the women get some food on."

Marv opened up the trunk of the car and pulled out a tent. From the back seat, he carried three boxes into the trailer. One he set on the small table, one he slid underneath, and the other he set on the bench. Helen patted Valentina's arm and said, "No mutton for you tonight. That must get rather monotonous. There are some cans of tuna in the food box we brought, but I brought a picnic for us. Fried chicken, potato salad, a can of olives, and a chocolate cake for dessert."

"Sounds wonderful. Are there any secrets to cooking mutton to make it more tasty? It is so greasy."

"I brought some potatoes, onions, and carrots. A little stew is a nice variation once in a while. Marv might have some suggestions. I've never really cooked mutton. Let me know if there is anything you would like."

"Cabbage and beets, if you can get them.

"Beets are not in season yet. I'll see if I can get some canned ones. I should be able to get some cabbage."

After the scrumptious dinner, Marv held Nancy on his lap and read her a book about a little Indian boy named Keeko, with lots of extraneous cat sounds that made Nancy giggle. Valentina prepared Nancy for bed, then fed her a bottle.

Marv said, "Well, I guess we need to bring you up to snuff about what's happening with you. Roadblocks were established the morning you left— but after you left. You were hot stuff in the newspapers. Ronald Schupe knew he had driven you to your home, but nobody knew where you had gone. It was like you disappeared into thin air."

"And that's all?"

"Oh, no. Only the beginning. Greg Bullock has been arrested."

"Arrested? Why?"

"Because he supposedly knew you were Russian. He was your bishop, was he not?"

"Yes. What will happen to him?"

"Some hotshot lawyer has shown up from Chicago and says he is going to defend him."

Marvin reached into a box and pulled out a newspaper, and Valentina realized the newspapers he had brought them were not just for starting fires. He spread it on the table before them, and Valentina gasped as she saw the picture of herself staring out at them. In her scramble to clean everything they would need out of the house, as well as anything that might identify them, she had completely forgotten about the picture still under the paper lining the top drawer of the chest. How stupid she had been! Now everyone knew what she looked like, or at least what she had looked like eight years ago. She wasn't as pretty as Alex had portrayed her, and her hair was now short, but an astute person might still be able to recognize her.

"It's unfortunate they found this picture. I don't know if we will be able to have you give birth in a hospital with everyone looking for you. The news reporters have questioned people who knew you and have speculated that you will be having your baby sometime in September."

"It's okay," Alex said. "Nancy was born at home with only me attending. We know how to handle that now."

"Nevertheless, we will be bringing everything we can that will be helpful."

*****

Greg was so grateful to be back with his family, but soon he was called to the University president's office. "I'm sorry, Greg. I have to send you before a state loyalty review board. Your past will be combed for signs of disloyalty, your students questioned for clues to any dangerous thoughts you might have."

"I am not disloyal to the United States."

"I am not in a position to judge that. The clamor is that in not revealing these people were Russian, you were being subversive. We will not knowingly employ a Communist or a member of any party or group which advocates the overthrow of the government of the United States. My hands are tied. I hope you have a good defense."

"I have a lawyer."

"I wish you the best. I don't know where you'll get a job after this."

Greg called Scott Hadley, and they met at the Bullock home.

"Don't worry about the loyalty review board. It will all work out," Scott said.

"I have a summons to appear before the committee on un-American activities."

"I'll take care of that. We are not going before the committee on un-American activities. I won't allow that. You would be asked to defend yourself against accusations without being allowed to cross-examine the accuser. You will be declared guilty just by virtue of the fact you knew Alex and Anita were Russian. We're going to full trial with witnesses and everything."

"A jury?"

"No. It takes too long to set up that kind of trial. We want just enough time to assemble the witnesses, and I think it is basically done on both sides. Also, you really haven't violated any kind of law which would justify a jury trial. We will be just before a judge, but the accusers are going to have to plead and prove their case that you have violated the law."

"But I did violate the law. I didn't report that Alex and Anita were Russian even though I knew it."

"The assumption the law is making is that all Russian refugees in the US are spies. It just simply isn't true. Our approach will be that there is a valid reason for not reporting them. It essentially would be condemning them to death since they get no trial before being repatriated."

A knock on the door interrupted the discussion. Greg opened it to a shower of raw eggs and shouts of, "Commie lover!" and "Traitor!"

Hadley slammed the door shut.

"I think I should send my wife and our kids to her parents. I can't subject them to this," Greg said.

"No. It is important that you conduct a normal life, that you stand up as evidence that you have done nothing wrong. It is crucial you present that face to the world. I will have men stationed in front of your home around the clock. Two others will be at your disposal to escort you, your wife, or children wherever they need to go."

"Yes, but I can't afford to pay for that kind of security."

"Oh, you'll pay, but not with money. This is going to be the most publicized trial I can make happen."

"But why?"

"It's not just you who is on trial, but also Alex and Anita, and every other Russian who has taken refuge in the United States. We need to make a statement that will be heard for all of them. I have an old debt I need to repay, and this is the only way I can see to do it."

That very night, a car was parked in their driveway and remained there around the clock, with husky fellows rotating the duty of occupying it. A different beefy guy camped in the backyard—sometimes with the children. The Bullocks' old friends were staying aloof, but they felt well-protected by their new friends.

16

The Forgotten Portrait

Working as a sheepherder was like a dream come true. Sasha could live in the mountains, work and provide for his family, and keep Valentina and Nancy with him. He was pleased with their efficient little home. No fuss, no bother. Just the basic necessities. It was life the way he liked to live it. He was even more pleased that the dogs spoke Russian and Kamchadal. He could bark a command, and they would respond, going just where he wanted them to go. They even understood the swear words that formed the bulk of the vocabulary of sledge drivers in Kamchatka. Valentina had requested he not use these words around her anymore, but the horses, dogs, and sheep did not object. He would gallop across the mountain top, loudly swearing and cursing in Russian, feeling happy and at home. He was ready to spend the rest of his life here.

One day as he rode with the salt bags out to the sheep, he came upon another man on horseback. The man greeted him, "I'm Sodie. Who ya herdin' fer?"

"Blacks."

"Oh. From Manti."

"I'm from the other side of the Muddy—Emery." Sodie drew a cigarette from his pocket and offered one to Sasha.

Sasha hadn't smoked since France, but only from lack of access to tobacco. He knew this would make Valentina unhappy, but she had accepted him as a smoker in Kamchatka and had even been a smoker herself. She'd just have to accept this. He took the cigarette. He visited a bit more with Sodie.

"Come and join me for some mutton and sourdough." Sodie invited. He told Sasha how to find his camp.

"I'll come tomorrow."

Sasha rode back for the mutton dinner Valentina was preparing for him. He unsaddled the horse, hobbled it, and strapped a bell on. He scooped Nancy from the playpen in the shade of the trailer and greeted Valentina with a kiss. She drew back in horror. "You've been smoking!"

"Yup. I met another herder. He gave me a cigarette."

"But, Alex, you promised."

Sasha shrugged. "I promised? When? Smoking is not such a big deal."

Valentina turned and ran from the trailer. She disappeared into the trees. Sasha could hear her sobbing as she went. He let her go. She would have to come to terms with this one. He had made up his mind.

He finished fixing the lunch Valentina had begun. He fed and changed Nancy and lulled her to sleep with a Russian lullaby. He pulled out his bird books and read, making a list of words for Valentina to define. Valentina still had not returned when Nancy awoke. Sasha felt growing anger at her. Was she going to force him to come looking for her, grovel at her knees, promise anew not to smoke, or she would not return? He would not do it.

It was time for him to ride around the sheep and bed them down for the night. He saddled the horse, put Nancy in the saddle in front of him, and rode carefully, holding her, so she didn't bounce against the saddle horn. Nancy loved it, but it was a lot slower than when he went alone.

The shadows were lengthening when he returned to camp. Reluctantly, he decided he would have to go find Valentina. As angry as he was with her, he couldn't feel good about her spending a night on the mountain, alone and pregnant. He went and got a jacket to put on Nancy and a crust of bread for her to suck on. It looked like someone was coming in the distance. He verified with his binoculars. It was Valentina. He put Nancy in the playpen, unsaddled the horse, gave it oats in a nose bag, and curried it. Valentina brushed past him without speaking. Her face was smeared and swollen from crying. She went to the water bucket and dipped herself a drink of water. Then she scooped Nancy into her arms and went into the trailer. Sasha finished with the horse, put everything away for the night, and carried wood in to refill the firebox. Valentina sat on the bench chewing some cold meat left over from lunch. Sasha built a fire and lit the lantern. Neither of them spoke. He opened a can of tomato soup, thinned it with some canned milk, and heated it. He set one bowl before Valentina and drank from a bowl himself. She daintily shared hers with spoonfuls for Nancy and then prepared herself and Nancy for bed. Sasha stayed up late reading, not caring that the light kept Valentina awake. If she wouldn't bend, neither would he. When he finally crawled into bed, she turned her back to him and moved against the back of the trailer. He did not try to touch her.

The next morning she slept or feigned sleep when he woke early to ride around the sheep. She was up and cooking his breakfast when he returned. She did not greet him verbally or with a kiss. She would not meet his eyes. He was willing to let her nurse her anger and hurt. He was confident he could outlast her. She would eventually resign herself to his smoking and give up her fight.

He played with Nancy as Valentina finished the breakfast. Both of them interacted with Nancy but not overtly with each other. As soon as Sasha finished eating, he said his first direct comment to her. "I'll not be back for lunch."

Her eyes asked why, but she did not voice the question, and he did not answer. He rode off feeling victorious. She was relenting, or she wouldn't have fixed his breakfast.

Sasha found Sodie's camp without any problem. They sat and smoked, and Sodie talked about the weather. Sodie pulled a slab of mutton from a drawer under the back of his trailer. He sharpened his knife on a whetstone and removed the mutton from a burlap bag. He sliced a few pieces and stoked up his fire. He took some mutton tallow from a can and put it in a large skillet on the stove. As it was melting down, he pulled out a crock.

"Ever made sourdough?"

Sasha shook his head. "I'll give you a start. Every self-respecting sheepherder knows how to make sourdough. Basically, it's some flour, soda, water, and salt."

Sodie put some flour in a basin that looked like a washbasin. Out of the crock, he scooped a gooey dough ball. He dumped it into the flour and kneaded it until he had a biscuit consistency. He poured some of the melted tallow into a dripper pan, rolled it around, and dumped most of it back into the skillet. Then he formed a small ball of dough, wiped the top, and then the bottom in the tallow. He put it in the corner of the dripper and repeated the process until the dripper was full of little dough balls. He slipped it into the piping hot oven.

Sodie placed the skillet back on the stove surface. He put the pieces of meat in the hot tallow and fried them. In between tending them, he handed Sasha a can of green beans and a can opener. Sasha opened the beans, and Sodie dumped them in a saucepan on the stove. Then he handed Sasha a tomato and a knife and told him to slice it.

Sodie set a trivet on the table and placed the hot frying pan on the trivet. He pulled the biscuits from the oven. He pulled a glass jar with butter in it and another with crystallized honey from a compartment under the benches. Sasha's taste buds were wide awake, just from the odors. The hot biscuits melted the butter and honey, and, in turn, the biscuit melted in his mouth. The meat was not cooked much differently from the way he and Valentina cooked it, but somehow it tasted different. He had never tasted anything so delicious. They cleaned up after dinner and had another smoke. Sasha was about ready to leave when Sodie asked, "Would you like a drink?"

Sodie withdrew a bottle from his storage. Sasha knew it contained liquor of some sort. He realized drinking would just add fuel to

Valentina's fire. He did want a drink. He accepted Sodie's offer. Sodie reminded him after a couple of glasses that they had work to do. They'd better not get drunk. Sasha left, enjoying the buzz of alcohol in his system.

He picked up his salt bags without going near Valentina and went to bed down the sheep. The odors in the air when he returned told him supper was being prepared. As soon as the horse was cared for, he walked into the trailer. He caught Valentina in an embrace and kissed her from habit before thought warned him. She pushed him away.

"Drinking too! Alex!" She opened the door to leave the trailer. Sasha caught her by the hand.

"We can't handle this by you running away. Stay here, and let's deal with it."

"Deal with what? That the promises you made to me mean nothing to you?"

He grabbed her other arm and backed her to the door. He was not yelling as much as she, but he was angry. "In Kamchatka, even you smoked and drank. When you seduced me in Kamchatka and lured me to follow you to Moscow, there was no hint that being with you would mean giving up smoking and drinking. Don't you think you're being a bit unreasonable? Haven't I given up enough to be with you?"

"You didn't have to marry me. You knew I didn't want you to smoke and drink before we married. You promised."

"The marriage covenant said nothing about smoking and drinking. I was a prisoner when we married. I couldn't talk to anybody but you. I couldn't go anyplace but the mountains. I had no access to cigarettes or liquor. It meant nothing to promise to not do something I couldn't do anyway."

"I wish you had just disappeared into the mountains and let me marry someone who would keep his promises."

"Well, I didn't just disappear, and neither will you. You don't know how to handle yourself out there, and Nancy needs you."

He turned her to the interior of the trailer and released her. She glared at him and rubbed her wrists. Tears streamed down her face. She climbed on the bed and slid to the wall, her back to him. He ate his supper, cleaned up, and cared for Nancy. He crawled into bed, placing Nancy between him and Valentina, and sang her some Russian lullabies until she slept. He lay awake, aware that Valentina was also awake. Neither of them was willing to cross the emotional chasm by offering a concession to appease the other.

*****

Greg Bullock walked to his seat in the courtroom, grateful he would not be ushered in by a court bailiff, with his hands handcuffed behind him. What a godsend Scott Hadley had been! Now his prayer was that, in the end, he would walk out equally free, with Anita and Alex still hidden from the grasp of the insidious law of repatriation.

The judge entered the courtroom, and everyone stood until he banged his gavel, and the bailiff said, "Court is in session."

"Mr. Brown, will you please read the indictment in this case."

Mr. Brown stood and read, "Gregory Henry Bullock is obstructing the requirement resulting from the Yalta Conference in March of 1945. He knew of the nationality and whereabouts of two Russian nationals and did not disclose this to the proper authorities. As these Russians could be Communist spies, this becomes an issue of national security."

"It will please the court if the prosecution will now make their opening statement."

Brian Bailey arose and stood, positioning himself to address the judge, then turning to address the spectators, said, "I represent the United States government. As is widely known, there is a genuinely dangerous subversive element in the name of the Communist Party in the United States, and this danger justifies extreme measures in rooting it out. Gregory Bullock is accused of knowingly shielding Russian spies from the authorities' knowledge in open sympathy to the Communist Party. Possibly he is even a member of said party himself. We will prove that he is worthy of censure leading to a prison term unless he will cooperate with authorities to discover the whereabouts of these spies still hiding within our community."

Greg groaned inwardly. This man was going to sentence him before a trial. How people on a witch hunt could twist simple compassionate facts.

"Defense, your opening statement, please."

Hadley stood, and Greg felt the gratitude wash over him as it had regularly since this man had appeared in his life. He still didn't understand why Hadley had come to be entangled in this problem, but it was obvious he needed the help. Hadley moved and spoke with self-assurance, inspiring confidence in all who heard him.

"Your honor, one cannot automatically assume that where there is smoke, there is fire. We must always remember that accusation is not proof and that conviction depends upon evidence and due process of law. More is on trial here than Gregory Bullock. Some of the basic principles of Americanism are on trial. We must stop character assassinations based on guilt by association. We must be open-minded enough to listen to circumstances that could have a bearing on any individual situation.

"Gregory Bullock served as a bishop in the Mormon Church. What he knows about Alex and Anita Drake was told him in the privacy of his office under the umbrella of his calling as a clergyman. While laws in the United States must be observed, there are relationships where the trust that must exist in confidential situations must also be observed. A Russian in the United States does not automatically mean that Russian is a spy for the Communist Party. Any Russian in the United States might be here seeking refuge from an oppressive government and in no way be a threat to our own. We will establish that there were good reasons for Greg Bullock to not disclose what he knew about Anita and Alex Drake."

"Will the prosecution please call their first witness?"

Douglas Parkins was sworn to tell the truth, the whole truth and nothing but the truth. Once seated on the witness stand, the prosecutor asked, "Are you now, or have you ever been, a member of the Communist Party?"

"I have not."

"Tell us, Mr. Parkins, of your interest in rooting out Communist spies in the United States."

"I was in Berlin as a soldier at the end of the war. I saw the savage Communists infiltrate into that city and vowed that I would do anything to keep these destroyers of freedom out of my own country."

"And how have you done that?"

"Initially, after the war, I kind of put it behind me. I came back and resumed my life. I met and actually started to date Anita Waters as she was known at the time."

"Did you have any idea she wasn't American?"

"She spoke English perfectly, though not with a Utah accent. She claimed she was from England, had no family in the United States. I believed her; I had no reason not to believe her. Some Englishisms would creep into her speech. For instance, she called the trunk of a car a boot, and she said 'Jolly'."

"Did you ever meet the man Alex, who is now her husband?"

"Not officially. That is to say, she did not introduce him. I did see him once. He looked like a wild man, unkempt beard, shaggy hair. She claimed he was her cousin."

"Did you speak with him?"

"No. I offered to punch him out, but Anita said to leave him alone."

"How did your relationship with Anita Waters end?"

"The newspapers announced the arrest of a Russian spy in New Jersey, going by the name of Janice Holmes. She had been teaching French in a high school there. A parent at a parent-teacher conference recognized her as a spy in England during the war. He knew she helped coordinate the spy efforts of the Russians and reported her to the authorities. She was later identified as Nina Pavlovna from Moscow."

"Your honor, exhibit number one is the said newspaper. Mr. Parkins, what did you do then?"

"I felt it was my time to act on my convictions. I told Anita that I was going to Washington, D. C. to help hunt down Russian spies."

"How did Anita react?"

"She didn't seem particularly interested or alarmed. I guess in her own spy training, she had learned to play the poker face."

"How do you know that she is a spy?"

"The newspaper reported that the Russian spy, Nina Pavlovna had a daughter by the name of Valentina Markovna, who served in France as a spy during the war. No one knew what happened to her after the war."

"Why do you suspect that Anita Waters is Valentina Markovna?"

"When I went to Washington D.C., I joined the Senate Internal Security Subcommittee charged with ensuring the enforcement of laws relating to espionage, sabotage, and the protection of the internal security of the United States. I became responsible for investigating employees of businesses and questioning them about their politics and affiliations. We kept cross-referenced lists of leftist organizations, publications, rallies, charities, and the like, as well as lists of individuals who were known or suspected Communists. Books such as *Red Channels* and newsletters such as *Counterattack* and *Confidential Information* were published to keep track of communist and leftist organizations and individuals. I was given training concerning how a Russian hiding in the US might accidentally let slip a clue to their origins.

"Anyway, after a time, I came back to Utah. I decided to seek Anita out. I had enjoyed dating her, thought we might renew our relationship. I asked about her, and a common acquaintance from the ward or church group I had been part of before invited me to go on a campout. I hoped Anita would be there. She was there, pregnant. Said she had married. Of course, I was curious to whom. Finally, I saw her with her husband at the campfire."

"Did you recognize him as the same individual you had seen at her place those years before?"

"No. He was groomed better, with a trimmed beard and short hair."

"How did you conclude they were Russian?"

"After the fire died down and many people had retired, he asked someone if he could use their "gee-tar." That was a red flag. Americans never say an "i" like a long e, but many foreigners do." Douglas himself said "foreigners" like "furners," revealing his own accent. "So with the fact that it was Anita's husband and obvious furn accent, my ears were perked. He started strumming on the gee-tar," Douglas stressed the mispronunciation Alex had used. "Part of my training to find Russians was to become familiar with Russian music if a situation such as I am describing should arise. I am a musician myself, so I remember things like this very well. He played two such songs. One is known as Ochee Chornaya, or 'Dark Eyes' and the other, Proshchai or 'Farewell.' I knew then that he was Russian."

"Did he sing the songs as he played?"

"He started to sing the second song in English. This is a tune which lends itself to the making up of words to fit the circumstances."

"So, what happened next?"

"Their child started to cry. They left the fire and went back to their tent. I decided to get some backup and then arrest them. My friend was unwilling to drive back to the city that night, and I could not find anyone else going that night. I decided I would have to arrest them myself the next morning. I went to their tent at 5:30 AM, and they were gone. I knew then that Anita was hiding him. She knew that they had better disappear before they were discovered."

"Thank you, Mr. Parkins."

"Does the defense have any questions?"

Scott Hadley arose and walked before Douglas, "Are there no other reasons why someone might leave the campout?"

"There is too much coincidental evidence to believe that in this case."

"Did Alex play any other pieces on the guitar?"

Douglas paused and said, "I think he played 'Lili Marlene.'"

"So would that make him American to play an American song?"

"Even the Germans were singing and whistling that by the end of the war. If this Alex had been a soldier during the war, and he must have been because I don't know how else he would have gotten from Russia to the US, he would have heard it."

"I heard Proshchai during my time as a soldier, so not only were the American songs heard and strummed by others, so were Russian songs."

"It wasn't on the radio."

"No, but Russians were in many prison camps with soldiers from all nationalities. A lot of music was passed back and forth in those camps. Even if you could establish that Alex is not American, what leads you to the conclusion that Anita is Russian?"

"First of all, in that drawing of her found in the house, her hair-do is so Russian and not at all American."

"And why does that lead you to believe she is Valentina, the daughter of Nina Pavlovna?"

Douglas smiled like the Cheshire cat, and a sick feeling went through Greg. Evidently, they had anticipated Hadley's questions and saved this information for this moment. "Because of my top-secret clearance as part of the Senate Internal Security Subcommittee, I requested local authorities' permission to take the picture. I went to the federal prison where Nina Pavlovna is being held and obtained permission to see her. I told her I was a friend of her daughter Valentina and she had requested that I give her this picture. Nina Pavlovna broke into tears and hugged the picture to herself. After she got control of herself, she asked where Valentina was and how she was doing."

Bad news. Greg felt as if he had been socked in the stomach. They hadn't known this. Hadley went on as if he were not fazed at all, although he too must feel knocked back.

"And what did you tell her?"

"That her daughter was married, had one child, another on the way. She was hungry to know any news about her daughter. I didn't tell her she was being sought as a spy."

"Snake," Hadley said.

"Objection!" Bailey screamed.

"Objection sustained." Judge Smith banged his gavel.

"Why do you think Greg Bullock had any knowledge of the background of Anita and Alex Drake?"

"After I saw Alex at Anita's home, I met with Greg Bullock and told him I thought Anita was living with a man. That is considered a sin in our religion, for a single man and woman to live together. He said he would talk to her about it."

"And that constitutes him knowing she was Russian?"

Greg knew they couldn't push too hard on this, as it probably would come out in the trial that he did know.

"I have a gut feeling that he did know."

"And do you have any evidence, other than your suspicions that Alex and Anita are Russian, that they are spies?"

"No, but I suspect Greg Bullock does."

"No further questions."

The next witness was Ronald Schupe.

"Are you now, or have you ever been, a member of the Communist Party?"

"No."

"How do you know Valentina Markovna?"

"Objection," Hadley sang out. "It has not been established that Anita is, in fact, Valentina Markovna."

"Objection overruled. If the Russian spy Nina Pavlovna recognized her picture, that is enough evidence, unless you have information to contradict that conclusion."

Greg did not know why Hadley had objected. They knew that Anita was Valentina Markovna. They just didn't know the others had known it, but at some point, he would himself be on the stand and likely to be asked the same question. What was he going to say under oath? He couldn't lie. He couldn't plead the 5th amendment on the grounds that it would incriminate him. That would be like a de facto confession. He would be labeled a "fifth amendment Communist." He had read of other individuals so labeled in the proceedings of similar trials, which

Hadley had given him. Maybe Hadley wasn't the sharp tack he had thought him to be.

Bailey repeated his question, "How do you know Valentina Markovna?"

"I don't know anyone named Valentina Markovna," Schupe replied.

"How do you know Anita?"

"She has been in the church congregation I've attended for the past few years."

Questions went on, and he revealed that he didn't know either Alex or Anita well but that he had given them a ride back to Salt Lake the night of the campout. He dropped them at their house. No, he didn't know what happened to them next. He knew that both claimed to be from Europe, but he didn't know where. Anita spoke English perfectly but with a different accent. Yes, Alex had trouble saying I's like long E's, and he didn't always get his TH's right. He didn't talk a lot. Hadley had no questions for Schupe.

Bailey's next witness was a fussy woman, wrinkly and skinny, named Mabel Snyder.

"Are you now, or have you ever been, a member of the Communist Party?"

"Objection. These people are not on trial."

"Objection overruled. It is routine in trials such as this to learn the political orientation of the witnesses where it might be pertinent to the case."

Mrs. Snyder worked with courthouse records and had the marriage license for Anita Waters and Alex Drake. It said that Anita was born in England and Alex was born in Indiana.

Bailey strutted, "We can clearly deduce from this that Alex is here under a false identity. Two people have testified he spoke with an accent which would not be characteristic of someone from Indiana. With the additional evidence that Nina Pavlovna has identified the picture as belonging to her daughter Valentina, we can conclude they are both Russian."

"Is there any record of Anita Waters registering under the Smith Act of 1940 as an Alien?" Bailey asked the woman.

"There is no evidence."

"Is there any record of Anita Waters of England becoming a Naturalized Citizen of the United States?"

"There is no record."

"It is obvious from the few records that do exist and those that do not that Anita is also here under false pretenses."

Hadley had a few questions for Mrs. Snyder, "Do you have any knowledge about Anita Waters or Alex Drake being Russian?"

"No."

"Do you have information about what Anita Waters or Alex Drake may have told Greg Bullock?"

Greg knew Hadley was establishing that it was not Anita or Alex who were on trial, and none of the witnesses really had any idea what either Anita or Alex had told him. Parkins only had his suspicions. Of course, the truth was more damning than even Parkins knew.

Bailey's next witness was a professional photographer who had taken a picture of Alex and Anita at their wedding. She still had the negative, and she had made a new print which was splashed over the newspapers the following day.

*****

Valentina was tense, wondering how the trial was going. Other than Douglas Parkins and Bishop Bullock, who knew anything? Would there be enough evidence to convict Bishop Bullock? What would his sentence be? And this was all because he had tried to help them. She felt like she was going to explode from the tension.

The Savages hadn't come this week, and she was actually glad. She didn't want to have to pretend everything was fine between her and Alex in front of them. He had continued his smoking and occasional drinking. When she asked where he was getting it, he just said, "Another herder." Their days had fallen into a silent pattern. She fixed his meals, tended Nancy, reminded him to get more water or wood, and followed him with hurt, swollen eyes. It just cut at the core of their marriage. She had been so hopeful after what she called her vision the day she had fasted and prayed about whether to marry him. Bishop Bullock had counseled her to write it down. She didn't at that time, because she was afraid someone might find it. She didn't dare leave anything personal like that in the house for fear it might be ransacked, just as it had been. She didn't dare keep it on her because she might be searched. She had written it now, in French, although there would certainly be people who could translate it and read it still. She kept it with her scriptures.

She read it frequently now, trying to remind herself that her vision was what had convinced her to marry Alex. It could yet be years before that might be accomplished. If the vision had been real, and she did believe it was, it told her several things. They would survive this somehow. They would have at least one son, and Alex would yet join the church. In spite of that, she felt like crying anew each time he came home with the odor of smoke or alcohol on his breath. Maybe it was the pregnancy that made her so emotional. She expected he would hold onto his position until she gave in. He was as solicitous, thoughtful, and helpful to her as possible, with the distance she created between them.

Valentina pulled out one of the newspapers the Savages had brought them. She felt a ravenous hunger for reading them. Even the advertisements were interesting. She liked to see the clothing, the prices. She saw another ad for the Samoyed puppies. She trusted Marv Savage had ordered her pair and wondered how soon they would be delivered. Would Alex see that as a peace offering? Not as forgiveness for his smoking and drinking, but as an apology for what she had cost him in luring him away from his beloved Kamchatka? Would he see it as a vote for their future?

She turned the page, and there, a very small, easily overlooked article announced NINA PAVLOVNA ABSOLVED OF SPY CHARGES. Her heart seemed to stop as she read the article: "Nina Pavlovna, charged with working as a Communist spy, has been cleared for lack of evidence. Accordingly, she will be repatriated to the Soviet Union per the terms of the Yalta agreement." Valentina's tears began anew in earnest. Her mother would be executed, as certainly as the sun rose in the morning. She wouldn't get to see her, to show her her grandchildren, to tell her she loved her. What terrible news. She had hoped it would not come to this.

Through her tears, Valentina did get Nancy up, changed her, and put her in her playpen, but she was bent over the newspaper sobbing when Alex returned. "No dinner tonight?"

"I can't."

He reached for the newspaper, and she looked at him in horror as he started to scrunch it for burning.

"No!" she screamed and grabbed the newspaper and dashed out the door, then she dashed back in and grabbed the whole pile of newspapers and dashed back out.

She heard Alex call behind her, "What is up with you? Get back here!" until she was too far away to hear his voice. She fell onto the grass and cried until the darkness cloaked her grief.

Valentina was startled awake with Alex placing a blanket around her. "Come. You're chilled out here." He lifted her and placed her on his horse. Then he picked up the lantern he had placed on the grass.

"My newspapers."

He set the lantern back down and gathered the newspapers, and handed them to her.

Alex led the horseback to the trailer, lifted her down, and placed her in the trailer. He poured her a cup of hot water brewing on the fire and added some of the herb she used to make her Brigham tea. He stepped out to tend the horse, and she assured herself that Nancy was safely asleep, her little thumb tucked in her mouth. Then Valentina sat, the blanket on her shoulders, warming her hands on the mug and blowing on the too hot water. Alex reentered.

"Do you want some milk and sugar in the tea?"

"A tiny bit." She set the mug down, grateful for his tender ministrations.

He poured in a little of the Carnation canned milk, dropped a sugar cube into the mug, and handed it back to her with a spoon.

"This isn't about me and the smoking and drinking, is it?"

"No, my mother," her voice caught. "They've decided she was not spying for the Soviets."

The tears spilled anew in earnest.

"But isn't that good?"

"No, it's disastrous," she choked out between sobs. "She is being repatriated. She will most surely be executed."

Ales gathered Valentina into his arms and held her until the sobs subsided. Then he removed her shoes and socks and helped her climb into bed.

******

When the trial resumed, Bailey's next witness was Russell George. Greg wondered how Bailey had known to seek him out.

"Mr. George. You are listed as the owner of the home where Valentina and Alex were living." Bailey felt he had substantiated that Anita Waters was, in fact, Valentina, whether or not he had sufficient evidence that it was true.

Russell George looked extremely uncomfortable on the witness stand. "I do not know her by that name, and I never met him, but yes, I own the home. I inherited it from my grandmother."

"Tell us how you came to rent it to them."

Russell shifted in the chair, looked down, ran his finger along the inside of his collar as if he were too hot and choking, and said in a subdued voice, "I met the woman you are calling Valentina in France during the war. We both worked in espionage. Our cover was a medical team. I am a doctor, and she a nurse. I went by the code name of Etienne, she, Marie Yvette."

"So she was a spy."

"For the Allies." Russell looked straight at Bailey as he said this. "As I said, so was I."

"Did you know she was Russian?"

Russell looked down. His reluctance to answer was palpable. "Yes. In the espionage arm of the service, we had representatives from all of the countries. Specifically, we had people fluent and schooled enough in French or German to be able to pass for natives."

"And what did Valentina speak?"

"French."

"How had she learned her French and English?"

"We didn't discuss it. We never discussed our private lives. We well understood, the less we knew about each other, the less danger we were to each other."

"How did she come to live in your house?"

"I did share my religious beliefs with her. She joined my church. At the end of the war, the personal danger for Russians to return to their native land was well known. Many of the American and British officers assisted these poor, unfortunate people to obtain false identities to be able to enter England or the United States."

"Did you assist Valentina in obtaining her false identity?"

"Not personally. I did suggest she do it. I gave her my contact information should she ever come to the United States."

"And so she did contact you?"

"Actually, she came in as a nurse. I requested a transfer for her to the States. I knew she would be in great danger if she were repatriated. When she came to the States, I worked as a doctor at the Schick Hospital in Clinton, Iowa. She came there, and we renewed our friendship."

"Did you have a romantic interest in her?"

"No. I'm married. We were just friends. I do esteem her highly. I think she is compassionate, very intelligent, and brave."

"And how did she end up in your house?"

"Uh," again, his discomfort showed in the way he glanced around the room and then briefly, heavenward. His actions reflected Greg's feelings. He wanted to tell the truth as he knew he would be asked to vow to do, but he also was afraid of endangering Alex and Valentina. Even Greg was beginning to think of her under that name. "We were working together when a telegram came to me, but for her, telling her that an injured soldier she knew was arriving at Fitzsimmons Army Hospital in Aurora, Colorado. I told her that if she needed a place to go, she could use my grandmother's home in Salt Lake."

"And did you keep up a regular correspondence after she left?"

"No. We knew she was still in danger, and the less I knew, the more protective it would be for her."

"Did you ever meet the soldier in question?"

"No."

"Did you know anything at all about him?"

"Only that it was someone she met in France."

"So you don't know if he were Russian or not?"

"No."

"What were Valentina's responsibilities in espionage?"

"Well, as she nursed the soldiers, she tried to pry information from the injured Vichy French in our care about the battles they had been in, plans for future battles, other information that could be useful in our own war effort."

"That's all?"

"She had the skill of typing, and so she typed up the reports of all of us."

"You all spoke French?"

"We all spoke English. Not all of us spoke French."

"Did she have anything to do with the Russians who were in the Russian Liberation Army?"

Russell sighed heavily as if he had hoped the questioning wouldn't go here. He seemed to be committed to answering any question asked, but he was not volunteering information. "Uh, yes. She met with those fit to go back into battle and recruited them for the allies to go back into the German army to encourage other Russians to sabotage the German effort. They also carried fliers they distributed urging the Russians to desert."

"So the soldier in question could have been one of these Russians?"

"I do not know."

"The prosecution rests."

"The defense?"

Hadley arose, again filling the space with the aura of his presence. "Mr. George, I notice throughout your questioning by Mr. Bailey that you seem extremely uncomfortable in answering the questions. Could you elaborate on why you feel that way?"

"While I admit that I know Valentina, as they are calling her, is Russian, I do not believe that she is in the United States as a Communist spy. I believe she is here as a refugee and that her life is in danger should she be repatriated to the Soviet Union. I would be most distressed should some ill come to her because of anything I have said."

"Do you know where she is now?"

"I do not."

"Do you fear for yourself in connection with knowing that Valentina is Russian and you let her stay in your home?"

"I suppose I am as guilty as Greg Bullock is accused of being in this. I think it is contrary to the spirit of our country to criminally accuse someone who has helped someone else in mortal danger, out of compassion."

"That is all, Mr. George."

******

Sasha didn't visit Sodie after learning the news of Valentina's mother. He felt the need to be solicitous of her in her vulnerability. The cold war that had grown up between them because of the smoking and drinking thawed, and they were once again warm and kind to each other. One day Sodie rode into their camp. "I've missed you. Is everything all right?"

"Yeah. I just had some home things to attend to."

"I brought you that sourdough starter I promised."

Valentina stepped from the trailer carrying Nancy. Sasha put his arm around her, "This is my wife, Valentina, our daughter, Nancy. Valentina, this is Sodie, another herder." He didn't add, 'the source of my cigarettes and liquor.'

"You didn't tell me you had a little lady," Sodie said as he bent over and kissed Valentina's hand. "And this gal is a charmer." He shook Nancy's pudgy little hand. She giggled and buried her face in Valentina's neck.

Sasha shrugged. No, he hadn't told Sodie.

He invited Sodie to sit down. Sodie did, and they chatted. Valentina sat next to Sasha, and he held Nancy. Sasha put his arm around Valentina, resting his hand on her shoulder in the recent comfortableness they had reestablished with each other.

"Sodie, would you teach Valentina how to make one of your mutton and sourdough lunches?"

Sodie graciously agreed. Sasha helped. Valentina talked, laughed, and smiled, not betraying either the recent grief she had suffered because of her mother or the anger his smoking and drinking had caused her. She must suspect Sodie as the source; the odor of cigarette smoke was heavy upon him. She asked questions so she could replicate Sodie's production, and she praised him for how delicious it was.

After the meal was cleaned up, Nancy slept. Valentina sat next to Sasha, her head on his shoulder, her hand in his. Sodie pulled out some cigarettes and offered one to Valentina. She declined. Sasha accepted. Valentina stood up, glared at him, and ran from the trailer.

Sodie looked after her, a deep sadness in his eyes. He put away the cigarettes without taking one himself. He stood, "You're going to lose your little lady," he said. "It's not worth it." He stood and left the trailer.

Sasha looked after him, wondering what he meant. He smoked his cigarette, stayed with Nancy, and waited for Valentina to return.

She did, eventually. The hurt was back in her eyes, swollen from more crying. Sasha didn't speak to her. His own anger boiled. She had been rude to his guest, to his friend. He shouldn't have to put up with this.

Still wondering what Sodie had meant, Sasha rode over to his camp after bedding down the sheep. He found him solidly drunk, sobbing over yet another glass of the numbing liquid. Sasha poured himself a glass, downed it, and wondered what to say.

"You will lose your little lady," Sodie slurred. "I used to have one. I loved her. I really did, but I also loved my cigarettes and drink. She'd get that hurt look in her eyes just like yours, and she'd cry and plead and beg and get angry and yell and deny me, and I just kept smokin' and drinkin'. It wasn't my problem. It was hers. She was one of them Mormons. She wanted me to be like them. Never smokin', never drinkin', not even coffee. It weren't my style. When I'd get drunk, I'd fancy she was runnin' around with one of them Mormon dudes. I started beatin' her when I was drunk. Then she started talkin' about leavin' me. I got mad and loaded her and the two kids in the car. A little boy, a little girl." Sodie's sobs overwhelmed him. He covered his face with his hands. After maybe five minutes, he continued, "We wrecked. I was driving drunk. She was killed. The baby girl was killed. The boy lies in a rest home with a broken neck, hatred in his eyes. He can talk, but he won't talk to me. Now I drink to forget, but I'll never forget. I can't forget. You'll lose your little lady. You will."

Sodie's words chilled Sasha through. He knew they were true. He'd lose Valentina if he insisted on smoking and drinking. Even if that only meant she never again would trust him in a promise. She would always know that maybe he would betray that promise later. He left Sodie to his misery and urged the horse to a gallop back to his own camp. Valentina was in bed, her face to the back wall of the camp. Nancy lay between her and the wall. Sasha peeled off his clothes, aware that he reeked of cigarette smoke and liquor. He crawled into bed and put his hand on her shoulder, "Valentina." She didn't answer. "I'm sorry I broke my promise not to smoke or drink. I promise now not to ever again smoke or drink alcohol, coffee or tea, again."

She turned to him. "Why?"

"I don't want to lose you." She placed her hand on the side of his face. "I love you, Valentina. I really do."

She moved Nancy to the side of the trailer against the wall and slid next to him. She kissed him and kissed him. Tears ran down her cheeks.

He gently wiped them away. "You cry whether I do or not."

"Thank you, Sasha." She snuggled up to him, and the baby in her womb kicked him.

17

Operation Keelhaul

Scott Hadley strode to the front of the courtroom, again exuding the take-charge demeanor so characteristic of him. Greg wondered who his witnesses were and where this would take him. He was charged with knowingly shielding Russians from the knowledge of the authorities. Although there was some doubt exactly who Alex was, there was little doubt, if any, that Anita Waters was, in fact, Valentina Markovna and that both Alex and Valentina were Russian. All that was left to be established was how much he, Greg Bullock, knew. If he were as candid as Russell George had been, that would be established within minutes, and then he would be summarily convicted and face, what? A prison term? A destroyed career and ruined reputation? Why had Scott Hadley come to town with great show and expense to do that? It could have all been accomplished before The Committee on Un-American Activities without all of this fanfare.

"Your Honor," Hadley began. "Gregory Bullock is upstanding in the community, trusted by his church with the highest position in his congregation, and a loyal US citizen who served as a paratrooper during the war. One must ask why would such a man withhold the knowledge of the existence of Russians in his congregation? To understand this, we must first understand the history behind the repatriation of Russians. To do so, I call upon Henry Walker as my first witness.

Walker was sworn in, and then Hadley asked, "What was your position at Yalta?"

"I am from the State Department of the United States of America."

"What was discussed at Yalta?"

"The heads of government of the United States, the United Kingdom, and the Soviet Union met near Yalta in Crimea, in February 1945. President Franklin D. Roosevelt, Prime Minister Winston Churchill, and Premier Joseph Stalin, respectively represented their individual countries for the purpose of discussing Europe's post-war reorganization."

"And as a result of the Yalta agreement, what was the position of the United States regarding the repatriation of Russians?"

"I now quote from the handbook issued by Headquarters, United States Forces, European Theater, September 1945:

> No United Nations' National, stateless person...or persons persecuted because of race, religion, or activity in favor of the United Nations, will be compelled to return to his domicile except for a criminal offense. Liberated Soviet Citizens... are excluded from this policy... and will be returned to the control of the USSR without regard to their individual wishes.
>
> Our Government policy has been established after long and careful weighing all of these factors, and the Army must carry it out to the best of its ability."

"Liberated Soviet Citizens were to be returned to the control of the USSR without regard to their individual wishes. Did I understand that correctly?"

"Yes, you did. They were to be returned without regard to their individual wishes.

"Thank you, Mr. Walker?"

"Any questions from the prosecution?"

"The people have no questions."

"I call as my next witness Philip Duckworth."

After Duckworth had been duly sworn in, Hadley asked him, "Please identify which branch of the armed services you were in, and your duties there."

"US Navy Aviation Rescue Swimmer."

"Are you familiar with the policy of the US government of repatriating liberated Soviet Citizens without regard to their individual wishes established at Yalta and enforced by the US Army?"

"Yes, I am. The US and British armies enforced it."

"What did the US call this forced repatriation?"

"The code name adopted by the leaders of our armed forces in the field for the forced deportation of the millions of refugees who found themselves in apparent freedom in the West was Operation Keelhaul."

"Will you explain what keelhauling means?"

"Keelhauling is the cruelest, most dangerous of punishments and tortures ever devised for men aboard a ship. It involves trussing a man up with ropes, throwing him overboard, unable to swim, and hauling him under the ship's keel from one side to the other, or even from stem to stern. Most of those thus keelhauled under water are already dead when their punishment is over."

"Were you ever aboard a ship where keelhauling was used as a punishment?"

"Heavens no! It was legally permitted as a punishment in the Dutch Navy. It was formally abolished even there in 1853."

"Objection!" Bailey sprang to his feet. "This man has no firsthand knowledge."

"He has the background to help us understand the meaning of the term, which is pertinent to this case."

"Objection overruled," the judge declared. "Continue, counselor."

Hadley turned back to Duckworth, "So it is not used by the US Navy as a form of punishment today?"

"It was never used by the US Navy."

"That our Armed Forces should have adopted this barbaric term as its code name for forcibly deporting millions of Russians who were already in the lands of freedom, to concentration camps, firing squads, or the hangman's noose shows how little the high brass thought of their longing to be free. Thank you, Mr. Duckworth."

"Any questions from the prosecution?"

"No questions."

"I call my next witness, Matthew Cope."

Matthew Cope, a squarish-shaped man with a prominent mole on his nose, swore to tell the truth and took the witness seat.

"Mr. Cope, please tell us what happened in Platting, Germany in February of 1946."

"About three thousand ex-Soviet veterans of the KONR Army were in the camp. During the night, American special commandos circled the camp with tanks. At five o'clock in the morning, the searchlights were turned on. At the same moment, trucks entered the camp. All inhabitants of the Russian barracks were ordered to form up in ranks in the glare of the searchlights. The very day before, we had promised them they would not be forcibly repatriated. American soldiers searched the Russians. I was one of those soldiers. We threw everything the Russian prisoners possessed in the mud: watches, bread, their last pencil, a photograph of a loved one that had been carried throughout the war. It was despicable. Then, the lists were read. Those named in the lists were driven onto the trucks. They were ordered to lie down on the floor of the trucks. As soon as a truck was fully loaded. American soldiers armed with billy clubs and machine guns climbed into the trucks. The prisoners on the floor were forbidden to move. If they did, they were beaten." Cope took a ragged breath. "The loaded trucks drove, accompanied by armored reconnaissance cars, to the railroad station in Platting. The prisoners were ordered to enter cattle cars of already waiting trains. The empty trucks returned to fetch another load of Cossacks. In a few hours, the work was done. Only who had sewed razor blades into their coats escaped when they slashed their wrists in front of their barracks under the glaring searchlights."

"Was this an isolated incident?"

"Heavens no. What happened at Platting was repeated in almost every other camp. There was no reason, no mercy."

"This seems to make you emotional."

"Force so brutal that American and British soldiers shed tears as they carried out the orders to club and blackjack prisoners into insensibility. We held them down at bayonet point, binding the cut arteries with which they had attempted to commit suicide rather than be returned to Stalin's 'justice.' We shot their feet so that they could not run. We tossed maimed and mangled bodies back into trucks after beating them into unconsciousness, or drugging them into insensibility. Shameful, pitiful story. Bloody details of the fate of these millions is terribly painful to remember. It was the most disgraceful thing I ever did as a soldier. I regret it every day. 'I should have let them shoot me instead,' I heard one of the Cossacks say, as he was loaded into the truck, 'The NKVD would have slain us with truncheons; the Americans did it with their word of honor. Blamed military.'"

"Thank you, Mr. Cope."

"Any questions, prosecution?"

"No questions, Your Honor." Then, under his breath, "but I still don't see the relevance," Bailey muttered.

Hadley addressed his next witness, a nervous, bespectacled man, "Mr. Henry Fox, I understand you were a journalist at Dachau, Germany following the war."

"That is true."

"What happened at Dachau with the Russians?"

"As reported in the New York Times January 20, 1946, ten renegade Russian soldiers, in a frenzy of terror over their impending repatriation to their homeland, committed suicide during a riot in the Dachau prison camp. Twenty-one others were hospitalized, suffering from deep gashes that they inflicted on themselves, apparently with razor blades, but no further deaths had been reported. Many suffered cracked heads from the nightsticks wielded by 500 American and Polish guards who were attempting to bring the situation under control.

"The practical certainty of the fate they would face on arrival in the Soviet area precipitated the disorder. It had its prelude in the inmates' resistance in one of the barracks when they were ordered to line up to enter trains waiting inside the former concentration camp. Even though threatened with rifles and carbines, they refused to leave the shelter, begging GI guards to shoot them rather than carry out the extradition order.

"Authorities in the United States Third Army's headquarters at Bad Toelz stated in reporting the riot that every possible precaution had been taken to deliver the prisoners in accordance with the Yalta terms."

Bailey continued to complain about irrelevance, and Hadley kept insisting that this was necessary background. Greg had not heard about many of these atrocities but felt more strongly than ever that he had been right in not reporting Alex and Anita.

Once Hadley's next witness was seated, he addressed him. "Mr. Thomas Hodgson, where were you in the summer of 1945?"

"I was one of several artillery officers in the 102nd Infantry Division. We were detailed to lead a convoy of all the trucks in my battalion on the mission of picking up Russian POWs from German internment camps and delivering them to the Russian officials at Chemnitz. For about two weeks, day and night, I led seventeen trucks on shuttle service all over Germany and France on this mission. There were thousands of other trucks doing the same. We soon found out that many Russians didn't want to be repatriated, and also found out why."

"Why, Mr. Hodgson, why did these Russians not desire to return to their homes and loved ones after being absent for several years?"

"They believed that any officer POW would face execution upon return and any non-com POW could face a term in Siberia. As a result, we stood over them with guns, and our orders were to shoot to kill if they tried to escape from our convoy. Needless to say, many of them did risk death to accomplish their escape.

"Thank you, Mr. Hodgson."

After Bailey waived his right to questions, Hadley continued, "I call Julius Epstein to the witness stand. Mr. Epstein, please tell the court your profession."

"I am a journalist."

"Mr. Epstein, it would seem contrary to common sense that these Russians did not welcome their opportunity to return to their home and loved ones. Was there really a basis to their fear that they would not be welcomed when they returned to Russia following the war?"

"Stalin's brutality was well known. In 1940 some 15,000 Polish Army Officers who had been prisoners of the war disappeared. In 1941, the German occupying army dug up some four thousand of their corpses buried in the Katyn forest. They had been hastily shot and carelessly buried in their winter uniforms, complete with identity cards and even letters from home in their pockets. Nazi propagandists charged Stalin with the crime, while Stalin laid the murders at Hitler's door. The US accepted Stalin's version, but the truth of the matter was they had been captured when Hitler and Stalin together attacked and divided Poland between them. The forest had been in Russian hands until Hitler attacked Stalin in June 1941, whereafter the Germans occupied it. Since they were buried in their winter uniforms, it was clearly in Soviet hands at the time of the execution of the Polish officers."

"Objection! This has nothing to do with Bullock and the case at hand."

"Mr. Epstein, does this have anything to do with the case at hand?"

"Oh, yes. It shows the ruthlessness of Stalin."

"Objection sustained. The treatment of Polish officers is no indication of what would happen to Russian nationals once they returned to Russia after the war."

"Mr. Epstein, please tell us why the Russians so feared repatriation," Hadley refocused his question.

"Stalin labeled any Russian taken prisoner during the war a traitor," Epstein answered. "Any Russian who has served in the war or even who emigrated from Russia twenty, forty, sixty years ago, any Russian who was captured by Germany and deported for forced labor into Germany, was now labeled a traitor to Russia. They were to be summarily deported to Russia either to face a life of hard labor or execution—which is probably the more merciful of the two. The horror of the labor camps was well known throughout all of Russia. No Russian would knowingly put himself in a position to suffer such a fate.

"When the war ended, the Soviet General Golikov promised these prisoners that everything would be understood, forgiven, and forgotten. Many believed, appeared at the points of assembly, and were sent to the USSR. However, through unofficial channels, news soon spread that nothing but hardships awaited those prisoners who returned. Those who wore German uniforms could expect torture and death. Yes, these unfortunate people knew what awaited them in the Soviet paradise."

"Thank you, Mr. Epstein."

Bailey had no questions, and Hadley continued, "One might think these were isolated instances which happened at the close of the war only in Europe. I would now like to call Jonathan Snarr to the stand. Mr. Snarr, please tell us what happened in Seattle Harbor."

"It was a horror at Seattle Harbor. I, among other American soldiers, some of us weeping, dumped Russian bodies knocked senseless with blackjacks into trucks. We subdued them with bayonets. We fished them up when they leaped into the water. We threw them on a Soviet ship where they fought with bare fists, disabling the engines. We helped the Soviet captors to subdue them and repair their engine."

"Why do you think this is so little known?"

"Everyone that participated was deeply ashamed of what they were compelled to do. We have all tried to conceal it under the cloak of secrecy. We were actually told that the unauthorized disclosure of this could result in serious damage to the nation."

"So you were ordered to commit these acts but not talk about what you had done?

"Exactly. We were told it could do exceptionally grave damage to the nation."

"Why do you think you were told to keep silent about it?"

"It goes against the grain of everything we think is American. It violates the very spirit of what we want to think our country stands for to engage in such activities."

Bailey had surrendered to the fact that he was not going to win through objecting to these witnesses he considered immaterial. He had no questions.

Hadley called his next witness, Sam Henderson. A tall, lanky man with a bushy mustache mounted the witness stand.

"Mr. Henderson, I understand you were at Fort Dix, in New Jersey. Can you pinpoint that date?"

"It was June 29, 1945. The day is forever emblazoned upon my mind."

"What happened there?"

"One hundred fifty-four Russians held at Fort Dix, New Jersey refused to be repatriated. That morning, these men were told that they would be loaded onto a ship that afternoon and returned to the Soviet Union. The men thereupon barricaded themselves in their barracks. To flush them out, American guards fired in tear-gas grenades; the men emerged brandishing mess-kit knives, table legs, and other improvised weapons. The skirmish lasted for 30 minutes, leaving three US soldiers and seven prisoners wounded. Inside those barracks, the Americans found three prisoners hanging from the rafters, and 15 empty nooses—their use forestalled by the tear-gas attack. The US State Department hesitated briefly. Two months later, the group was shipped out."

Again Bailey had no questions. Hadley continued, "So we see that this forced repatriation of Russian citizens was carried out not only on European soil but upon our own. We must ask ourselves if this is still going on. As evidence, I submit the Salt Lake Tribune, the date July

11, 1950. The individual who has been identified to this court as Nina Pavlovna was repatriated to the Soviet Union because," and Hadley slowed down, emphasizing each word, "there is no evidence she has served as a spy for the Communists in the United States. This reprehensible practice continues today. We may or may not learn what happens to her upon her return."

"Now," Hadley resumed the following day, "we need to look at a particular group of those repatriated to the Soviet Union. I call Mr. Ronald Steggler to the stand."

"Mr. Steggler, I understand that you worked with the Soviets flushing out those who became members of what is known as the ROA following the war. Is that correct?"

"Yes, sir."

"And what was the ROA?"

"Objection. This has nothing to do with the case."

"Excuse me, Mr. Bailey, you have intimated that the individual we are calling Alex might well have been a member of the ROA."

"But that has not been substantiated."

"It may be in further testimony."

Judge Smith said, "I suggest that if you have a witness who can substantiate that Alex was in the ROA, that he come forth now."

"Very well," Hadley said. "May it please the court that we first establish what the ROA was?"

"Continue."

"Mr. Steggler, please explain what the ROA was."

"ROA are the initials for the Russian words meaning the Russian Liberation Army. They were a group of predominantly Russian prisoners of war captured by the Germans subordinated to the Nazi German high command during the war. Former Red Army general Andrey Vlasov organized the ROA. The idea was that these prisoners of war, as well as White Russian emigrants following the Russian Civil War, would help Germany win the war with the Allies, and then the

Germans, in turn, would help free Russia from the Communist regime in the Soviet Union. Russian divisions not under the German command were known as KONR."

""To refresh our memory, Mr. Cope told us what happened in Platting, Germany to veterans of the KONR," Hadley inserted. "Russian soldiers who joined the ROA or the KONR took up arms and fought on the side of the enemy against their own country and its allies."

"Yes."

"Why would they do that?"

"They may have been actuated by local patriotism taking the form of separatism; by racial, religious or political ideologies, or merely by a desire to save their own skins under enemy pressure, or even by the greed of gain. Whatever their motives, it is hard to see how, in such cases, forcible repatriation can be avoided, or, indeed, why it should be avoided. Even when their motives were pure, these men fought against their own country and against their country's allies. Their actions may well have prolonged the war, cost extra lives, and caused untold suffering. Moreover, the obligation of a country to its allies seems here to be paramount and inescapable."

"So you feel that, in the case of the ROA soldiers, forced repatriation was fully justified."

"I do."

"Was it because of Germanophilia that they joined the ROA?"

"Probably not in most cases."

"I read in the New York Times that some fifty-thousand Russian POWs starved to death in German camps, often as many as six hundred a day. Why were they treated so poorly?"

Steggler appeared to squirm. "Well, Stalin called them traitors for being captured. In those cases, I might extend some mercy. Many of them were subsequently captured by the Allies and recruited to fight against the Germans, so I guess some came full circle."

*****

As the days went by, Sasha found it easier to make a resolution than to keep it. That brief interlude of again smoking and drinking had awakened in him a ferocious desire. He came to Valentina for help, afraid he'd lose the battle if he tried to face it alone. She pleasured him, encouraged him to pleasure her, read to him, walked with him, prayed with him to help him through. He clung to her for support and drew strength from her. Sasha did not dare go see Sodie alone, and he felt it unwise to put Valentina on a horse so advanced in her pregnancy. Sasha went out of his way to run into Sodie on the range. He invited Sodie to visit them. Sodie came hesitantly and then frequently as Valentina warmly received him. Sasha was glad he could see the love between them. There was no offer of cigarettes.

*****

The next day Hadley called Greg to the witness stand. Greg still didn't understand Hadley's strategy. He had been so relieved when Hadley showed up and sprung him from jail, but it was becoming increasingly clear that Hadley had his own agenda, that for Hadley, he was only the means to an end. Greg had not had any idea of the extent of the abuse the Russians suffered in repatriation, and he was even more certain he had done right in not reporting Alex and Valentina. Greg placed his hand on the Bible and swore to tell the truth, the whole truth, and nothing but the truth, with an inaudible prayer that he wouldn't be asked to tell anything he didn't feel comfortable in revealing.

Hadley began the questioning, "Mr. Bullock, please state your profession, your service during World War II, and the circumstances under which you met the individuals being identified in this court as Valentina and Alex."

"I have been a professor of history at the University of Utah. I was part of the 82nd Airborne Division and parachuted into France shortly after D-day. I was injured when my parachute snagged on a tree. After recovering from my injuries, I switched to a non-combatant unit where I served until the end of the war. For the last two years I have served as a bishop to what the Mormon church calls a ward. Valentina was a member of that ward. We called her Anita Waters. She asked to speak to me."

"And what did she discuss with you?"

Greg felt like squirming like Russell George had. "She disclosed that she wanted to live pure before the Lord as she had promised to do at her baptism, and she felt she was living a lie and sought counsel on what to do."

"What lie was she living?"

"That she had a Russian man living at her home, that she herself was Russian, and that she was Nina Pavlovna's daughter, Valentina."

Both Doug Parkins and Bailey's eyes bulged, and a smile lit their faces. Their case had just been made. His own tongue had just verified everything the indictment accused him of. The surprise in their expressions told him they hadn't thought he knew who Valentina actually was.

"You knew all of this."

Greg nodded.

"Did you not know the requirement to report all Russians living in the United States to the proper authorities?"

"Yes, I knew I was supposed to report them."

"Why did you not report them?"

"I prayed about it and tried to listen to the promptings of the Holy Ghost, which I firmly believe in as a means for God to communicate with man. Since Valentina had come to me of her own volition, my feeling was strong that I should hear her out. I had had no inkling she was Russian before her first visit to my office, and I did not know of the man living in her home."

"Had anything prompted her to come to you?"

"Yes. She had been dating Douglas Parkins."

"Excuse me, this is the Douglas Parkins who brought the accusations against you?"

"Yes. The announcement had just come out that Valentina's mother had been picked up in New Jersey on suspicion of spying for the

Communists. Douglas announced to Valentina that he was going to help root out the Communist influence in the US."

"To your knowledge, did he have any idea that Valentina was Russian?"

"She did not believe he did at the time."

"Did you ever meet with the man known as Alex?"

"Yes."

"What is his real name?"

"Alexander."

Hadley smiled. "So. What did you learn about him? Had he been in the Russian Army?"

"Yes. And he was captured by the Germans, nearly starved to death, joined the ROA, and finally was recruited by Valentina to fight with the Allies against the Germans. He was in this employment until the end of the war, when he came to the US under a false identity."

"Did Valentina and Alex know each other prior to coming to the United States?"

"Yes. They knew each other in Russia, had been lovers."

"So, they continued that relationship once they were here?"

"No, not exactly. She had joined the Mormon Church and had committed to waiting for marriage for a sexual relationship. They just lived in the same house. He didn't speak English."

"How did you communicate with him?"

"When my parachute snagged on the tree, I was rescued by a Russian," Greg debated whether to reveal whether it was Alex and chose not to. "I had been severely injured and, when recovered sufficiently, I didn't return to combat, but instead went to the military language school. I studied Russian and developed a moderate fluency. Valentina translated whatever I could not understand."

"After hearing their story, what did you counsel them to do?"

"Get married. And I counseled Alex to learn English. He had been resisting it rather strenuously up to that point."

"Why was that?"

"Well, I think he thought we would find some way to get him back to the Kamchatka peninsula where he came from, and it wouldn't be necessary."

"But instead, you counseled them to get married. Why?"

"It felt like the right answer."

"But it didn't really solve anything."

Greg smiled inwardly. That had been Valentina's response to the suggestion they marry as well. "It didn't solve many things."

"Thank you, Mr. Bullock."

The judge said, "Counsel for the prosecution?"

"Mr. Bullock, have you ever been a member of the Communist party?" Bailey strutted before him, exuding confidence.

"No, sir."

"Do you have acquaintance with anyone who is a member of the Communist party?"

"No, sir."

"Do you have any sympathies with the Communist party?"

"No, sir."

"But you knowingly broke the law when you knew the whereabouts of two Russians in the United States, and you did not report it to the proper authorities. You admit that."

"I knew they were Russian, and I did not report it."

"Did you ever tell anyone?"

"No."

"Not even your wife?"

"Not until the FBI came for me."

"Why?"

"Then I would just be putting the same burden of secrecy on someone else's shoulders. They wouldn't be able to tell anyone else, or they might report Alex and Valentina."

"But it is the law that they be reported. I thought Mormons, especially Mormon bishops, were law-abiding citizens."

"And I am, but Valentina realized that deportation would mean either death or hard labor for them. There was nothing in what they told me to indicate they were here as spies, merely as refugees. They wouldn't get a trial, they would just be sent back."

"Her mother got a trial."

"Yes, and was found innocent of spying and now has been repatriated. Now she will probably be executed."

"That is supposition. I request it be stricken from the record." Hadley spoke up.

"Request granted."

"Do you know where Valentina and Alex are now?"

"I do not."

"Do you know who might have helped them go into hiding?"

"I do not."

"How did they support themselves?"

"She worked as a nurse at the VA."

"The VA indicates she terminated employment in April of last year. Do you know what they did for employment then?"

Greg felt like squirming again. They were getting close to the issue that he didn't know if he would tell the whole truth about. "Alex got employed."

"For whom?"

"I do not know."

"You didn't ask?"

"I asked not to be told."

"Why?"

"I feared this day might come. I thought the less I knew, the better for them."

"That is all."

Greg gave an inward prayer of thanks. He had neither been required to reveal nor lie about Alex's skill as an artist, nor his ability to call birds. Although Greg didn't know who Alex worked for, he strongly suspected that somehow knowing that bit of knowledge about Alex could lead a curious person to Alex's employer and hence, require that person to cover up what he knew or reveal them. Greg strongly suspected Alex's employer had aided in their disappearance. Who else could have? If he were identified, Alex and Valentina would be discovered, and all would have been in vain.

*****

Valentina both yearned for and dreaded a change from their predictable days. Alex rode around the sheep in the morning. She tended to Nancy, diapering and dressing her, feeding her and playing with her. Then breakfast, chores around the camp, the never-ending laundry, and finally the long, lazy afternoons where she could read while Alex studied his English. A nap beckoned her more often than not, and Alex spent his time out with his birds and drawings. Then there was the evening meal, clean up, and Alex riding around the sheep again. Not much different day in and day out, week in and week out.

Things would change, in one way or another, and soon. The baby was due. The trial was drawing to a close. Although every newspaper brought to them carried detailed accounts of the trial, so far none of the few who knew where they were, had sought the sizable reward for turning them in. If convicted, and he obviously was guilty, Bishop Bullock could suffer greatly for keeping the knowledge of them secret, and things would still not be over for her and Alex. Those who hunted them still knew they were out there somewhere and would watch and wait until something or someone revealed their whereabouts. Would it ever end for them? Were they destined to live out their lives and raise their children in this isolated sheep camp? Tangled thoughts. They could drive one crazy.

She put the pot on the stove and filled it from the bucket of water. Every day required washing diapers. What would it be like with two babies? How she would love to have one of those electric washing machines that agitated by themselves, and a wringer to pass the clothing through, which removed most of the water. Would such luxuries so commonplace in America ever be hers? Then there was winter. She didn't even dare think about it. She would have to bundle herself and the two babies up just to get out of the confined space occasionally. But what would they do out in the cold and snow? Maybe it was good their father had grown up in Siberia.

The diapers dried on the bushes, Alex tried out the watercolors he was trying to master, and she lay on the bed, watching Nancy sleep, her little lips puckering as she breathed in and out. Valentina's breath caught as she heard the car. Was it the authorities coming to take them, someone bringing supplies, or someone just wandering around the mountain and thought they would stop in to say hello? No one in the last category had ever come yet, but Valentina dreaded them the most. If anyone did just happen by, it could be the end of them. She gave an audible sigh as she recognized Aaron Dickenson's red pick-up, in which they had ridden to the sheep camp. "It's Aaron," she said to Alex. He left his painting drying on the table as Valentina clumsily tried to heave herself off the bed. She felt like an enormous beetle on its back.

Aaron was busy unloading the usual boxes. Valentina knew there would be replenishing of food, hopefully, some new books and hand-work, maybe some things for the baby. Helen had asked what she needed. Aaron kissed her on the cheek and then winked at her as he unloaded a wooden crate.

"What's that?" Alex asked.

"Open it and see."

Alex pried a slat from the top of the crate, and a little white puppy head stuck out, and a tongue licked him.

"What...where?"

He pulled the puppy from the container and snuggled it to him. Valentina smiled at his obvious delight. Aaron pulled out the second puppy.

"Just like my pups in...at home," Alex corrected. She suspected that had he been a tad more emotional, she would have seen tears in his eyes.

Aaron then handed her a book. "Helen sent this for you."

Valentina held the book reverently. *Constellations: Stars and Stories.* Tears did come to her eyes.

*****

"Today, we will hear the final arguments in the trial of Gregory Bullock. Mr. Bailey, you will go first."

"Mr. Bullock has been accused of knowingly withholding the whereabouts of two Russians hiding in the United States, which is in violation of the law requiring all citizens to communicate this information to proper authorities. By Gregory Bullock's own admission, he did this. These Communists are a threat to the very warp and weft of our society. We have seen the increasing restrictions imposed on the Germans in the Russian occupied zone. Now, we have in our own community individuals such as Gregory Bullock welcoming and shielding these people. I ask the court to make a firm statement that the US government and the state of Utah will not tolerate this, and the full exercise of the law will be executed in the instances of individuals violating this law. Thank you, your honor."

Hadley strode solemnly to the stand, "Your honor, I realize it is not customary to submit additional evidence in the final statements but something central to this case came out in this morning's Salt Lake Tribune, page 4.

"Objection! No new evidence can be admitted at this point of a trial."

"It is very pertinent to the case. May I proceed?"

"Yes. Objection overruled."

"It is entitled "Russian Spy Executed." and the article reads, "As reported in Izvestia, a Russian newspaper, Nina Pavlovna, recently repatriated after being absolved in the United States of accusations that she is serving as a spy for the Soviet Communists, was hung Thursday past for treason against the Soviet Union.

"Sir, first, I want to clarify that Gregory Bullock has violated no law of the United States. As I read in the beginning, it was the US military's policy to repatriate all citizens of Russian origin irrespective of their personal wishes. It had been the assumption that all US citizens were under obligation to aid in the enforcement of this policy. It is not a law that they do so. I feel the real issue in the case against my client, Gregory Bullock, is not whether Alex and Valentina were Russian, but whether they were Communist spies. We as a country seem to have accepted the definition that nationality equates with spying, but the very case of Nina Pavlovna indicates that there are times it does not so equate. Still we repatriate individuals seeking refuge in the United States from the kind of dictatorship which exists in Russia. The prosecution has submitted no evidence that Alex or Valentina are here as spies, and they could not because there is no such evidence.

"As we hear stories come out of Germany, is it the patriotic, law-abiding German who turned in his Jewish neighbors that we extol as heroes? No. It is the individual who fed, hid, and aided the Jew at the risk of his own life that we call a hero. We wish we would have the moral integrity to be like the German who aided the Jews if such a challenge came to us. Gregory Bullock is such a man. He stands strong before the God he believes in, doing what he feels in his heart is right, against a policy of the land he believes is misguided and wrong. Many of us, including Gregory Bullock, Douglas Parkins, Mr. Bailey, and myself, risked our lives fighting a war to guarantee the perpetuation of free-dom in this world. How can we then turn around and deny that very freedom to individuals who face not freedom but death or forced hard labor in their own country because they were willing to join with us as allies against the tyranny of Germany? In all due respect, I request that the charges against Gregory Bullock be dropped for doing what we all should do in this situation. The defense rests."

"Is there any rebuttal from the prosecution?"

Again Bailey strutted to the front, smiling as if he had bagged the treasure, "The defense is wrong when he says no law has been broken. The Alien Registration Act or Smith Act of 1940 made it a criminal offense for anyone and I quote 'to knowingly or willfully advocate, abet, advise or teach the desirability or propriety of overthrowing the Government of the United States or of any State by force or violence, or for anyone to organize any association which teaches, advises or encourages such an overthrow, or for anyone to become a member of or to affiliate with any such association.' Hundreds of Communists and others have been prosecuted under this law. Eleven leaders of the Communist Party were charged and convicted under the Smith Act last year. Ten defendants were given sentences of five years, and the eleventh was sentenced to three years. All of the defense attorneys were cited for contempt of court and were also given prison sentences." He shot a triumphant glance at Hadley.

"And Mr. Hadley, any rebuttal on your side?"

Hadley went to the front, not looking the least bit fazed, "While it might be argued that Alex and Valentina did not register as aliens in the US, no evidence whatsoever has been presented that they have any intention of doing anything which would lead in any way to the over-throwing of the Government of the United States. Gregory Bullock has not assisted in any way in furthering any plans or intent against our government. I move that he be acquitted of all charges."

"Thank you, gentlemen. We will have a recess, reconvening at two in the afternoon for the verdict." Judge Smith banged his gavel.

Greg went nervously to the courtroom. He was guilty of the charge. Bailey had suggested it, Hadley had drawn it out of him, and he had admitted it. So what could the judge do but find him guilty? Unless Hadley was right and no law had been broken.

They all rose to their feet as the judge entered the courtroom, then sat as he banged his gavel. "Court is in session," the bailiff announced.

They all sat, looking expectantly at Judge Smith. "When a trial is before a judge only, he hears the testimony of the witnesses of each side. He also needs to be aware of judgments in other courts relating to similar issues for any precedents set, as well as statements made by the lawmakers of our land. Mr. Bailey has referred to the Alien Registration

Act or Smith Act of 1940, but has produced no evidence that Gregory Bullock has violated this law. Merely withholding information about Russians who are here as refugees does not constitute a violation of this law. We saw in the case of Nina Pavlovna that there is a clear and present danger to Russians repatriated under the Yalta agreement.

"President Truman has said, 'In a free country, we punish men for the crimes they commit, but never for the opinions they have. It is the corruption of truth, the abandonment of the due process of law. It is the use of the big lie and the unfounded accusation against any citizen in the name of Americanism or security. It is the rise to power of the demagogue who lives on untruth; it is the spreading of fear and the destruction of faith in every level of society that destroys the freedoms we value.'

"On June 1, 1950, Senator Margaret Chase Smith, a Maine Republican, delivered a speech to the Senate she called a 'Declaration of Conscience.' In a clear attack upon McCarthyism as this frenzied search for so-called Communists has been dubbed, she called for an end to 'character assassinations' and named 'some of the basic principles of Americanism: The right to criticize; The right to hold unpopular beliefs; The right to protest; The right of independent thought.' She said, 'freedom of speech is not what it used to be in America,' and decried 'cancerous tentacles of 'know nothing, suspect everything' attitudes.'

"Continuing to quote: 'The present law proceeds on a principle repugnant to our society — guilt by association. What happens under this law is typical of what happens in a police state. Teachers are under constant surveillance; their pasts are combed for signs of disloyalty; their utterances are watched for clues to dangerous thoughts.' End quote.

"Gregory Bullock has not in anything presented, spoken out in favor of anything we would consider anti-American. He did in good conscience protect two individuals from the very tyranny of law that President Truman and Senator Smith speak against. No evidence has been presented that Gregory Bullock, in protecting the whereabouts of the individuals identified as Alex and Valentina, has done anything that endangers our nation's security. I therefore dismiss all charges against Gregory Bullock. Court is dismissed."

With the crack of the gavel, Gregory Bullock breathed again.

Scott Hadley shook Greg's hand as they left the courtroom.

"Why did you really come?" Greg asked.

Scott smiled, "I was in Platting, Germany with Matthew Cope. It was the most shameful, painful thing I have ever been asked to do. I vowed then as sort of an atonement, that if I ever had the opportunity to save a Russian from the horrible fate of repatriation, I would do it even if it required me to put my own life on the line."

Greg understood. It now made perfect sense.

Greg tapped the receiver of the phone in his hand with a smile on his lips. Reinstated at the university with an apology. He hung the phone up only to have it ring again. A man's voice he didn't recognize said, "I'm going to visit some common friends and wonder if you would like to come along."

"Who is this?"

"The guy who knows where our friends are. Are you still being watched in hopes that somehow you might inadvertently lead them to our friends?"

"I think so."

"Come to the church on Friday morning. Go into the men's restroom. Change into the ragged suit you will find in a bag there. Put the hat on. A man will wheel you out in a wheelchair and transport you to where I'll be waiting. Someone else will pick up your personal stuff. My wife will call your wife to see if she would like to accompany us. If so, she will make arrangements to rendezvous with her. When we are certain all is safe, we will journey to where our friends are hiding. The baby is due soon. I don't know if it would be safe to put her in a hospital with all of the publicity about them. We also need to tell her of the death of her mother. What a low blow, but maybe that was the clincher for your release. You know her a lot better than I do. I know him."

"I'll be there on Friday," Greg smiled again as he hung up. He had undoubtedly just spoken to Alex's employer. He would not have to live in indefinite suspense, wondering what had happened to them.

*****

Valentina's time drew near. They were anxious to hear the outcome of the trial and expected someone to visit them soon. Sasha, confident from Nancy's successful birth at home, was not unduly concerned about the birth of the baby. Valentina went into labor at the sheep camp two weeks before anyone expected. Sasha and Valentina were alone with Nancy. Valentina urged him to go tend the sheep. "I'll need you later. I won't want you to leave then. I won't be able to care for Nancy then. Please go now."

Sasha went but not to the sheep. He went to Sodie's. "Cover for me." he said. "Valentina's having the baby."

Sodie nodded his assent, and Sasha urged the horse to a run back to camp. The hours dragged by as Valentina coped with the intensifying pain. Sasha wished he'd insisted Valentina go to a hospital, although he didn't know how they would have gotten her there. He'd forgotten how terrifying this was to see her so unable to handle the pain and be so helpless himself. Sodie came and fed and played with Nancy until his evening chores called him away. Valentina lay on the bed, tossing and crying as each pain racked her body. Sasha stood helplessly at her side, wiping her brow, offering sips of water, giving words of love and encouragement. Sasha left Valentina only when Nancy's cries from the playpen grew so loud that they were obviously adding to Valentina's pains. "Go to her," she urged as she caught her breath between contractions. Sasha changed Nancy, put her in her warmest clothes against the evening chill, fixed her a bottle, and put her back in the playpen just outside the door, wishing Sodie would come back and care for her.

When Nancy's cries again urgently demanded attention, Valentina did not hear them, and Sasha shut them out. Valentina was pushing, claiming she was too exhausted to push anymore and then pushing again. Sasha caught his second daughter in his hands as Valentina's push brought success. He laid the babe at her mother's side. He kissed Valentina, grateful she could finally rest. He decided to wait for the afterbirth before tending to Nancy's wails. As he waited, he noticed there was blood, much more blood than he remembered after Nancy's birth. How did one stop internal bleeding? He couldn't put a tourniquet on it. How would he apply pressure to it? He pushed on Valentina's abdomen. She cried out. The afterbirth expelled, but the blood continued. More and more. Valentina was bleeding to death, and he didn't know how to stop it. She cooed to the new infant, oblivious to the imminent danger she was in. Plugging the vagina from the outside wouldn't help. She would just fill up on the inside. What could he do? He was going to lose her. Death was going to steal her away. After all he had given up to have her, he was still going to lose her. She became still beside the infant as if she were sleeping. Sasha knew there was not much time left now before she would be gone. Gone in death, forever irretrievable, and still, the blood came.

"Merciful God!" he hollered. "If you are there, if you exist, do not take her. I need her! I want her! I'll do whatever you ask. Don't take her!"

Sasha tried to wipe up the bright red blood. It seemed it was slowing. Maybe he imagined it because he wanted it to stop so badly. He couldn't tell. The infant fussed. Nancy screamed. Valentina laid there white, quiet, calm as if she were asleep.

"Valentina! Valentina!" He shook her. She did not respond.

Sasha paused. He heard a car. Maybe God had heard his plea. Maybe there was a God who cared, who sent help. "Valentina! Someone is coming. There is help coming! Don't die! There is help! There is hope!"

There was no hope. It was too late. No one could help her now. Sasha felt no breath, no heartbeat. It was too, too late. The infant cried; Nancy wailed; Sasha clasped Valentina in his arms and sobbed.

The car stopped. Sasha heard voices. A woman's voice crooned to the screeching Nancy. Marv Savage and Bishop Bullock appeared in the door of the tiny trailer. "She bled to death. The baby's okay, but she is dead." Sasha looked at them wearily.

"Let us see her," Marv said gently. Sasha moved down the narrow aisle and out of the trailer to allow them to Valentina's bedside. The women stood wide-eyed in the doorway. Bishop Bullock pulled a vial from his pocket. "What's her full name— her real name— her Russian name?"

"Valentina Markovna."

"Say it slowly so I can hear the sounds."

Sasha repeated the name slowly. What did her name matter now anyway?

"Is Markovna your last name?"

"No. Nikoliayevich."

Bishop Bullock knelt upon the bench and poured a drop of what looked like oil from the vial onto her head. Marv stood in the table space and stretched to place his hands with Bishop Bullock upon Valentina's head. "Valentina Markovna Nikoliayevich," Bishop Bullock slaughtered her name with his broad American accent, "In the name of Jesus Christ..."

Sasha pushed past the women in the doorway and ran into the gathering darkness. He had pleaded with God to save Valentina, and God had sent men with words. They were performing some sort of last rite over her. That was God's answer. She's happy now. She's beyond pain. What good was a God who came too late? Sasha crumbled at the base of a tree. His sorrow overtook him. He sobbed until it seemed he could sob no more. What now? What was life without Valentina? Maybe the Bullocks or Savages would raise his daughters. How could he ever love the new one? Her life had cost him Valentina. He didn't want to hold her, caress her, validate her existence by giving her a name. He just wanted her gone— gone. Never to have come, so Valentina would not be gone. Let them take her. He would never want to see her, never want to hear from her again.

Nancy, he would miss. Maybe they would bring her to visit him. But she would be disgusted with the sodden drunk he would become, trying to drown his sorrows in liquor. Drinking to *sabytsa*, to forget himself. It would be better if she knew him only through pictures. He would go where no one knew him, no one could find him— maybe Alaska, the closest he could get to home, to Kamchatka, without being home. He would drink, and drink, and drink until he could not feel, until he could not think, until death took him also.

"Alex," Marv's hand was on his. "Valentina wants you."

"The dead have no wants."

"She is not dead."

"I saw her. I know death when I see it. Don't taunt me. I can't bear it."

"Please come."

It was with the greatest of reluctance that Sasha arose and followed Marv back into the tiny trailer. He supposed he had to do this before they took her body away, before they took the girls away, before they took his life away. Maybe now they would assist him to get to Kamchatka. Maybe he could do it on his own. He had plenty of money, and he spoke and read English well enough to be able to make his way.

Bishop Bullock met him on his approach. The lantern showed brightly from the trailer, and he could hear the crackle of a fire and smell the odor of chicken cooking. Why would they celebrate death in this manner? It seemed heartless. The only sensible food to partake of would be liquor, and, of course, they would not violate that law given to them by the God they claimed loved them.

He stepped into the trailer and saw Valentina, but she was not lying supine, her skin a pasty white, her eyes closed as if asleep, her hands folded across her abdomen, No. She sat up in the bed, the clothed infant contentedly sucking at her breast. Her eyes lit up as she saw him and she extended her free hand to him, "Come, Sasha."

He stood rooted in dumbfounded disbelief. His tongue could make no utterance.

"You called me back, Sasha when you pleaded with God to spare me, and they brought me back by the priesthood, God's power which they hold. Come, I'm fine now."

This time he moved to her. Gently touched the reality of her, and then lay his head on her other breast and sobbed while she soothingly ran her fingers through his hair. He could not comprehend what had happened, or how, but she was not dead! She was not gone, and his life was still here with her.

"Well, I guess that is about it, Kenrushka," Sasha said.

Kenretta could tell from the quirk of his smile and the twinkle in his eye that he knew full well it would not be acceptable to her to end their story on this note. She so loved this man and played along with him for his pleasure. "No, no, no, Papochka! You can't end a story like that."

"Just say we lived happily ever after."

"Except you didn't. That's fairy tales, and no life is a fairy tale."

"Well, our lives' stories don't end until our lives are ended, and according to Mamochka," he put an arm around Valentina and hugged her to him, "It doesn't end even then."

"And you believe that too now, and that is another of the loose ends to this story we must tie up before we can declare it finished. Let's start with how you finally got off your mountain retreat."

"I'll explain how we got off the mountain," Valentina said. "Really, the question is: How did it become safe for Russians to be refugees in the United States without fear of repatriation? Even though Bishop Bullock had been acquitted, McCarthyism was still running full tilt. The fear and discrimination began to end when McCarthy accused the army of being soft on communism, and there were thirty-two days of hearings on national television."

She glanced at some papers in her lap. "Even though I roughly know the story, I don't remember all of the names and dates without reminding myself. I'll read from this: 'Senator Joseph McCarthy began hearings investigating the United States Army, which he charged with being 'soft' on communism. These televised hearings gave the American public their first view of McCarthy in action. His recklessness, bluster, and bullying tactics quickly resulted in his fall from prominence.'"

"We didn't see this since we had no access to television." She went back to reading from her newspaper article, "'The most famous incident in the hearings was an exchange between McCarthy and the army's chief legal representative, Joseph Nye Welch. On June 9, the thirtieth day of the hearings, Welch challenged Roy Cohn to provide U.S. Attorney General Herbert Brownell, Jr. with McCarthy's list of 130 Communists or subversives in defense plants 'before the sun goes down.'

"McCarthy stepped in and said that if Welch was so concerned about persons aiding the Communist Party, he should check on a man in his Boston law office named Fred Fisher, who had once belonged to the National Lawyers Guild, which Brownell had called 'the legal mouthpiece of the Communist Party.' In an impassioned defense of Fisher that some have suggested he had prepared in advance and had hoped not to have to make, Welch responded, 'Until this moment, Senator, I think I never really gauged your cruelty or your recklessness.'

"When McCarthy resumed his attack, Welch interrupted him: 'Let us not assassinate this lad further, Senator. You've done enough. Have you no sense of decency, sir, at long last? Have you left no sense of decency?' When McCarthy once again persisted, Welch cut him off and demanded the chairman 'call the next witness'. At that point, the gallery erupted in applause, and a recess was called.'"

Valentina glanced up from her reading. "The people had gotten tired of McCarthy. He played as a bully on TV, and he lost all credibility."

"Then Stalin died in 1953," Sasha added. "The public became less committed to send anyone Russian back to the Soviet Union."

"So, when did you leave your mountain retreat?" Kenretta asked.

Valentina answered. "Eisenhower was the president in 1956. At first, he had supported the repatriation of Russians, but by then, the United States was involved in the Korean War, and issues of repatriation of those in Asian countries came up. President Eisenhower reversed his position completely. He gave a message to Congress concerning the Russians. Let's see, here's the date on that, February 8, 1956. Let me read this. It is very important:

" A large group of refugees in this country obtained visa " by the use of false identities in order to escape forced repatriation behind the Iron Curtain; the number may run into the thousands. Under existing law such falsification is a mandatory grounds for deportation. The law should be amended to give relief to these unfortunate people.

"Senator Watkins of Utah introduced an amendment on the same day, and repatriation formally ended. Then, we finally felt safe."

"Was Watkins aware of your situation because of the trial?"

"He may have been. We do not know," Valentina answered. "By then, we had accumulated quite a bit of money, between the sheep herding and Papochka's work for Marv Savage, so we were able to buy a home in the Rose Park neighborhood of Salt Lake City, where we raised our family."

"It must have gotten crowded in that little trailer before you left. You had three children by then, didn't you?"

"In the winter, we were stationed not too far from Delta, Utah, in what is called the West Desert. They rented a small house for us there, so it wasn't too bad," Valentina said. "In the summer, we did live in the sheep camp, but we all spent much of our days outside. By the end, we had a camp that had two double beds. One slid under the other. We didn't seem too crowded then, and it is full of fond memories for us."

"After a couple of years, we bought a little car, and both learned to drive. We could drive into Delta for groceries, and Valentina and the children began to attend church," Sasha added.

"Did the people in Delta know who you were?"

"Either they didn't know, or they pretended not to know," Valentina said. "Actually, at least one did know. A woman by the name of Anna from church came to me all excited to announce the end of repatriation."

"We need to include details about your growing family in this story," Kenretta said.

"After the birth of Nina," Sasha picked up the story. "I was willing to deny myself and Valentina rather than risk her death with the birth of yet another child."

"Yet on my side, while I was dead, and I had been dead," Valentina added her vital part to the story, "I had what is now called a near-death experience. I saw my mother and my three brothers, so I knew my mother was dead. They all seemed happy and at peace, so I had no further anguish over their deaths. Bishop Bullock and Marv Savage felt it important that I know that my mother had been executed. They didn't want me to learn it accidentally from a newspaper as I had learned of her repatriation. However, with all of the trauma of the birth, they didn't feel it was the best time to tell me. They told Alex before they left and asked him to tell me. Before he told me, I told him that we needed to name the baby Nina to honor my mother since she was dead. He was astounded that I knew and even more surprised that I wasn't all broken up about it.

"I don't remember seeing anyone other than my mother and brothers in my vision, but I seemed to know that we would yet have three more sons and three more daughters. I did not fear for my life if I were to conceive another child. I also wasn't afraid of death because I now knew it to open a door into a beautiful place where loved ones dwelt. The problem was to convince Papochka that it was alright to have additional children. I told him that God had communicated to me that we would have more children, and he need not fear. He was not convinced. I told him that nursing without supplementing with a bottle would prevent conception. He would occasionally give in to his desire. For a while, the nursing did suppress ovulation but eventually, I became pregnant with Andrei. He was born in a hospital, and I did hemorrhage again. After that, Papochka didn't trust nursing as birth control. I didn't know what to do, so I prayed about it. I wasn't willing to tell Papochka about condoms. They were called rubbers in those days. Sometimes, still, the desire would get the better of him, and he would withdraw without giving me his seed. This loving act had become a source of considerable tension in our relationship. Tell her what happened next."

"Well, you know it is interesting to talk to your son's wife about conceiving her husband," Sasha winked at her.

Kenretta suspected he was not at all ill at ease in talking to her about it, but maybe he thought that she might be uneasy. There was a time she would have been, but three children of her own had done a lot to erase that naivete. Then again, this was for posterity, some of whom were definitely too young to read it. If they were mature enough to handle the war, they should be able to handle this.

"One time, while we were making love, as you young people call it, I had what I call a vision. I saw two little boys in bib overalls playing by a stream. Just as I was going to withdraw, the elder of the two looked at me and said, 'Please, Papochka.' I was so astonished that I didn't withdraw, and Lex was conceived. I knew immediately she was pregnant, and so did she. By this time, I was on the cusp of joining the church, and I knew I had to trust the Lord. Besides, there were two little boys, so she wouldn't die with the first if they were both to be my sons. After joining the church, I knew I had to give her the second son also. Now that was an act of faith. She didn't fear for her life because she assured me there were still three little girls. No way, I thought. I only saw two little boys."

Valentina picked up the story, "I had wanted to name a son after each of my brothers. But since we named Lex after Papochka, we named Dmitri, Dmitri Mark, as I knew that would be my last son."

"And what about the three daughters?" Kenretta knew the answer but wanted it in their words.

Valentina replied, "I hemorrhaged so badly when Dmitri Mark was born that they performed a hysterectomy to preserve my life. That solved the sexual tension between us, but I still wondered about the impression that I would yet have three daughters. Of course, you know the story, but for the sake of the grandchildren, Natasha, whom we had called Nancy until we could openly be Russian, died in childbirth from hemorrhaging in the birth of her third daughter, so we raised them as our own. It was bittersweet, but, because of my near-death experience, we knew it to be foreordained."

"Lastly, how did you come to join the church?" Kenretta addressed Sasha.

"Well, it wasn't instantaneous. I had promised God I would do anything if he would spare Valentina's life in the sheep camp. After she lived, I didn't take my own promise too seriously. We have continued to have regular contact with the Savages and the Bullocks. Both men were examples of the type of man Valentina hoped I would become, men of God. I held them both in high esteem but didn't see myself becoming like them. I mellowed over time. I allowed Valentina to read the Book of Mormon to me and the New Testament, so I knew of Christ and his mission and our need for redemption. Once we left the mountain and bought our home in Rose Park, Valentina saw that I became active in the scouting program and the ward choir, so Church members basically surrounded me. Their acceptance of me, their interest in me, and their kindness to me won me over. Then, when I had the vision, if you want to call it that, of Lex and Dmitri, I became convinced there was a God who interested himself in human affairs and who can communicate with humans in ways they understand. Also, I was tired of the pleading looks Valentina always gave me as my resistance dragged on. So I was ready for a different stage of our relationship. I became active in the church. Eventually, I was baptized and have become more convinced of its truthfulness ever since."

"Did you finally decide what love means?" Kenretta couldn't resist asking this.

Sasha chuckled before answering, "Love is a many splendored word and much abused in the language of today. It is not that feeling of unrequited desire—what is that you young people say?"

"Twitterpated?"

"I guess so. It is not that. Even though that desire was a thread in our relationship from the beginning, it wasn't until we had to sacrifice ourselves for each other that we really began to understand what love was. The biggest sacrifice I had to make was to give her another baby, even though it might mean losing her. That was heart-wrenching. Each pregnancy after Nina was basically nine months of terror."

"Any last words?" Kenretta turned to Valentina.

"Only that one must always trust God. He is in control. He knows us, he loves us, and he knows the time schedule that things must happen."

Foreign Language Vocabulary

I have tried to minimize the use of foreign words in this book, but I think a little bit adds flavor that the characters are not native English speakers and they find themselves in different circumstances where they hear and sometimes speak foreign languages. I tried to make it so that when a foreign language is used, either the reader gets the translation at the time, or can figure it out from the context. Other times, the meaning is really not important. Nevertheless, here are translations for the foreign words. I apologize if I have missed some. In the text, if I use the same foreign word over and over again, I do not italicize it after the first time.

Kamchadal

Tétk oun, oukhtchitch--Watch out! A girl!
Enokitch?--What?

Russian

Ah, moya malen'kaya ptitsa.Ya tui lyublyu--My little bird. I love you.

Avos--a string bag carried 'just in case' one comes across something to carry, or especially, something to buy.

babushka--Grandmother but it is also generally used to refer to an older lady

balagans--conical shelters standing like hats with wide brims on high pole pedestals

balalaika--A balalaika is a Russian stringed musical instrument with a characteristic triangular, wooden, hollow body, fretted neck, and three strings

banya--bath

besprizhorniki--political orphans

brodovshchiki--homemade snowshoes

chort--is considered to be an anthropomorphic demon of total evil and of doom, with horns, hooves and a skinny tail. This word is used in the book as an exclamation of exasperation.

dedushka--Grandfather

kolkhoz--collective farm

kuklianka--the traditional knee-length, winter, outer-garment made of reindeer skin

kulich--a sweet cylindrical bread made at Easter

Mamochka--Mommy. In the book it is used to mean this as well as Valentina calling herself this to her children and grandchildren.

Matushka--Mama

nasha luchshaya--ours is best. Common patriotic saying in Russia.

Nyet--No

Papochka--Daddy. In the book, Valentina calls her own father this but also Sasha is called this by his children and grandchildren.

pokazuka--little braggart

proshchai--farewell (for a long time)

roubles--Russian coins, bills

sabeysta--To forget. I can't find this online but in the books I researched, I found the word used this way.

sheltok--egg-yolk yellow paint

Spokoynoy nochi , moya malen'kaya Goodnight, my little one. Literally, "quiet night, my little girl".

sudba--fate

ushaka--a Russian fur cap with ear flaps that can be tied up to the crown of the cap, or fastened at the chin to protect the ears, jaw, and lower chin from the cold.

valenki--felt boots

Vozhd--the leader

Ya tui lyublyu--I love you

Zdrasti, tovarich!--Greetings, Comrade

French

bonjour--hello

freres and soeurs--brothers and sisters

Je suis tres desollée--I am very sorry

Les diables!--The devils!

ma belle--my beautiful one

meres et peres--mothers and fathers

mes cheres--my dear ones

O, mon Dieu!--Oh, my God!

Tu es tres intelligente, petite fille--You are very intelligent, little girl

Une Funambule--a tightrope walker

voila ton--here is your

German

Bei der Laterne wollen wir steh'n Wie einst Lili Marlene.--We want to stand beneath the lamplight as before, Lili Marlene.

Für Sie ist der Krieg vorbei!--For you, the war is over.

kaput--broken

Operation Barbarossa--red beard. The name the Germans gave to their attack on Russia

willkommen--welcome

Author Statement

What's Real, What's Not

This is a work of historical fiction. Because it is historical, I have done extensive research about other times and places. It is very difficult to answer all of one's questions through research. Some things I knew nothing or very little about. In these instances, I tried to tell the story of someone these things actually happened to, so they are accurate to that extent. All of the horrors of war in the book did happen sometime, someplace, to someone, during World War II--the Russian deserters on the trains, the crucifixion of the pregnant woman, the mistreatment of the prisoners in German POW camps, even the bleeding out of French children by German doctors. All real. Also, it really was a senator from Utah, Arthur Vivian Watkins, who introduced the bill to end the repatriation of Russians from the United States.

The main characters are fictional. Having a medical spy team is fictional. As far as I know, no such teams existed. Russian spies working for the Allies is historical. The Russian Liberation Army is historical. Repatriation is historical. Russian refugees being viewed as spies in the US after World War II is historical. Even the mistreatment of liberated Russians by the US and British military is historical. Julius Epstein is historical, though he never testified in a trial in Salt Lake City. The trial is fictional, but all the quotations from historical figures quoted during the trial are real.

Bibliography

This book first began with wanting to have a character for a yet unpublished novel (Sasha and Valentina's son) from 'an exotic' place. I looked at a map and liked the sound of Kamchatka. I hadn't even played Risk at this point and don't recall having ever heard of Kamchatka. The first book I read was Kennan's *Tent Life in Siberia*. Kennan is poetic, funny, and a great read. He writes in a way that most of us are not capable of writing these days.

Internet then was not what it is now (it was the 1990's), and I went to the library and began to request every book on Russia. Another book I absolutely loved, but it had no bearing on this book was Mark Jenkins' *Off the Map*. I finished reading it and immediately told my husband that we needed to read it together. We read it out loud together. and it is one of our all time favorite books. Mark is an adventurer that if it can't be done, he does it and then writes about it. I've since read everything that he has written that I can get my hands on. Another of my favorites is his visit to hades in Greece. This is a short article in a collection. I am not certain which of his books it is in. Just read Mark Jenkins. You'll find it..

The book that ultimately set this book on its course was Julius Epstein's *Operation Keelhaul*. I probably had this book half-written, and in a sense, didn't know what it was about, until I read Epstein's book about repatriation. That gave me the framework within which to construct my story.

A Day in the Life of the Soviet Union, (May 15, 1987), Collins Publishers, Inc., 1987.

Bethell, Nicholas, *Russia Besieged,* Time-Life Books, 1977

Bobrick, Benson *East of the Sun*, Poseidon Press, 1992

Bookbiner, Alan, Olivia Lichtenstein & Richard Denton, *Comrades,* New American Library, 1985

Dabars, Zita, *The Russian Way,* Passport Books, 1995

De Lesseps, M., *Travels In Kamtschatka.* Originally published by J. Johnson, St. Paul's Chruch-Yard, 1790. Reprint Edition 1970 by Arno Press, Inc.

Encyclopedia of World Geography, Volume 14 Russia, Northern Eurasia, Marshall Cavendish, 1994.

Epstein, Julius *Operation Keelhaul* The story of Forced Repatriation, The Devin-Adair Company, 1973.

Russian Folksongs, Folkways music

Funcken, Liliane and Fred *Arms and Uniforms*, The Second World War pt. 1-4, Prentice-Hall, Inc., 1976

Gippenreiter, Vadim, *Kamchatka, Land of Fire and Ice*, Laurence King, 1992.

Grossfeld, Stan, *The Whisper of Stars*, Globe Pequot Press, 1988.

Hautzig, Esther, *The Endless Steepe*, Thomas Y. Crowell Company, 1968

Jenkins, Mark, *Off the Map*, William Marrow and Company, 1992.

Kalashnikoff, Nicholas, *The Defender*, Walker and Company, 1951.

Kempe, Frederick, *Siberian Odyssey*, G. P. Putnam's Sons, 1992.

Kennan, George *Tent Life In Siberia*, originally published by G.P. Putnam's Sons, The Knickerbocker Press, 1910. Reprinted by Arno Press & The New York Times 1970.

Krasheninnikov, Stepan Petrovich, *Explorations of Kamchatka*, Reprint by Oregon Historical Society, Portland 1972.

Laloy, Jean *Yalta Yesterday, Today, Tomorrow*, Harper & Row, 1988.

Lincoln, W. Bruce, *The Conquest of a Continent*, Random House, 1994.

Lucas, James, *War on the Eastern Front*, Bonanza Books, 1979.

Markovna, Nina *Nina's Journey*, Regnery Gateway, 1989.

Newby, Eric, *The Big Red Train Ride*, St. Martin's Press, 1978.

Petrov, Vladimir *My Retreat From Russia*, Yale University Press, 1950.

Piumini, Roberto, *The Knot in the Tracks*, Tambourine Books, 1982.

Rachlin, Rachel and Israel, *Sixteen Years In Siberia*, The University of Alabama Press, 1988.

Rybakov, Anatoli *Heavy Sand*, The Viking Press, 1981

Sevela, Ephraim, *We Were Not like Other People*, Harper & Row 1989

Shinkarev, Leionid, *The Land Beyond The Mountains*, Macmillan Publishing Co., 1973.

The World At War, Vol. 5 Barbarossa June-December 1941 (Video)

Wittlin, Tadeusz, *A Reluctant Traveller in Russia*, Rinehart & Company, Inc., 1952.

Ziemke, Earl F. *The Soviet Juggernaut*, Time-Life Books, 1980

Murie, Margaret E. *Two In the Far North* (Book about Alaska), Alaska Northwest Books, 1979

Acknowledgements

I acknowledge God's hand in this book. The involvement has been subtle but there. I didn't get the job I was seeking in education and ended up substituting in high schools where, once I got the students onto the task of the day, I could do my own thing. I researched and wrote. Before cell phones became common in every kids' hand, they would ask me if they could use my computer to check their email. I said I did not have internet. They would say, "What do you do on a computer without internet?"

I felt God's gentle nudging to find the books to read to create this book. I have sensed his hand when I prayed about giving up writing and investing my time in other endeavors. I've noticed that many times, people were put into my path to teach me skills to enhance or use technology to aid me in my writing. I pray that my stumbling efforts might add to his work and glory in bringing his children unto him.

I thank Jennie Hansen for loving my story and being willing to review it.

I thank my husband, Donald Fallick, for his unfailing support, love, and editing expertise.

I thank Daniel Forbes for designing the cover, Daniel is also an author and can be checked out at Twitter @DanielsTales.

About Barbara Sorensen Fallick

Barbara grew up in the rural towns of Emery and Manti, Utah. Her father herded sheep in the hills above Manti, and she remembers visiting him in his sheep camp with her mother and siblings. She currently lives with her husband in a mining ghost town, in a cabin built by her husband. She has also lived in Arizona, Idaho, Illinois, Maryland, Virginia, and Washington State, as well as in France, The Dominican Republic, and Chile. She enjoys reading, watching birds and deer, family history, and her many grandchildren.